KU-636-037

For Rose, Poppy and Jasmine

The Honey and the Sting

The Honey and the Sting

E. C. FREMANTLE

MICHAEL JOSEPH
an imprint of
PENGUIN BOOKS

MICHAEL JOSEPH

UK | USA | Canada | Ireland | Australia
India | New Zealand | South Africa

Michael Joseph is part of the Penguin Random House group of companies whose addresses
can be found at global.penguinrandomhouse.com.

First published 2020
001

Copyright © E. C. Fremantle, 2020

The moral right of the author has been asserted

Set in 13.5/16pt Garamond MT Std
Typeset by Jouve (UK), Milton Keynes
Printed and bound in Great Britain by Clays Ltd, Elcograf S.p.A.

A CIP catalogue record for this book is available from the British Library

HARDBACK ISBN: 978–0–718–18050–8
OM PAPERBACK ISBN: 978–1–405–92014–8

www.greenpenguin.co.uk

Penguin Random House is committed to a
sustainable future for our business, our readers
and our planet. This book is made from Forest
Stewardship Council® certified paper.

My honey lost, and I, a drone-like bee,
Have no perfection of my summer left,
But robbed and ransacked by injurious theft:
In thy weak hive a wand'ring wasp hath crept,
And sucked the honey which thy chaste bee kept.

Shakespeare, *The Rape of Lucrece*

The girl appears to float in the low brume. Her skin is transparent. Veins tick in her temples, mysterious as the workings of an opened clock. Oblivious to her sister watching from the fence, she gazes entranced at her hands, which are blanketed in something dark and moving.

An anxious crevice forms between the sister's moth eyes. Instinct, a twist in her gut, tells her to bolt, to run back to the house and slam the door, to throw herself into the solid embrace of her father. She can imagine the rough wool kiss of his jacket against her cheek, the safe squeeze of his arms.

But her father isn't there. He left before dawn, with the groom, to visit a patient. She had heard, through a haze of half-sleep, the hollow timpani of the horses' hoofs on the cobbles. When he is absent, she feels a desperate emptiness, as if he might never return and she will be left to care for her sisters alone, adrift in a world she does not yet fully comprehend.

Her father's voice is in her head – *Melis is different. You must take special care of her, or she will be crushed by the world.* She turns, almost expecting to see him close by, but there is nothing, just the snap and hum of insects in the crisp air. She shivers, calling to her sister.

Melis doesn't respond, is entirely bound into her own impenetrable universe.

Hester girds herself, climbing over the fence, jumping

down into the dew-drenched grass, the cold of it smacking her bare ankles. The wet soon clogs her canvas slippers, her hem absorbing it thirstily, making her skirts heavy as she approaches her floating sister.

'What in Heaven's name . . . ?' She can see now that Melis's hands are encrusted with bees, a great agitating mass that obscures her skin, spilling down her wrists and up her sleeves.

Without looking away from the swarm, Melis whispers, 'I have their queen.' She has a disturbing, feverish air about her, and Hester wishes she knew what to do. She feels the fast, hard thump of her heart. They knew of a child in Oxford once, who'd fallen into a bees' nest and died of the stings.

A few of the insects break away, vibrating close, as if to learn whether Hester is friend or foe, close enough for her to feel the disturbance of air against the skin of her face. She resists the temptation to bat them off, standing stock still until they leave.

'They sing to me – tell me secrets.' Melis transfers her stare momentarily towards Hester, who releases an involuntary gasp at the sight of her sister's horror-struck expression. 'The blackest secrets.'

'You're imagining things.' Hester does her best to muster her common sense but her thumping chest is making her feel lightheaded.

When Melis looks back again, her expression is transformed, now serene. 'Watch this.' She opens her fist. A small bullet flies out, disappearing into a bank of nettles. The swarm moves after it directly, in a great dark cloud, leaving only half a dozen confused malingerers on Melis's white lap.

The girls watch the bees depart in silence, and only once they have disappeared does Melis inspect her open palm. 'She can sting as many times as she wants. See!' She thrusts her hand towards Hester. 'And survive.' There are several angry-looking welts, bright pink against the pale skin. 'But the workers die if they sting. They defend her with their lives.'

Hester doesn't know how to respond.

'Why such sacrifice? It must be something to do with there being only one queen in a hive. Did you know that, Hester? Just one queen.'

'How do *you* know?' Hester asks.

'They told me so.'

'They? Who?'

'The bees, of course.' Her eyes widen, the pupils expanding – drops of treacle spreading on a plate.

'Come inside.' Hester holds out her hand. 'Please.' She breathes into her cupped hands to warm them. 'You'll catch your death.'

But Melis's eyebrows ruffle, like birds drawn by a child, and her lids slide open. The tormented look has returned, causing unease to seep into Hester, right to her core.

'Don't you want to know what the queen said, what she showed me?'

Hester is tugging at her sister's hand now but Melis shakes herself free. 'I saw Father.'

'What do you mean?'

But Melis has crumpled, is scratching at her eyes and dissolving into strange, anguished sobs. 'Help me, Hessie. You must help me. They show me things I don't want to see.'

Hester slides down to take her tightly in her arms,

rocking her back and forth. Beneath her hands, Melis feels insubstantial, breakable. 'You're safe. I'm here. I won't let anything happen to you . . .'

The quiet is shattered with the hammer of approaching hoofs – closer and closer.

The girls huddle together.

A vast shape vaults the orchard fence and comes to a halt, quivering and striated with foam, head tossing manically. It is their father's horse.

Hester begins to unravel but forces the frayed parts of herself together as she approaches the petrified animal.

He backs away.

'Poseidon. Here, boy. Here.' She makes a quiet clucking sound, waiting, motionless, for him to drop his head and inch towards her. Finally he allows her to stroke his muzzle lightly, and blows his hot, heavy breath into her hand. 'What's happened, boy?'

Melis is still rocking back and forth, emitting a low moan, almost a song, almost a dirge. From the side of her eye Hester notices the small form of their half-sister toddling towards the orchard gate.

'Stay there, Hope.' She dashes towards the infant, foreboding rattling round her head like a dried pea in a pan. She picks Hope up, heaving her onto her hip, just as the groom clatters into the yard.

He is running, calling to the girls, and leading his own horse by the reins.

Something heavy is slung over its back.

Hester can see the boots she had polished the night before hanging limply against the chestnut flanks.

Hope, too young to understand, prods at their father. 'Wake up, Papa.'

Melis has drawn beside her sisters and is staring, tears coursing silently down her face.

'Poseidon bolted.' The groom is distraught, his face ashen. 'Your da fell. Cracked his head.' He rips off his cap. He's young, can't even grow a beard yet. 'It were quick. He wouldn't have known nothing about it, God rest his soul.' He presses a hand to his heart.

New distress breaks over Melis's face, her voice cracking. 'I – I saw his head hit the ground.' She twists her fists into her eyes, as if to rub the vision out of them.

Hope, understanding now that something is wrong, begins to howl.

Hester can't speak, can't think, can't move. Her smallest sister is inconsolable in her arms, the other is raving, and she must keep the fragile edifice of their family from tumbling, while her every crevice crowds with dread.

An Unwanted Visitor

Or are you like the painting of a sorrow,
A face without a heart?

Shakespeare, *Hamlet*

Hester

Twelve years later

A heart-stopping shriek comes from the orchard.

I hurtle around the house, the top of the tall cherry tree coming into view, with Melis perched high on one of its branches. My immediate thought is that she intends to fling herself off.

'Don't move,' I shout, fear crashing through me, but my voice is lost in loud peals of wild laughter.

'Higher! Higher!'

I realize I have misinterpreted the situation as I see my son, Rafe, beneath her, on a makeshift rope swing, squawking with delight as he careers back and forth. 'I'm flying.' Hope is pushing him into the air, up, high, too high, until there is nothing but sky behind him.

'Stop!' I shout, managing to grab his shirt as he swings down towards me, banging into me, flinging me into the grass, where I lie, half winded.

I can see the soles of Melis's dangling feet far above.

'Are you out of your mind?' I call up to her, hauling myself to my elbows. 'What if you fall? And Rafe . . .'

Rafe slides off the swing, face set in a screw of disappointment as he stalks off. 'You always spoil everything.'

'Don't speak in that way to your mother,' Hope calls

after him. 'Are you hurt?' She crouches over me, dark eyes full of concern.

'No. No, I'm fine.' My response is blunt with annoyance.

'I'm sorry,' she is saying, brushing debris from my skirt. 'It was foolish – dangerous.' But I know this wasn't Hope's idea.

I watch Melis scale down from branch to branch, agile as a squirrel, heaving a breath of relief as she finally jumps to the ground.

'We were just having a bit of fun, Hessie.' Her face is flushed, eyes flashing.

'One of you might have fallen to your death.'

'Must you be such a doomsayer? Don't you remember? We used to swing from this tree as children.'

I do remember. I remember Father's large hands at my back, the exhilaration, my squeals of excitement, the sensation of flight. It is a long time since I have allowed myself to think back that far. I have become the sensible one, the killer of joy. But one of us must hold everything together.

'Back to work, I suppose.' Melis walks towards the hives at the far end of the orchard.

Inside, Hope and I swaddle ourselves from head to toe in vast canvas aprons and roll up our sleeves. In Orchard Cottage kitchen no surface is left uncovered and everything is sticky. It is the end of July and we are in the middle of harvesting the wildflower honey.

As I trim off the good comb and lay it carefully on oilcloth, Hope scoops the rest into the press, wrapping it into an oozing muslin parcel. I still think of her as a child but she is sixteen now, tall and dark, with a boyish muscularity, so unlike we elder sisters, pale and small as mayflies.

'Do you want to help me work the press?' Hope asks

Rafe, who is skulking on the back step. He positions himself with a grin, small hands gripping the handle. They whisper to each other and he glances towards me. It is my birthday today. I said I didn't want a fuss made but suspect they've been plotting a surprise.

I stop a moment to watch his glee as the golden liquid flows into the pail below, first a trickle, soon a gush. It is a moment I relish, too, seeing the fruits of our labour.

Melis appears, her face hidden behind the gauze veil of her apiary hat, cradling a large bee skep. She shoves things aside to make room for it on the table. 'That's the last of it for now.' She removes the hat, peels off her gloves, and has settled down to extract the combs when the afternoon is interrupted by the sound of a horse trotting up to the back door.

Melis's eyes meet mine. Even after so much time, unexpected arrivals bring back the memory of Poseidon galloping riderless into the yard, stitching dread through us all.

'Is anybody here?' comes the call from outside and the door is pushed open to reveal a tall, straw-haired young man, who introduces himself as the steward of a manor on the other side of Oxford. 'Where is the man of the house?'

'What's your business?' I set down my trimming knife and approach him, becoming aware of his eyes wandering over Hope as he explains that his employer is entertaining a houseful of guests and they are in need of more candles than they can make.

'I was told I might procure some here.' He looks briefly to me, then back to Hope. 'Is your husband here?'

'I am a widow,' I say. It is a lie.

I am not, as a rule, given to deceit but this particular untruth is a necessity for the smooth running of our daily lives at Orchard Cottage. I would not have been made welcome on returning to Iffley nine years ago with a distended belly, a craving for pickles and no husband. But as a widow no explanation has ever been required.

We never talk about Rafe's father.

'You women live here alone?' He sounds surprised.

Melis makes a snort of annoyance and throws him a scowl. I ask her to look in the store cupboard to see how much stock we have before she blurts out of turn. She will have interpreted his comment as a criticism and has a tendency to say exactly what is on her mind. The steward, though, seems hardly to have noticed her disapproval, and is still gaping at Hope.

'We can certainly provide you with candles.'

'Don't do that, Rafe. You'll cut your tongue.' Hope is carefully removing my trimming knife from Rafe's hand to prevent him from licking it. She only now notices the young man's gaze and I see her react with a flickering glance of her own. I make a mental note to talk to her. I have scarcely noticed that she is on the brink of womanhood and ripe for trouble. It worries me that she has been kept too sheltered and is unequipped to deal with the inevitable attentions of men. Her dark hooded eyes and pitch-black curls make her stand out from the whey-faced Iffley girls, and I have learned that desire is drawn to novelty.

Hope takes after her mother, whom none of us knew. I discovered from Father's papers after his death that she was the outcome of an illicit union between a salvage diver from Guinea and the wife of the Deptford merchant who had employed him to recover a consignment of precious stones from the wreck of one of his ships. It was a story to ignite the imagination. What had brought her into Father's orbit was unclear, but he'd loved her. That much I deduced from the unsparing way in which he doted on Hope.

Hope doesn't remember him – she was only four when he was taken from us – but I remember, as if it was yesterday, him arriving home with the tiny bundle that was my youngest sister. He had a woman with him. It turned out she was the wet nurse. I recall the squeeze in my heart at the first sight of the crumpled little face with its bush of inky hair. She burst into a sudden angry scream, pink toothless mouth gaping wide. The wet nurse made a great fuss, wondering what could have caused it. Melis shuffled back slightly, her lips tightly pursed, and I wondered if she'd pinched the infant. I supposed she didn't want to give up her place as youngest but I was already ten and determined to become a little mother to the tiny newcomer.

I negotiate a price for the candles, handing him a packet of fresh-cut honeycomb, saying that if his employer is ever in need we have ample. 'We can undercut the price at market. We take in needlework too. Embroidery, invisible mending. My sister can work magic with a needle, can't you, Hope.'

Hope, arms piled with packages of candles, looks embarrassed. Rafe insists on helping load them onto the cart, leaving sticky fingermarks on the wrappings.

'You the man of the house?' The steward amiably tousles Rafe's hair. Melis gives him a narrow-eyed look, which he ignores, vaulting onto the cart, thanking us and waving as he trundles away.

'You could try to be a bit more welcoming,' I say to

Melis, as we walk back inside. 'He might bring us more business.'

'The way he was acting,' she narrows her eyes, 'you'd have thought we intended to put a spell on him and turn him into a toad.'

I laugh. 'He seemed a perfectly decent fellow. There's really no need for you to be so suspicious.' Frankly, though, I would rather the suspicious Melis; it is when she disappears inside herself that I worry. She has been so well recently, with none of the voices and visions that periodically beset her. Our quiet life here at Orchard Cottage suits her.

'Goodness!' calls Hope from the parlour at the front, where the clock lives. 'It is six already. The Cottons will be here in half an hour and nothing is ready.'

We are all spurred into a frenzy of tidying in preparation for our visitors.

'Go and open the door for your godfather,' I tell Rafe, when I hear the click of the front gate, and I watch from the window as Ambrose Cotton takes my son's hand and they walk up the path together, laughing – a sight that makes my heart swell.

In the wake of Father's death, Ambrose, his dearest friend and mentor, had become our Heaven-sent protector. He was a royal physician then, with illustrious affiliations, and arranged for Melis and me to be placed in service in the Buckingham household, while Hope was taken into the care of Ambrose's housekeeper at Littlemore Manor. The idea, I suppose, had been that I might attract a well-connected husband at court, but the placement didn't end well and Ambrose came to regret it.

They spill into the parlour with smiles and greetings, his wife Bette proffering a bunch of wildflowers picked along the route. Littlemore is a good league away and it surprises me they didn't bring the carriage, but Ambrose is keen on the merits of fresh air and exercise.

We sit to eat early, so they have time to walk home before nightfall. The two have the happy air of newlyweds, though at least five years have passed since they came together. Bette is pale and has a sharp cough that interrupts her as she ribs him about being an untidy eater, plucking a breadcrumb from his beard, while he tells us of the convalescing patient he visited recently with a gift of fresh strawberries that made her come out in hives. 'The road to Hell is paved with good intentions.'

'At least your heart was in the right place,' Melis says.

'As a matter of fact it is not – literally speaking.' He launches into a long and convoluted story about how he came to discover that his heart was set to the right rather than the left of his ribcage, and invites Rafe to listen to his chest. I am wondering how it is possible to have known him all my life yet be unaware of this invisible quirk.

'Talking of matters of the heart,' Bette says, 'I met a nice young man the other day,' she is picking delicately at her plate, not really eating, 'with fifty acres the other side of Oxford.' I know exactly what she means by this. 'He's in the market for a bride and you've been a widow long enough.'

Ambrose shoots me a knowing glance. He has kept my secret, even from his beloved wife. Bette, being uncommonly happy in her marriage, wants the same for me.

Melis laughs. 'Hester doesn't want a husband, do you, Hessie?'

'Probably not. I have enough on my plate, without a husband to look after.' I make this sound like a joke but it is the truth. Besides, we three sisters are in the fortunate position of having Orchard Cottage, which provides our modest living and leaves us in charge of our own destinies.

'But a companion – would you not want the companionship of a man? It has brought us such contentment,' says Bette, taking Ambrose's hand.

'Men like Ambrose are a rarity.' My voice sounds clipped, defensive.

The talk has caused memories of Rafe's father to flood back, filling me like a storm gutter in a squall. There he is pulling my skirts up, pressing a vast beringed hand over my mouth to quash my protestations until my head swims for want of breath. The smell of his pomade clogs my head. In the wake of that first time, when I railed, he told me it was a privilege to be the recipient of his attentions, that I was his chosen one.

It didn't feel a privilege to be taken against my will. *How much do you want this?* he would ask, his voice low and hot with desire. He coerced me, little fool that I was, into saying I wanted him. I quickly learned that the sooner I said it the sooner the ordeal would be over. The only answer acceptable to him was: *Very much. Very, very much.* And then he would say, *I knew you were a filthy little whore, Hessie*, as he finished his business. *Don't you have a smile for your George?* I would manage to crease my face into an approximation of happiness. *If you ever tell a soul about our special friendship, I will wipe that smile off your face quicker than the flick of a lamb's tail.* One day, he discarded me without explanation.

Bette will not let the topic of marriage go. 'If Hester hasn't the mind to wed then we might find a husband for

16

you.' She is talking to Hope, who blushes to the roots of her hair.

'She's much too young,' I say, though I met girls at Lady Buckingham's who went off to wed at fourteen and Hope is already two years past that. But they were girls of better breeding than us, who were obliged to do as they were told.

'What about Aunt Melis?' pipes up Rafe. 'She is old enough.'

Hope shushes him. A dense silence ensues. We all eat or pretend to. No one ever mentions that Melis's erratic nature makes her an unsuitable candidate for matrimony. But you wouldn't know it were you to encounter her this evening, radiant in the full flush of her considerable beauty, her inner torments hidden from view.

I place my hand over hers as reassurance but she hasn't noticed the awkward hush, has begun to talk about her hives and the quality of the honey this year.

'It must have been the wet spring,' says Ambrose, moving the subject tactfully on and serving himself a second helping.

'What is it that draws you so to beekeeping, Melis?' Bette is asking.

'There is a pleasing harmony to a hive. All serve the queen without question, while she ensures the colony survives.' Melis's delicate hands flutter as she speaks, her eyes fervid. I cannot help but be reminded of finding her in the orchard, those hands blanketed in insects. I push away the memory.

Hope and Rafe slip into the kitchen and return holding a cake decorated with almonds and wild strawberries, wishing me a happy birthday.

'I decorated it.' Rafe is puffed up with pride, happy pink circles lighting his cheeks.

'So that is what you and Hope were whispering about earlier,' I say, hauling him onto my lap.

'What did you wish for?' he asks, as I cut the first slice.

'For your good fortune.'

'If you say it, it won't come true.' It is Melis who points this out.

A look of worry flits over Rafe's face until I declare Melis's statement nonsense.

'This is for you.' Rafe puts a small soft object in my hand. It is a little woman with a child in her arms, crudely carved in wax. 'It's you and me. I made it all by myself.'

I want to preserve this moment, sealed tight, like bottled fruits that taste of the sun when the winter draws in. 'I will treasure it for ever, my darling boy.' I hug his small body close and he tucks his head into the crook of my shoulder.

Looking around the table, I feel touched by good fortune, surrounded by those I love, all in good enough health, and am brimful of gratitude.

Hope

Hope was in the sun for half an hour without her hat this morning and her complexion has turned – enough for the sour-faced cheesemonger to comment, 'Been licked by the tar brush?'

Hope stares silently at the woman's big folded fists, chapped and red, with ridged yellow nails. The church bells start to ring. Hope lets the sound swallow her, counting out each of the ten chimes until the woman's comment fades to almost nothing in her mind. It reassures her to know exactly where she is in the day.

Reaching out for a cheese, Hope touches its rind to test for firmness. It is velvet soft under the tip of her finger.

'Hands off,' snaps the vendor. 'I know your sort. You'd disappear that cheese into your sleeve the moment my back was turned.'

'How dare you?' Melis glares at the woman. 'We'd rather starve than give *you* our custom.'

The woman mutters something under her breath, making a sweeping gesture with one of those ugly hands as if the two of them are flies to be swatted. Melis hooks her arm tightly through her sister's, marching her away. 'Don't listen to her. She's only envious.' Her tone is clipped with indignation. 'She has a face like a turnip and you . . . well, you would make an angel seem wanting.'

Hope knows she's saying it to be kind because who has ever seen an angel with hair as black as coal? She silently curses that half-hour in the sun. Sometimes she takes the small looking-glass down from the shelf by Hester's bed and scrutinizes herself, seeking similarities with her sisters: the high forehead, straight nose, and the shallow dip at the centre of her chin that must all have come from their father.

Hester and Melis have a portrait of their mother. It is the size of a prayer book and hangs in the parlour near the clock. She is a woman folded from finest parchment. At a glance it might be a likeness of Melis but a closer inspection reveals the mud-brown eyes of Hester. There is no portrait of Hope's mother. She imagines her strong, hewn from oak, like the beautiful carved figures in the altar screen at church, but it is difficult to conjure an image of someone you know nothing of.

Occasionally, more often when she was small, the sight of that portrait would open a void inside her. It isn't jealousy or sadness or even a sense of loss, because how can you lose what you never had? It is a feeling of unsteadiness, as if she is only tenuously attached to Orchard Cottage, though it is as much her home as her sisters'.

They make their way to the other cheese stall across the square, passing a group of girls gathered on a low wall, talking, laughing and throwing crumbs for a flock of sparrows.

'See what she's wearing,' giggles one girl behind a cupped hand, just loud enough for them to hear. 'Does she think she's a duchess?'

Melis is oblivious or is giving a perfect impression of it. She is the object of their ridicule in her silk dress, utterly unsuitable for a trip to the market. But that is Melis, wearing what pleases her, speaking her mind, not wanting to be bound by convention. Hope admires this about her middle sister but not now when it makes her the object of ridicule by association.

They are just the Iffley girls Hope has seen at church every Sunday since she can remember. One flicks a disdainful glance her way. Hope looks ahead. She is not one of them and has stopped agonizing about the reason. 'Most young girls have a very narrow outlook,' is what Hester says of it. Hope made up her mind long ago that it didn't matter.

They buy their cheese and deliver some finished needlework to the tailor on the square, before setting off for home. But as they walk, Melis becomes increasingly quiet, seeming to disappear into herself.

It is not a good sign.

When they are through Iffley and have reached the vast oak a quarter-mile from home, Melis stops dead. Hope shakes her arm, attempting to draw her attention. But she doesn't respond, appears trapped in some fugue state, staring right through her sister as if she doesn't exist. The basket drops from her hand, all the produce scattering over the ground, onions and apples rolling away, a pat of butter slumping into the long grass.

Hope does her best to gather everything up, trying to make light of it – 'Oopsy-daisy' – in the face of her sister's strange, dense silence.

Melis stretches her hand to the tree, tilting her temple against the bark, eyes tight shut, lips moving silently.

'What is it?' Hope knows what it is. She has seen it before but Hester has always been there and knew what to do. 'Tell me what's wrong.'

Melis shushes her brusquely. 'I can't hear.'

Hope notices a small crevice in the trunk beside Melis's ear, like a mouth. She seems to be trying to listen to it, deep in concentration, as if it is telling her a secret.

They are close enough for Hope to run home and fetch Hester but she is loath to leave Melis alone, even for a moment. She has seen Hester sometimes manage to force Melis's attention to something else, if she catches it early enough, and is furiously wondering what she might do or say to achieve this.

But it is too late as Melis turns to her, eyes snapping open, glaring with a terrifying intensity. 'So hot.' Her voice is trimmed with panic and a gloss of sweat blooms over her forehead. She sinks to the ground, as if her legs can no longer support her, skirts billowing out. A bright grass stain marks the place where her knees have met the earth. Hope can't help thinking it will be impossible to clean.

'It's all in flames.'

'What is in flames, Melis? What can you see?'

Melis begins to gasp, struggling for breath, like a drowning woman. 'I can't see for the smoke.' She is coughing, her body racked, and muttering things Hope cannot hear properly.

'There's no smoke, Melis. No fire.' Wanting to reassure her, Hope crouches and takes her hand.

Melis recoils with a cry, as if scalded. 'Rafe's inside. He'll be burned alive.' Her arms are flailing, batting away the invisible fire. 'Can't you hear his screams?'

Hope is at a loss, fear prodding her.

Then, from one moment to the next, Melis returns from whatever hell she has been in. She is holding her head, and looks up at Hope with bloodshot eyes. There is a red mark on the side of her head where it has been pressed against the tree.

'It's nothing to worry about. Only your imagination. You've been seeing things again.' That is what she's heard Hester say to Melis many times in the past but, nevertheless, an image of Orchard Cottage in flames inserts itself into her uneasy mind.

Her throat tightens as she is sure, now, she can catch the faint smell of burning in the air. She pulls her sister to her feet, running, half dragging her along as fast as she can.

At the bend in the lane, breath short, a stitch jabbing sharply at her side, Orchard Cottage comes into view. The place is intact, no sign of any fire, no smoke emanating from the thatch, only a thin trail rising from the kitchen chimney. Rafe is seated on the front step playing with the cat, while Hester is crouched over the vegetable patch pulling up weeds. Hope bends double, gasping for breath.

'Why the hurry?' Hester stands, approaching her sisters. 'And where is the produce from market?' Hope realizes that, in her rush, she has abandoned the basket.

As she says this Hester looks at Melis, seeming instinctively to understand what has occurred. She guides Melis inside.

Hope sits on the doorstep beside her nephew. The cat pushes its face onto her hand with a rattling purr. She strokes it absently, the vestiges of fear still jangling through her.

'Is Aunt Melis mad?' Rafe turns his round sparrow eyes on her in great seriousness.

'No, sweetheart. She sometimes has a funny turn, that's all.'

'Because I heard the maid at Littlemore say she was mad as a bag of snakes.'

'Well, *we* know her better than the maid at Littlemore. she seem mad to you most of the time?' Hope thinks of Melis defending her so robustly from the cheesemonger's insults in the market earlier.

He shakes his head. 'But what *is* a funny turn?'

Hope doesn't really know any more than Rafe does. 'It's like having a bad dream when you're awake.'

He seems satisfied with this explanation, as he goes back to playing with the cat.

She knows she ought to go and reclaim the basket but can't bring herself to return to that place alone, as if the great oak, with its whispering mouth, might put a spell on her.

Hester

Melis is sapped of spirit, sitting and staring into the kitchen hearth after supper, watching carefully for stray embers. When one pops onto the floor she reaches with her foot, quick as a frog's tongue to a fly, to stamp it out. Hope told me what had happened on the road back from Iffley, and I am thankful it is summer so only the kitchen hearth is lit. Otherwise Melis might be in a frenzy of worry, rushing from room to room to check for signs of fire.

Hope comes down from putting Rafe to bed. She is still shaken, casting occasional worried glances towards Melis, hiding it by chatting with forced levity as she joins me in washing the dishes from supper. She then sets to work brushing the dirt off Melis's overdress, tutting at a grass stain that resists her vigorous scrubbing with diluted white vinegar. It sends a sharp unpleasant scent through the air and I want to tell her to stop, that no amount of scrubbing will make her sister better.

We hear the faint rumble of distant thunder, though the evening is still and balmy, and go out together to put the pony into the barn. Outside the sky is a livid purple. The animal is agitated, sensing the coming storm as I lead him inside, while Hope shoos the chickens into their pen and ensures the hatches are fastened.

'Try not to worry,' I say. 'It's all in her imagination. I

know it can be distressing to witness, but her visions never come to pass. You know that, don't you?' It is what I tell myself every time, and it is true, or almost true. I have never found an explanation for that first vision – *I saw his head hit the ground* – which still squats at the back of my mind, like a curse. It has never been discussed, not with Melis, not with anyone, and Hope was too young to remember.

I want to call it coincidence but I have occasionally wondered whether time can fold in on itself and allow some people, if they are sensitive enough, a glimpse of the future. Some are more receptive to the invisible workings of the world, can intuit things in the way a dog can smell fear. It is often called a gift but to me it seems more of a blight.

'Remember when she predicted the river would burst its banks and flood the village? It never happened.' I list a few other examples, careful to conceal my own misgivings.

'She seemed so . . . so caught up . . .'

'I know. I think her visions can be vivid, as if she is living through them. That's why she becomes so distressed. It'll pass in a while.' The first drops of rain are falling and we hurry towards the house.

'Why is it she only ever predicts bad events?'

'I don't know.' I have wondered about this too and have no answer. Melis is special – that is what our father used to say. Even when she was small it was clear that she was different, more fragile, angrier, as if the world was an ill fit for her.

Melis barely notices us as we come back in and pass through the kitchen into the parlour, where I fasten the front door for the night and close the shutters. Hope winds the old clock. It is a daily job she has taken upon herself since childhood. Hope learned to read a clock face almost before she could read a book. She likes to keep track of the time and the date, always the one to remember birthdays and anniversaries. It appeals to her sense of order, I suppose, to know exactly where we are in time.

'I'm going up,' she says, with a yawn, opening the door to the staircase.

'Will you look in on Rafe?' She studies my face to see if I am worried. I smile but I *am* worried. Despite myself, I, too, have a niggling fear of the house going up in flames. My mind snaps back again to the day our father died – the terrible look Melis had worn.

'Goodnight, then.' The old stairs creak as she mounts them, disappearing into the dark.

'I'll be up soon. Melis had better sleep with me tonight.'

Back in the kitchen Melis hasn't moved. I put a few leaves of lemon balm, her favourite, to infuse in hot water, pour a measure for each of us and take the chair beside her, picking up my needlework. I can hear the trickle of rain outside, comforted at the thought of the thatch soaking through.

The light is fading, so I take a candle, touching its wick to the low flames in the hearth. Melis watches me, alert, as I press it into the holder. It burns with a steady clean flame.

'I'll keep a close eye on it,' I say, as I squint to thread my needle.

'I'm so very grateful to you, Hessie.' The distraught look in her eyes is dissipating. 'You take such good care of me.'

'What happens to you when you have one of your turns? What is it like?' I want to understand the nature of her torment.

'It's as if I go to another place.' She fixes me with an intent gaze. 'Voices draw me there. They show me things . . .' She falters and I reach out to touch her hand. It is stone cold, despite the proximity of the fire. 'I fear one day, Hessie, that I will not find my way back from there.'

'You always do return. You must trust that.'

We are quiet for a while, just the sound of the eaves dripping and the whisper of thread pulling through fabric.

'Rafe hasn't a candle in his room, has he?' She sounds a little less anxious but has clearly been pondering this.

'No. Hope's made sure of that. You've nothing to worry about.'

'It was terrible. I could hear him screaming for help. It was such a relief to find . . .'

'I know.' I reach for her hand again and sense her slowly returning to her normal self.

'Do you remember when you discovered you were pregnant with him?' She is half smiling, as if it is a good memory. At the time, she was so angry on my behalf, but perhaps she doesn't remember that. Perhaps it seems a good memory to her because it marked our departure from Lady Buckingham's household: a grim place indeed for two parentless girls who were not quite well enough bred to fit in.

It is not a good memory for me.

I kept my suspicions to myself for some weeks, creeping towards the edge of an abyss, as every day I expected my monthlies, which never arrived. Each moment was lived in the hope that I was mistaken. I struggled to complete my household duties, explaining away the morning sickness and the encroaching fatigue as the results of sleepless nights. I hadn't told a soul, not even Melis, but she became increasingly concerned for me, so reluctantly I confided in her.

'I don't understand.' She was deeply upset on my behalf, her pale eyes stuttering. 'How could he do such a thing?'

'It is what happens. Men have appetites they cannot control.' I believed this at the time. It was what he had told me. *If pretty little creatures like you will smile at me, how can I be expected to prevent myself?* I hadn't wanted his attentions, had tried to refuse him, but I was too young then and too afraid.

'But it is wrong . . . so unjust.' Melis had always struggled to accept the inherent unfairness of the world. The sudden loss of our father had affected us in different ways: where she railed against injustice, I immersed myself in responsibilities. 'He must be made to pay.' Her upset was transforming into anger and I regretted confiding in her.

She insisted on coming with me to his study, where we household servants were forbidden to go. The door was of polished walnut and smelt strongly of beeswax. I stood before it, nipped with dread, waves of nausea buffeting through me, wishing myself anywhere else on earth. Eventually I mustered the courage to knock, but Melis pushed it open before I had the chance to stop her and marched in. She was too young to understand that her well-meant support of me risked making things worse for us both.

He was inside with his elderly mother, who cast us a glance, sharp as a serpent's tooth. 'What do you think you are doing?' She was outraged by our insolence. 'You haven't permission to be in here. Get back to where you belong. I will not tolerate disobedience in my household.'

I girded myself, dropping into a deep curtsy, pulling

Melis down with me, an apology on my lips, explaining that I had something important to discuss with her son. He was leaning against the wall, watching, seeming faintly amused by my distress.

'Important? I hope at the very least someone has died.' There wasn't even a fleck of kindness in that woman.

'I'll see to this,' he said to her.

'As you wish. I was leaving anyway.' She heaved her considerable form out of her chair, departing in a rustle of black silk and making a comment about the ills of taking in girls of the wrong breeding. 'Orphaned daughters of a country physician. I should have known . . .' The door swung shut with a clunk.

'So?' He stepped towards us, sweeping his hair back with an equine toss of the head, and stood, legs apart, arms folded, lips twisted into a sneer.

I couldn't find my voice but Melis spoke into her collar. 'You've got her with child.'

'Speak up.' His voice snapped like a whip.

She repeated it, but louder, with a snarl in her tone.

He took her by the scruff, as if she was a dog, lifting her from the floor. 'If I was you, I'd watch my tongue. Bad things can happen to girls who tell tales.' He let her go. She stumbled backwards. I grabbed her to keep her from falling. 'Now get out of here. Wait outside. This is between your sister and me.'

She turned, slicing him with a sharp glare as she left.

Once the door was shut he confronted me. 'Is it true?'

'It is.' I kept my eyes down, fixed on his shoes, which were of kid, tooled in an intricate pattern of vines and fastened with elaborate silver buckles. A new wave of nausea racked me and I feared I would spew all over them.

'There are powders you can take to get rid of it. They work in some cases if you catch it early enough. I shall make arrangements.'

'But that is a sin.' I was horrified by his suggestion, made without so much as a turned hair, as if the life growing inside me was nothing more than an inconvenience.

He spat out a laugh. 'One more sin for a little hussy like you won't make much difference when it comes to Judgement Day.'

I found my courage then and firmly said, 'Never!'

'Don't claim I haven't tried to help you.'

'I don't want your help.'

'Why are you here, then?'

'I thought . . . I thought . . .' In truth I didn't know what I thought. If I had expected his sympathy or kindness I was mistaken and should have known that.

'You seek payment?'

'No . . . no.' I was dismayed that he thought me so mercenary.

'You do understand that you can't remain here? There is no place for pregnant whores in my mother's household. How am I even to know that the child is mine?' It was impossible to see even the smallest vestige of his famous beauty. The cold, hard creature before me, father of my unborn child, had become repulsive.

It was the moment I grew up.

'You and your sister will leave first thing in the morning.' He swiped his arm over the piles of papers on his desk, scattering them across the floor and, looking directly at me, said, 'See what you've done.' I knew better than to contradict him. 'Pick up this mess and make yourself scarce. I have things of importance to see to.' As he was about to leave, he turned to me with a disturbing huff of laughter. 'If it's a boy, and I like the look of him, I might want him for myself when he's grown.' The door slammed and I was left to crawl around the floor retrieving his paperwork.

That was nine years ago, the last time I saw George Villiers. Even though I told myself he had said it only to taunt me, those words – *when he's grown* – had sat niggling at the back of my mind, like a debt to a wicked fairy.

Hope

Hope flings open the kitchen door. The morning is clear after the rain and everything smells fresh. The little pasture beyond the orchard is a brilliant green and she is infused with relief that the night has passed without mishap.

She can hear Hester upstairs, getting Rafe dressed and ready to go to Littlemore for his lessons with Ambrose. She prods the hearth to see if she can find any embers still alive to rekindle but it is dead. Melis must have ensured so last night. She sweeps out the ash and lays a new fire, setting herself down with the tinderbox as Rafe and Hester clatter in.

Hester sits Rafe at the table, buttering a slice of bread for him and pouring a cup of milk, then goes to let the hens out, returning with a clutch of eggs.

'Can I go to Littlemore on the pony?' Rafe asks, between mouthfuls.

'I don't see why not. Now sit still.' Hester is attempting to tug a comb through his tangled hair. He is complaining, ducking away from her, refusing to sit still.

'Very well, then. As you wish.' Hester puts down the comb with a sigh. She rarely refuses Rafe anything and, secretly, Hope has opinions about that. Even she, who has little knowledge of such things, knows that a child shouldn't be overindulged.

Melis comes in, still in her nightdress, rubbing her eyes. They all turn, regarding her anxiously.

'No need to look at me as if I'm a lunatic. I'm perfectly well.' She sits beside her nephew and begins to slice the loaf, asking if anyone else wants some, taking a drink from Rafe's cup and tickling him when he protests, making him laugh. 'This butter's on the turn.' She sniffs it with a grimace, the vivid yellow reflecting on her pale skin. 'Didn't we buy some yesterday?'

Hope can't help but remember the fallen pat of butter that had been filthy and crawling with ants when she'd finally gone to collect the basket of produce. She shrugs, saying they must have forgotten it, not wanting to drag yesterday's worries into today.

She goes out to saddle up the pony, has just put the bridle over his head, when she sees one of the Littlemore servants striding across the meadow, skirts bunched in her fist, waving with her other hand. Hope crosses the orchard to meet her, racking her mind for the girl's name, unable to remember it.

'Dr Cotton asked me to come and tell you that there will be no lessons today.' There is a smudge of dirt on her apron, her shoes are scuffed and her hair is escaping untidily from her cap. 'The mistress is ailing and he doesn't want Rafe there in case it is contagious.'

Hope is remembering Bette's hacking cough the other evening. 'Oh dear. It's kind of you to come. Will you tell her we send our best?' The girl is about to turn on her heel when Hope adds, 'In fact, would you mind waiting? I'm sure Hester would like to write your mistress a note.'

As they enter the house, the maid casts her eyes around with disdain. She seems surprised by the mean dimensions

34

of the Orchard Cottage kitchen, as if she'd expected them to be more elevated, the family being such close friends of her employer.

Melis, who is carefully pouring hot wax from a pan into candle moulds, must have noticed the girl's expression too. 'Are we not grand enough for you?'

The girl looks down, hot red blotches blossoming on her throat. The forgotten name springs into Hope's mind: Joan. Now she has remembered it seems obvious: she looks like a Joan, with her red face and bitten nails. She sits, nervously tapping a foot against the table leg, while Hope fetches Hester, who writes a hasty note to Bette. Hope can't help but notice Joan's shoes are dirty and each time she taps a little chip of dry mud breaks away to land on the newly swept floor.

'Do you mind?' says Melis, pointing to the scattering of dirt. 'That floor was clean.' The girl mumbles an apology. Hester frowns at Melis, but Hope is just happy that her sister is back to her usual outspoken self.

Hester, ever the diplomat, seeks to put the girl at her ease. 'Never mind. It's just a bit of dust.'

Once the visitor has gone, the three sisters settle to their mending. Rafe is restless with the day's plans thwarted, fidgeting and taunting the cat. Hester suggests he tidy the needlework box. He sits on the floor, tipping it to spill the jumble of contents onto the flagstones, at last becoming absorbed in sorting the buttons and hooks, untangling the spools of thread and arranging all the pins in the pincushion.

'You're such a help, sweetheart,' Hester says, watching him fondly. He basks in her approval. Hope wonders if it is good for him to lead a life so mollycoddled, whether it might be better for him to go to school and meet other boys his own age. It is not the first time she has thought about it, and once she had brought it up with Hester, who said she'd consider it but never mentioned the subject again.

A squeal shatters the peace and the sound of buttons skittering over the floor. Rafe has flung the newly tidied box to the flagstones and is holding his thumb aloft. A bead of blood is swelling where he has managed to prick himself on one of the sharp leatherwork needles.

'Why don't we take the pony up the lane, get some fresh air?' Hope suggests, to distract him.

Rafe kicks the piebald into a trot. 'Don't go too far ahead,' Hope calls. 'Wait for me at the oak.' He is a confident rider, looks good in the saddle, straight-backed and taller than he really is. Hope ambles in his wake, collecting scented herbs into a posy as she goes.

At the oak there is no sign of the previous day's incident, not even a slick of butter in the grass. It makes her question whether it happened at all. The hole in the tree gapes. A bee wavers nearby, disappearing inside. An involuntary spasm runs through her and she feels compelled to get away from the place. 'Let's go back.'

They arrive home to find Hester and Melis outside the front door, laughing about something, heads thrown back in happy abandon. The feeling is infectious and the unease she had felt only minutes before wanes.

'Someone's coming,' says Rafe, craning his neck to see over the high yew hedge, as they become aware of the jangle of horses approaching down the lane. Two eventually come into sight, not the nags usually to be seen around

Iffley but great big beasts, glossy with long, crimped manes and silver-beaded browbands that catch the light. The two riders are as fancy as bishops, one in a scarlet suit with an ostrich feather in his cap. As for the other, Hope has never seen the like. He is garlanded with pearls and his jacket gleams with gold thread, as if he is a god.

Hester's eyes narrow.

The air thickens – you could almost ram a pin into it.

Something is amiss.

'Take Rafe to the back.' Hester's voice is reedy.

Hope doesn't argue, though her curiosity about the visitors is almost too much to contain, and pulls Rafe, protesting, towards the kitchen door.

Hester

I recognize George Villiers immediately, dread dropping into me, rooting me to the doorstep as, speechless, I watch him dismount and saunter up the front path.

I can't find my voice. It is Melis who speaks. 'What are you doing here?' There is no need to ask: he can be here only for Rafe, who is now, thankfully, out of sight.

He ignores her. 'Aren't you going to invite me in?' He walks past us over the threshold, taking claim of the space. His head almost brushes the low beams of the parlour. I wish he would crack it against one.

I feel the pulse, deep within, of a monster so far buried I had forgotten its force. It stirs, opening an eye to watch him, bedecked in jewels and pearls and gilded gewgaws, as if an ember has broken off the sun and fallen into my home, threatening to burn it to the ground.

'Ah! Little Hessie, quite the woman now.' His smile mocks.

I would like to take my pet name out of his mouth and smash it to pieces on the floor so it can never be used again.

He removes his hat and shakes out his hair. He was always proud of his chestnut curls. Now grey strands run through them and I notice, with a shameful jolt of satisfaction, that he has become a little paunchy.

'What brings you here?' I can't bear to say his name. It's

all I can do to prevent myself spitting on the floor by his feet and sending him packing.

Melis steps forward to stand beside me in sisterly solidarity. We both know there can be no good reason for this visit.

He looms between us and the door with the light at his back.

Beyond him I can see Hope trying to contain Rafe, who has broken from her grasp and is running towards the horses. George's man is leaning against the wall smoking a pipe, eyes on Hope, who gives him a flirtatious smile. He is wearing a foppish jacket the colour of raspberries and blows out an ostentatious chain of smoke rings, seeming the type to be exactly aware of how good-looking he is. Rafe is gazing up in awe at the imposing pair of Holsteiners, slurping loudly from the trough, putting our own stocky piebald pony to shame.

'I'm here to see my boy.'

My hackles rise. I don't respond and will Rafe to return round the back, out of sight.

'He must be growing up.' George says this in a manner that suggests he means something by it.

'He's *eight*!' I understand the implication. Keeping an eye firmly on Rafe, I watch him stroking one of the animals, a vast hunter, black and shiny as tar. Hope is distracted, deep in conversation with the foppish manservant.

'Nearly nine, by my calculation,' he counters.

'We don't want you here. Stay away from Rafe,' spits Melis. I give her ankle a sharp kick. It will make things worse if George is riled. But he seems more amused than annoyed and runs his eyes over Melis, who returns his look with a scowl.

39

As he moves to sit I nudge the door half shut with my foot to block his view of the front path. He brushes his knees with a quick flick of his fingers though his breeches are spotless. I wonder how he managed to travel all the way from Whitehall to Iffley without acquiring so much as a speck of dirt.

'I was rather surprised to hear you'd named him Rafe.' He says the name as if it has a bitter taste. The implication is that he'd expected our child to be named for him.

'I called him after my father.' Sliding a hand into my pocket, I find the soft contours of the wax figure Rafe made for me.

'You always were a headstrong little thing.'

A memory comes to me, something I haven't thought of in years, of an incident back at Lady Buckingham's. One of the pages was wearing a neckerchief embroidered with rosemary sprigs, unusual enough for George to remark on it.

'It was given me by my mother,' the boy told him, 'before she died.'

'May I look?' George had produced his most beguiling smile as the boy untied the scarf for him to inspect. 'Silk.' He ran it through his fingers. 'It really is rather lovely.'

'She was known for her skills at needlework.' The boy swelled with pride but I remember feeling uneasy, for the kerchief was not so remarkable as George was making it seem, only a thing of sentimental value.

'What I would give for something like this.'

'Then it is yours.' I saw the flicker of regret cross the boy's face once the words had been said but it was too late. He couldn't rescind the offer and George knew it.

'Such generosity will surely reap great rewards.'

When the boy had gone, George threw the kerchief onto the fire. 'Hideous thing.'

It reminds me who I am dealing with.

'Where are you hiding him, then?' His tone is light, teasing. 'I caught a glimpse of him before you hustled him off.'

The air in the room thins, suspicion threading through it like spider's silk. Beyond the sliver of open door I can see George's man about to help Rafe onto the back of the vast hunter. Melis, seeing it too, gives my hand a squeeze and says, 'You must both have things you need to discuss.' She slides past George and outside towards Rafe. She has smelt the danger, too, but I fear it is too late.

Before I have had the chance to close the door behind her, George has twisted in his seat. 'There he is. My boy.' A shadow of disappointment passes over his face. 'He's rather small for his age.'

'He takes after me.' Defiantly I keep my eyes trained on George. Everyone says how like me Rafe is. *If I like the look of him.* I hope against all hope that this will mean George rejects him.

'Why so prickly, Hessie?' He makes a kind of amiable half-shrug, smacking of false innocence.

It is a gesture I remember, one he used to make when he wanted something. George always got what he wanted. And if he ever met with a refusal, he would simply help himself. That was how he got me. He helped himself to my virtue. He would never have considered that he hadn't the right to take any of the girls in his mother's household. He would never have considered that my cries of 'No!' meant anything at all.

My monster stirs again, yawning, stretching.

41

'My people have been keeping an eye on you.' He says it as if it is a privilege. I feel stripped bare. Everyone knows of the Duke of Buckingham's network of informers but I'd been naive enough to hope I wasn't of sufficient importance to merit such attentions.

The silence is astringent. I watch Melis hustling Rafe and Hope out of sight and hear the kitchen door shut at the back of the cottage.

'His birthday is soon, isn't it?'

'I'm sure your *people* have informed you of that.'

'Of course they have.' George expels a short laugh and seizes my waist, pulling me down onto his lap. 'The fourteenth day of September. Holy Cross Day. He will be nine. Hasn't time flown? It doesn't seem nearly a decade since . . .' I try to wriggle free, but he has me fast and he is strong. His smell is horribly familiar. He still wears the same pomade – lilies. The smell of funerals.

'Don't you want me to see him?'

I know if I refuse him his determination will be roused, so I say nothing.

'He needs to learn how to be a man,' continues George. 'Not be cosseted by women. He'll go soft.'

'He is tutored by Dr Cotton.' I have a horrible certainty about the outcome of this visit.

'I'm aware of that. I don't approve of Ambrose Cotton.' Red patches flush his cheeks and he tightens his clasp on my waist until I fear he will bruise my ribs. I would rather die than let him know he is hurting me.

I find my voice. 'Dr Cotton is an upright man. He is Rafe's godfather and very dear to us. He took us in when our father died.' I consider that, of course, George already knows this.

'I will not have *my* son raised by a coven of women.' Anger leaks from behind his veneer.

'We are far from a coven, my sisters and I.' It is all I can do to prevent the alarm from sounding in my voice.

'You keep yourselves to yourselves.' He has tempered his tone. 'It makes people talk.'

'We live quietly, that is all.' I don't point out to him that I have to couch myself in a lie of respectability to ensure I am a welcome member of the parish. I suppose he knows this about me, too, but I will not cast my situation as anything other than ideal.

George is talking, asking if we aren't cramped living here, but I am not listening as a sudden new panic has taken hold of me: that while George has engaged me in conversation, his manservant has stolen Rafe away. I twist my neck to gain a view through the crack of the door and, to my great relief, the man is still leaning against the gatepost, smoking.

'Listen,' George continues, loosening his grip with a disingenuous smile. 'I have a proposition.'

I meet his twinkling gaze with a blunted stare, girding myself. 'Go on.'

'When he is nine, Rafe will take his place in my household. It is the right age for him to begin his education in the ways of court.' I don't point out that it is an order, not a proposition. 'Six weeks will give you ample time to prepare him.' He is smiling, taking pleasure in my pain.

I won't be cowed. I have no intention of losing Rafe to the deceits of court where he will learn to hate me for my modest means. 'You have a son with your wife. Why would you want —'

'Ah!' He doesn't let me finish. 'So, you *do* follow my affairs.' His tone is triumphant.

43

'The whole country knows your business, George.'

He softens his tone. 'Don't be like this, Hessie. You were fond of me once. Have you forgotten?'

His face is the image of sincerity and I understand something about George I had never realized before: that he has absorbed the lies he tells himself until they have become indistinguishable from the truth. There is no point in reminding him that he took me against my will or telling him that I never felt anything for him but hatred: he cannot see beyond the dense cladding of falsehood he has built.

'I don't think you understand.' He begins to rub my back with the flat of his palm. I flinch beneath his touch. 'As my son he will have all the advantages. He will take precedence over all but those of my children born to my wife.' He looks around the house with a barely disguised sneer. 'You wouldn't want to deny our boy the kind of advantages I can give him, would you?'

'If you knew me, you would understand that I find such ambitions meaningless.' I am aware I should give him the impression at least that I intend to concede to his demands. But I can't bring myself to do so. 'Rafe is happy and safe here with us.'

He releases a sardonic gust of laughter. 'I'd forgotten quite how wilful you could be, Hester.' He pushes me off his lap with a pat on my backside.

I step away from his reach, hands tightly fisted.

He shifts and I think he is going to stand but all he does is uncross his legs and re-cross them the other way. 'I'll make it worth your while. Set you up in decent fashion – a manor, an annuity.'

I lift my chin and stand firm. 'My son is not for sale. Not at any price.'

'I could simply take him. You do know that? Of course you do. But I don't want things to be like that.' He tilts his head to the side, his eyes widening with false sincerity. 'Surely you don't either.' He is toying with me, as a cat with its prey.

I know that vanity is George's weakness. Even when he took my virtue, he sought to believe I gave myself freely, wanted to hear me say so. *How much do you want this?* I see now it is the same with Rafe. He wants my agreement to satisfy his own pride. I will not give it as long as I have breath in my body. Rafe is not some silk kerchief to be thrown into the fire.

'How do you manage here?' He waves his arm in an arc, with undisguised disdain for the ordinary surroundings.

'Since your people have been "keeping an eye on me",' I say pointedly, 'I'm sure you already know the answer to that.'

He raises his eyebrows, making no attempt to hide his amusement, and picks up the book that is on the table, opening it to read its title: '*The Feminine Monarchie, or a treatise concerning bees.* So, Mr Butler's book is where you learned to keep bees?'

'My sister is a gifted apiarist. It is her book.'

He snorts derisively and reaches to pinch the fabric of my dress between his thumb and forefinger. 'You still manage to turn yourself out well on your meagre income.'

I am sure his implication is that our industry extends to something more nefarious than beekeeping and needle-work. 'We make an honest living here.' My voice is steady despite the rage seething beneath my surface. 'Now that you have said what you wanted to say, I would be grateful if you would kindly take your leave.' Stonily, I gesture towards the door.

He relaxes further into his chair. 'So much for English hospitality. I haven't even been offered a drink. You weren't always so ungenerous with me.' His leer drills deep. 'I will leave when I'm good and ready. I have not yet had the pleasure of meeting my son.'

He has risen to his feet and is pushing open the door that leads to the kitchen.

Melis moves to put herself firmly between him and Rafe. I cast my eyes round the room, instinctively thinking of what might best serve as a weapon should I need it.

But George has benignly squatted on his haunches and beckoned Rafe over, so he can pretend to make a coin appear from behind his ear. Rafe laughs and looks in wonder at the gilded stranger. 'Keep it,' George says.

Six weeks, I am thinking. Six weeks.

Hope is gazing agog at George and I am reminded of when I first set eyes on him. I was more or less the same age as she is now. Sixteen is too young to see beyond the end of your nose. That was his effect, everyone falling in thrall to him, as if he'd been dipped in the Styx, like Achilles, and rendered half god. I had quickly learned the dangers of such bedazzlement.

'What do you say, Rafe?' I won't have him forget his manners whatever the circumstances, and he mumbles a thank-you, pocketing the coin.

'I saw you admiring my horse, young man. Do you like to ride?'

'I do, but we have only a fat pony, nothing like your horse.'

I watch my son, heart bloating until I ache with love. I

46

can't find any resemblance, nothing at all of his father. He is all mine. It feels like my victory, rather than Nature's, and I will do anything to prevent even the smallest part of that man from rubbing off on my sweet boy.

'I have a stable full of animals just like him. Would you like one of your own?'

Just as I think I am going to have to defend Rafe against a barrage of persuasion, Melis steps up to George, standing inches from him. 'Leave us alone.' Her face is painted with loathing, her eyes directed at his, and she points her finger a hair's breadth from his chest. 'I know what you are.'

I try to drag her away but she shoves me off without removing her stare from George. 'Traitor,' she hisses.

I am in turmoil but plaster a smile onto my face, as if it is nothing.

George laughs dismissively, but I can tell he is angry. Beads of sweat have formed on his brow and his voice cracks slightly as he looks at me to say, 'I should have thought by now that your sister would know when to keep her mouth shut.' I can see the menace beneath his surface, his words needle sharp. Melis has touched a nerve.

'Come, Melis.' I try to persuade her away but she won't be moved.

'We have proof. Proof of your treachery.'

'Stop, Melis.' My heart collapses. She seems not to realize the trouble she's stirring for us with her outburst. 'She doesn't know what she's saying.' I try to sound light.

'I *do* know what I'm saying.' Her prodding finger makes contact with his breast.

'ENOUGH!' George's façade fractures as he barks the command.

'You're not making sense, Melis.' I try to sound placatory. But she *is* making sense. That is what has nettled George.

'Don't make the mistake of believing yourself immortal,' she says, and marches out into the yard. I can see her through the window, making for the orchard and her hives.

George has regained his composure. 'I'd advise you to keep your sister under control. Most wouldn't tolerate such aspersions being cast.'

'Don't mind her,' I say, with a gesture that implies my sister is not entirely in control of her faculties.

His expression is as hard and cool as glass. 'No?' He runs his knuckles slowly over my cheek and the air seems to coagulate, like beaten cream.

'Melis imagines things.'

'Even so, there are punishments for slanders such as that.' He pinches my cheek hard. 'You know that, don't you?'

I nod. 'She doesn't understand what she says.'

'I may consider letting it go.' He is back on firm territory, his eyes boring into me before shifting to Rafe. 'Prepare him well for the change of circumstances. Wouldn't want it to come as too much of a shock to him ... would we?' Something sharp lodges in my breast. 'Would you kindly tell my man to make the horses ready?' he says to Hope, his voice velvet smooth.

Fixing his eyes on mine he says, 'You will be hearing from me.'

'Who was that?' asks Rafe, when he has gone.

'Someone you should take no notice of.'

'He promised me a horse.'

48

'He didn't mean it, darling.' I stroke his shiny conker hair and the soft skin of his neck, feeling his disappointment as if it were mine. I would sell my soul to save him from upset. 'One day you shall have a horse even better than that.'

Hope is still suspended in wonder. 'To think the duke was standing here in this kitchen.'

Hope knows George only by reputation: the great man depicted in the news-sheets as more powerful even than King Charles.

'That man is none of our business,' I say bluntly, then go upstairs to find my writing box.

Opening it, I pull out all of the papers and tuck my fingernail under the base, lifting up the false bottom, drawing out a bundle of correspondence, yellowed at the edges and pocked with age. I flick through it, making sure all the letters are there in George's distinctive, forward-thrusting handwriting and the replies bearing the Spanish ambassador's seal.

I am back in his study at Whitehall, on the floor gathering up the mess of fallen papers. He must have assumed me too ill-educated to understand what they were, probably assumed I couldn't read. I *could* read and was perfectly able to deduce from the pages I skimmed over that George had been passing state secrets to our enemy, Spain. To what ends, I still don't understand, but it was treason, of that I had no doubt.

His carelessness in leaving such sensitive material open even to the eyes of a maid he assumed illiterate might have seemed surprising to someone who didn't know him. But you had only to know him a little to understand the profound belief he held of being untouchable.

I'd selected a few of the more incriminating pages, which I stuffed under my dress, spending that final night at White-hall wide awake and petrified that he would spot they were missing. I might have been young and ignorant but I was never so much of a fool to believe I might not need to pro-tect myself. From what exactly, I didn't know at the time. It was my orphan's sense of self-preservation, I suppose.

Looking through the papers now, I wonder if the years that have passed have rendered obsolete their potential to damage him. But treason is treason, and in the intervening years George has accrued powerful enemies who would be glad of such potent ammunition.

I return them to their cache, and don't mention them when I write to Ambrose, asking his advice on my predicament.

Ambrose's reply arrives early the following morning. *We must get you away from Orchard Cottage before Rafe's birthday*, he writes emphatically. *I can make arrangements for you to go some-where safe. Prepare to leave by the end of the month and don't advertise your departure to a soul.* The words *Burn this, once read* bring home to me the reach of my adversary, but I am relieved at least that Ambrose has a plan for us.

That afternoon, Mr Worley, George's foppish manser-vant, arrives with a package for Rafe. It contains a suit of clothes, stiff and ugly with embellishment. The sight of it angers me, as does the book of etiquette that is packed with it and the letter with detailed instructions for Rafe's preparation.

Worley hovers, with his irritating air of contempt, sug-gesting I might wish to reply to the duke. I snap at him, telling him to wait in the kitchen. Taking out my writing things, I am subsumed with a terrible sense of hopeless-ness. We can hide but George will find us eventually. I begin to write, the pen scratching deeply into the paper as my misery turns to rage.

It is only as I watch Worley leave at full-pelt for White-hall with the reply – *I would rather die than hand my son into your care* – that my anger subsides, giving rise to the sicken-ing feeling that I have made an irreversible and terrible mistake. My gut contracts, painful as colic, with the recol-lection of what else I wrote: *I can prove you once committed treason and I am not afraid to use that knowledge, should you try to take my son from me.*

Threatening George will ignite every last ember of his malice. Running out into the lane, I shout for Worley to wait. He doesn't hear. He is galloping away out of sight.

I shout again but my voice is lost in the thunder of hoofs.

'Is something the matter?' It is Hope, who has found me clinging to the gatepost, unable to move.

'It's nothing. Just a little lightheaded, that's all. I didn't breakfast this morning.' I attempt a cheerful smile – I don't want to worry her. We walk together towards the house where Rafe is kicking a ball repeatedly against the wall. Thump, thump, thump, the sound like a hammer inside my skull. I turn on him, my misplaced rage undiluted. 'For pity's sake, stop that!'

Rafe turns his eyes towards me with a sideways frown, picks up the ball and skulks off, while Hope guides me inside.

'If he'd been a girl,' I state baldly, 'none of this would be happening.' It is the truth. Girls count for nothing, unless they are wealthy.

The house feels stuffy and dark, and I am sure I can still

smell George's lily-scented pomade, as if he has marked the place, like a dog. I try, but fail, to convince myself that perhaps he will desist in his mission to take Rafe from me, that perhaps I have done the right thing in standing up to him.

I scribble a quick note to Ambrose, informing him that we need to leave urgently, first thing in the morning. I ask Hope to deliver it to Littlemore and set to preparing for our departure, unable to shake off the creeping panic, as if I have been stabbed in the stomach and await the imminent arrival of death.

Hope

Hope lies in the dark, recalling the events of the previous hour or two. She can still feel his hands exploring the secret pockets of her body, can hear him: 'I must leave you, precious girl. Your sisters mustn't find me here.'

She wanted to confide in him that they are leaving Orchard Cottage in the morning but Hester has forbidden her to speak of it. In fact, Hester has been infuriatingly abstruse about their plans. Hope doesn't know where they are going – she doesn't even know *why* they are leaving in such a hurry. Her sister thinks of her as a child but she is not, not any more.

It was her first time. She is supposed to regret it. She doesn't. How could she wish away such pleasure? And he so tender, making her feel things she has never felt. For a moment she wonders if she didn't dream it, but her thumb finds the hard contour of the ring he gave her. It is too big for the correct finger. He has promised to have it altered.

'Gold,' he had said, kissing the back of her hand, 'just right for your complexion. Most girls don't suit gold but it's perfect on you.' His words had coiled around her tightly, making speech impossible. No one had ever said anything like that about her complexion. She only ever received insults. Gypsy, they would call her, and worse.

But not him. No.

He had said, 'There is no one like you, Hope. I want to make a wife of you, give you the position in the world you deserve,' and buried his face in her curls, breathing her in, then removing her clothes, carefully, like someone peeling an apple in a single spiral.

She floats away on the thought.

Then comes the collapsing feeling of loss, of separation, the tug of want, so strong, as if every part of her has his name etched through it.

Now she understands what people mean when they talk of love.

A sound interrupts her thoughts, a scuffling, a small cry, perhaps a fox. But, no, it comes from inside the house.

She sits up, alert now.

There it is again.

She pulls herself out of the bed, listening in the corridor, feeling her way through the dark to the nook where Rafe sleeps, thinking he might have had a nightmare and cried out. He has been unsettled since the duke's visit. Carefully drawing back the bed curtain, she reaches down to stroke his hair. Her hands find nothing but an empty expanse of pillow, still warm, and a hollow where his head should be. She feels around the bed, finding only the monkey she had sewn for him from an old stocking, its button eyes hard rounds beneath her fingers.

She considers all the possibilities that might have drawn the child from his bed in the middle of the night. He might have gone to get a drink, he might have slipped into his mother's bed, he might have sleepwalked somewhere. But she has never known him to sleepwalk before.

A door scrapes downstairs.

She hears, distinctly, the sound of Rafe calling, 'No!' accompanied by a scuffling sound. 'Leave me alone.'

She knows the firm voice that tells him to hush.

Guilt has her in its claws.

She runs down the stairs, shouting for help. At the bottom she hears Rafe's protestations, muffled now, and imagines the hand over his mouth – the same hand that was . . . The thought is too appalling to allow.

She flings open the door to the kitchen. It bangs loudly against the wall. Worley is struggling with the window latch, Rafe in his grip, kicking and writhing. She can hear her sisters upstairs, roused by the noise.

'Sweetness,' he is saying to her. 'It's not what you think. I found him down here, quite distressed.' He smiles but she knows what she sees.

'Lies, all lies!' Mustering every shred of her strength, she grabs a heavy pan from the table, rushing at him, striking him hard over the head.

A blunt thump sounds out.

He staggers back, swaying, then staggers further, grabbing the edge of the table to prevent himself from falling. He still holds Rafe by the arm.

'Let him go this minute!' comes a shout from behind her. It is Hester. Rafe breaks free, running into the arms of his mother.

Worley, still stunned, touches his head, looking at his hand, seeming surprised to find he is not bleeding. She cannot seem to move. He crumples to the floor. She is horrified, believing she has killed him, but he scrambles back to his feet. Something bright in his hand catches the moonlight.

He has a blade.

Hope screeches like a harpy, charging at him again, swinging the pan, its weight giving it momentum as it whacks across his back with force.

A choked cry explodes from him as he pitches forward, winded.

He thrashes frantically with the knife. It whistles through the air, close. Hester reaches for the poker. Hope thumps the pan against his arm. Something skitters across the floor. It is his blade, coming to rest in the far corner, out of his reach.

She glances to Hester, gesturing towards the pantry. Its door is open just behind him. Between them they can back him in and secure the door. Escape will be impossible from the small windowless space.

Hope edges forward. He steps back, as if they are in a dance. Then, in one swift sudden movement, he lurches to one side, heaving the full weight of his shoulder into the window. It swings open, glass shattering. In an instant he has vaulted out and run off down the lane, with the big yard-dog barking in his wake.

Turning back to the room, Hope sees that Melis has joined Hester, who has her arms wrapped round Rafe's shoulders: three white faces, staring through the gloom. Heart still rattling, Hope sinks to the floor. Feeling a tickle of pain on her hand, she sees a dark smear: it is blood. Worley's blade must have nicked her. She sucks at the cut. Her mouth is flooded with the taste of metal and her guts seize as the fear she should have felt minutes ago finally catches up.

'How did he get in?' Melis says.

Hope shrugs, looking at the floor as she registers the need to explain how Marmaduke Worley came to be upstairs in the house in the middle of the night.

Hester is talking to Rafe, soothing him, asking him what happened. His response is slurred and incomprehensible. He seems in a stupor, eyes half closed, head lolling, and she can't get any sense out of him.

Worley must have sedated him.

Hope is appalled by what she has allowed to happen, drowning in her own stupidity.

'How did he get in here?' Hester asks this time, her face pallid in the gloom.

'I'm sorry, so, so sorry.' Hope hauls herself to her feet to make her confession, berating herself, preparing for the worst. 'It's all my fault. I let him take me for a fool.'

'He seduced you?' Hester's suppressed rage is evident in the tight clipping of her words.

Hope says nothing, gazes at her feet, holding onto the faint tick of the hall clock that penetrates the heavy silence.

'We can't stay here.' says Melis. 'It isn't safe.'

'We need to get to Littlemore,' announces Hester.

'That's the first place they'll look for us if we're not here,' says Melis.

'Ambrose knows of somewhere we can go. Come,' Hester chivvies them. 'There's no time to waste.'

Hope has the yard-dog on a lead for protection, and Worley's knife is tucked into Hester's belt. There is only the one mount, the sturdy little piebald, which Rafe, still dazed, is slumped over like a sack of grain.

As they set off across country, it is barely light but the first birds are already singing. They avoid the roads. Dawn arrives with layers of cloud, thick as porridge, that begin to leak rain, and their clothes are soon heavy with wet hems trailing in the mud.

Hope's conscience weighs heavy.

Worley's ring mocks her.

She removes it. She can sell it, at least. But it has left a dark, greenish smudge on her finger – so, not gold but brass. What a fool to think true love can alight in a matter of days.

She throws it into the undergrowth and trudges on through the wet, hauling her burden of shame, hatred simmering for the man who duped her. With each small sound, each crack of a twig or rustle in the hedgerow, she glances back, half expecting to see a flash of crimson jacket dipping behind a tree.

Hester

We reach Littlemore Manor a bedraggled group, weary and wet through. The rain becomes sparse and the bank of cloud rips open, shafts of light forcing their way through so the puddles glisten and wink. A rainbow shimmers above, mocking us with its promise of good fortune.

I bang on the door several times, and when there is no response, I shout and rap at the downstairs windows until the servant girl opens up. It is the same girl with the dirty shoes whom Melis was so sharp with the other day, holding a finger to her lips with a grave expression.

'Has the mistress shown no signs of recovery?' In the panic I had all but forgotten about Bette's illness.

The girl lifts a shoulder, raising both palms to face upward. 'It's not smallpox, at least.'

We shuffle inside, quietly, and she leaves us in the hall to wait. Ambrose's hound, Caesar, lollops over to lick my hand with his warm tongue. I stroke the dome of his head. Even he seems subdued. We cluster close to the hearth, though the fire is not lit, somehow imagining we might find some warmth there.

Eventually Ambrose appears, descending the stairs, eyes ringed in shadow, dark as bruises.

He attempts a smile, just visible behind his beard, which has become wild and untrimmed. 'What brings you here so early?' He is well aware that only trouble could bring us to Littlemore at the crack of dawn. 'I received your note, saying you needed to get away this morning, but I didn't expect . . .' He is desperately agitated, his hands fumbling together. 'I'm afraid you find us in disarray. Bette has taken a turn for the worse.'

A gulf widens between us. He would normally open his arms and enfold me in an embrace but today he advises me to keep my distance in case of contagion.

'Come in here, where we can talk in private.' He opens the door to his study and asks the maid to take the others to the kitchens. 'Give them something to eat, Joan, and dry out their clothes.' I peel off my damp coat and dig around in my bag for a shawl.

Once we are inside Ambrose's study, he closes the door. The room is warmer, a fire burning. I stand near to it, the smell of damp wool rising off me.

'How is she?' I ask.

'She's reaching the crisis. If she survives until tomorrow, we have reason for optimism.' His face shows the opposite of confidence.

'I'm so very sorry, Ambrose.' He'd always said he was waiting for the perfect woman and had found her eventually in Bette.

'Now, will you tell me what's going on?'

As I explain about the attempted kidnapping, Ambrose looks increasingly perturbed. 'I must confess, Hessie, when you mentioned that the duke had visited, I was worried he might try something underhand. But I thought Rafe was to go to him on his birthday. That's still some time off.' He runs his palm over the ashy stubble of his hair. 'I don't understand.'

'Circumstances have changed.' I can't quite admit to him that it is my own fault matters have become so urgent. Silently I curse myself for my folly.

'Why didn't he simply send a few armed guards to fetch the boy? You would have been powerless to prevent them from taking him.'

'I know George better than you. To him it would be an insult to his vanity. One of the guards would have been sure to say something to someone and word would have got round that a lowly rural doctor's daughter had refused him, the great duke, custody of his own son.' I give a sardonic snort. 'Sending a trusted agent to steal Rafe allows him to craft the story he wants everyone to believe.'

'I see.' Ambrose looks at me directly. 'He must not only have everything he wants, but it must be seen to be given willingly.'

'Correct.' I hold my hands over the fire, thawing them.

'You can't stay here. It will be the first place he'll look.'

'You said in your letter that you knew of somewhere we could go.'

'I do.' He sits at his desk pulling a leaf of paper from a stack. 'You know what my opinion is of the duke. He could murder a man in the middle of the Strand on market day and get away with it. No mud sullies George Villiers.' He uncorks his ink and dips his pen. 'We shall have to make you disappear.'

'It might be the moment to show you these.' I reach inside my clothes and draw out the sheaf of yellowing correspondence I have harboured for nine years.

As he reads, consternation spreads over his face. 'These are real?' He inspects the pages, back and front, and the seals, holding them up to the light the better to see. 'Where did you get them from?'

'From his mother's house, when I was in service there.' My voice sounds hard and cold, as if it belongs to someone else. 'I thought I might one day need something to bargain with.'

'Dear God, Hessie. It would be a perilous path to try to blackmail him. You'd likely end up dead.'

The pit of my stomach contracts. 'That is why I haven't used them before now.' I still can't bring myself to confess to him what I have done.

'I've always known you were no fool, Hessie, but this.' He waves the papers. 'This is proof of treason. Incontrovertible.' He hands the correspondence back to me. 'I don't understand why George would pass state secrets to an enemy. What could he have gained? Unless . . .' he seems to be thinking aloud, '. . . they paid him an astronomical sum. It might be as simple as that – money. And influence on the Continent, playing off the Catholics against the Protestants, perhaps. Is there any way these might be forged?'

'There's no doubt of their authenticity. I found them among his own papers.'

A small cough sounds from the direction of the door. We turn. The servant girl has appeared without a sound, as if by magic, making me wonder how long she has been there and what she might have heard of our conversation. She hovers nervously half in, half out of the room, holding a large plate of bread and ham.

'Goodness, Joan, you startled us,' says Ambrose. 'Is everything as it should be?'

'Yes, sir.' The girl reddens, barely speaking above a whisper. 'I was just wondering if you wanted something to eat.'

'Yes, please.' He begins to clear a space on the desk. 'You can put it down here.'

The girl leaves the food and slips away.

'Do you think she heard us talking of the correspondence?' Anxiety twists into me. 'Can she be trusted? She might have caught a glimpse –'

'Of course she can be trusted. Don't you remember Joan? She's the daughter of our cook. She was brought up here. Even if she did see them, she wouldn't have understood a thing. She's not the brightest button in the box, that one. I don't think she can even read her own name.' His confidence is reassuring. I have become suspicious of every small thing.

'We need to get you to safety. Then we can form a plan of action. Keep these safely in case we have need of them.' He taps the letters. 'But for goodness' sake, Hessie, they are dangerous. Make sure you keep them well hidden.'

'What are we going to do?' Despair nips at me.

'I know someone who has the duke's ear, someone he respects. Initially it might be best if I approach him discreetly to see if he can make George see reason.'

The likelihood of George ever being reasonable seems infinitesimally small and any hope I might have had begins to drain away. 'There's something I must tell you.' I finally blurt out the contents of my angry missive, the threat I made.

He doesn't tell me how foolish I am but silently draws his hand over his head, his mouth tightening in desperation. 'What's done is done. It might make him more willing to compromise, now he knows you have the letters. Something to bargain with in the last resort.' It is apparent he is attempting to find something positive to say. 'We've no time to lose. You do understand' – an apologetic line folds into his brow – 'much as I'd like to, I can't accompany you.'

'Of course.' I hold a hand aloft, indicating he has no need to explain.

'When she's recovered I'll join you and, in the meantime, I can work out how best to approach the situation.'

'Yes, when she's recovered.' The likelihood of Bette not recovering hangs in the air unspoken. 'So, where is this place you know of?' I recall George's words, my heart sinking: *I've been keeping an eye on you, Hessie.*

Ambrose has begun to write and, without looking up, begins to describe an old hunting lodge buried deep in a Shropshire forest that was bequeathed to him by a cousin. Signing off the hastily scrawled letter, he marks it as urgent and calls in one of his grooms to deliver it to the carrier. 'We'll get you to the Lamb and Flag in Oxford where you can hire horses. From there . . .' He reels off a list of towns and the names of their coaching inns, writing each one down, ending with Ludlow. I have little idea of where Shropshire is but clearly it is distant.

'It will take at least three or four days,' he hands me the list, 'with time for detours to foil any attempts to follow you.'

I find myself folding the piece of paper over and over again as I fight feelings of defeat.

'I'll send instructions to Gifford the caretaker to meet you at the Feathers in Ludlow and guide you to the lodge. It's dilapidated and, without knowing the way, almost impossible to find. That's what makes it so safe. You must travel under aliases. I think it might be wise, too, for Rafe to be dressed in girls' clothes and one of you got up as a man.' He looks me over, deep in thought. 'Neither you nor

Melis could make a convincing man, you're both too small, but Hope would. They'll be looking for three women and a boy.' He's right: two women with a young man and a girl might throw them off the scent. 'We can find suitable clothes for them. Now, have you enough funds?'

I feel weighed down. The idea of several perilous days on the road when I am already exhausted is almost too much to bear, but I must brace myself. 'We have our savings.'

He reaches into a coffer on his desk and brings out a purse, handing it to me. 'You'll likely need more than you think.'

The purse is heavy, and I begin to protest, but he says, 'Listen. I promised your father I would act as protector to you girls. That doesn't end simply because you are grown up.' He takes a wooden box from a shelf, opens it and produces an object wrapped in a cloth. It is a pistol.

'There's little point in giving me that. None of us has ever handled a firearm.' The very idea seems absurd.

'Gifford will teach you how to use it when you get to the lodge. I'd show you myself but we don't want to attract unwanted attention, with the neighbours so close here. You could explode a hundredweight of gunpowder at the lodge and no one would hear.'

I feel daunted. Seeing the firearm brings home to me the extent of the danger we are in.

'I'll find someone to guard you. Gifford's rather long in the tooth, you see. I'd send my groom with you but I'm not entirely sure of him. He hasn't been with me long.' He is absently tapping his fingers on the desk.

The thrumming enters my head, like the sound of horses arriving. It makes me jittery and I am grateful when he stops.

'I have someone in mind, a man I trust, an officer called Bloor, but it may take me a day or so to contact him.' He pauses, resting his chin on the heel of his hand, deep in thought. 'See this ring?' He holds out a finger. 'Take a good look.' It is a black-enamelled band, like a mourning ring. 'I'll give it to the man I send to you, so you'll know he comes from me.' Peering closer I see that it is inscribed with a motto: *Veritas nunquam perit* – the truth never dies.

Death Foretold

Through darkness diamonds spread their richest light.

John Webster, *The White Devil*

Felton

The pungent reek of saltpetre stings his nostrils and his head rings with noise, shouting, chaos, terror. Someone calls his name through the thick fog. A flare lights the sky and the blanket of smoke is a sudden hellish pink. He staggers, losing his footing, crashing to meet the ground, dirt flying up into his eyes, his mouth. As he scrambles to his feet, a jolt shudders through him, the snap of shattering bone, the searing pain, his breath knocked right out of him.

He wakes with a lurch.

'Lieutenant Felton!' The landlady is thumping repeatedly on the parchment-thin door of his room. 'Lieutenant Felton, there's a delivery for you. Says it's urgent.'

He waits a moment to gather his thoughts, his fear dissipating as he takes in his surroundings: the filthy room with its mean furniture, the overflowing piss-pot in the corner, the relentless metallic hammering of the blacksmith next door, the squeal of the winch on a nearby building site. He is not back on the battlefield but in the Budge Row boarding-house in London, where he has been staying since he returned from the war in France. He was lucky to survive the siege at Saint-Martin; thousands didn't. But the horror remains, waiting for him to drop his guard. He must have fallen asleep as he wrote his journal:

he is slumped forward with a crick in his neck and his ink-pot is on its side, a black runnel dripping to the floor.

Pain shoots through his injured arm as he rises to open the door. It has been several months and the shattered bone has knitted, albeit misaligned, but the wound still refuses to heal. The moon-faced landlady is on the threshold.

'You don't look the sort to receive fancy correspondence from Whitehall.' She is holding out a letter of spotless stiff vellum bearing an important-looking red seal.

He takes it from her, recognizing the arms instantly. 'George,' he says, under his breath. He rips the letter open, scanning it. It is a summons. A spark ignites in him.

'Who's it from, then?'

'That is *my* business. You got anything to eat?' He is lightheaded with hunger.

'It'll cost you extra.'

'Add it to my account.'

She makes a tutting noise. He owes her a month's rent. He had been fretful about joining the ranks of beggars lining the streets of the capital, mostly soldiers who, like him, haven't been paid in months. But this summons will surely change everything.

'And bring me a basin so I can wash, if you would.'

'About time. You don't half stink.'

He returns to the table to read the letter. It is to the point. *His Grace, the Duke of Buckingham requests your presence at Whitehall early on the morrow . . .*

This must be it: his promotion, the captaincy he had long given up on. The times he has tried and failed to reach George, and just as he is at his lowest ebb, this arrives. He knows he's useless for soldiering now, what with his injured arm, had been wondering how he would find a way to earn his living, his options diminishing rapidly. But a captaincy, a leader of men – at last his skills as a martial strategist will be recognized – a place in the world.

'George needs me,' he says to the empty room, heart light as a cloud. George and he were equals once, and close, very close – it was first love for them both – but time and circumstance had separated them. Felton has spent a decade and a half fighting on every battlefield of Europe, for anyone who would pay him, working his way up to the middling role of lieutenant. War has been raging for a decade now: the old faith, the emperor with Spain against the Protestant alliance, a multitude of states spread over northern Europe. It was all good business for a mercenary. While Felton was ankle deep in European mud and gore, George had elevated himself with indecent swiftness. He'd barely arrived at the English court, in his borrowed suit, when he was warming King James's bed.

Felton first met George in France, where they were being trained in the martial arts: horsemanship, the use of firearms, fencing. Everyone knew, even then, that George was destined for great things, not for his intellect, for he hadn't that, but for his extraordinary magnetism. Felton finds himself becoming a little wistful as he thinks of those days and how close they had been. Most would have been envious but Felton had always accepted George's unquestionable destiny.

He turns the vellum to see if George has written a personal note but it is blank. Taking a small phial of opium tincture from his pocket, he removes the stopper with his teeth to swig a measure and then a little more, careful not to finish it. He hasn't the means to buy another bottle and it is the only remedy he has found that stills the pain of his injured arm. But the summons has given him hope that his fortunes are shifting.

There is another knock at the door.

'Come,' he calls, and the landlady's son, Joseph, backs in, balancing a tray of food on a basin of water. He grins broadly as Felton takes the basin to the table, peeling off his shirt and sluicing his face and torso, rubbing his armpits.

The pain has mercifully receded to a dull throb and his head is beginning to swim pleasantly. Joseph puts the tray down but doesn't leave. 'Is there something else?' Felton turns, rubbing himself dry, looking at the young man, noticing how lithe he appears, his shirt tight against the lean muscles of his chest as if he has grown out of it. His own body, with its useless arm, seems cumbersome in comparison. On another day he might have been distracted by the sight of Joseph in his room, with his ill-fitting shirt, but his head is filled with George.

'What's this, then?' Joseph has picked up his summons and is inspecting it. He has become rather familiar lately – they have shared the occasional game of dice and cup of beer. Felton doesn't really mind: London can be a lonely place. 'The Duke of Buckingham? What does he want with you?'

'None of your business.' Felton snatches back the letter, noticing, to his annoyance, a greasy thumbprint.

Joseph meets Felton's irritation with a smile. 'Buckingham's doctor, the one they called his wizard, he was murdered near here.'

'You mean Dr Lambe, his *adviser*.'

'I heard he had his finger in all sorts of devilish schemes.'

Felton has heard the rumours, too, of Lambe's occult practices. He doubts any of it is true. George isn't foolish enough to get involved in such things. 'You don't want to believe everything you hear.'

'Know what happened to that Lambe fellow? A mob set on him, tore him apart.' Felton is well aware of what became of Lambe but Joseph is warming to his topic. 'I saw him with my own eyes that night, couple of months back. Not long before you arrived here. I'm having a drink at the Windmill, minding my own business, and in comes this elderly cove, eyes wheeling like a horse at the knacker's – got to be eighty if he's a day. He's twitchy as anything, looking behind as if he's being followed. And he seems to know the landlord cos they go upstairs together.

'Next thing I know a gang of a dozen ugly fellows piles in the door, all rowdy like, and looking about. I keep my head down, don't I? Can tell their blood's up. They order a flagon of ale and I can hear them talking about the duke, laughing, saying, "Someone needs to stick him with a knife for the sake of England," and, "Needs teaching a bloody lesson." Anyway, they leave and it's the morning after, I hear that the old doctor was killed. Pulled apart, wasn't he, down on Old Jewry? Eye hanging on a sinew, arms pulled out of their sockets, kicked black and blue –'

Felton raises a palm. 'That's enough, Joseph.'

'I only say it cos you wouldn't want to be getting involved with the duke's business if that's the kind of –'

'No need to worry about me. I know how to stay out of trouble. Now get lost,' he says amiably. 'I've business to attend to.' He hustles the young man out of his room.

Truth is, Felton hasn't any business, unless it's pondering on his lack of it. But being reminded of Lambe's fate has rattled him, made him wonder about the safety of his old friend George, up in his gilded palace. He may still be feted at court but the public have turned on him lately. Felton recalls an image in a recent news-sheet of a tiny King Charles as a puppet, operated by George, ignorant of the coins falling from his pockets and the dead soldiers scattering the ground.

It was the disastrous siege, under George's command, with so many casualties, a litany of mistakes and costs escalating beyond control, troops unpaid, the country bankrupted, that had made public opinion turn.

He takes a few bites of a pork pie but the tincture has quashed his appetite. He moves the tray, exposing the packet of papers that has sat unopened on the table since he collected it from the notary three weeks ago. It is his mother's will.

He had had word of his mother's death soon after his return from France. He can't face opening it. She had nothing to leave him and he has no desire to confront the pathetic list of mended furniture and threadbare dresses she has most likely left to the parish poor. He and his mother had been estranged for many years. They had never been close, even when he was a child, but he couldn't forgive her for neglecting to tell him of his beloved twin sister's death. He had been a thousand miles away on a distant battlefield when word got to him. Bridget had been dead three months and was long buried by then.

When he managed to travel home, every scrap of her had been erased, just a mound of red earth in the corner of the churchyard. He had commissioned a stone to mark the grave but had never been back to see it. His mother had made it clear he wouldn't be welcome. The year is branded on his heart: 1614. Fourteen years have passed but he still feels the vacuum of Bridget's loss.

Time is collapsing, memories churning him up. The languid summer when he and George had returned home to Playford Hall from the school near Rouen where they had been transformed from cocky boys into martial men.

The crossing to Ipswich had been delayed and they had arrived in the dead of night, had had to wake Bridget by throwing pebbles at her window. She had let them in wearing her nightgown, dishevelled from sleep, and had thrown herself immediately into her brother's embrace.

'Who is your friend?' Her eyes took in George then. Felton saw what he always saw when people first met George and were staggered by his beauty.

'George Villiers.' He stepped forward to kiss the back of her hand. He was just plain George Villiers then, minor gentry, as were the Feltons. But still Felton always felt the need to impress him. 'Your brother has told me so much about you that I feel I know you already.' He turned to Felton. 'You two are like peas in a pod.'

Felton felt an astringent pang of jealousy. He had so wanted George to love Bridget but, seeing them together in that moment, he was struck with a sudden desperate worry that George's desire would turn away from him to his twin.

His concern was unfounded. The three spent an idyllic summer together at Playford before they went their separate ways: Felton to fight in the Adriatic, George to court and his meteoric rise, and Bridget, it galls him to dig up his long-buried grief – Bridget to the grave.

He stuffs the unopened package into the bottom of his travelling chest, angry with himself for allowing his thoughts to run away with him, the pain of loss as sharp as ever. Taking another measure of the tincture, he kicks back on the narrow bed and turns his mind to George and their meeting tomorrow.

Hope

Hope practises her swagger.

The suit had once belonged to Ambrose Cotton's nephew and the minute she'd put it on she'd felt different, taller, stronger. It fits surprisingly well, but the wool smells slightly of mildew and it is thick, much too warm now the morning heat has burned off the cloud after the early rain.

She sits on the box seat, sweltering, beside the driver, hat pulled over her eyes, while Hester, Melis and Rafe travel inside the carriage. Rafe, with his slight frame, makes a convincing girl. It had been a struggle to get him into the brocade gown, and the effects of Worley's sedative have not yet quite worn off, making him fractious, his mood not helped by the yard-dog's absence: it had become lame and was left behind at Littlemore. The green smudge on her finger mocks Hope, a reminder of her own stupidity. She balks to think what might have happened to Rafe and is relieved to see, through the small window behind, that he has dropped off to sleep, lolling against his mother.

Before long they are wheeling into the yard of the Lamb and Flag. The place is bustling with life. The post-coach must have recently arrived. Its passengers mill aimlessly about the stable-yard. Hope is surprised that the stable-boy doesn't offer his hand to help her down, then remembers she is meant to be a young man.

She scans the yard for anyone seeming shifty and is thrown into panic when she spots a familiar red jacket slung over one of the stable doors.

'Could that be Worley's, do you think?' she whispers to Hester, who agrees they need to check and pulls her hat low to shadow her face, suggesting the others do likewise. Fear prickles over her, like nettle rash, but a man they don't recognize appears, taking the jacket and shrugging it on. Hester leads the way inside to find the landlord.

He is surrounded by a clamour of people all wanting rooms, or food and drink, or fresh horses. Hester pushes through to hand him the letter of introduction from Ambrose. At the mention of the doctor's name, he ushers them to an anteroom, ignoring the complaints of his disgruntled customers.

'Any friend of Dr Cotton gets privileged service from me.' He couldn't have been friendlier. 'He saved the life of my daughter, so I'm ever in his debt.'

The man offers them a drink, which Hester politely refuses, saying they are short of time. 'We must get to Aylesbury today and from there to Bedford, to make Cambridge in time for our mother's birthday celebrations.' She smiles at him. 'I wonder if you might recommend an inn at Aylesbury. Somewhere clean.'

Hope is impressed at the ease with which Hester tells the lie. She adds small details to elaborate the story, making it seem more authentic. She would almost believe it herself, were she not aware that they intend to head in the opposite direction, towards a place called Burford. The innkeeper appears entirely convinced and, anyway, there is no reason for him to doubt their plans. Even so, Hope cannot shake off the feeling that they have 'fugitive' shot through their bearing.

Although it is Hester who initiates negotiations with him, each one of his responses is directed to Hope. 'Yes, Mr Hope, of course. I'm more than happy to let you have a pair of horses. Will the ladies be comfortable on horseback? I can provide a small carriage if they would prefer.'

'Do we look like the kind of women who can't ride?' Melis says, and Hester is obliged to apologize for her discourtesy.

Acclimatizing to her masculine role, remembering to drop her voice, Hope adds, 'My sisters are both accomplished horsewomen.'

Two hardy-looking animals are procured immediately, to the annoyance of a party who comment loudly that they have been kept waiting more than two hours.

It is already past midday when they finally set off again. They are obliged to travel initially, a good mile in the wrong direction, keeping alert for anyone who might be on their tail. It is market day so the route is busy, making it easy for them to double back inconspicuously and loop round to meet the Burford road outside the city.

Hester is annoyed with Melis, riding in silence for some time, saying eventually, 'Can you try not to be rude? It attracts attention and the landlord was only being helpful.'

Their quarrel is soon forgotten and they reach the Bull at Burford before dark and without event. The place is hosting a wedding party and the only room left is a tight space beneath the eaves, dominated by a large bed that is impossible to get into without banging your head on the sloping ceiling.

Hester bolts the door, top and bottom, saying that at least up in the attic they need not worry about the security of the windows, while Hope flips back the covers to check for unwanted visitors. She had heard of a woman who found a whole nest of mice under a pillow at an inn.

Despite her exhaustion, Hope lies awake, her mind cluttered with qualms, listening to the noise of carousing downstairs, the sounds filtering up through the building. Each wedding toast provokes a more raucous cheer than the one before. After a while a fiddle starts up and the guests begin to dance, drunkenly, if the erratic thumping is anything to go by.

She hears a racket on the stairs, a clash of loud laughter, and supposes the newlyweds are being put to bed. She wonders if she will ever marry, now she has been spoiled. No one wants a girl who has given herself to the first taker without a second thought.

She can hear the sharp jab of an argument on the landing and the slam of a door, after which the place falls silent. Her thoughts continue to swirl, pushing sleep further and further away because she can't help imagining someone scaling the building, creeping in through the window and murdering them all while they sleep.

Rafe has a nightmare, sitting bolt upright with a cry. She tucks her arm around him, stroking his head and quietly singing a lullaby until he has settled.

Still she lies awake, mind swirling with jagged thoughts. Deep in the night she hears the sound of an arrival, the jangle of keys, quiet conversation and footfall on the stairs. She slips to the door to make sure it is bolted fast, though she checked it twice before they went to bed. Her heart continues its desperate thudding, even once the place has fallen silent.

She wakes Hester at dawn, telling her of the late-night visitor, and they pack quickly, creeping down the stairs. The place is dead but they find the landlady slumped asleep in a chair in the hall surrounded by debris from the wedding party. She appears not to have been to bed and wakes as they tiptoe past.

'Where are you off to so early?' Her breath is still high with last night's drink.

'We have to make Southampton by Wednesday.' Hester constructs an elaborate story about crossing to the Low Countries where her husband is waiting.

The landlady levers herself out of the chair. 'You'd better take some of these.' She wraps up some victuals left over from the feast and sends them on their way.

They travel through the early morning in silence, keeping close to the hedgerows, alert for sounds, glancing back every now and again to be sure they haven't been followed.

Felton

George is in black, a mourning pin attached to his jacket – a skull with diamonds for eyes. The atmosphere is close as he and Felton regard each other without speaking. Felton detects something different in his old friend, a small fissure in his pristine veneer that only someone who knows him as well as Felton does would notice.

'I am sorry,' Felton says, pointing to the death's head, 'about Dr Lambe.' His words seem woefully inadequate in the face of the horror of the old doctor's death. He wants to reach out, touch him, draw him close as he used to, but a gulf of time squats between them.

A small tic at the corner of George's eye reveals that he has committed his feelings about the murder to somewhere unreachable. 'Terrible business.' He touches his fingers absently to the pin. 'Wanted to get at me.' George's clipped tone suggests that it will take more than the murder of his personal adviser to 'get at' him but the flicker of fear in his eyes tells a different story. 'In my position it is inevitable that I will accrue enemies . . . the price of power. The King is unpopular and people want to blame me for it.'

That news-sheet image springs to Felton's mind. 'You must step carefully.' His first instinct is to protect his old lover. He is well aware that there are many who would like to see George meet a similar end to his adviser. People are fickle. It is not so long since he was feted.

George runs his gaze over Felton, taking in his ragged state, the threadbare coat and injured arm, wrapped in a bandage and strapped into a makeshift sling. His condition is so miserable the guard hadn't initially recognized him: he had tried to send Felton packing as a vagrant until he'd seen the duke's letter of summons.

'Fiske,' he'd said. 'Don't you remember me?' Fiske had served under him at Cádiz.

'Lieutenant Felton?' The man regarded him for a moment. 'You look a fright.'

'You've gone up in the world.' Felton eyes Fiske's smart uniform, the polished sword at his hip.

'Duke's personal guard. Reward for bravery.'

'I'm glad for you,' Felton said, as Fiske opened the gate to let him pass.

He feels slightly unsteady on his feet. He is in terrible pain and trying to hide it. He finished the last of his laudanum earlier and its effect is wearing off.

'What happened to you?' says George, placing a hand on Felton's shoulder, his fingers touching the bare skin of his neck.

'Cannon shot, as we pulled out of Saint-Martin.'

'I plan to raise more troops and return to finish the job.'

This is it, thinks Felton, waiting for George to say: *And I won't be able to succeed without your expertise.*

'I want you to perform a service for me.'

'Anything.' Felton is barely able to contain himself, palms sweating in anticipation.

'You won't be aware that I have a natural son.' Felton is

perplexed by the turn of the conversation, disappointment dropping into him like a stone.

'I want you to bring the boy to me. I sent Worley to fetch him but . . . Well, let's just say the man can be unreliable.' He smiles at Felton – the smile that could melt the devil's heart. 'Not like you.'

'I thought . . . I thought . . . I thought you wanted to offer me a martial role.'

'A command? It hadn't crossed my mind.' Felton is crushed. 'This is far more important. I don't think I explained. It is not the boy alone I want. His mother and her sister have threatened me.' He draws in a sharp breath, with a pained expression. 'And they have the means to bring me down.'

'Are you sure of this?' It seems to Felton so implausible that two women could be bent on his destruction, one of them the mother of his bastard.

'Look! Look at this!' He draws a dog-eared scrap of paper from inside his jacket, thrusting it under Felton's nose, tapping it with his finger.

It appears to be a letter in which a few sentences have been underlined. *I have proof that you once committed treason and I am not afraid to use that knowledge, should you try to take Rafe from me.* 'Rafe is your son?'

'Yes.' He snatches back the paper.

'How do you know she's not making it up? What proof could she possibly have?'

'That is what I wondered when I first received it but I investigated further. The women have letters, forgeries, but in the wrong hands . . .' he pauses to take a sharp inhalation '. . . they could light the fuse to bring all this down.' He sweeps an arm in an arc to indicate the splendid room, then forms his hand into a fist, banging it to his chest. 'It could be the end of me, Felton. Those letters must be destroyed. I would hardly send you on such a – a –' He seems unsure of the word.

'Mission?' suggests Felton.

'Yes, exactly, mission. You yourself said only moments ago that I should watch my step, that I have too many enemies. Well, this is me stepping carefully.' George fixes him with a pleading stare. 'I need you, Felton. I need some-one with your skills of subtlety for this undertaking. Those letters must be destroyed. The women stopped. I trust only you for this.' He pulls open the front of his jacket and takes Felton's hand to place it over his heart. 'Hold you here!'

Felton's disappointment melts away. He can feel George's heartbeat, the warm skin. 'You know you have my loyalty.'

'I'll pay you well. Well enough to set you up . . . There's a manor north of the city, brings in a good living. It will be yours.'

'I understand.' A spark of suspicion ignites in Felton. Something seems awry. George's offer is too generous. 'And if I refuse?'

'Why would you?' George knows Felton too well. He is not in a position to refuse.

Besides, after so many years in the wilderness with nothing but uncertainty, he has a glimpse of a future bask-ing in George's favour. 'And the promotion?'

'Are you taking advantage of me?' George looks to the floor, then up again with a half-smile and kisses Felton's hand before letting it drop.

'I could be an asset to you, with fifteen years' martial experience.' It is true. Felton has served under some of the most gifted commanders in Europe and George knows it.

'You're right. We could make a formidable team.' George pauses. 'Deal with the mother and her sister, get rid of the letters, and bring the boy to me. Then you shall have your captaincy.'

'*Deal* with?' Felton feels as if he has swallowed a shard of glass.

'Make it seem accidental.'

'I can't do that. *Women!*'

Now the façade cracks open, revealing the full extent of George's fear. 'Those women would send me to the block.' His expression is haunted. 'Me . . . *your* George.'

Felton tries to tame the confusion of emotion roiling within him. 'I don't think I can –'

George interjects, 'You've seen the threat to me in black and white.'

'Can't you have them imprisoned?'

'If only it were so easy. Those two hussies will cast aspersions and I can't risk people asking questions or those forged letters falling into the wrong hands. God knows what might . . .' His desperation is clear. 'There's no other way. They must be silenced.' George hooks his arm round Felton's waist, pulling him close. 'Remember how we were? Life was so simple then. I miss those days.' Their foreheads touch. George takes Felton's hand, turning it upward to expose the ugly jagged scar at the base of his thumb, opening his hand too, to reveal his own neat silver scar, pressing them together. 'Blood brothers. Our secret. Remember?'

'Of course I remember.'

'It's not as if you haven't taken a life before.' George's tone has sharpened.

'On the battlefield it is different.'

'You know what I mean. I protected you when you needed it. You can't have forgotten that.'

The past comes crashing back – the young man Felton killed in France, those dead eyes staring out. It had started as a fight over a game of dice but his adversary was smaller, younger, and something had come over Felton, a streak of cold violence. He had knocked the boy to the ground and booted him over and over until his head was caved in.

It wasn't anger or any common reaction but a perverse desire to know if he was capable of taking a life. He was. Had George not sworn they were together elsewhere, he would have hanged for it: it turned out the boy was the magistrate's son.

They are silent for several moments while Felton's thoughts percolate.

'It's them or me. Just because they belong to the fairer sex doesn't make them immune from treachery. Would you wish the fate of Dr Lambe on me, the one who loved you first, whom you loved too? You did love me, didn't you?' George's eyes are vast and dewy and for a moment Felton thinks he is on the brink of tears.

'I did, George. I do. Of course I do.' An image asserts itself in his head of George crouching over the block, his hair falling forward. The sound of the axe thuds in his ears.

'You know me,' says George, 'better than anyone.'

Felton remembers vividly the George he knew, the loyal young man who risked himself to protect his friend, and he is back in that idyllic summer with George and Bridget before they parted ways. It was the happiest time of his life. 'I do know you.' He might balk at the task but he is a soldier: he knows death and he knows killing. Indeed, it is all he knows. This is just another commission, he tells himself. He knows he cannot stand back and watch George brought down, George who is all that is left of his past.

The axe thuds again. 'I'll do it.'

George slaps him on the back. 'That's my man.' He outlines the circumstances, saying that the women were last seen with the boy's godfather. 'One of his maidservants is in my pay, a young girl named Joan, but you mustn't solicit her help. I don't want her compromised. You won't find the women or the boy still there. They have moved on. You shall have to find out where. I'll give you directions to Littlemore Manor. Dr Cotton may be willing to speak, given the right . . . *encouragement*.' He speaks the word in a pointed tone that makes Felton wonder, once more, what he is getting into.

'Once you find them, don't rush things. Inveigle yourself into their company. Befriend my boy. Seek out the forged letters and destroy them.'

'How will I identify them?'

'My informant tells me they bear the stamp of the Spanish ambassador and *my* stamp, faked by some knave. The devil only knows what libels they contain.' He has removed the mourning pin from his jacket and is absently prodding the pointed end onto the surface of the table where it leaves small indentations in the fine marquetry.

'Once the letters are destroyed, move on to the other business,' he continues. 'There is a third sister, younger, part-mulatto. Worley tells me she doesn't know much but that she is easily manipulated – might prove helpful. But,' he meets Felton's eyes with a crystalline look, 'it's imperative that it appears to be an accident. I can't have it coming back on me. You do understand?'

Felton nods. 'And should I need support, is there some-one I can call on?' He is beginning to understand the complexity of the mission and the practicalities involved. 'Someone trusted.'

'There's Worley, I suppose. He's suffered a rather bad concussion lately but should be on his feet again before long.'

'You said Worley was unreliable.'

'He wouldn't be my first choice. *You* are my first choice.' George's smile catches Felton, sending memories of their old intimacies running through him once more. 'Worley may not be the most efficient of men but he's absolutely loyal and doesn't balk at much.' The way George says this suggests he has some kind of hold over the man. But that is neither here nor there for Felton. 'Bear in mind, though, that Worley is known to the sisters so they mustn't see him.'

'I understand. Once I know the women's destination, I will send word for Worley to be dispatched to a place nearby, should I have need of him.'

'I knew you were my man. Leaving nothing to chance.' George's gaze is on him, intense and warm. 'I will be ever in your debt if you rid me of this threat and unite me with my boy. My own boy! A son should be raised by his father, don't you agree?'

'Indeed.' Felton imagines the child, a miniature of George.

George opens a drawer, taking out a purse, which he tosses over. It chinks as Felton catches it with one hand. 'To be going on with. Clean yourself up and keep a tally of your expenses. I'd loan you one of my good horses but it would attract too much attention. Better you travel discreetly.' He lists his advice as if this were a mere ordinary commission. 'It goes without saying that this stays between us.'

'Of course.' Felton hasn't a soul to tell. He has no one, no family, no lover, no children, not even a bastard somewhere in the world to seek him out. George must know this.

'I almost forgot.' George stands, going to a bookcase from which he slides out a slim volume. 'I thought you might like a copy. Bacon has revised his essays.' He holds up the book. 'Do you remember?'

Felton is catapulted once more to that summer at Playford, lying in the warm grass, reading passages to each other. It had been Felton who had introduced George to Bacon. It would seem hard to believe for anyone encountering them now that Felton had once been the more sophisticated of the two men. '"It is impossible",' he starts, George chiming in to complete the quotation, '"to love *and* be wise."' They laugh and the heavy atmosphere is lifted.

'Let me put something in it.' George opens the book to scrawl a note inside, then hands it over, appearing not to notice the mourning pin fall to the floor. Felton stoops to pick it up and follows him to the door, where George is suddenly serious once more. 'And I don't want any harm to come to my son. I don't want him frightened. I mean it.' He brings a hand to stroke the side of Felton's face. 'So make things as smooth as possible for him. I don't want him resenting me before he's even here.'

Felton replaces the pin in George's jacket, forcing its sharp point through the thick fabric, and takes his leave.

Hester

The latch rattles. I lift my head to listen, gooseflesh prickling its way up my arms. I can see nothing at all, not even my hand when I hold it in front of my face. Then I hear the definite scuff of feet against floorboards.

Someone is in our room.

Cold sweat springs up over my brow.

I feel for Rafe in the bed, relieved to find his warm body. Beneath the pillow my fingers come into contact with the brittle papers hidden there and also the steel contours of Ambrose's pistol. I draw it out, breath held. I don't know how to load or fire it but it might scare someone off . . . unless they, too, are armed.

Trying to quash that thought, I jump up, holding the pistol ahead of me. 'Who goes there?' My voice booms through the quiet. I imagine firing, a flare exploding outwards like a firework, the thud as the bullet meets its mark, the slump of a body. I don't know if I could, even if the thing were loaded.

I begin to see vague shapes in the darkness and, grasping the bed frame, feel my way towards the door where I can see a pale figure emerging from the gloom. The latch rattles again. Whoever it is is trying to leave and seems unable to open the door.

Hope stirs. 'What's going on?'

'Who goes there?' I repeat, taking several tentative steps towards the door, pistol brandished, until it meets resistance against the intruder's back. I give it a hard shove. 'Don't move. I'm armed.'

'Where am I?' It is Melis calling, not from the bed but from the door. 'What's happening?'

'Melis?' I reach out, feeling the thin fabric of her nightgown, and retract the gun. 'What are you doing?'

'I don't know. Where are we?' She sounds befuddled.

Hope is up and opening the shutters, allowing the grey dawn to filter into the room. 'We're at the King's Head.'

'Oh.' Melis slumps onto the bed, rubbing her eyes. 'I thought we were back at Orchard Cottage. I couldn't open the door.'

I feel my exhaustion now, my whole body aching from days in the saddle and lack of rest.

'You were sleepwalking.' I describe how we came to be here and she slowly returns to her senses. She used to sleepwalk as a child but hasn't done so for years. I hope it isn't the precursor to one of her episodes. That is the last thing I need when I have so much else to worry about.

A bell chimes from a nearby church and I hear another, more distant, like an echo.

'Five o'clock,' says Hope.

'We may as well get going.' I try to sound positive. 'There's no point in dallying here.' The idea of another day of travelling and then another after that, stalked by dread, makes it hard to muster my spirit.

'Good idea,' says Melis, who begins to gather our things together. She catches my worried scrutiny. 'I'm all right. No need to watch me like a hawk.' There is a slight edge of impatience to her tone, which reassures me. I smile. She returns it, her annoyance draining away.

'Like an oven in here.' Hope opens the window to air the stuffy room. Despite the heat we hadn't dared leave it open during the night, as the room is on the first floor with a tree close by that would have been easy to climb.

Telling myself it will be over soon, I tuck the letters safely out of sight into my bodice. They are my only hope, but changing George's mind, even with Ambrose's help, seems impossible. If I allow my misgivings free rein, all I can see lying ahead is a landscape of fear stretching into the far distance, an endless fugitive life.

I watch Rafe for a moment, still asleep, his hand clutched around his monkey, the dear curve of his mouth twitching minutely. Gently, I shake him awake. He is bleary-eyed and thrusts the toy at me. 'Why did you think I wanted this? It's for babies.' I stuff it into my bag, knowing he will ask for it again.

I try to lighten his mood as I help him dress, but my words ring with insincere brightness. Shaking out the brocade gown, filthy with dust from the road, I see it has been torn from neck to hem, making it unwearable. 'How did this happen?'

Rafe shrugs, insouciant, saying he doesn't know.

'I'll tack it back together quickly, shall I?' suggests Hope, rummaging for the sewing things.

'I *won't* wear it.' The firm jut of his chin is clear indication that he is ready for a prolonged protest.

'There isn't time and it won't hurt for him to wear his own clothes for one day.'

'Don't you think . . .' begins Hope, then seems to think better of it. Without finishing her sentence, she emits a snort of disapproval and stuffs the torn dress into one of the bags.

'There's been no sign of anyone following us and we're so far from Oxford now . . .' My words trail off. Even I am unconvinced it is a good idea to let him go undisguised, but if he makes a fuss about it he will draw unwanted attention to us. 'I don't understand how it was torn.'

Hope is looking at Rafe, clearly assuming him the culprit. Certainly the evidence points to him but I can't imagine it. It's such a wilfully destructive act.

'It wasn't me,' he says vehemently. 'Aunt Hope thinks it was.'

'We believe you.' I stroke my hand over his cheek, noticing that he shrinks slightly from my touch. 'Don't we, Hope.' I look at my youngest sister, whose back is turned, pointedly.

'I'll go down and see that the horses are fed,' says Melis, who is by the door, bags packed already. I wonder if it is possible that she ripped the dress in her sleep last night. She has done stranger things.

Rafe puts on his usual clothes and offers me a quick-silver smile. George may think he is growing up but to me he is still so young, everything about him out of proportion, his body still too slight for his head, awkward gangly limbs, the pair of new front teeth dominating his mouth. He is still a nestling, in need of my protection. I cannot imagine that one day he will be a man.

Hope and I lug the bags downstairs, Rafe following, and out to the yard where Melis is already preparing the horses. We slide quietly out into the dawn, plodding steadily towards the north-west. According to Ambrose's instructions, with luck and good conditions, we ought to reach Ludlow by nightfall.

We stop every now and again so the horses can drink, and by midday we are at a small inn, suitable for an hour's respite and a simple meal. Once we have eaten, we sit outside to rest awhile in a small meadow at the rear of the building.

Rafe and Hope, their quarrel forgotten, doze off in the long grass, Rafe's head resting on his aunt's lap. Melis is drawn to inspect a row of hives set in a wooded area, while I find myself contemplating a colony of ants marching up and down a nearby tree, marvelling at their order and their ability to carry vast objects over uncertain terrain with apparent ease. They are relentless to the point that when one of their troop becomes injured, or is unable to continue its task, the others simply climb over, or make a path around, their suffering comrade. I wonder what lesson God intended by putting them on this earth – the example of industry, perhaps. They are absent of either conscience or empathy yet their colony appears the apogee of efficiency. Were humans also lacking in those qualities the world would be in chaos, though I can think of one in whom they are absent.

A sudden disturbance jolts me from my thoughts and I become aware of Melis rushing towards me. Scrambling to my feet, my hand goes instinctively to the pistol. She is dashing through the grass, wild-eyed. 'There is a wasp in our hive. We must be rid of it.'

I notice, to my dismay, that her behaviour has drawn the attention of a group of travellers, who have stopped to gawp. She must seem to them like a creature possessed.

Desperate for her to stop, I slap her briskly around the face, stunning her into an abrupt silence.

Her hand at her cheek, she regards me in shock, tears welling. I am shocked too. My palm is smarting, my nerves shredded. I have never before lost my patience with her so violently. 'I'm sorry,' I say quietly. 'You were attracting attention.'

The ogling travellers are now in an avid semi-circle, several paces away from us, nudging one another and making tuts of disapproval. I turn to them with an attempted smile. 'All is well now. I have it in hand. My sister is ailing. There is no need for concern.'

A voice comes out of the group. 'Don't I know you from somewhere?'

I freeze, unable to respond. The man who spoke wears a clergyman's cassock and collar and is vaguely familiar but I cannot place him. Finally, I find my voice. 'I'm not aware of having met you before, reverend.'

Leaving his companions, three women of varying ages, he approaches. My stomach lurches with the abrupt notion that he might have been George's mother's chaplain and remember me from when I was in her household.

I glance over to the long grass where Rafe and Hope are stirring. Turning to Melis, now calm in the wake of my slap, I tell her beneath my breath to keep the others away.

'I never forget a face.' He is standing quite close now, and seeing him properly I remember, with no small relief, that he is the vicar of a church to which we occasionally supply candles. Mostly I had dealt with the sexton but eventually recall dealing with this man once, briefly.

'Aren't you the vicar of St Laurence at Cowley?' I am astonished that there is not so much as a wobble in my voice.

From the corner of my eye I am thankful to see that the others have wandered away towards the wooded area at the end of the paddock.

'Indeed I am.' He appears delighted that I have remembered him. 'I must apologize for my lack of manners, but I find I cannot quite place you, Mistress . . . ?'

I cross my fingers behind my back. 'Mistress Holtby. My family worshipped at St Laurence for a month or so when we were living nearby.' I tilt my head with an obliging smile. 'I remember you principally for the quality of your sermons.'

He puffs up under this nugget of praise. 'Which in particular?' He is scrutinizing me carefully.

'Much as I would like to discuss such things with you, sir, I'm afraid duty calls. My husband awaits me in Worcester.' I count up the lies I have told since our journey began, silently begging God for lenience. Worcester is where we travelled from this morning. 'He will be wondering where we have got to.' I dip into a small, respectful curtsy and bid him goodbye.

As I marshal the others in preparation for a swift departure, I hear the vicar's companions ask how he knows me. 'One of my congregation,' he replies, pricked with pride. 'An enthusiast of my sermons.'

I hurry my small party, making haste to leave before his memory is jogged.

Felton

When he lifts his eyes over the lip of the sill, Felton can see the shadows of the two men moving about in the pale glow of the lamplit interior. He is concealed in a yew bush under the window of what appears to be Dr Cotton's study, or library, considering the books around the walls.

The weather is hot and dry but there must have been a downpour in the last few days as it is damp in his hiding place, where the sun doesn't reach. He has been there for some time and his body is stiffening, the familiar pain pulsing through his injured arm. Feeling for the phial in his bag, he swallows a liberal measure of his tincture, leaning back against the cold wall, and waits for the discomfort to recede.

A door bangs at the back of the building. He can hear two male voices talking, about women, he gathers, which of the maids they would like to 'vault'. They are smoking. The smell wafts through the thick vegetation of his hideout making him crave a pipe of tobacco. He vaguely wonders which of the several maids they mention is George's informant.

Before long, his pain is banished to a place where he can recognize yet not feel it – akin to the place his conscience hides. His head swims pleasantly and a glorious feeling builds in him that he is capable of anything and impervious to everything.

He had watched Dr Cotton's visitor arrive at Littlemore Manor a good two hours ago, when it was still light. The man had the straight posture and meaningful stride of an officer. A business-like sword was attached at his waist and, from the way his coat hung off kilter, Felton could tell he was carrying a firearm. He would recognize one of his own kind at a hundred yards.

He is about to take another peep into the room when the gravel crunches nearby, the pipe smell strong now. It must be one of the smoking servants walking about nearby, doing the evening rounds, perhaps. He makes himself small, hackles up, primed for a fight, touching his fingers to the knife he wears tucked inside his belt.

The footsteps recede and Felton relaxes, removing a hunk of bread from his bag. The satchel holds a small firearm with ammunition and the purse of money, both given to him by George, a tinderbox and the precious tincture, more of which is in his small travelling box left at an inn in Oxford: the Lamb and Flag. George had informed him that this was the place Dr Cotton's groom had been instructed to take the women. However, according to the landlord, whom he had quizzed thoroughly, no group fitting their description has passed through the inn recently. Either George has been misinformed or the man is lying.

He creeps up to peer inside again. The two men are deep in conversation and he sees Dr Cotton hand a roll of papers to the other before they both rise and leave the room. Felton drops down into the dark.

Almost immediately the front door opens. Felton is close enough to hear the scuff of the visitor's shoes on the stoop. There is the merest sliver of moon, casting a thin, cool light over the night, like a dusting of frost. The man turns to face the doctor, whose hands alone are visible. He is removing a ring from one of his fingers.

He taps the roll of papers. 'You have directions and this will serve as proof that you are sent by me.' He hands over the ring. 'In the meantime I shall attempt to open negotiations with the duke.'

'Understood.' The visitor, shifting from one foot to the other, slips on the ring, tucks the papers into his jacket and clicks his heels, then marches briskly down the drive.

'Take care of them, Bloor,' calls the doctor after him. 'They are most dear to me.'

Felton waits for the door to shut, then follows, creeping from one dark hulk of yew bush to the next where they line the drive. Bloor stops a moment, crouching, appearing to tie his bootlace, then continues. Felton allows him to go ahead fifty yards, knowing there is only the one way out of Littlemore Manor. He can easily catch him up if necessary.

He hears something. The quiet crunch of another set of footsteps. The servant must be about again. Glad of the thin moon and its mean light, Felton presses himself into the arms of the foliage. A small cough sounds close – too close. Felton stands immobile, breath held.

Someone jumps at him, forcing him to the ground with a great thud, winding him and pulling his bad arm up and back by the wrist. The sudden searing pain forces a guttural cry to burst from his windpipe.

'Who in Hell's name are you?' Dr Cotton's breath is hot in his ear, the weight of his body holding Felton down, face in the dirt.

Felton struggles, flailing and kicking. Each twist rips renewed agony through his injured arm. He spits out a wad of earth. The doctor thrusts his forearm under Felton's chin pulling his head up off the ground, pressing into his gullet.

He sputters, grabbing at his breath. A knee crunches agonizingly into his gut. He expels a cry. A fist meets his ear, exploding, a constellation of stars in his head.

With sheer force of will he manages to stay conscious and wriggles his good hand to his waist where it meets with the hilt of his blade. He summons all the strength he can muster and, with an almighty roar, he forces his attacker off, rolling onto him, kneeing his groin and plunging the knife deep between his ribs.

The doctor thrashes his legs, pounding at Felton's head, calling for help. Felton claps a hand over his mouth. The doctor bites. Felton winces, staunching the cry that wants to burst out of him.

He holds the knife firm, can feel hot blood on his hand, waiting for the man's writhing to subside, feeling now his strength sapping.

Everything drops to silence, save the fading stutter of the doctor's breath.

He falls limp.

Someone shouts from the house. 'Who's out there?'

Felton hears the door go and sees the dark shape of a figure holding a lit torch searching the drive. Leaving his knife, he scrambles into the shadow of the nearest bush, crawling from one to another until he reaches the gate and from there runs as fast as he can to catch up with Bloor.

Hope

'Would you help me hitch this boy to the cart, young man?' Gifford walks a grey gelding into the yard. From the moment they arrived at the Feathers in Ludlow the previous evening, he had seemed entirely convinced by Hope's disguise.

Gifford is an ancient, bow-legged man with a broad face and very few teeth. She helps him haul the cart round. An ungainly vehicle, it looks as if it might be even older than its owner and is no more sophisticated than an open box with plank benches on either side and two large wheels that sport several broken spokes.

The hired horses are to be sent back, leaving their party with just this grey, sturdy enough if ill-proportioned, and the dependable piebald, to take them from Ludlow to their destination.

Hester has referred to it mysteriously as 'the Hall in the Forest', sometimes just 'the lodge', and all Hope has gathered is that it is so deeply buried, its location so secret, that it can't be found without either a guide or detailed instructions.

The Feathers is handsome, and recently built, so the smell of sawdust still lingers. Unlike the poky old inns they have stayed in on the way, with their low ceilings and sagging roofs, it has a double-height hall and a large staircase that sweeps up and up to the bedrooms, which, the land-lord had told them proudly, are each furnished with new feather beds. Hope felt like a duchess as she made her way up and sank into that cloud of down.

It was her first proper sleep since their departure and she feels better for the rest. Indeed, they all seem to have relaxed. Rafe's mood improved the minute his mother allowed him to abandon the hated dress, which Hope is almost certain he ripped on purpose. She didn't say any-thing. Though none of them has articulated it, there appears to be no evidence of them having been followed. But a threat that doesn't show its face is all the more sinis-ter and they are still strung out with worry.

They load the cart with their few belongings and the supplies that Gifford bought at market: a large bag of grain, a barrel of salted fish and some other parcelled items. Hope is preparing to get onto the cart and Melis is on the mount-ing block, one foot already in the stirrup, to climb onto the piebald when Rafe begins to complain.

'I've ridden pillion all the way. I want to ride by myself. I'm a good rider, aren't I?' His mouth is set stubbornly tight.

Hester puts up no resistance. 'Very well, sweetheart, as long as you're tethered to the grey. You don't mind sitting in the cart with us, do you, Melis?'

They are all relieved he is safe, Hope as much as her sisters, and it is understandable, given all he has been through, but Hope still thinks Hester should indulge him less. She wishes Melis would say something, as Hester might listen to her, but Melis is a law unto herself.

Rafe takes the reins, his expression transformed. Hope, making much of her disguise, leaps onto the cart, holding out her hand to each of her sisters in turn as they clamber into the unwieldy vehicle, before she takes her place at the front beside Gifford.

They move away. The castle, a vast edifice high above, seems to watch their progress as they wind through the jumbled streets of Ludlow, alert for anything suspicious. The houses soon thin out until they are in the open countryside, where there are few places to hide.

The sky, a merciless blue, heralds yet another airless day. Hope has abandoned the wool jacket, wearing just a shirt and breeches, sun falling across her back, like spilled blood. Thankful for the wide-brimmed straw hat that protects her face, she arranges her handkerchief beneath it to protect her nape and draws her cuffs down over her hands: a few minutes exposed and they would turn dark as medlar jelly. They pass gilded fields of wheat. The verges throb with life, the song of crickets, the scuffle of rodents, and there is not a spot of shade, only wobbling pools of disappearing liquid in the track ahead and parched hills that roll out before them towards the distant Welsh mountains, purple and hazy.

She has the sense of moving further and further from civilization, towards a daunting nothingness, so she trains her attention on the rhythmic plod and trundle, the hard bench beneath her. Keeping an eye on the position of the sun, to hold her in the world, she arranges the days in obedient rows in her mind: it is the sixth day of August and four days since they left Orchard Cottage.

Before noon they enter an immense forest, its gloom a welcome reprieve from the relentless brightness. Smooth loam softens the motion of the cart, its mulchy scent rising as they move over it. Trees tower above, where birds flit and chat, light leaking through in channels to stipple the ground. The path narrows, winding and complicated, low branches forcing them to duck. For the first time since they left, calm falls over her, making her feel distant from her mistakes, as if they happened in another lifetime.

They pass round ham, bread and cheese, and a thin brew of beer, not wanting to stop, sensing their destination now. She notices Hester making notes on a fold of paper and asks what they are for.

'I'm marking points on the route.' Hester appears different, the strain filched from her eyes. 'You know the story of Theseus and the minotaur?'

Hope does not, or can't remember, but doesn't want to seem foolish, so she nods as if everything makes sense when nothing really does.

They return to their comfortable silence, moving deeper and deeper into the forest. Melis has fallen asleep, her head resting on Hester's shoulder, but is jolted awake when the cart comes to an abrupt halt.

A dark shape jumps into the path ahead.

Hope cries out, startled.

It is a creature, man-shaped yet monstrous, grey eyes staring from a dark face and great mats of knotted hair falling in clots over its shoulders. It is clothed but in rags, like streamers.

Hester grabs Rafe by the waist, pulling him from the pony's back into the cart where they all cower together, waiting for the creature to move or speak or do something.

Inexplicably, Gifford laughs. 'That's only Hywel. Harmless, he is.' He picks up the left-over remnants of their food and jumps down, walking towards the creature, who takes them, mumbling something incoherent and scurrying away into the undergrowth.

'Hywel's nothing to worry about. Just a vagrant who likes to keep himself to himself,' says Gifford, as he returns. 'My daughter, Margie, leaves food out for him, so he won't starve. Mind you, wouldn't think it to look at him, but he can hit a sparrow with a slingshot at twenty paces, so he finds enough to keep heart and soul together.'

'So, he's some kind of hermit?' says Hester.

''S right, mistress. Been about here a long time. I remember him when my Margie was still a girl and he was not a young man even then.'

Hope wonders what kind of man Hywel might once have been, whether he had a family, a trade. She tries to imagine what it would be like to discard the past, like an old coat, what could have caused the choice – madness or shame. Maybe he had done a terrible thing.

'He won't tell anyone about us, will he?' Hester sounds firm.

'Oh, no, mistress, no chance of that. There's no one for miles. And Hywel doesn't like company.'

Hester seems satisfied as her expression mellows, and she fields questions from Rafe about how to kill a bird with a slingshot. 'I imagine it must take a great deal of skill,' she tells him.

It is not long before they arrive at a fence too high to see over and a gate, tied open, giving on to the lodge. Hope doesn't know what she had imagined, but not this.

It is an imposing brick house, drenched in sun, tall as the surrounding trees with four symmetrical rows of windows, shuttered tight. The windows increase in size towards the top floors, giving the whole place an ungainly air, like a beautiful woman whose head is too large. The decoration in her hat is a dovecot set on the highest point of the steep slate roof.

A sweep of stone steps rises to a central door, a great studded slab of oak. And high above, right at the top, is a large wooden balcony where vines that have wound their way up the face of the building are woven through its balustrade, like garlands.

A dog barks lazily as they ride into a large fenced enclosure with a scattering of outbuildings and a paddock, where a few goats and a grizzled mule are huddled in a patch of shade cast by the barn.

'Goodness!' says Hester, seeming as surprised as Hope. 'I hadn't thought it would be so . . .' She doesn't finish and both sisters seem to have noticed that what at a distance had seemed excessively grand is unkempt now they are closer. A few panes are broken in the windows, like missing teeth, and the bricks are deeply pocked and crooked. Plants have seeded in the mortar and the vines run amok up the walls, interwoven with other climbing plants, all fighting for supremacy.

They dismount and a woman appears from the barn. She is as tall as a man, plainly dressed, with a skein of sun-bleached hair coiled into a knot and stabbed through with a long pin. She approaches them but seems to cast her eyes away as if the visitors are too bright to look at. It takes Hope a few moments to realize that she must be blind.

Gifford introduces her as his granddaughter, Lark. They free the grey from the cart, and Lark takes him, with the pony, into the shade. 'So, who are you, then?' she asks the piebald, producing a carrot, which she snaps in two, offering half to each.

Hope finds she cannot drag her gaze away from the strange girl.

Gifford is swinging a ring of keys from his hand. He leads the way up the steps, unlocks the door and they are swallowed into the shady interior. As Hope's eyes adjust to the gloom she feels, as the heavy door swings shut, a palpable sense of relief to be somewhere safe at last.

They are in a large, badly lit hall. Hope imagines it was once hung with tapestries but its walls are bare now, save for a few abandoned pikes arranged above the large stone fireplace, which is empty except for a nest that must have fallen down the chimney. It contains the broken blue shell of what looks like a robin's egg.

A large white cat darts by, disappearing up a flight of wooden stairs that rises to a gallery. The place has a sad, neglected atmosphere, and several hulking pieces of dark brown furniture squat about the room, filmed with a coating of dust.

A door bangs, and a woman emerges from behind the stairs. She introduces herself as Margie, 'With a hard *g*,' she insists. She is solid, with a frizz of red hair and freckled, damp skin, like cheese left out in the sun.

They follow her up the stairs, past a small chapel that is on the turn of the second flight. 'I've put you at the top,' she says. 'It's safer up there and you have the view. These rooms,' she says, of the firmly closed doors on the middle landings, 'haven't been used in years.'

At the top of the stairs they see the small carcass of a dead finch, tiny claws furled around an invisible twig. Margie scoops it into the pocket of her apron. 'Cat brings them in.'

Behind the first of three doors at the top is a large

bedroom with a sagging ceiling and an enormous canopied bed. Hope runs her finger over the top of the bed head. It is dusty and the windowsills are silted with dead insects, a few flies but mostly bees, and she itches to clean the place.

'There's another small bedroom next to this,' says Margie. 'But you may prefer to be together. This bed's certainly big enough.'

'This room'll do for us.' Hester flings down her jacket, pulling off her boots and stockings and abandoning them on the floor.

'I could take the small room,' Hope suggests, but Hester is firm in her insistence that they stay together.

It is hardly surprising.

The third door off the top landing leads to a large, bright chamber that Margie calls the 'blue room', most likely because of the ceiling, which is a grimy blue and flecked with faded stars. There is a chimneypiece on the far wall, where an old clock squats in a niche, measuring out thimblefuls of time with an insistent tick. It is already almost seven, yet outside there is no sign of dusk.

A lone bee loops lazily round the space, escaping when Margie opens the doors onto the balcony, from where they can see far over the tops of the trees that spread out in a blanket of endless green.

'At least from up here we'll know if anyone's approaching,' says Hester, who has unpinned her hair, shaken it out, and pads about the balcony barefoot.

Hope looks out in silence. She can see Lark far below, herding the goats into the barn. It is that still moment of the evening, when the light gleams and everything sharpens as if summer is holding its breath, waiting for something to happen.

Rafe insists upon his mother lifting him up so he can look down. He leans precariously over the balustrade. Hester is so slight, Hope fears he will slip from her grip and fall.

To her relief, Hester hauls him in, puts him down and, suddenly serious, turns to Margie. 'Dr Cotton told me there was a priest-hole somewhere here. Will you show me?'

Back in the blue room, Margie crouches in the fireplace, heaving away the iron back-plate to reveal an empty alcove behind. They squat to peer in but there isn't anything to see, just a dark space the size of a tomb. There is nothing on the outside of the house, with its perfect symmetry, each window carefully placed, that suggests the possibility of this hiding-hole.

'You won't make me go in there.' This is almost the first thing Melis has said since they left Ludlow that morning.

'You may have no choice.' Hester's tone is blunt, like a heavy object dropped on stone.

They stand, wrapped in the swirl of their private thoughts, staring at the hole without speaking for some time.

Felton

Felton has frantically searched Oxford and the surrounding villages for two days, but Bloor is nowhere to be found. He had lost him after the incident with Dr Cotton and has been searching for him since. Time presses. No one of Bloor's description has been seen at any of the inns, or the stews or the back-street taverns where the wastrels flock.

He even returned to Littlemore Manor, crouching unseen in the woods beyond the gate, to see if Bloor had been informed of Dr Cotton's death and gone to pay his respects. The only activity he witnessed there was the arrival of a draper's cart and the unloading of several bolts of black material – funeral hangings, certainly.

It is Sunday now and he walks from church to church, in the hope of sighting his quarry among the worshippers, but the trail is dead. Walking back to the Lamb and Flag, a hunched and cheerless figure, he is plagued by the thought of returning to George to confess that he has not only lost Bloor but also managed to eliminate the doctor. He remembers George's scathing attitude towards Worley and imagines being consigned to those George deems unreliable. Not the first choice any more. Like sand into an hourglass, despondency dribbles into him.

The only small mercy in his situation is that he has money in his pocket and enough opium tincture to keep his pain at bay for several weeks. He finds the landlord, orders a measure of ale and sits to weigh up his options, which seem vanishingly few. The drink is cool and delicious, offering fleeting succour from the doldrums. He closes his eyes, his mood lifting temporarily as the strong brew winds its way to his head where it mingles drunkenly with the tincture.

Opening his eyes, he believes he must be in the grip of a hallucination, for there, sitting a mere arm's length from him, nursing his own draught of ale, is the very man he's been looking for. His back is turned. Felton doesn't need to see his face. He instantly recognizes the neatly ordered hair and the erect posture. And there is the ring on the hand that holds his drink. He hears the dead man's voice – *This will serve as proof you come from me*. A charge of excitement catches in his breast, more intense and thrilling than any arousal of the flesh.

He waits. Planning. Watching. Wondering what good fortune brought the man back to the Lamb and Flag. Perhaps news of Cotton's fate had turned him back on the road. No matter the reason, Bloor is here. Felton wipes his sweaty palms on his breeches and drains his drink.

The landlord brings Bloor a plate of food, which he eats fast and efficiently, as if the meal is army rations, not the Lamb and Flag's famous capon pie. What a waste of fine food, Felton can't help thinking. But he concedes that it is only fair for a condemned man to have his last meal.

Finally, when they have both availed themselves of a second cup of ale, the man rises, stretches his arms with a loud yawn and, tossing a tip to the landlord, makes his way towards the stairs. Felton falls unseen into his slipstream, following him up and along the jumble of corridors on the first floor. Bloor is teetering slightly and holds his hand to the wall to steady himself.

He stops finally outside a bedroom door, fumbling with his key. Felton waits at the turn of the corridor, his fingers wound around a length of sturdy twine in his pocket.

The key cranks in the lock, the door falls open, and Felton is upon him, nimble even with only one arm, flicking the twine around his neck, drawing it tight, shoving him into the room, kicking the door shut. Bloor gurgles and flails for breath as Felton tightens the makeshift noose.

Pressing his mouth tight to the man's ear, Felton says, 'I know who you are, Bloor, and whom you have been charged to guard.' He loosens the string slightly. Bloor coughs, his body heaving desperately. 'Tell me where to find Buckingham's son.' His voice is menacingly reasonable, as if it is an ordinary question, asked in ordinary circumstances.

Bloor struggles to reply, managing to croak, 'I don't know what you mean.' The man is brave, if nothing else.

'Don't play the fool with me.' Felton thumps his knee into Bloor's kidney. The officer releases a guttural cry. 'Tell me.'

Felton expects him to beg for his life but he remains stubbornly silent.

Bloor holds firm as Felton asks and asks again. Another sharp prod meets his lower back. He expels a grunt. 'Ready to talk?'

'Never,' he rasps, as his terrified eyes flick involuntarily towards a satchel slung over a chair.

'Thank you,' says Felton. He has played enough games of cards with enough hard-nosed soldiers over the years to have learned when to spot a tell.

Bloor looks confused and, for an instant, he seems to

believe he will be set free, until the noose jerks tight. As dread surges into him, his pupils gape, as if sighting a beloved rather than staring death in the eye.

Felton waits for the body to slacken, then a little longer to be sure the job is done. It is a long time since he has been obliged to kill a man who wasn't also trying to kill him.

It is surprisingly easy.

He feels for a pulse.

The skin of the man's neck is rough with bristle.

There is nothing.

He pulls the ring from Bloor's finger, has to tug it with some force so dark bruises appear on the knuckle, and slips it onto his own finger for safe-keeping. Then, riffling swiftly through the satchel, he finds the roll of papers that will lead him to the women. He removes the few valuables, a purse of coin, a silver hat badge with a gemstone set into it and the man's jacket, a superior replacement for his own, which is threadbare.

He considers taking Bloor's firearm, a heavy flintlock apparatus, and his sword, but decides against it as he already has the better, lighter, newer pistol, given to him by George, and the sword is too cumbersome. He pockets a serviceable poniard, which will replace the blade he left embedded in Dr Cotton's ribcage. Before he leaves, he wraps a blanket around the window latch to deaden the noise as he bludgeons it with the hilt of the flintlock, creating the appearance of a break-in.

By the time anyone finds the body, Felton will be miles away.

Hester

Glad of a few minutes alone, I stand on the balcony, looking out. Indolence has descended over the afternoon. Melis and Rafe are playing cards in the bedroom, Hope has dropped off in a chair in the blue room, head lolling, sweat beading on her upper lip, and the Giffords are somewhere downstairs.

Beyond the gate a dead trunk, a naked old man, guards the path, prodding with several gouty fingers towards the dark hollow in the vegetation where the track begins. A trio of poplars soars above the rest, heads together, whispering, sharing secrets – so many secrets. If I focus my eyes into the green depths I can see the silent movement of antlers between the foliage and something, a buzzard or a kite, screeches, almost the sound of a human infant in distress.

There is barely a breath of wind, all life suffocated by the heat, which hasn't let up since our arrival five days ago. If anything it has intensified. The air is as thick as aspic and we are entombed in it, like banquet vegetables. A flowering vine reaches its fingers up the building, spreading its heady soporific scent. Only the bees, dusted with pollen as they dip in and out of the brazen blooms, continue their industry. Even they dither, seeming half intoxicated, too, by the cloying vine, finding themselves drawn into the shade of the interior from where only the fortunate escape, the others leaving their desiccated little carcasses on the window ledges.

The house seems to have a sad life of its own: its crevices are filled with mice and its beams squeeze out tears of resin, its old bones creaking and complaining at night, like an arthritic old man. We are so remote here, without even the sound of church bells to remind us of God and time.

I have no choice but to decide to feel safe. The alternative is a fate I cannot bear to confront. But a small cog of fear clicks and whirs perpetually, deep in my mind. I tell myself I will feel better when Ambrose Cotton's guard has arrived.

In the meantime we have become absorbed into the small routines of life. Margie's domain is the kitchen, where she is almost always to be found, sleeves rolled up, muscular forearms deep in flour, kneading. She is a good cook and makes cheeses that stink and sweat in the cellar but taste smooth and delicious spread on the coarse bread she bakes daily. Margie is superstitious, always touching her head for wood, and says the house hides her things deliberately, when she has misplaced them. Gifford, who indulges his daughter's beliefs to her face but chuckles at her behind her back, tends the vegetable garden, creaking into the kitchen with earthy clumps of potatoes or carrots that Margie swiftly transforms beneath her sharp kitchen knife.

I have noticed that Hope, when she is not scrubbing the life out of the laundry, or dusting the bedchamber as if she can clean our lives into order, has struck up an incipient friendship with Lark. The two have taken to perching on the fence in the evenings, talking.

Lark's realm is the barn, where she tends and milks the goats and other livestock, so surefooted that it is easy to forget she cannot see. The Giffords' yard-dog has a large, lolloping puppy that has taken a shine to Rafe. He has called it Captain and it has teased him out of the doldrums. The shock of the attempted abduction had left its mark, and it is a relief for me to see my son's mood lighten.

Melis has taken it upon herself to revive the neglected hives in the corner of the paddock and seems quite content to busy herself mending the dilapidated skeps. In the evenings we sit in the kitchen telling stories and playing cards, using pebbles for wagers, always keeping one ear open for the bark of the yard-dog, hailing an unexpected arrival.

There is a certain allure to this unobserved life and, were my circumstances different, I might enjoy a simple existence away from the eyes of the world. We have fallen swiftly into the routine of the place. I collect the eggs each morning from the henhouse, a folly of a structure designed in miniature imitation of the house itself, dovecote and all. Big enough to house at least forty brooders, it is a reminder of what this place once was, filled to the rafters with guests. Now a mere dozen hens nest there and a noisy cockerel lords it over them all.

Its wood is rotten and paint peeling, but it was someone's labour of love once, with each tiny brick and slate picked out, each window brought to life with a spot of white to mimic a splash of light. Only the balcony is missing, just a few splintered struts hanging where it must once have been.

The old clock spits out its high-pitched ping, marking the quarter-hour. I feel as if I have already been in this place

117

half a lifetime. Hope half wakes, shifts and settles back to sleep. If it were up to me, I would lock that clock, with its infernally loud tick, in a cupboard and let it run down. I would like to forget altogether about the passing of time but Hope seems to have become attached to it, carefully winding it each day as if all our lives depend on it.

I see something, a distant ripple between the trees. A flash of vivid colour, crimson, tells me it is not an animal, or that old mendicant we encountered. A dreaded image pops into my head of Worley and his red coat, and my legs feel as heavy as lead.

I tell myself it must be Ambrose Cotton's man but we must take precautions.

'Wake up,' I cry, shaking Hope and running to the bedroom to warn Melis and Rafe. 'For God's sake, all of you, hurry!'

While Hope pulls on her breeches and tucks her hair under a cap, I ram our clothes and other belongings into a cupboard out of sight and stuff the letters into my dress. I hold out the pistol for Hope, who looks at it a moment before taking it and concealing it under her clothes. Taking Rafe by the hand, I pick up his toy monkey and half drag him to the blue room, Melis in our wake. Together we heave away the heavy back-plate.

On seeing the dark opening, Melis's breath comes fast, in shallow rasps, and her eyes flick back and forth. 'I can't go in there. I can't.' She is wringing her hands and shaking her head desperately.

'We've talked about it, Melis.' My own fear nips at me, I am weighing up whether I can risk leaving her outside – it is Rafe George wants and I am the one standing in the way, not Melis – but I can't, of course I can't.

The dog starts up a rapid volley of loud barks.

'It won't be for long. I'll be with you.'

Melis, chewing her nails, doesn't seem reassured, and I can feel Rafe's body tighten as if he is preparing his dissent too.

'It's the safest place here.' I sound absolutely confident, though I am not – not at all. Really, I am sick with fear.

Leaning round the balcony door Hope says, in an urgent low voice, 'There's a man in the yard, talking to Gifford.'

I abandon my coaxing and shove Melis into the space, bundling Rafe in behind her before he, too, has a chance to protest, secure in the knowledge that Lark and the others have been primed to say nothing of our presence.

'Can you cope?' I ask Hope pointlessly. We have been over the drill. There is not space for us all in the priesthole, so she will greet the visitor in her man's disguise and feign no knowledge of us. 'Remember the ring. If he has a black enamel ring he is Ambrose's guard.'

She offers me a wan smile and a nod.

I shuffle after them into the tight space, feet first. The air is stale and smells of ash and dread. There is just enough room for the three of us to sit huddled tightly together, arms cradling our knees. Melis is shaking.

Hope pushes the iron plate back into position with a loud scraping sound and I have a final uneasy glimpse of her face. Then the light is gone. I am entombed in a darkness so intense I lose my bearings and seek some source of light, however vague, a tiny slit where the back-plate meets the wall, a space between the floorboards giving onto the room below. There is nothing but a blanket of black that is at once limitless, spreading out for ever, and suffocating, closing in around us. In the darkness all noise is amplified. The tick of the hated clock reaches in, beating through the quiet, counting out each long moment.

I feel the wing-beat of panic in my throat, but I cannot give rein to my fear or I will unleash chaos. I must focus on keeping Rafe and Melis from succumbing to their demons. My sister grips my arm hard enough to leave a bruise. I gently release her fingers one by one and lean to kiss her cheek. It is as clammy as wax. 'Don't worry. I'm here.' Useless words that cannot stem her fear but she is mercifully quiet.

It is as hot as a furnace and Rafe is panting like a wary dog. I pull him onto my lap, holding him in the crook of my body, like a baby. Just when I might have expected him to make trouble, he heaves a long sigh and relaxes into my embrace. I think I can hear the suck of his thumb in his mouth, something he hasn't done since infancy, and am glad I remembered his monkey. My love for him swells, subsuming me. It is not a mere tender affection but a fierce warrior love, strong and whetted on retribution. I would protect my child to the death.

Sweat blossoms under my clothes, spreading out through my body, trickling down my face. I wipe it away, catching a whiff of saltpetre, the residue left on my hands from when Gifford taught us all how to shoot a firearm that morning. I think of Hope with the pistol. She had met the target first time, much to Gifford's surprise. He had refused to believe she was a novice.

I try to remember the sequence of loading: the powder poured down the barrel, then the square of ticking to cradle the lead ball, all pressed in behind the powder with the ram-rod. 'A gun should be handled as if you mean it,'

Gifford had said. 'Imagine it is a fowl for the pot and you must break its neck.'

So many words to remember: the flintlock, the frizzen pan, the dog lock, the powder horn. 'Carry it angled upwards – don't want the lead falling out – and never set it to full-cock unless you intend to fire it.' Holding the loaded pistol had infused me with a new sense of authority. I was shocked to find myself imagining how that feeling would multiply, were I pointing it at George.

'Can you hear it?' Melis murmurs, drawing me out of my thoughts. Her breath is coming in short, agitated bursts. I offer a silent prayer that this is not the first salvo of one of her episodes. Not that. Not now.

I stroke her hair, whispering more platitudes.

'Can you hear it?' she repeats. 'There is something in this house. Something evil. Can't you hear it? It has stolen the song of the bees.'

'You're not making sense.' I try to counter her outburst with pragmatism but I am rattled – I can feel how tense she is. If she has an episode she will give us away. 'Hush.' I continue to stroke her hair, trying to calm her, tight as a bowstring myself.

'You must be able to hear it.' She still won't temper her tone and now Rafe is stirring too.

'*Be quiet.*' Rafe's voice bursts out of him, too loud and edged with alarm.

Not knowing what else to do, I press my hand over his mouth. He struggles but I hold fast. 'Please. It's not safe.'

'It's everywhere.' Melis is now rocking slightly back and forth. 'Can you not hear it? You must be able to hear it.'

We fall silent and, to my horror, I begin to hear a kind of rhythmic buzzing throb that seems to echo round my skull, now faint, now loud, making me fear Melis's auditory hallucinations might be contagious. A worm is crawling into my ear and feeding on my mind.

I tell myself firmly that it is nothing more than the hush ringing in my ears. But the sound seems to be gaining momentum and volume.

Hope

The man stands at the bottom of the steps facing away from Hope. On seeing the red of the jacket slung over his shoulder, her heart cranks up but as she nears it becomes clear that this is not Worley. This man is bigger.

Seeming to intuit her presence, he turns to face her with a greeting. He has a kind face, framed by a wildly unkempt burst of russet hair and several days' worth of beard. The jacket, she sees now, is made of peat-coloured felt with silver buttons and is half inside out, displaying its red lining. If this man is Ambrose Cotton's guard, she wonders how much use he will be, as his left arm is in a sling.

The puppy bounds up to him and he stoops, ruffling its ears. 'Who's a handsome fellow, then?'

Hope remains on the top step. He waits for her to say something, scrutinizing her with what appears to be suspicion. As she is about to speak, he smiles, saying, 'I come in friendship,' and she is struck dumb because his expression is transformed. The smile overtakes his entire face, the lines of it catching as far up as his temples and even including a slight lift of the shoulders. It exposes a friendly gap between his front teeth. Despite trying to look directly at him, in a masculine manner, she is too shy to meet his eyes, which are the same fox-coat colour as his hair, making him seem more animal than human.

She finds her voice, remembering to deepen her tone. 'May I ask what your business is here, sir?' She picks nervously at her fingernails and is glad to see Gifford nearby, his ancient musket under his arm, keeping an eye on the visitor.

'I have been sent by Dr Cotton of Littlemore Manor to ensure the safety of Mistress Hester, her son and her sisters.' He huffs a small gust of laughter. 'I sincerely hope I have come to the correct place, as there seems not to be another house in the vicinity and this is where my map led me.' He opens and lifts the palm of his good hand.

'No. There is nowhere else.' She realizes too late that he meant it as a joke of sorts – it is plain to see there is nothing but trees for miles around.

'And you are . . . ?' she asks.

'Lieutenant Bloor.' He turns back to Hope, pulling a ring from his finger, holding it up. 'Dr Cotton instructed me to present this as proof I come on his orders.' He takes a step up and simultaneously she takes a step down, realizing now the heft of the man, as he is still taller than her, though two steps below. His shirt is pulled tight across his shoulders revealing his broad bulk, and she revises her first impression: even with one good arm, he could surely floor an attacker with ease. But there is something about him, too, something broken, not just his arm but something more profound that she senses, and which sparks her compassion.

Now he is closer she can smell him. He smells strong, like a horse after a gallop. She takes the ring. It is a plain band inset with black enamel and engraved with some words in what appears to be Latin.

'If you could please show it to the mistress of the house?'

He smiles again and looks intently at her, making her feel as if she is having her pockets searched. It is not an unpleasant feeling.

'Would you be so kind as to wait here?' She indicates to the hovering Gifford that he keep watch, and whips herself away, up and up to the blue room, taking a look from the balcony to make sure he is still there. He is, exactly where she left him.

She taps on the chimneypiece. 'Can you hear me?'

Hester's voice comes faintly, as if from deep in a well. 'Who is he?'

'He's called Lieutenant Bloor, says he's been sent by Ambrose, gave me the ring. It is black enamel as you described.'

'Thanks to God.' Hester's relief is manifest. 'Get us out of here, Hope. It's unendurable.'

Hope inches the heavy plate away and the three crawl out, blinking in the bright light. They are filthy with smut and ash but none of them seems to care. Melis is pale as bone, her face set rigid, and she has bitten her fingernails so far to the quick there are smears of blood on her cuffs. Hester inspects the ring and says nothing but appears to be satisfied, attaching it to the locket chain she wears around her neck.

Melis leads her nephew out onto the landing wordlessly, while Hope and Hester push the fire's back-plate into place. Hester stops a moment and pulls a bundle of letters from under her dress, brown and spotted with age, which she slips into the hiding place before the two of them close it up.

'What are they?' Hope's curiosity is roused.

'It's better you don't know.' Hope's frustration must

register as Hester says, 'I only keep you in the dark for your own safety. You're very young. It wouldn't be fair to burden you.' She then takes on a formidably stern tone. 'You're not to tell a soul about them. Not a soul. Is that clear?'

'Quite clear.' Hope tries to imagine what the letters might contain that could make her unsafe and wonders what other secrets Hester is keeping from her, all the things she doesn't know, all the hazards. The lieutenant is here now, she tells herself, and he will protect them.

Felton

Two women and a child come outside to greet him. They are a ragged bunch, smeared with dirt, which one of them – the mother, he supposes – explains away with the excuse that they have been digging in the vegetable garden.

This is a lie. The dark smudges look to him more like ash than earth.

Both women are very slight and it is almost impossible to imagine them as a threat to anyone, least of all the formidable George. But Felton is well aware that danger can be wrapped in unexpected packages.

Looking at the mother with her unremarkable features – he can't help but notice she goes barefoot – it is hard for Felton to believe that George has sired a child with her. Initially he had assumed it was the other one, who is better put together and holds a passing resemblance to his own sister, Bridget. It seems an insult that George might have been drawn to this plain woman, who appears entirely unabashed to display her dirty toenails.

'We are very glad to see you, Lieutenant Bloor.' She fingers the enamel ring, which is now suspended from a chain around her neck. 'Tell me, how is Dr Cotton? And his wife? She was very unwell when we were last at Littlemore.'

He gives her a noncommittal reply, suggesting that

Dr Cotton's wife is recovering steadily. He can't help the memory of his hand saturated in the doctor's blood, right up the wrist and into the sleeve of his old jacket, abandoned in favour of this smart new one, with its scarlet lining and silver buttons – Bloor's jacket.

It doesn't take him long to gather that the younger sister is not quite right. It is not immediately apparent but lurks in the subtle air of distraction in her bearing and a gaze that skims the edges, avoiding directness. He has seen something like it in soldiers who have witnessed too much horror. They become loosed from their bindings, unpredictable, and are often the first to be killed in combat.

'What happened to you? Is it painful?' The mother indicates his injured arm and he responds with a vague explanation, assuring her it will not affect his ability to carry out his duty.

'I didn't mean that.' Her brow is ruffled with what appears to be genuine concern. 'If it's still painful after so many months it must be infected. I can dress it for you. Make a compress to draw out any impurities.'

'That's very kind of you, madam, but . . .' He hates her for her pity.

'I won't accept a refusal.' Behind her smile there is a glint of steel. Felton is wary of becoming too familiar as it might impede his ability to fulfil his mission. However, she gives him no choice but to consent to her care and he has an inkling that she will be a more formidable adversary than she first appeared. 'And please call me Hester.'

She calls over the caretaker, a doddering creature, asking him to show Felton around the grounds. The man carries an old musket – the kind of inaccurate weapon that is more likely to dislocate your shoulder with its kick than meet its target.

'Perhaps your son would like to join us.' He might as well start by gaining the boy's trust.

'What a good idea. He's so tired of the company of we women.' She seems delighted by Felton's suggestion.

Felton wonders about the youth who greeted his arrival. Surely he has been male company for the child.

'Are you a soldier?' the boy asks. 'Have you got a gun?'

'I have.' Felton opens his jerkin to reveal the pistol tucked inside.

'Have you ever killed anyone?'

Hester laughs uncomfortably, apologizing to Felton and telling her son that it is not the kind of question you are supposed to ask.

Felton squats down to the boy's level. 'I see you have an enquiring mind. There is nothing wrong with that.' He glances up at Hester, who returns his smile. 'It's a sign of intelligence.'

He and the boy follow Gifford as he trudges around the perimeter fence at an agonizingly slow pace, pointing out where it needs mending, while Felton quizzes him on the daily routines. 'I need to know everything if I am to keep them safe.' The heat is stifling and Felton's arm is beginning to twinge. The entire place has an air of dilapidation, as if it is on the brink of being engulfed by the forest that laps so close.

'How often do you travel into town?' he asks the old man.

'I'd say about once a month. To take the eggs and cheese to market and fetch supplies. Won't have need to go for a while yet. Was there to collect the ladies not long ago, see.'

He hadn't expected the lodge to be quite so isolated. He'd written to George, explaining he would be close to Ludlow and for him to send this Worley fellow to the inn there to wait for his word. He took the precaution of leaving a letter with the landlord at the Feathers giving instructions for Worley to lie low there, and also copied out detailed directions to the lodge for him in case of emergency. He realizes this safeguard is as good as useless. If he were to encounter problems and needed Worley's help, he'd have no way of contacting the man. It had taken him the best part of a day to get here from the town.

In the barn, it is mercifully a little cooler. They find Gifford's blind granddaughter skulking in the gloom. Swallows dart about under the beams, flying in and out of a hole in the wall where the brickwork has crumbled away. Gifford is telling him about Lark's gift with animals while Felton watches her pouring milk from a bucket into a larger churn, noticing how confident she seems with the task and that not a drop is spilled. She looks up suddenly, as if in response to his gaze, training her eyes directly on him.

'How much can your granddaughter see?' Felton asks, once they are out of earshot, unsettled by the look she gave him. 'She seems to have some vision, at least.'

'Nothing, nothing at all. She was born that way.' Gifford doesn't hesitate in his response but still Felton wonders if it is the truth.

Rafe closes his eyes, holding his arms out in front of him, apparently trying to find out what it would be like to be blind, not getting very far before he trips over the puppy. 'Daft boy,' Gifford calls him.

He can't be aware that the child is the son of the Duke of Buckingham, thinks Felton, or he'd never have used such a familiar tone. Though there seems to be a complete absence of ceremony in this place. He is thinking of Hester's bare feet and the women's dirt-smeared dresses, loose like night-gowns, and her insistence on given names.

Gifford points out a large henhouse, someone's now dilapidated folly, where a few brood-fowl are pecking about. As they walk on, a black and white pony, a dappled grey horse and a decrepit mule watch them lethargically from a small parched meadow, where he notices at the far end that Melis is busying herself with some shabby bee skeps.

At some point on their rounds, Rafe slips his hand into Felton's. It is a strange gesture for a boy of his age but he supposes the child has been mollycoddled by the company of women. As they walk hand in hand, Felton is surprised to discover a tender feeling burgeoning in his chest.

He has never fathered a child, has never thought about such things. He has always lived such a hand-to-mouth life, moving from one conflict to another, without feeling the need to settle, but this small gesture carves a window into how it might be to have a son of his own. The vision of a possible future rolls out in his mind, commanding an army, marrying, fathering children. A new life detached from his past, from the acts he is about to commit. He crushes his sentimentality.

As they round the corner of the house a few rabbits scamper away as the puppy bounds towards them, barking. 'I can show you how to set a rabbit trap sometime, if you'd like,' Felton suggests to the boy. 'We'd have to go out into the forest. What do you think?'

'Mother wouldn't let me. She says it's too dangerous to leave the house and its grounds.' His small shoulders are slouched in disappointment.

'I'm sure I can persuade her.' The boy brightens. Felton doesn't think he'll have much difficulty bringing the child to his side. He seems eager enough for adventure.

At the back of the house a bovine woman is sitting outside the kitchen door, shelling peas. Gifford introduces her as his daughter, Margie. She asks him if he is hungry. He hasn't thought about food since breakfast.

Gifford points out the door that leads to his family's quarters.

'The three of you sleep in there, do you?' Felton says. 'I only ask as a matter of security. If I know where everyone tends to be at night, I can better protect the women and the child.'

Gifford answers that they do indeed bed down there, 'But if one of the animals is ailing, Lark likes to sleep in the barn.'

He makes a mental note of everything. So many different things he must take into consideration, and attention to detail is what will make a success of this mission. He will need a little time to get the lie of the place and its occupants before he acts and must do his utmost to avoid the suspicions of the Giffords.

'The sisters and the boy all sleep upstairs, I assume.'

Margie nods. 'Yes, at the top.'

'There is a third sister, I believe, whom I have yet to meet. And what of the young man who greeted me? Where –'

The old man interrupts him, laughing for no apparent reason, his peg-toothed mouth wide, breath sour.

Margie puts her bowl of peas on table, giving a handful to Rafe. 'That *was* Hope –' she is also laughing – 'in breeches. Had you fooled, didn't she?'

'That was the third sister?' He is picturing the dark young man, handsome, smooth-skinned, remembering the stirring he'd felt, now refiguring the image in his mind as that of a girl. He feels as if he's been duped. She is the one George described as a 'weak link'.

'That's my aunt Hope,' says Rafe.

Felton forces out a chuckle, resenting the Giffords' laughter, feeling ridiculed.

Forcing his focus back to his mission, he indicates a low door in the corner of the kitchen. 'Where does that lead?'

'Down to the cellar. You won't find much in there of interest. Just the food store, last year's preserves, some fruit and beer, and my cheeses, of course.' She seems very proud of them. 'And eggs. We've more eggs than we know what to do with.'

'I wouldn't be doing my job properly if I didn't take a look down there.'

'You'll need a lamp, then.' She touches a rush-light to the embers under a cooking pot in which something is simmering. 'And take care. Those steps are hazardous.' She seems distracted. 'I can't find my sharp knife any-where. Have you seen it?' she asks her father, who is in the process of sitting down, with a long wheeze, and blotting the sweat from his face with a rumpled handkerchief. 'This house likes to hide things from me.'

Felton opens the cellar door, poking his head into the cool dark, the stench of old fruit and mildew assailing him.

Holding out the light, he can vaguely see a steep flight of steps.

Rafe follows him, saying he's never been down to the cellar, his voice bristling with eagerness. Felton warns him to tread carefully. The last thing he needs is for any harm to come to the child on the stairs. Margie was right, they are uneven and treacherous, and George's voice whispers through his mind: *It's imperative that it appears to be an accident.*

He stamps his feet hard several times when he gets to the bottom.

'What are you doing?' Rafe asks.

'Scaring off the rats.'

'Rats?' Rafe repeats, his tone more fascinated than scared.

Felton feels his way along the dank walls, searching for loose bricks, potential hiding places for the incriminating letters George has instructed him to find and destroy, but reasons that only a fool would stash paper in such a place, where the damp would eat away at it in no time.

'How big are the rats?'

'Some can grow as big as dogs.'

The child's eyes widen. 'That big?'

'No, little fellow. I'm only teasing.' He cuffs the boy's shoulder, drawing a giggle from him.

There is a cobwebbed door in the far wall. Felton imagines finding a secret passage out into the forest. How convenient that would make his task. But he finds only a dusty, airless space, stacked with a few broken barrels, which must once have been used as a still room.

Returning to the bottom of the steps, he calls up to Margie, 'Do you need anything brought up?'

'I could do with a jar of honey. On the shelf above the cheeses.'

Felton makes a cursory search of the shelves, still finding no sign of the hidden correspondence, then picks up a pot of honey and takes it up to the kitchen.

Margie takes over the tour of the interior, saying her father finds the stairs difficult. She leads them to a large hall and, before following her up the stairs, he returns to the front steps to pick up his bag, only to find, with a flicker of concern, that it is no longer where he left it.

''Spect one of the sisters took it up for you,' says Margie, when he asks if she's seen it. 'Hope probably. She's very efficient. Can't stand to see anything out of its proper place . . . Unless the house has been misbehaving again.' Clearly she is one of those country people with peculiar ideas. 'They want you to sleep upstairs near them, I'm told. For safety,' she explains, tapping her head. 'Touch wood, they won't need you.'

The house is tall, with several suites of gloomy rooms on the middle floors that are unused. Felton continues to keep an eye open for possible hiding places where the letters might be. He hadn't expected the place to be so large and they could be anywhere but he can't risk leaving it until the other task is completed, as he might be obliged to leave in a hurry.

A white cat slinks about in the shadows, watching them with its green gaze, a grey mouse in its jaws. The child stoops to stroke it and it lashes out, leaving a raised pink scratch on his hand. Rafe retaliates, kicking out at it. It is too quick for him and is gone.

'Shouldn't approach a cat when it has prey,' says Margie. 'They don't like it.'

Felton has never liked felines either, has the sense they can see through to his soul and read his sins.

As they mount the final flight of stairs, they can hear the voices of the women and Rafe runs ahead. Felton stands for a moment, looking down the stairwell and pondering its unhindered view of the flagstones below. He collects his thoughts, the beginnings of a plan formulating.

Margie points out the door to the women's bedroom, then opens another beside it. 'This is where you will bed down.'

It is a small, sparsely furnished room, like a monk's cell, with a high east-facing window. Felton is relieved to find his bag but dismayed to see that someone, the 'efficient' Hope, he supposes, has already unpacked his few belongings.

He feels stripped naked and checks the lock of his small chest, thankful to find it has not been opened. It houses his journal, and the unopened folder containing his mother's probate papers, either of which risk the exposure of his true identity. When he checks, he is relieved to find the key still tucked into the small hidden pocket of his bag and berates himself for having taken such a risk when he has been there barely an hour.

'Everything as it should be?' Margie has noticed his unease.

'Yes, yes. This arm's giving me bother, that's all.'

Margie seems to think it is a cue for her to ask how he was injured, and he tries to quash his irritation as he briefly recounts the circumstances.

'I heard dreadful things about the siege,' she says. 'Gossip even reached Ludlow about all the dead. Is it true seven thousand men went and only two thousand returned?'

'Something like that, I think.' He knows the numbers only too well. Too many of his comrades were killed.

'They say it's the duke's fault. I'm glad I don't have a son to be drawn into one of that varlet's needless wars.' Her expression is tight and bitter. His fist clenches involuntarily, and he has to hold himself back from a spontaneous defence of George.

'I see you have books.' She is surprised, her eyebrows arched quizzically. He has often come across such a response. By the look of him no one would take him for a cultured man.

'Yes,' he says, pretending a friendly smile. 'And Rafe, does he read?'

'Of course I can read.' Felton jumps, turning in surprise. He hadn't been aware of Rafe entering the room, quiet as a thief.

'I'm sure you can, young man.' He collects his thoughts as they follow Margie back out onto the landing. 'Can you write as well?'

'Of *course* I can.' The child is indignant.

'I expect your mother has a writing box somewhere with paper and ink. Does she let you use it?' He watches the child's expression carefully.

'I am forbidden to look inside it.' Rafe's eyes move involuntarily towards the closed door of the women's bedchamber, telling Felton all he needs to know.

'And, finally, the blue room.' Margie opens the third door on the landing. 'It's where the mistress likes to sit.'

Felton takes in all the detail: a pistol on the table, a clock above the hearth, a pan of old ashes. Someone has swept out the fireplace. He remembers the older sisters in their ash-smeared dresses, wonders if they might have been burning something. He touches a finger to the surround. It is cool.

They step out onto the balcony where the three women are sitting. The old boards creak under his weight, riddled with worm. The whole place is neglected, its bricks so deeply dinted that birds could comfortably nest there. It's a wonder that the house is still standing. He glances over the edge at the stone steps far down in the yard. Now, if you were to fall from here . . .

'Have you seen everything?' Hester interrupts his thoughts. She is lounging back, feet tucked under her, in a chair that dwarfs her small frame. 'You will find us very informal here . . .' She continues asking questions about whether he has everything he needs, how his journey was – on and on. She is apparently the kind of woman who will talk just to fill a silence.

Contrarily Melis gives him a silent, penetrating stare, with eyes pale as water in a white bowl, which makes him feel a little uneasy, as if she can see into him and read his thoughts. The third sister appears now, apologizing, saying they haven't yet prepared the bed in his room, making to return inside. She is wearing a dress now, crisply starched and neatly laced, like a cats' cradle, over her front.

He moves into her path. 'That won't be necessary.' She is close enough for him to smell her. Her scent is clean and brisk, her dark curls tamed into plaits, her mouth soft and generous. It is impossible now to imagine her as a boy. 'I can do that myself.' He doesn't want her in his room again, not until he can hide the key to his chest properly.

'It's no trouble,' she says, looking at her hands rather than at him.

'I must insist.' Felton is firm.

'Leave him be, Hope,' says Hester. 'He doesn't want you fussing over him.'

He can see now why George had suggested the youngest of them might be useful to him. Willingness is spread all over her, a desire to help the stranger in their midst.

Hester

The interior of the henhouse is dry and smells of straw.
When I feel in the nest boxes, each warm clutch of eggs is
like treasure. I sit for a while on the floor, closing my eyes
to absorb the peace punctuated only by the soft parp and
chuckle of the hens and the rustle of their feathers. Even
the cockerel is quiet. We have all been a little calmer since
the arrival of the lieutenant yesterday, all but Melis, who
has disappeared into her impenetrable world. I am afraid
our spell in the priest-hole has roused her demons.

I walk back across the yard with my basket full of eggs.
The air is sullen, already dense with heat, though the sun
is barely risen. Something invisible rustles and barks deep
in the forest, causing me to stop for a moment. An involuntary shudder runs through me. We are like rats in a sack
in this place. Anything, anyone – an entire army – could
hide unseen among the trees and none of us would know.
My gaze is drawn towards the top of the house and there
is the lieutenant, waving to me from the balcony. I am
reassured to know he is keeping watch and wonder if he,
too, has trouble sleeping. The pain of his injured arm must
keep him awake.

It was a terrible mess when I dressed it the previous
evening, a putrid reek emanating from it as I removed the
bandage. His good arm was well-shaped and muscular,

like his chest, but the other hung ghostly white and strangely twisted at the elbow as if the bone had once been shattered and mended badly.

There was a half-healed wound near the inner side of the joint, raised and suppurating in places with angry bulbous veins spreading out around it. I thought it a wonder he didn't seem more ill. I'd become suddenly uncomfortable. It had felt too intimate, looking at this strange, sullen man's undressed body.

'I'm going to make something to draw out the infection.' I began to gather together what I needed for the poultice.

He made no attempt to hide his doubt. 'I've had all manner of cures. Nothing seems to have much of an effect.'

'You've never tried my bread and milk compress.'

He made a snort, not quite a laugh. 'Old maids' remedy.'

'As a matter of fact, it was taught to me by Dr Cotton. It'll ease your pain. Just you wait and see.'

He enters the kitchen at the same time as me, placing a book and a magnifying-glass on the table. I notice he has shaved and is a good deal tidier than he was on his arrival. He offers to scramble some of the fresh eggs in a pan, saying it was what he used to do when the army was on the move, marching through Europe. 'We'd take the eggs from the local farms and cook them over an open fire.'

I watch him crack the shells single-handed. He is surprisingly deft, stirring, adding a little milk, a knob of butter. The eggs are vivid yellow, delicious, and I feel restored.

'Is it you who collects the eggs every day?' he asks. His implication seems to be that, as the mistress of the house, it is a task I stoop to.

'I enjoy it.' I can't help my defensive tone. 'We all help here.'

'I only ask because, if I am to protect you properly, it is vital I have an idea of where everyone is and what the routines of the place are.'

'Of course. I see.'

Once we have eaten I change his dressing, peeling away the compress, releasing the stench of rot once more, though it is less pungent than it was. Much of the infection has been drawn out and there is a black fragment of matter on the dressing. He takes his magnifier to inspect it.

'Piece of shot,' he says.

'No wonder it wouldn't heal. I'll make another poultice this evening in case there's more to bring to the surface.'

'I have to concede to the effectiveness of your remedy. I didn't believe it would work.'

I tear a strip of fresh linen and dab salve on the wound, chatting to hide my awkwardness. 'Thank you for being so kind to Rafe. It's good for him to be in male company. You're very good with him. Do you have children of your own, nephews, nieces?'

A fleeting sorrow passes over his face. 'No. No children. I had a twin sister who was very dear to me but she was taken by an ague many years ago.'

The atmosphere has become heavy, so I change the topic. 'Rafe mentioned you'd offered to take him out and set rabbit traps. But I'm not sure it's such a good idea for him to leave the grounds.'

'Of course.' He nods. 'I understand. Perhaps I could simply teach him how to tie the snares. Would you mind?'

'That's a very good idea.' He returns my smile. 'Rafe told me you like reading.' I point to the book beside him.

He nods, his eyes following me as I pick it up. It is a volume of essays by Francis Bacon and falls open to a passage about love, where the corner of the page has been turned down to mark it.

Surprise must register on my face because he says, 'Didn't expect a rough old dog like me to have refined tastes?'

'I suppose I didn't.'

'Alas, I'm reliant on this for reading now.' He holds up the magnifying-glass. 'My far sight is excellent, but close to, all is a blur.'

'I can barely thread a needle without a magnifier.' I turn to the inside cover of the book, seeing a note scrawled and signed. The words *'your devoted'* spark my curiosity, but he snatches it back before I can read the rest, stashing it inside his jacket out of sight.

The door bangs open, startling us, and Hope appears. She is holding Margie's kitchen knife at arm's length, as if it will bite.

'You've found it. Margie *will* be pleased. Where was it?' I become increasingly aware that something is not right. Hope's expression is taut. 'What is it, Hope?'

'It was upstairs . . . in *our* bed, right inside it.' Hope sits, dropping the knife onto the table, pushing it away from her. 'I almost cut myself on it when I was making the bed.'

At that moment Margie walks in. 'It's like a furnace in our rooms.' She stops, taking in the scene, saying, 'Goodness me, has somebody died?' She picks up the knife. 'You found it! Where was it?'

When I explain, Margie's cheerfulness fades. 'I tell you, things disappear in this place.'

'I can't imagine how it got there,' I say.

But Hope snaps, 'You know perfectly well who it was.'

She waits for me to say it but I won't. Everyone has noticed Melis's strange brooding mood.

Melis is not out at the beehives where I expect to find her, or in the barn, and Margie tells me she hasn't been through the kitchen. I climb the stairs, feeling a pall of tiredness fall over me. The heat is intensifying, sapping me of energy.

On the middle floor I hear a scratching coming from inside one of the unused rooms. My mind transforms it into something ugly and malevolent. I throw open the door, determined to face this imaginary creature. The cat slips out, curling round my ankles in gratitude for its freedom.

I laugh at my own silliness, for allowing myself to be unsettled, putting it down to the sleepless nights and the burden of responsibility weighing heavily.

Melis is in the bedchamber lying on her back, fanning herself with a piece of paper and gazing vacantly at the ceiling. 'There you are,' I say. 'I've been looking every-where for you.'

'I've been here all morning.' She sounds completely her-self. But as I near her, I see clusters of raised swellings running up her arm and onto her neck.

'What are these?' I point to the swellings. 'They look like stings.'

She ignores my question, tugging down her sleeves to cover the welts. 'How old do you think this house is? Do you see how the ceiling sags?'

'Melis?' I am loath to broach the subject, but I must.

'Yes.'

'Margie's knife . . . did you put it in the bed to make you feel safer? I understand –'

'You think it was me,' she interjects angrily. 'Hope has already accused me of this. I suppose it's what everyone thinks. Mad Melis, the demented sister. That's what they think, that I'm loose in the head. It's what you think, too, isn't it?' She regards me with simmering indignation.

'I don't think that.' I sit on the bed. 'Really.'

We are silent for a while.

'I told you. You wouldn't listen.' She is perfectly calm now, quite matter-of-fact. 'There's something bad in this house. You know it, don't you, Hessie? You've felt it too. I know you have.'

'The danger is out there.' I point towards the window. 'We are as safe as we can be here. Being cooped up in this place is bound to set us all on edge.' I sound as if I have more conviction than I do. She has been right before. But only once, I remind myself, only once.

'You never believe me.' She begins to button her night-dress right up, so the collar covers her neck, and pulls on a pair of white gloves and, in the absence of her beekeeping hat, drapes a length of fine muslin over her head, then leaves the room without a word.

From the window I can see the men, Rafe with them, mending the fence, while Hope and Lark hobble awk-wardly over the yard carrying a heavy churn between them. Margie is hauling a bucket of water up from the well, the winch rasping with each turn. A faint smell of fresh-baked bread wafts up from the kitchen.

I watch Melis picking her way determinedly past them and across the paddock towards the skeps, looking like a crazed bride. Even from this distance, I can see how they look at her suspiciously as she passes, even Hope.

Hope

Days collapse into moments.

Minutes stretch into hours.

Hope keeps her eye on the time to prevent it from playing these tricks. She winds the clock in the blue room, ordering the minutes, forcing them to behave. They have been at the lodge for six days already.

She tightens the laces on the front of her dress and tells herself firmly that Melis is losing her mind, that when she looked Hope in the eye earlier and told her there was something bad in the house, she didn't know what she was saying. Hester had told her to take no notice, reminded her that Melis was convinced Orchard Cottage would burn down with Rafe in it and that hadn't happened.

It didn't happen, it didn't happen, she repeats silently, with each tick of the clock.

She can hear her two older sisters on the balcony, with their sewing, chatting playfully. 'Look at this. You can't even see where it was torn,' she hears Melis say. She couldn't sound saner. If anything, it is Hope who feels she is becoming detached from her common sense.

She picks up the basket of laundry on the landing. It creaks against her hip as she descends the stairs, rushing past the middle floors. The idea of those empty rooms, dark and looming and oppressive, sets off her imagination again.

She settles on the kitchen step at the washtub and sets to scrubbing at the laundry until her hands are raw. The lye stinks and burns her eyes.

'You're a hard worker, Hope,' comments the lieutenant, as he passes with Rafe. They settle on the other side of the yard in the shade of the barn. She can hear Rafe chatting happily, like a sparrow, so much better now he has the company of a man. The lieutenant is showing him how to make rabbit snares, endlessly patient as he demonstrates again and again how to tie a slipknot – 'This end over, that end under' – good-naturedly unpicking the twine when Rafe tangles it and becomes exasperated.

She finds herself gazing at the man, wet linen hanging forgotten from her fist. His hands are large and capable. He catches her staring. She looks away sharply, her skin bristling, heat flushing over her face and under her arms. But she has seen him looking at her, too, on more than one occasion. Desire makes itself known inside her, patting in her chest and prodding at her belly.

He couldn't be less like Worley, with his smooth, feminine hands, the carefully barbered beard. Thinking of Worley makes her insides tangle with shame. He is her only measure for desire but she knows she desires this rugged man more.

Lark steps past her. 'Is that you, Hope?' When she responds, Lark reaches out a hand. It wavers in space, finally meeting Hope's shoulder and she levers herself down to sit beside her.

They fall into easy conversation, Hope finding it a relief to have someone to talk to, with Melis so unpredictable and Hester treating her like a child. She finds herself confessing the details of what had happened between her and Marmaduke Worley.

'I truly believed we loved each other, fool that I was.'

'Not a fool.' There is not even a splinter of judgement in Lark's tone. 'It sounds to me as if he knew exactly what he was up to. I'm sure he was very convincing. What a vile creature to seek to harm someone as lovely as you.'

'Lovely? Not really.' Hope is embarrassed by the compliment.

'I mean it.'

Hope changes the subject. 'Don't you ever get lonely living here?'

Lark seems to ponder for a time. Then: 'I've never really thought about it. I suppose you don't miss what you don't know. But I like having you here.' She leans in slightly against Hope and they fall into an easy silence, punctuated by the rhythmic scrub of linen against washboard.

Hope can hear the lieutenant describing to Rafe the best place to set a snare.

'What do you think of him?' Hope asks quietly, so she can't be overheard.

'I don't know. He seems . . .' Lark presses her hands together, whispering, 'I don't think I trust him.'

'What do you mean?' Hope feels personally affronted. 'What makes you not trust him? He's so patient with Rafe.' How would Lark know anything about anyone, she asks herself, since she knows so little of the world? She is regretting her previous confession.

'Just a feeling.'

Hope would like to say that if we all went on feelings we wouldn't get very far. 'Well, *I* like him.' She can't prevent herself from sounding defensive.

'I can tell.' There is a tone in Lark's voice that makes Hope conclude she might be jealous of the attention the lieutenant has paid to her, that Lark might want him for herself. That would explain why she thinks badly of him. 'I'm not usually wrong about people.' She holds Hope's forearm. 'What if he's another Worley?'

'He's not. I know he's not.' Hope wonders how many people Lark has even met but doesn't want to make her feel challenged by asking. 'I wouldn't be taken for a fool twice.'

Lark doesn't reply, just makes a small sigh.

Hester comes out to call for the lieutenant. 'How is your arm after yesterday's treatment?'

'It's much better,' he calls back.

'One more dressing and it'll be as good as new.'

It will not be 'as good as new', thinks Hope. She has seen the wound and it is clear that he will never regain the full use of that arm. It ignites a raw sympathy in her and, if she is honest, it makes her like him more. If he has a flaw, it makes her past misdemeanour matter less.

'Hope, would you nip downstairs and get me . . .' Hester lists the ingredients for her compress.

It is blessedly cool in the cellar and the tang of old fruit and ripe cheese hangs in the air. A dim light spills from her candle into the gloom and a little more from the open door at the top of the steps. Her eyes take some time to adjust, so she waits, leaning back against the damp wall, for the chill to seep through her dress to her skin. Unlike Hester and Melis, who go about in little more than their linen shifts, Hope continues to dress properly. She doesn't approve. In only six days they have practically become savages, so Heaven only knows what they will look like in ten. Like that man who lives in the woods.

She picks up an apple from the trestle where they are

stacked. It is waxy and wrinkled beneath her fingers, like a grandmother's skin. She moves to the shelves, where the produce is stored, carefully parcelled in oilcloth or preserved in jars.

A sudden thud sounds, as the door at the top slams shut. She gasps loudly, dropping the candle, which sputters and dies. She is pressed into the dark, her imagination igniting. 'It's just the wind. It's just the wind,' she repeats to herself aloud. But in the back of her mind she knows that the weather is thick and hot without even the slightest gust of a breeze.

Arms outstretched, she inches her way back to where she thinks the steps lie, but she cannot tell where she is in space. Something brushes over her face, catching in her hair. She cries out and scrambles with her hands, meeting feathers, realizing it is only a brace of pigeons suspended from a beam.

As she steps away from the birds, something falls, scattering objects across the floor.

Did she knock against it?

She doesn't know.

Flailing in thin air, her bearings altogether lost now, she drops to her hands and knees, grateful for the solid floor beneath her, feeling her way across it. Fallen things at her fingertips are turned monstrous in her mind. She tells herself they are nothing more than onions and turnips but she picks one up and it is neither of those things. It is soft and chilled and slimy. Flinging it away, she crawls blindly until her hands meet the wall and feels her way along it, eventually coming to the stone slab of the bottom step. Shaking as she clambers to the top, she shoves the latch up but it will not budge.

She bangs desperately, shouting for help.

After what seems an age of panic, the bolt clicks and the door swings open. Light gushes in and the large shape of Margie is cast dark in the frame.

'Whatever's the matter? You look as if you've seen a ghost.' Hope cannot find her voice to reply. 'You need to clip the door back, see,' Margie is saying, as she slots a long hook into an eye on the wall. 'The hinges are skewed, so it's prone to slamming and the latch sticks.' She casts her gaze to Hope's empty hands. 'You've not brought anything up, daft girl.'

The ordinary scene in the kitchen doesn't match with her simmering alarm. The lieutenant and Melis are playing slapjack at the table with Rafe, who giggles triumphantly as he smacks his hand over the pile of cards, and Hester is preparing the charcoal burner to make the compress. Margie announces briskly that *she* will fetch the ingredients.

She returns only moments later. 'You might've told me you'd knocked over one of the trestles. I could have tripped on it and broke my neck.'

'But I didn't.' Hope's voice is a croak. 'I didn't touch the trestle.' She can't remember whether she might have brushed against it or not. Her mind is all a muddle.

Margie's hand claps to her chest. 'The house is making mischief again.' She seems thrilled, laughing, as if it is all a great caper. Hope wants to shake sense into her, force her to see it is not a laughing matter if a house has a mind of its own.

'Come and sit down,' insists Hester, moving up to make space for her on the bench.

'I'm sure there's a perfectly ordinary explanation,' says the lieutenant.

Melis, beside her, cups a hand over her ear and murmurs, 'There's not an ordinary explanation. I told you there's something bad in this house.' Hope's insides shrivel.

Hester, doing her best to hide her exasperation, says through pursed lips, 'Stop making things worse, Melis.'

The lieutenant holds Hope with a benevolent look. 'Don't be afraid. In the darkness everything seems strange. More than likely the door slamming caused it. And those trestles are on their last legs.'

Felton's rational explanation, his kindness, allows Hope to see how she had let her fears get the better of her. Hester takes her hand with a smile. 'He's right. Why don't you go out and help Lark with the goats? It'll distract you.'

Hope pulls herself together. If Hester can manage to keep a level head, when she and Rafe are the targets of the real threat, then Hope is determined not to let her imagination addle her and make things worse for them.

As she leaves the room, she glances back to see if the lieutenant is watching her.

He is.

A delicate bubble of elation inflates in her breast.

In the evening, as Hope takes the clean laundry up the final flight of stairs to the top landing, she can hear a noise coming from the bedchamber. Someone – something – is moving about, the rustle of paper, the creak of a floorboard. Sweat blooms cool on her brow. In her head she accounts for everyone in the house. Her heart gutters. They were all in the kitchen save for the lieutenant, who had gone out to do his evening round of the perimeter fence.

She creeps up, inching closer, pushing the door silently open a crack, peering in.

'What are you doing?' She flings the door wide. The lieutenant turns, startled, with a fistful of papers from Hester's writing box. 'Those are my sister's private things.' Alarm is ringing through her. 'Did she send you to fetch something?'

Deep in her gut Hope knows that she is seeking a benign explanation because she is sweet on him. Her spirits sink, as she absorbs the scene. 'Are you stealing? She has nothing of value, you know.'

'It's not what you think.' He steps towards her. He is close, too close, and his body is drawn tight, his eyes flashing with a dark look she can't read.

Hope is wary but a little flicker of arousal runs up her spine. Perhaps, she allows herself to think, that look was desire.

He leans round her, snapping the door shut. 'Can I trust you?' A little crease of sincerity cuts through his forehead and she wants to, she really does. 'What I am about to tell you is of the utmost secrecy, Hope. It concerns the safety of your eldest sister. You can't tell a soul. You must promise me that.'

'I can't promise you anything.' She is trying her best to sound firm. 'But I'd like an explanation.'

'Dr Cotton instructed me to find some letters your sister has in her possession. He didn't tell me what they contain, only that they could put her in grave danger. I am to destroy them. It will make her safer. You want that, don't you?'

Hope picks up the upturned writing box. Hester had said herself the letters were dangerous. 'Why, if these letters are such a risk, can you not tell her to destroy them herself? Surely –'

He doesn't let her finish. 'The doctor was adamant that if she knew, she would prevent me, in spite of the danger.' He looks so forlorn and there is a plea in his tone that seems authentic.

'I don't know.'

'I understand why you would doubt me but you must believe I have your best interests at heart – all of you.' He smiles and she can't help but smile back. '*Your* interests particularly.'

'*Mine?* I'm not the one in danger.'

'Don't you feel it, too, what I'm feeling?' He takes her hand then and she can't bear the idea of him letting it go, that bubble of desire swelling. She *can* feel it – she can – but daren't give in to her desire so easily, not this time.

She looks at him again. He is the image of sincerity. 'She has letters. I've seen them.' Hope is trying to contain her elation. Her hand is alive in his grip. 'I don't know what's in them.'

'Where does she keep them?'

Hester's firm instruction not to tell a soul is ringing round her head. He lifts her hand to lightly kiss it. 'They're not in here.'

'Then where?'

She shakes her head.

'I don't mean any harm. I just want to protect you all the best I can.'

There is nothing about him that seems insincere and, after all, Ambrose Cotton sent him to protect them – Ambrose who is as good as a father to her and her sisters. 'Follow me,' she says, leading him out of the room.

He casts a look over the banisters and follows her into the blue room, where the balcony doors are open and the indigo dusk is spread out across the sky. She starts to drag aside the fire's back-plate.

'Let me,' he says. It moves easily under his strength. 'So, this is why they were covered in smut when I arrived.' It is as if he is talking to himself.

She ducks inside. The tight space is horribly close, and she can't imagine how it might feel to be shut inside. She feels around the walls, eventually finding the package of papers tucked into a niche. Crawling out she looks at them in the light. They are crisp with age and have several large important-looking seals attached to them.

She questions once more whether Hester shouldn't be the one to decide their fate. He must notice her hesitation, as he says, 'God only knows what they must contain to put the holder in such grave peril.'

She knows how wilful Hester can be and can imagine her insisting on keeping them, putting herself in greater peril. So, she hands them over.

After a cursory look, he stashes them under his clothes. 'I'll burn them later. I don't want to rouse any curiosity by lighting a fire now.'

He pushes the iron plate back into place, then, placing his good hand on her shoulder, looks her directly in the eyes. The bubble swells further.

'You've done a good thing, Hope.' He leans closer – she cannot move – and closer still, tucking his nose almost into her neck, without quite touching, and says, under his breath, 'This is our secret.'

He pulls back then, looking at her clothes, which are smeared with soot. 'You'd better change. You do that, while I go down. We mustn't let them think we've been together alone. I don't want anyone thinking your virtue has been compromised.' He puffs out a gust of air that is almost, but not quite, a laugh.

Was he laughing because he can see that her virtue is already as stained as her dress? The thought makes her heart dip but, she consoles herself, wrapping her arms about her torso. *A secret. We have a secret.*

Felton

Felton stays awake until the house is silent, reading the letters. How easy it had been to convince the girl, her big dark-brown eyes believing almost without question. The letters are the work of an uncommonly gifted forger. Felton knows George's hand as well as he knows his own and this is a flawless imitation. They are apparently between George and the Spanish ambassador, dated back some years. Much of the script is faded and hard to make out but what is clear is that they seem to imply George has sold state secrets to an enemy of England. There is no doubt it would be seen as treason and, even at this distance in time, could be proof enough for his enemies to bring about his fall.

He scrutinizes the handwriting once more, questioning whether they are truly forgeries. As doubt arises, he quashes it. He is not here to judge George's actions.

It is small wonder that George wants them destroyed, and if Felton had held any prior vestige of misgiving about whether these feeble-seeming women truly were the menace George believes them to be, it is now thoroughly dispelled. He had seen for himself the threat Hester had made in her letter to him. He was right – danger can come in unexpected guises. The sisters – charmingly dishevelled, their butter-wouldn't-melt expressions, their kindnesses and pity – are lethal as hemlock.

He lights a pile of kindling in the small hearth of his room and watches the papers burn with a thrilling sense of achievement at the ease with which he has completed this first task. Now he must prepare carefully for the next.

His plan is forming in the shadowy architecture of his mind. The idea came to him earlier that evening when he was doing a round of the premises. He had passed the henhouse and noticed its missing balcony. Looking back and up at the balcony on the house, he conjured in his mind's eye the image of the two falling shapes, could hear the sound of flesh and bone meeting stone, could see the two broken bodies on the steps. He sees them again now, their white dresses stark against the slate, with perhaps an ooze of blood emanating from a cracked head and an arm bent back at an inhuman angle. It will require some careful choreography.

Once the fire has burned away the last of the incriminating words, he sweeps up the ashes, tipping them out of the window to be scattered by the night air, and settles down in his bed content in the knowledge that George is a little safer. He drifts off, allowing himself the indulgence of imagining his and George's old affinity being rekindled.

The following morning he observes the usual routines of the house, which proceed with clockwork regularity each day. Hester collects the eggs, Melis tends the hives, Lark milks the goats, Margie bakes bread for the day, the old man waters his vegetable garden with the waste water from the women's ablutions, and Hope puts the washing to soak. He supposes her soiled dress is in there somewhere.

He takes the boy out to help him continue mending the

fence. Hope, seated over the washtub, tries to meet his eye as he walks by but he won't be drawn. It wouldn't do for someone to notice anything pass between them. He can sense her gaze boring into his back – those besotted eyes.

The boy chats to him, asking questions as he holds the bag of nails, handing them to him one by one. 'How do you skin a rabbit?'; 'How painful was it when the shot hit your arm?'; 'What is it like being drunk?' As he answers one question, another comes in its wake.

It is no wonder the boy craves to understand the world when he has been cloistered with his mother and aunts. If only he knew the splendid life that awaits him as the recognized son of the most powerful man in the land. The world will be his for the taking.

The child likes him. It will make things much easier when the blow comes.

He hammers in the last loose panel and, taking some off-cuts of timber, nails together a pair of wooden swords. 'Want to learn how to fence, little fellow?'

Rafe's eyes glimmer as he takes the weapon.

'Where are your mother and aunts? I'm sure they'd like to watch you.'

'Up there.' The child points to the balcony. Just as Felton had suspected. 'Except not Aunt Hope. She does the laundry all morning.'

'How can you be so sure they are there? I can't see them from here.'

'They sit there every day, with the sewing and darning, until the sun comes around.' He calls up, 'The lieutenant is teaching me to fence. Come and watch,' and the two women appear high above, at the balustrade.

'Every morning?' Felton asks nonchalantly. 'Why?'

'Mother says it is too hot to do anything but sit in the shade and sew.'

He shows Rafe how to hold the makeshift sword, the rudiments of how to place one's body to avoid injury and how to make an opponent misread one's intentions. 'You have to be crafty, keep one step ahead, anticipate the way your rival will go.'

The child learns fast and is soon ducking swiftly as he swipes the sword low over his head, jabbing and lunging, then jumping away, backing Felton up to the fence, holding the wooden point to his stomach. Felton laughs. 'You'll make a fine swordsman one day.'

Rafe puffs up with pride. 'What does it feel like to kill a person?'

He is taken aback by the question, as if the child has seen through him, but it is only his curiosity. He certainly has a taste for darker things. 'It is mostly relief, when that person is trying to kill you.' He can't help but be reminded of the surge of excitement and sense of power, too, thinking of Bloor's terror, of Cotton's warm blood spilling over his hand.

'Has anyone died that you knew well?'

'Oh, yes. Many of my comrades. In battle.'

'When you kill someone, is it like butchering an animal?'

Felton, wishing the boy would stop talking, glances up at the women and for an instant, instead of Melis, who has the same pale colouring, a vague resemblance, he sees Bridget watching him. His heart is wrenched out of place. 'No, it's not the same.' He pushes the boy's wooden sword aside brusquely and begins to gather the tools that are still scattered about. He doesn't want to think of Bridget now, to look into the abyss of grief that he has held at bay for so long.

'But how is it different?'

He feels exposed, as if pure, perfect Bridget is watching him from beyond the grave and she can see his soul, so clogged with sin it is unrecognizable as that of her beloved brother. She has seen Dr Cotton bleeding to death and Bloor struggling and writhing for breath, and can see, too, the terrible future acts he is set on committing. He forces the thought away – can't allow a crisis of conscience when everything is falling so beautifully into place.

He marches into the house, without answering the boy, who trots behind him to the door of his room, asking if he can come in. Felton tells him to go to his mother. Disappointment registers on the child's face.

He shuts himself in, swigging his tincture, then unlocking his box of papers and pulling out his neglected journal into which he has entered only the barest notes of late. He can still sense his sister hovering. He opens a virgin page and dips his pen. The ink is down to its dregs, dense and viscous, daubing unwanted marks and distorting the letters as he writes like a man possessed. On and on, pages and pages, unburdening himself, accounting for every misdeed ever committed, each detail, all his future crimes explained.

When he has finished, he carefully returns everything to its place, locking the box and placing the key high on the top of the door surround. He feels purged, better, more robust, committed once more to the fulfilment of his mission. It is the living he must think of now and ensuring George's safety.

*

After they have eaten and all retired to their separate quarters, the house is as quiet as the grave. Felton steals out to the balcony. He stands for a moment, looking out to where the waxing moon has cast its cool glow over the blanket of trees. The air is dead still and hardly less close than it is in daylight hours. Every day they expect the weather to break but the heat continues to thicken, sucking the life out of the forest and the godforsaken house buried at its core.

A door bangs outside. He tucks himself into the curtain of vines, watching as Lark comes out of the barn, a ghostly shape, and disappears out of sight, returning a few moments later. Remembering she sometimes sleeps out with the livestock, he assumes she must have gone to relieve herself. He waits awhile, until he can be sure everyone is sound asleep, then sets to work.

He has helped build enough wooden structures, war machines, scaffolds and the like, to know what he must do. Working as quietly as possible, he removes all the supports of the balustrade. The wood is so rotten in places it's a wonder the whole structure hasn't crashed to the ground long ago. That is what people will say when it does collapse.

He props up the struts carefully, contriving that they appear untouched, disguising his handiwork by draping fronds of vine over the handrail. Then, returning inside, he leans through the window, balancing on the sill to loosen the nails from the buttresses that support the body of the balcony. Once done, he surveys his invisible work and, satisfied, returns to bed.

Hester

Rafe is up early and perched on the back step, carefully inspecting the carcass of a blackbird. I ask him where he found it.

'On the kitchen floor.' He is opening its wings and fanning the feathers, scrutinizing them.

'The cat must have brought it in.'

Hope is talking to the lieutenant inside. I have noticed how she looks at him and warned her that I believe he has a sweetheart somewhere. Surely it is the case, given the manner in which he snatched back his book before I had a chance to read the note written in it. I worry that she is too open-hearted for her own good, and pray she has become less vulnerable to the attentions of men after the Worley incident.

Rafe is turning the dead bird over in his hand, peering under its feathers, fascinated.

'What are you doing?' I ask.

'Don't know.' He shrugs, taking a small folding penknife from his pocket and beginning to cut into the joint of the wing. 'I want to know how it flies.' He twists it then, as if jointing a chicken, exposing a ball of white gristle. 'I see.' He bites down on his lip in absolute concentration as he pulls away the flesh, exposing strings of sinew. 'These are what make it flap, I think.'

'You take after your grandfather.' I am remembering my father and his fascination with the natural world. He always used to say it was what had led him to become a physician. There is still a shelf of his books at Orchard Cottage, with diagrams displaying the skeletal and muscular systems of different mammals. I have a pang of longing to go back and show them to Rafe. 'It's a shame he never knew you. He'd have loved to see you so interested in such things.'

Dipping my handkerchief into the water-butt, I squeeze it out and press it to the back of my neck, relishing the moment of cool it brings, and watch Rafe for a while more, rapt in the task of butchering the bird. 'Be careful with that penknife. Where did you get it anyway?'

'This?' He holds it up. 'The lieutenant gave it to me.'

'Gave it?'

'Yes. He said it wasn't much use to him any more.' He turns his gaze on me, looking up through lashes as long as a girl's.

'I don't think it's a good idea for you to carry something so sharp.'

'He gave it to me because it's blunt now.' He demonstrates this by running the tip of his thumb over the blade. I wince inwardly, imagining it cutting through his skin when it doesn't leave so much as a mark. 'See? He's going to teach me how to skin a rabbit.' I can see his eagerness to learn such things – male things.

It is true, I baby him. It's easy to forget my little boy is growing up. I mustn't hold him back. He will soon be nine and I know of boys sent into apprenticeships at not much older than that. One day I will have to let him go. The realization twists a screw of sadness into me.

'As long as you keep it folded when you're not using it and take great care.'

I call Felton, taking him to one side so Rafe is out of earshot. 'It's very kind of you to have given Rafe your old penknife but I'd rather he didn't have sharp objects. He might hurt himself.' I watch my son lining up the various parts of the dead blackbird on the step.

'I didn't give him a penknife.'

'Oh.' I look at him in confusion. 'But he said . . .' My words are left hanging as Melis comes tearing into view from the direction of the hives. Something is wrong. She half climbs, half vaults the paddock gate and trips, falling face first onto the hard ground, but scrambles back up, barely breaking her stride.

As she nears, I can see the wild look in her eyes but she doesn't even register my presence as she rushes past. She is covered with scratches and her nose is bleeding, blood soaking into the white linen of her dress in great bright blots, like poppies.

I try to take hold of her but she flails, running straight through the kitchen. She crosses the hall, stopping momentarily to snap up the latch of the front door, throwing it wide and descending the steps two at a time.

'This is the place.' She has stopped dead at the bottom, is crouching and slapping the stone step. 'This is the place. They told me. They showed me.'

The others have followed us out and are gaping at her. 'Don't worry,' I tell them. 'I'll see to this.' They don't move but stand agog, all but Hope open-mouthed as Melis unfurls her fist, releasing several bees from her palm.

Margie gasps in shock. 'What's she doing?'

I take hold of Melis's shoulders, speaking gently, attempting to reassure her, but she looks right through me and struggles away once more, running first towards the main gate but seeming to change her mind and returning to the front steps where we are all still standing, not knowing what to do.

She grips her hands tightly about her head, crying, 'Stop it,' over and over again before ripping open the buttons of her nightdress, to expose her torso, where her silvery skin is stippled with great angry stings. She seems to calm then, sinking onto the bottom step, saying again, 'This is the place.'

I sit beside her and can feel the others creeping closer, can feel their fascination, their repulsion. 'What is it, sweetheart? What is this place?'

Melis looks up at me. I remember that look, dread stamped through her eyes, pupils like burn holes. 'This is the place that will bring my death.'

I try to take her in my arms but she pushes me off. I am aware of Hope and Margie trying to draw Rafe away, back into the kitchen. 'We should leave them alone,' Hope is saying, but Rafe refuses, until the lieutenant squats down and speaks very quietly to him, whereupon he obediently follows the women into the house.

The lieutenant is still hovering. I ask him to leave us alone but he says, 'If I might offer a small suggestion.' His head is tilted kindly and concern is etched plainly over his features. At my wit's end now, I tell him to continue. 'It may be a good idea,' he says, 'if we keep this door bolted and use only the back entrance. It will mean your sister never need use these steps. They seem to be the cause of her distress. It is easily done and will save her from worry.'

'Thank you.' I am deeply grateful for such a sensible proposal. He slips tactfully away, and I hear him slide the bolts across and turn the key, securing the doors from the inside.

Hope

They sit round the kitchen table in a malignant silence, shaken by the scene on the steps, all but Rafe, who is on the floor playing knuckles, seemingly unperturbed. After some time, Hester appears, leading Melis by the hand. Without a word they pass through the kitchen and up the stairs.

Margie eventually resumes the kneading she abandoned earlier and Gifford returns to his vegetable garden. They are not the sort to ask questions. For that Hope is thankful.

'Come.' Lark breaks through her thoughts, tugging her outside to sit on the fence. 'Listen to the forest birds,' she says. 'It will soothe you.' To Hope it is a chaos of noise but Lark is able to tease out threads of barely audible sound, identifying each singer.

She tells Hope to close her eyes, that she will hear better. 'When you dull one sense the others spring to life.'

It is true. After a while, Hope finds she can distinguish individual distant strands of song. She begins to understand that so much lies beyond the ordinary scope of her senses – so much untapped wonder.

'Hear that?' Lark is pointing to the three poplars by the gates, from which Hope can hear a distinctive plangent melody, a few phrases, then silence, as if the bird has for-gotten the words of its own song. Lark whistles back, mimicking it almost exactly. It responds as if in conversa-tion with her. 'Stormcock,' she says. 'Its flesh is said to be a cure for madness.'

The lieutenant interrupts them, asking if he might have a private word with Hope. Something like disapproval passes over Lark's expression as Hope assents. He guides her to the well that is set in a quiet place away from the house. She looks in. The water far below is a winking eye. They sit side by side on the edge. Aware of the deep void behind her, she feels safe with the gentle pressure of his palm at the small of her back.

It is some time before he speaks. 'Have you seen your sister behave in such a way before?' He seems agitated, tapping his foot, jigging his leg.

She explains about Melis's visions, how distressing they can be for her. 'She believes she can see the future.'

He says nothing for a while, plucks a stalk from a nearby sage bush, pulling off its leaves and shredding them. It gives off a pungent scent, like fresh-dug earth after rain. 'Can she?' He looks at her, his brow puckered with concern. He seems so very worried about Melis, his compassion making Hope like him all the more.

'She never has.' A little of the tension seems to fall from him. 'But . . .'

She can feel the heat of his body close to hers, almost touching. 'Sometimes I think . . .' She pauses.

'Sometimes you think what?' His voice is so gentle.

'I know it sounds senseless, but I do wonder if she has a gift. She says there is something bad in this house.' Hope dares snatch a look at his eye, then casts her gaze back to

169

her hands. 'I sometimes think I believe her when she says there's something evil here.'

Instead of ridiculing her, he says softly, 'Your sister is sick. You mustn't let her stories run away with you. Don't worry about anything. We shall take care of Melis.' He smooths his hand up and down Hope's back. 'Make sure no harm befalls her.'

'I'm so thankful you are here to look after us,' Hope says, leaning in to his touch, daring to imagine what it might be like to kiss him.

But then she remembers Hester's mention of his sweetheart.

'I'd better go in. I may be needed.' She stands abruptly, shrugging him off.

'Wait!' She turns. 'You haven't told your sister about the letters, have you?'

'No . . . I gave my word.' It upsets her to think he doesn't trust her. She has nursed their secret for two days.

'Good girl,' he says, with a smile.

Our secret, she thinks.

Hester

In the bedroom I undress Melis and wash away the blood and dirt. I untangle her hair carefully, anointing the bee stings and scratches with a salve. She is as biddable as a child, doing exactly what I ask. Once in her clean shift she curls up on the bed and closes her eyes.

I sit with her, shaken by the episode. I haven't seen her so bad in a long time and am afraid this might be the precursor to worse.

To distract myself I write to Ambrose. Surely someone will make the day's trip to Ludlow and be able to send my letter before long. The Giffords must have to go there to sell their produce. I think of the eggs amassing in the cellar and the great wheels of cheese maturing beside them.

I ask after Bette's health, and inform Ambrose of the lieutenant's safe arrival, what a great reassurance he has proved to be. I am impatient to know if he is on his way here, as he promised, whether he has managed to make my case with George. As I write it, I am struck once more by the unlikelihood of George ever seeing reason, making me thankful for the letters. Signing my name, I realize what folly it would be to send such a missive. I screw it into a ball, noticing, with a stab of regret, that the wax figure Rafe gave me has melted in the sun on the windowsill, its form completely lost.

Melis stirs, sitting up, seeming almost herself again.

'Feeling better?' I ask.

She offers a bright smile. 'What do you mean?' It is as if she has completely forgotten what happened a mere half-hour ago, as if the incident never was. 'Listen,' she says. 'Isn't that Rafe?'

'So it is.' I can hear him calling me from down in the yard.

'Mother, Aunt Melis, come and see what I can do.'

'I expect he wants us to watch him fencing again,' she says. 'He was so pleased with himself yesterday.' She rises from the bed. I am still astounded that nothing of the earlier distress remains in her disposition. 'He's happier since the lieutenant arrived, don't you think?'

'I've noticed that too.' I am glad I haven't imagined it.

She shoves her feet into a pair of my slippers and, not caring that they are too big, scuffs across the landing towards the blue room.

I follow her.

Rafe's voice rises up to us through the open balcony doors. 'Come and watch me.'

Hope

Hope can hear the lieutenant outside ask Rafe if he'd like a fencing lesson before it becomes too hot. 'You won't improve if you don't practise.'

She makes for the stairs, thinking she will be able to watch them from the balcony. Nearing the top, she hears her sisters talking as they cross the landing, Melis seeming quite recovered.

Hope follows them into the blue room.

Rafe is calling from below.

Melis steps onto the balcony, leaning out over the balustrade to wave at her nephew.

Hester is behind her when an ominous crack slices through the air.

Melis emits a terrible hollow shriek.

Hope rushes towards the balcony door, panic jittering through her, to see Melis hanging tight to the balustrade, which has broken away, swinging down, attached only from a corner.

She screams too now, her voice shrill.

Hester is clinging to the vine that crawls up the wall as the balcony jolts, tilting like a ship in a storm. Grabbing the windowsill, Hope tries to reach Melis, who is suspended in mid-air, feet thrashing.

'Hold on.' Hope inches forward, afraid to lose her

own grip, but it is no good. Another crack snaps through the air.

'Help her, for God's sake!' cries Hester, who is flailing, trying to gain a foothold on the planks, which are listing beneath her, on the brink of collapse.

'I can't reach!' There is nothing Hope can do but watch helplessly as the balustrade breaks away, taking Melis with it.

She falls silently, her dress opening like a bell.

A *whump* sounds as she hits the ground.

'Keep hold!' Hope shouts, turning to Hester now, but the vine is detaching from the wall as she loses her grip, first one hand, her other arm at full length, tips of fingers slipping.

Rigid with fear, Hope reaches out into space, managing, miraculously, to grab Hester's collar, clasping it tight in her fist.

But the seam gives, Hester falling a little further as each stitch snaps, her scream becoming a long howl.

With a sudden lurch, the ripping stops where a few stitches have been over-sewn. Hope remembers mending that seam.

Hester hangs on those few threads.

And Hope, finding some vestige of superhuman strength, hauls her back into the room, just as the wooden struts beneath her feet explode onto the stone steps below.

They collapse inside, onto the floor, clinging to each other, racked with shock, the breath knocked out of them.

'Melis!' cries Hester, coming to her senses, scrambling to her feet, pulling Hope up with her. They fly down the stairs. At the door, Hester pushes and heaves at the vast slab of oak, forgetting it is locked. Hope pulls her aside, sliding the bolts, turning the key, hauling it open just as the remains of the balcony crash down, plank by plank.

Then silence.

Melis lies on the steps, half covered with debris, her body twisted out of shape. Felton runs to crouch over her. A slipper is lying a yard away in the dust. It is one of Hester's.

With a lurch of dread, Hope realizes her sister has fallen on exactly the step that caused her so much distress barely an hour ago. The place she said would bring her death. The knowledge paralyses her, her limbs suddenly heavy, the skin on her neck and arms chilling, a void opening inside, the only sound the puppy making a terrible high-pitched barking, as it careers back and forth manically.

Felton

The stupid girl is frozen on the steps watching blankly as Felton and Hester try to move the injured woman into a more comfortable position. She shrieks with pain. It is apparent that several of her bones are broken at the very least.

He rages at himself inwardly for the failure of his plan.

'Opium tincture!' says Hester, turning to him. 'You have some, haven't you? Is it in your room? Hope, fetch the lieutenant's tincture. Where is it exactly?'

'Let me –' Felton makes to stand. He doesn't want the girl in his room.

'She can go.' Hester has his wrist. Her grip is surprisingly strong. 'I need you here.'

'It's a small brown phial, on the shelf.'

Hope scurries into the house.

Hester is impressively calm, quietly talking to Melis, who seems to be slipping into and out of consciousness. It is manifestly clear to Felton that she will not survive. She must have internal injuries. It's a wonder she is alive at all. It's more a wonder that the other woman is unscathed.

Rafe is sitting on the steps, his face in his hands, shoulders quaking. Felton calls him over to help lift some of the broken timbers that have fallen onto Melis's body. The boy comes obediently. Felton is surprised to note that the child is dry-eyed. Shock makes people behave strangely. He's seen enough stricken soldiers to know that – men laughing hysterically to see their legs blown off or mewling like infants at the unexpected crack of gun salute. Rafe stoops to take one end of a plank, waiting, mouth tight, for Felton to count to three before they heave it away.

Margie bowls round the side of the house, her father hobbling behind. 'Oh, my good Lord!' She stops in her tracks, both hands over her face, eyes wide and round and horrified. 'This is exactly where –' She doesn't need to say it, they are all thinking it. Felton has been trying not to think about it. Melis had predicted this. God only knows what other revelations she is liable to envisage and whisper to her sister before she dies.

His thoughts want to spiral out of control, but he reins them in. He must keep a clear head if he is to complete this mission. Still doubt niggles at him. How could she have known?

He realizes Margie is talking to him, telling him she will make a bed in the hall for Melis, asking if there is anything else they can do. He enlists Gifford's help with the careful shifting of the rest of the timbers to clear a path up the steps.

'Riddled with worm, this wood, all of it,' Felton remarks. 'It's a wonder the structure held together at all.'

'If it weren't for the vine . . .' Gifford stops a moment, looking up to where the creeper has half fallen away from the front of the building and hangs, creating a suspended arch of green.

'She's bleeding from her ear!' Rafe is staring at his aunt, seeming fascinated by the trickle of bright red. Hester rips off her sleeve to staunch the flow.

Glancing to the injured woman, her face knotted with

177

pain, Felton is struck by some disturbing trick of the mind in which his sister is lying distraught on the steps. He shakes his head to free himself of the vision but his mind is erupting with painful memories of the last occasion he saw Bridget alive.

It was the end of that idyllic summer at Playford. George had departed for court on the previous day and Felton was leaving to join an army in the Adriatic. He had found Bridget alone in the garden, weeping desperately. Taking her in his arms, he felt the heave of her tears. She blew her nose noisily on his big handkerchief and he noticed a painful-looking, bruised swelling on her wrist.

'What's that?' He'd pointed to the mark.

She snatched her arm back. 'It's nothing. I was taking a jar from the high shelf and it fell on me.'

'But what's the matter? What's the cause of all these tears?'

'Nothing. I can't . . .' She met him with a look of distraction. Her eyes were red and swollen with dark smudges beneath.

'The knock on your wrist may be nothing but this is clearly not "nothing". You can tell me. We have no secrets.' That wasn't quite true: he had never found a way to confess to her about the dead boy in France. She would have been appalled to learn that.

She had expelled a jagged sigh and, after some persuasion, opened up. 'I can't bear the idea of you going into such danger. So much death.' She sounded like an actor reciting lines, as if to engage with her sadness might set her off again. 'I'm so afraid for you.' She had his arm tightly gripped in her fist, her knuckles ridged and white. 'I wish you didn't have to go.'

He was unsure how to respond to her distress, had never seen her so unravelled.

'You'll have to kill people.' Her expression was horrified.

'Not *people* – the enemy. It's what I've trained all these years to do.'

'What if . . . what if . . .'

He had known what she was unable to say. She was inconsolable, twisting her necklace until the fine chain broke. 'I'll be back before you know it.'

He wonders, thinking about that last encounter with Bridget, if she hadn't had some instinct, some sense of foreboding, that they would never see each other again, for that had been the case. The irony assails him now that it was she who had died, not him.

'Lieutenant.' A tugging on his sleeve brings him back from the past. 'Is this the right tincture?' Hope is waving the phial in front of his face.

Hester takes it from her and drips it into Melis's mouth. Felton feels its desperate draw, resisting the urge to snatch it from her and drain it himself. They wait in silence for it to take effect, while Felton agitates over how he will be able to instigate a second accident without rousing suspicion.

Hester will not leave her sister's side and the others hover silently nearby, like wraiths. As well as the opium tincture, Melis has been given some kind of strong sleeping draught, procured by Hester, so she lies like a corpse on the big table in the hall, which has been turned into a makeshift bed. A little too much of that draught would surely put her out of her misery. The bottle sits nearby but Felton can't get a moment alone with the injured woman to finish her off. It occurs to him that it would be the humane thing to do but he is thinking primarily of his own convenience.

They all hover, with nothing to do but wait.

Rafe appears to have cast off his initial hysteria and, restlessly, throws a ball for the puppy. Felton is pleased to note this steel in the child, though he might not be so quick to recover when his mother meets her end.

The dog's claws clash and skid loudly against the flagstones, returning the ball, yapping excitedly for it to be thrown again. Hester, exhausted with grief, suggests Felton find some means of occupying the boy.

'Can we go and set rabbit traps?' Rafe's timing is impeccable. His mother's defences are down. He knows exactly how to get what he wants – just like his father.

'This isn't the time, Rafe.' Felton doesn't want to leave his watch, not now. What if she comes round? If she was able to see her own fate she may also be able, by some devilish skill, to expose him.

'I don't know.' Hester dithers. 'It may be a good distraction.' Hope makes a small disapproving cough. Felton has noticed before how the youngest sister is critical of the way the eldest yields to her son's wishes. He makes a mental note of it as something he may be able to exploit. 'As long as you are armed, Lieutenant, I can't see it doing any harm. The diversion will do him good.'

Both Hester and Rafe are looking at him expectantly.

'Or perhaps I could teach you to play dice?' The child's face sinks.

'Take him out, Lieutenant.' Hester smiles wanly. 'I'd appreciate it.'

He is left with no choice.

*

180

Rafe, judging by the spring in his step, is glad to escape the oppressive atmosphere of the house and the grim wait for his aunt's death. They meander a little way off the main track onto a narrow path banked by nettles that reach across in places. Felton attempts to break off a slim stick of willow to beat them back but it is green and stubbornly resists his twisting and bending. 'Shame we don't have a penknife,' he says casually.

'I have one.' Rafe produces a small folding blade from his pocket, which cuts easily through the young wood.

'That's a useful tool. Where did you get it?'

'Mother gave it to me,' he replies, without missing a beat.

So, the boy is a liar as well as a thief. He cuts off another stem, hands it to the child, and they walk, thwacking back the nettles on either side. Rafe is stung and they find a dock leaf to rub on the rash.

'If you grab a nettle's leaves firmly, they won't sting you,' Felton explains, surprised the boy doesn't know this already. 'Like pinching out a candle.' He demonstrates by gripping a leaf hard, then opening his hand to show the boy he is not hurt. Rafe, without hesitation, grabs a fistful, laughing, seeming delighted with this new piece of knowledge.

'What's that on your hand?' Rafe points to the ugly mark on Felton's palm.

'Just an old scar.' He doesn't want to be reminded of the past, his blood pact with George, but inevitably he is.

It occurs to him that the grabbing of nettles makes a good metaphor for life. Perhaps he has not taken hold of life firmly enough. He once had aspirations. He had allowed his spirit to be crushed by that one event, the fulcrum on which his fate swung.

He thinks of George's climb to greatness. Had Felton not killed that boy and allowed his guilt to divest him of spirit, who knows what he might have become, what doors might have opened. He is nobody now, just a hunk of muscle with a useless arm, hired as an assassin, a failure to boot. To think he'd envisaged himself in charge of an army. He still holds stubbornly to this hope. That is why he is here, he reminds himself.

As they walk on, something catches Felton's eye. His hackles rise. He is as sure as he can be that it was a shadow in the shape of a man flitting between the trees, some fifty yards away. He puts his hand in front of the boy, indicating for him to stop, and presses his index finger over his lips, his hand going to the pistol in his belt. All he can hear is the cry of a buzzard. It has taken to the sky and is circling above.

'What is it?' whispers the boy.

There is no sign of movement now, and he wonders if he imagined the shadowy figure. 'Nothing. Must have been a deer.' He makes himself sound calm but his nerves are still clashing.

They reach a clearing where he can see several rabbit holes among the roots of an oak and points them out, crouching to show the boy how to recognize a rabbit run, where the grass has been flattened making a hollow passage through the vegetation. He demonstrates how to suspend the loop of twine across the hollow. They set several snares, the boy following his instructions, taking the task with absolute seriousness.

'So, the rabbit runs in, and the slipknot tightens round its neck?' Rafe has his hand pressed to his throat.

'That's right.' Felton stoops to place one last trap.

He appears thoughtful. 'Like a hanging.'

'I suppose so.'

'Have you ever seen a hanging, Lieutenant?'

Felton can't prevent himself from snapping that of course he's been to a hanging. 'Hasn't everyone?' He has been reminded of the man who was hanged in his place for the death of that boy in France and guilt grabs his innards, as if it was yesterday.

'I haven't.'

'You're still too young.' He wishes the child would stop his comments and questions. 'We'll come back tomorrow morning and see if we've caught anything.'

'Tomorrow?' Rafe's disappointment is clear, his shoulders drooping. Felton remembers being a boy and how a single hour seemed an eternity, let alone a whole day and night.

'It's the way with traps. Takes time. We can come out early, before anyone else is up.' He tries to make it seem exciting.

An idea is forming. His mind is alive, whirring, as he pieces his plan together.

'I wonder if your mother would like to come with us. Take her mind off things.' He realizes that the chance of getting Hester to leave the house is very small, while she is in the throes of grief for her dying sister. His mind plots. Hester can't refuse her son anything – it is her Achilles' heel. It must be the boy who asks her to come into the forest. How will he distract the child once he has lured her out? He will think of something.

Hester

The hall is as quiet as a morgue, Melis's breath coming in laboured rasps through the stale air. She is pallid, the colour of despair. But the fine structure of her face is intact, her beauty persisting where her body is a map of bruises. The sleeping draught has put her into an uneasy slumber, her eyelids twitching, scribbled with veins, as if a child has taken a pencil to them.

I sit beside her in limbo, waiting and praying, my heart squeezed out, like an old dishcloth. As a physician's daughter, my immediate thought was to send for a surgeon but I knew the moment I saw her on the steps – no, before: I knew the moment she fell – that there was no hope. She had seen this. A day's ride to Ludlow and back would be pointless. Now all I can pray for Melis is swift oblivion. I try to picture her soul, imagining it as a filament of vapour, barely visible, reaching upward from her breast.

It chills me to consider how close I came to facing my own end. Hope saved my life. She is sitting nearby in a state of quiet agitation, shredding the edge of her cuff, scattering white lint over her dark dress. I can't hold Hope together too, not now.

Rafe and the lieutenant return. I don't want my son to have to witness the heavy approach of death, so I ask Hope to take him upstairs. The lieutenant refuses to sit, standing beside the door like a sentry.

Time wavers. Margie tries to press food on me and some kind of pungent infusion of herbs. 'For shock,' she says. I can't eat but sip the drink, which is as bitter as a bad almond.

Melis's lips take on a blue tinge, her lids are still and I fear she has died while I was distracted with the bitter drink. I lean in to listen for a sign of breath when her eyes pop open, she grabs my arm and is somehow levering herself to sit up, as if risen from the dead.

Her voice is straight and clear, eyes chips of glass, sliding from side to side. 'I can see George.' Her mouth crumples in disgust, as if she can't stomach the taste of his name.

'You're imagining things, my love.' All I want is for her to be in peace, not racked any more by hallucinations.

'I see his death. An assassin's blade, his blood spilling. He's falling to the ground.' She stops to catch her breath, and the ghost of a smile plays over her lips. 'There will be rejoicing in the streets. I know the day. It flies to us. He will not see September. The twenty-third day of the eighth month will be his last.'

Understanding alights, fragile as a butterfly. It is my sister's fantasy. She wants to leave this world believing her family will be safe. If only it could be so.

The lieutenant, behind me, makes a small incomprehensible sound. He is close, too close for this private moment. I ask him to leave us alone. He seems reluctant to go. I say it again, a command this time, surprised by the force of my tone, and he breaks away towards the door.

Melis, her grip inhumanly strong, pulls me close. She

185

whispers, 'You know I've seen death before. You remember, don't you?' Her breath stutters.

'What do you mean?' I pretend not to know she is referring to her vision of Father's accident and am forced to consider that, as she also correctly predicted her own, she might truly have seen George's death. 'Lie down or you will suffer more.' She doesn't appear to be in pain, though, seems to have reached a place beyond suffering.

She still grips my arm. I can smell death on her now. 'This time you . . . you must make it happen. You think there is a reward for goodness, Hessie. There is not. God sees far beyond.' It is a relief to hear her speak of God: I had feared her lost to Him. She has fixed me with a stare. 'The bees know it – honey and sting. Sweetness *and* sharpness. That is what you need.'

'Yes, sweetheart,' I say to soothe her, even though my mind is completely muddled and I don't understand what she is trying to tell me with her riddle, what it is I must make happen.

'It will come clear.' Her body stiffens and she spits out a single, final word, 'Justice!' before collapsing back with a quiet hiss of breath, the hair's-breadth moment between life and death breached.

'Justice?' I repeat, at a murmur, desperate now to bring her back so she can explain, so she is not gone. But she *is* gone.

I cannot cry. I fear if I do we will all drown in a life's worth of unspent tears. I feel nothing at all. My existence makes no sense. She, Rafe and Hope were the three legs of my stool. Now the stool has only two legs and I do not know how it will stand.

*

We all gather in the chapel, where coloured light from the windows falls over her in a carnival of stripes.

The lieutenant suggests we say a prayer and I kneel, docile, glad someone else is making a decision. I recite the only prayer that hasn't flown my mind. 'Guide us, Lord, in all the varieties of the world . . .' The words seem heavy and God distant. When the prayer is said we are silent for a long moment, in which I stare at Melis's glass eyes, unable to accept she has gone.

The lieutenant reaches out a hand to close them. Hope is weeping, floods of heaving tears. I am not crying. Why can she cry when I cannot muster even the smallest sob? I am dried out, like an old riverbed, without even the memory of moisture.

'I understand,' the lieutenant says, putting his hand on Hope's shoulder and offering her a crumpled handkerchief. Turning to me, he adds, 'I, too, lost a beloved sister.'

I want to tell him he couldn't possibly understand the contradictory muddle of my emotions, for I don't understand it myself.

I can hear Margie and Gifford discussing in whispers that she will have to be buried quickly because of the heat.

'If you have anything to say, say it to me directly.' I don't hide my anger. Melis's words are circulating in my head: *Honey and sting. Sweetness and sharpness* . . . I have scrawled them on a scrap of paper. Perhaps one day they will make sense. 'I won't have her buried in unsanctified ground, like a sinner. We'll take her to Ludlow. Prepare the cart, Gifford.'

'With respect, madam,' Gifford clasps his cap in his hands, 'I think it unwise for you to leave the safety of the lodge.'

I turn on him, my nerves too frayed to keep my self-control. 'It is not for you to decide.'

He stands his ground. 'I beg you. It is too late in the day to think of travelling so far.'

I know he makes sense and regret my snappish response to this man who has been nothing but kind. 'Very well, then, Gifford. First thing in the morning.' As I say it, I realize there is no question of my leaving Rafe alone here, even under the guard of Felton, and it would be equally unwise to take him to Ludlow with us. There seems no solution and I'm too crushed to think about it now.

They all tactfully file out, leaving me and Hope. I am glad that Melis will not be buried in the Iffley churchyard, where the entire village would cast furtive glances at each other, pretending to pray but whispering behind their hands. In Ludlow it will be anonymous. It will simply be the sad burial of a beautiful stranger, whose time has been cut tragically short.

Lark returns, sliding quietly into the room, drawing Hope aside to comfort her. I can hear their hushed voices. I am glad, for I haven't anything left in me to offer Hope by way of consolation. Eventually they leave and I sit, suspended in time, with my thoughts.

When I finally leave the chapel, I am surprised to find it is dusk and Rafe is already tucked up in bed, fist furled around his toy monkey, the puppy at his feet. I haven't the heart to push the animal off the bed.

I watch my son sleeping, the occasional twitch of his lips or sigh of breath proof he is alive. I feel love expanding in my chest, painful as heartburn, and sense, more intensely than ever, the looming threat from George, distant though it may seem in this remote place.

Hope

Hope is shattered by the day's horrific events, numbed by sorrow. She left the others in the kitchen, thinking she wanted to be alone, but now that she is, she can't stop thinking about her sister falling, the sound of her body breaking against the ground.

She can't get Melis's words out of her head: *There's something bad in this house.* Hope has heard talk of houses that turn on their occupants and always believed it was nothing but stories, but now she knows differently.

She feels panic crashing through her. If she keeps her mind on the lieutenant, there will be no space left for the other thoughts, no space for the 'something bad' that killed her sister.

But it is hard to keep thinking of him. Fear renders threatening everything that is ordinary – the puppy scratching at the door becomes a clawed devil, each creaking beam the cry of a trapped soul, the bowed ceiling in the bedroom the pregnant belly that will birth a demon, and the strange hum that rings through her ears is the song of a siren that will force her to fling herself from the window.

Stop.

She forces her thoughts back to him and how kind he has been to her.

The image of Melis's body laid out in the chapel returns.

Don't think about that, she tells herself. Think about him. Think about *him*. Think about our secret.

She finds herself outside the door of his room, impelled to enter, to look at the place where he sleeps, see the dip in his pillow. She picks up the laundry basket to give herself an excuse should she need it.

It is dark inside, the shutter pulled to. She swings it open, allowing the last of the gloaming to cast its thin light over the small space. He is scrupulously tidy, as you'd expect from a soldier. His few things are neatly ordered, one or two books on the shelf, bed linen folded. The phial of tincture is back exactly where she had rushed to grab it from a few hours ago.

She lies on the bed, her face sinking into the sheets, breathing in his smell, listening for sounds on the stairs.

His locked box sits beside the bed. When she had seen it earlier, she knew in her bones it must contain some clue to him, to who he is, to whom he loves. She *must* look inside, cannot help herself. His bag hangs from the back of the door. She rummages through it, searching for the key, each interior pocket, right into the corners, thinking she has found it. But it is only a silver hat badge, set with a garnet. She searches the shelf, behind the books, beneath the mattress, in the pockets of his coat. Sewn inside the collar is his name: Bloor. She wonders what his given name is.

There is a pouch containing ammunition, a powder horn, patches, a packet of lead shot and a ram-rod, all familiar to her since Gifford taught her how to handle a firearm. Everyone was surprised because she met the target first time, despite the kick causing her to stumble. Gifford had assumed she'd used a pistol before, but she never had.

She hears something. A creak. A scuff. She jumps to her feet, picking up the basket, standing absolutely still. Her heart is tapping so loudly she fears it will give her away.

But everything falls silent, just the hum of silence and the very faint tick of the clock in the blue room, matching the tick of her heart. She returns to her search but there is nowhere else to look. She stops for a moment, to consider where she would hide a key if she really didn't want it to be found. Looking round the room, her gaze alights on the lintel above the door and, on tiptoe, she can just reach to skim her fingertips along the top. The key falls, glinting, into her hand.

A quick glance round the door at the silent landing and she returns to unlock the box. A strong vinegary smell assaults her on opening the lid. A bottle of ink, its stopper oozing, is the source. She lifts out a stack of papers and a leather-bound ledger, looking underneath for trinkets, a perfumed letter, a locket, a pressed flower in a fold of paper, a sonnet. She riffles through the pile of papers, bills and receipts mostly, as far as she can tell. At the bottom are several more phials of his tincture and under those is a sealed packet of papers, stamped, appearing official, as if it might come from a notary's office. She considers opening it but changes her mind and turns to the ledger. She flicks through its pages. It appears to be some kind of journal, as there are dates written at the top of each page. Her heart beats faster. This will tell her all about him.

'What do you think you're doing in here?' Hope jumps up, dropping the journal. Hester is standing in the doorway, holding a candle. The light throws itself over her face at a strange angle, making her seem ghoulish. 'Put that back. You have no business . . .'

Hope does as she is told, returning everything to the chest, closing the lid, locking it and replacing the key.

'Now come out of there.' Hester pulls her by the arm, shutting the door firmly. 'What, in Heaven's name, do you think you were doing?' She waits for an explanation, her expression stern.

'I don't know. I was curious about him.' She wants to cry over her own stupidity. 'You said he had a sweetheart and I wanted to know –'

'You have no right, Hope.' Hester is clearly still aggravated, her composure frayed. 'And, besides, Lieutenant Bloor has enough to do keeping us safe, without you mooning after him like a lovesick calf.' She looks half dead with anguish and Hope feels terrible for adding to her burden.

'I'm sorry.' Her voice is thin as a reed. 'I didn't mean to –'

She thaws, taking Hope in her arms. 'We're all grieving. All turned upside down.'

Hope feels the sorrow flood back into her.

A sudden thud sounds from the floor below – the empty rooms – followed by a clatter.

Hester tears down the stairs, Hope following more tentatively, a noose of fear gripping her throat.

The door is slightly open and Hope racks her mind to remember if it was closed when she passed it a few minutes earlier.

The lieutenant has also appeared, the Giffords behind him, and pushes it open with his foot. 'Who goes there?'

Quiet hisses back.

Hester follows him in, her candle throwing a yellow glow into the gloom that kisses the hulks of fabric-shrouded furniture. Dark shapes are scattered over the floor. The lieutenant stoops to pick one up. It is a pewter drinking vessel. Hester holds the candle up higher to illuminate the back wall, where, they can all see now, a tall dresser has fallen forward, casting the cups and plates that must have lined its shelves all around the room. Its linen cover lies to one side, like a ghost's discarded shape.

No one speaks.

Margie breaks through the silence. 'Must have been jolted when the balcony fell. Or else it's that wretched cat.' They all laugh in relief, except Hope, who can barely breathe, or move, or think.

'What happened?' It is Rafe's sleep-shot voice, coming from the stairs.

'Sweetheart!' Hester calls to him. 'It's nothing to worry about. The dresser fell down in here, that's all.' She takes Hope firmly by the hand and, telling everyone to leave the mess until morning, marches up to where Rafe is standing, his monkey hanging from his hand. He seems small and frail, much younger than his years.

Inside the bedroom, Hester and Hope straighten the bed. Something clangs to the floor.

The sight of it knocks the breath right out of her.

'What's the matter?' asks Hester. 'Hope?'

Hope tries to reply but can't form the words.

'It's Margie's knife.' Rafe picks it up, seeming more curious than perturbed. 'How can Aunt Melis have put it here again, when she is dead?'

Rafe is the first to use the bare word, not 'passed', not 'gone', but 'dead'.

'She must have done it this morning . . . before the accident.' Hester takes the knife from her son and puts it on the cabinet beside her writing box.

It seems to Hope as if Melis fell from the balcony days

ago but only a handful of hours have passed since. Time is playing tricks again. She wants desperately to go and fetch the clock, so she can keep an eye on it, but the idea of traversing the dark landing alone and going into the blue room, with its collapsed balcony, fills her with dread. She placates herself in the only way she knows: it is the fourteenth day of August, twelve days since they left Orchard Cottage, eight days since they arrived here.

Counting days, like a silent prayer, she undresses, folding her dress and pulling a clean shift over her head. Then she squats with the small broom and sweeps up the insect carcasses that are scattered along the skirting beneath the window. Every day there are more – yesterday she counted thirty bees and this evening there must be double that.

Getting into bed, she is horribly aware of the cold empty expanse between her and Rafe. She doesn't want to lie in Melis's vacant place, as if her sister's cold body still occupies it. 'Can't we all go to Ludlow together tomorrow?' she whispers. 'Go somewhere else. I don't feel safe here, Hessie.'

'The Ludlow trip is postponed.' Hester's voice is clipped but mellows when she says, 'This really is the safest place for us. It won't be for much longer. Ambrose will come and . . .' She leaves her words hanging, which makes Hope wonder if she believes what she is saying.

Before blowing out the candle, they lie in silence. A crack, fine as a hair, has appeared, running across the bulging ceiling and something seems to be oozing from it. Resin from the beams, she tells herself, but in the fading light it looks like blood.

Felton

Felton waits.

He can hear the women talking quietly. If he presses his ear to the door of their bedchamber, he can just about make out what they are saying. Hope is pleading to travel to Ludlow, but Hester is firm. If the pliable girl knew she'd end up in a forest grave, she wouldn't be so keen.

Tiptoeing back to his room, his thoughts whir as his plan comes clear. He will have to find some other pretext to lure Hester into the forest, now she is bent on staying put. Grief hasn't addled her as much as he'd hoped.

He waits for the house to fall silent, Melis's garbled death-bed vision of George's murder returning to him. He does his best to dismiss the thought. But she predicted correctly the place of her own death. Coincidence, he tells himself firmly. The woman barely knew if she were coming or going. Despite his pragmatism a stitch of unease catches in him.

He settles down to write in his journal. Laying himself bare on the page, however futile it may be, brings some small sense of respite for his cankered soul and he continues to spill his confession over the virgin pages. Eventually all he can hear is the scratch of his pen. Everyone is asleep.

Locking away his writing things, he tucks Bloor's blade inside his jacket, ensures his pistol is loaded and secured in his belt, then pinches out the candle. He moves stealthily down through the house, feeling his way through the dark, keeping close to the walls where the boards are less likely to creak.

He uses the front door, not wanting to pass through the kitchen, too close to the Giffords' quarters. The bolts slide back easily. He had smeared a little goose grease on them when he was doing his rounds. He stands a moment on the steps until his eyes accustom to the vague moonlight. The remains of the balcony are stacked to one side and the vine has been hacked away, where it had been hanging loose. He retrieves Gifford's shovel from where he had tucked it earlier among the piles of rotten timber.

The yard-dog rouses with a low growl. Felton squats, whispering to the animal, scratching its neck until it settles down again. He doesn't use the main gate but squeezes through one of the rotten panels in the narrow space behind the barn, slipping unseen into the forest and finding his way onto the main path. After walking a short distance he leaves the track and pushes into the undergrowth, tying small lengths of twine to the trees he passes so he can find his way back. He comes, eventually, to the perfect place, a large evergreen bush with a hollow space inside its jacket of foliage.

Hanging his shirt from a branch to avoid having to explain away any dirty stains, he begins to dig. His bad arm is feeling somewhat better and he is able to use it a little, thanks to the ministrations of the woman whose grave he is presently digging. Though the ground is hard, he chips away at the surface, building a rhythm, until the earth gives more freely. He is reminded of nights digging trenches to hide in when setting ambushes for raiding parties. He enjoyed those missions, the camaraderie, the careful strategy, and became something of an expert in stealth and surprise.

196

He constructs a story in his mind, imagining arriving back at the lodge without the woman, painting a look of panic over his features. *Hester is missing! She left to answer the call of nature. She was only alone for a moment and then she was gone. I searched and searched. I heard wild dogs. In packs they can be horribly* . . . He will leave it hanging, allowing their imaginations to fill in the gap, and toys with the idea of bringing back a torn remnant of her dress, perhaps smearing it with rabbit's blood, or leaving such an item to be found by someone else when they go out to continue the search.

He hears something. The crack of a stick. Footfall. He stops digging, holds his breath, crouching in the fresh-dug hole, and slides his pistol from his belt, inwardly cursing the metallic click as he sets the dog-lock. The thin light of dawn filters through the trees above.

'Oy!' It is a male voice, one he doesn't know. 'What's going on?' A dark shape looms over the grave.

Reflex-quick, on instinct, Felton fires. A flare of light and a clap of thunderous sound cracks through the night. He is temporarily deafened, his ears ringing. The shape slumps forward, falling in on top of him. Felton heaves it off. The stench is pungent, of urine and animal, strong enough to quench the sulphur smell of the blast.

He feels great mats of woolly fibre beneath his fingers. It is a man's snarled hair. Bile surges in his throat. Sliding his hand down to the neck, he is unable to find a pulse and neither is there any sign of breath from the crusted lips.

He can hear the yard-dog barking in response to the shot. Felton hauls himself out of the grave, hurriedly scraping in just enough soil to cover the body for the meantime. The woman will have to share her final resting place with this stinking creature. Leaving the spade hidden, he tugs on his shirt and runs back towards the house, brushing the dirt from his breeches as he goes, working out how he will explain away the gunshot.

On entering the yard from behind the barn, he sees Lark running out of the house. The place is in a commotion. The cockerel is on the roof of the henhouse, strutting back and forth while emitting an alarmed crowing, the goats are bleating inside the barn and the yard-dog is still barking madly, careering back and forth along the fence.

'Who goes there?' she shouts.

'It is I, Lieutenant Bloor.'

'Oh, thank God!' She reaches out a hand to touch him, as if to be absolutely sure. 'Did you hear the shot?' She is deathly pale in dawn's blue light. 'I've been in to warn them. They are in the hiding place.' She leans towards him, seeming to sniff at his clothes.

'There's no need for that.' He thinks fast. 'No need to worry. It was I who fired the shot.'

'I thought I could smell sulphur on you . . . But why?'

He feels bored through by her look and has to keep reminding himself she is blind. 'I couldn't sleep and heard a terrible racket coming from the dog. It was what roused me from my bed.' From the paddock the grey horse watches him, as if it can see right through his lie. 'A fox was trying to get into the henhouse. I chased it out and fired. Missed it.'

'You sure it was a fox?'

'I saw it.' He nods emphatically, even though she cannot see him.

'I thought I heard the shot before the dog started up.'

'You must be mistaken.' It was an error to say the dog woke him, he realizes, but all he can do is reaffirm the lie and hope she will accept it.

Lark stands awhile, saying nothing, as if about to challenge him, but seems to change her mind. 'Perhaps I was still asleep when the dog first barked. And I'm sure I heard footfall earlier. Long before the shot . . .' She still seems doubtful.

'The footfall you heard will have been me giving chase to the fox.'

'Anyway, I must go up and tell Hester what's happening.' She turns towards the house. 'She'll be out of her mind with worry.'

'I'll take a look around. Make sure there's nothing untoward, now it's getting light . . .'

Felton goes to the back door to sluice his face in the water-butt and wash any evidence from his hands. The butt is almost empty, just the gritty dregs, as it hasn't rained in at least a week. He lifts his head to be confronted by Margie, who is standing on the stoop, arms folded.

'Bloody foxes,' she says.

She must have overheard his conversation with Lark and Felton feels suddenly as if it is impossible to do anything in this place without someone seeing or hearing.

'It might have been Hywel, who set the dog barking,' Margie says. 'He does tend to creep about at night, that one.'

'Hywel?'

'Just an elderly vagrant who wanders the woods. I leave scraps out for him so he doesn't starve.'

'Why wasn't I told about him?' Felton sounds angry. He is, but mostly at himself for his reckless lack of caution. He acted rashly in shooting the man and resolves to keep a better grip on himself. 'How can I be expected to do my job properly if I'm not fully informed?' He is thinking that at least the man he has killed won't be missed.

Hester

Rafe and I sit huddled in the darkness of the priest-hole. In the rush I had remembered to pick up the kitchen knife and my hand is gripping its hilt so hard my knuckles ache.

All falls quiet, just the clock's tick, like water dripping onto the tight skin of a drum, resonating around the small space, a slow torture.

Rafe is completely silent. I can hardly even hear his breath. My mind turns over and over the possibilities of what the shot in the forest might have meant, and why, when I banged on his door just now, the lieutenant was absent. I have no answers.

The darkness gropes, and I imagine I can hear that sound again, creeping into my head, the low thrum – Melis's sound. Rafe is now so still and so quiet I have to bat away irrational thoughts that he may be dead, that we both may be. I don't know how much time has passed before he whispers, 'If I went to live with my father, we wouldn't have to hide like this, would we?'

'I won't let him take you.' I hold his small body tight to me but he wriggles out of my grip, expelling a huff of air.

'But he was nice.'

I don't know what to say. The George he met that day didn't seem the kind of monster who would kidnap his son and hound us like this. All Rafe saw was the splendid glittering George – the mirage.

'He promised me a horse.'

'He can't be trusted, sweetheart.'

Despair warps me out of shape. I sense my strength beginning to sap and silently pray for Ambrose to reach us. I fumble, feeling around for the niche where I hid the letters. My fingers meet dust. Urgent now, I run my hands over the walls and the floor, into every crevice. Perhaps we pushed them into the back when we crawled inside. The clock chimes. The letters are gone.

A stab of dread splits me open, spitting out a thousand unanswerable questions. Hope is the only one who knew where they were hidden. Even Melis didn't know. Why would Hope move them? Why? Or did someone else see us put them there? Who?

I begin to weep, desperate, silent, drooling sobs, over which I have no control. I haven't cried since I can remember. I didn't cry when Father died, I didn't cry when George ruined me, or when he rejected me, I didn't cry for Melis, and now I am crying for them all, a vat of hopeless, useless tears.

Hope

Hope sits with the gun in her lap cocked, barrel angled up so the shot stays in place.

She is afraid of the gun.

She will not allow herself to think of the 'something bad' in the house.

The hand of the clock snaps into the half-hour. It is half past five and already getting light. She is trying to calculate how long it is since Lark roused them: it can't be more than ten minutes.

The birds are singing, as if it is an ordinary dawn.

She can hear the puppy's pathetic half-whine, half-howl, shut in the bedroom. And she can hear footsteps.

Someone is mounting the stairs slowly and deliberately.

She stands, holding the pistol tentatively, afraid to set it to full-cock.

Her heart thumps – too fast – her head light, spinning.

She steals to the door, feeling as if her legs might give way beneath her, opening it a chink.

The footsteps reach the floor below.

A silent prayer for protection is on her lips.

The steps reach the final turn of the stairs.

'Stop! Who are you?' She tries to sound authoritative but her voice quakes.

'It's Lark.'

'Oh, thank God!' Relief knocks the substance from her, makes her want to sink to the floor.

Lark appears, spectral and indistinct in the gloom of the unlit staircase.

'What's happening?'

'The lieutenant fired at a fox. It was trying to get in at the hens but he missed it.'

'So, all is well?' Hope is wondering why Lark seems to look concerned, as if there is something she is not saying. 'Where's the lieutenant?'

'Gone back out to "survey the area", he said.' She reaches out, fingers fumbling over Hope's wrist and down to grip her hand. 'I don't fully trust that man. I've said it before.'

'You have.' Hope doesn't want to contradict her, or tell her that she is mistaken, but that is what she thinks. She is wondering if Lark's dislike of the lieutenant is clouding her judgement.

They hear him calling then, 'All clear,' from the bottom of the stairs.

Lark helps her release Hester and Rafe from the priest-hole. They emerge, bleary and confused, Hester with Margie's kitchen knife and Rafe's bedraggled monkey pressed to her torso like a bridal bouquet.

The lieutenant is mounting the stairs, his heavy foot-fall unmistakable. He reaches the landing, noticing the pistol in Hope's hand with a nod, as if to say she's done well. She flushes, looking at the floor, her heart slipping like hot wax.

'Just as I thought. Nothing more sinister than a fox out there.' His own firearm is hanging in his hand. 'It won't be back in a hurry.'

'Is it time to go and see if we've caught any rabbits?'

Two pink circles of anticipation appear on Rafe's cheeks beneath the smears of dark under his eyes.

'Leave the lieutenant be.' Hester is unusually firm with Rafe. 'I should think he's exhausted.' And, turning to the man, she asks, 'Did it get any of the hens?'

'No, nothing like that.' The lieutenant crouches in front of Rafe. 'I'd be very happy to take you out a little later, young man, but I have to be sure your mother hasn't decided to go to Ludlow, after all.' Rafe looks up at her.

Mention of the Ludlow trip has caused the atmosphere to sharpen, reminding them all that Melis is dead and her body is in the chapel.

'No,' says Hester. 'We're all staying here.'

'You're certain about that?' The lieutenant's expression is off-kilter. 'You would feel so much better to know that your sister is laid to rest in peace and that prayers have been said for her. Would it help if I were to offer to accompany you?'

He places his palm to his breast and Hope notices his fingernails are filthy. She can't help imagining those hands on her. Heat flares beneath her nightdress. She feels exposed, wishes she was laced into her day clothing.

'There will be no Ludlow trip today,' Hester says, not inviting further discussion.

All Hope can think of now is what will happen to Melis's body in the heat, she can't expel the thought from her head.

'Then I can take you out to the traps in a while.' The lieutenant ruffles Rafe's hair.

'Surely you must need to rest, Lieutenant,' says Hester, exhaustion and impatience infusing her tone. 'You've been out half the night chasing vermin.'

'It was barely an hour, and almost dawn when I was

204

roused.' Despite what he says, he looks dog-tired, as if he hasn't slept at all, and Hope imagines him tossing and turning, thinking of her in the night.

'I'd be happy to take him,' he adds. 'With *your* permission, of course.'

'I don't know that it's such a good idea.'

'But, Mother,' Rafe turns a gorgeous beam on Hester, 'if we don't get the rabbits today, they will rot in the heat, or that fox will eat them. Isn't that right, Lieutenant?'

Hope knows Hester will relent and so she does, on the proviso that they have an hour's rest first. She wishes Hester would be firmer with the boy, make it clear that 'no' means no.

'Can I persuade you to join us?' the lieutenant asks Hester. 'It might do you good to get out of here for a while. A change of scene.'

Hope is prodded by a small finger of jealousy. *She* would like to be the one to go out with them, and when Hester refuses curtly, despite another attempt by the lieutenant to convince her, Hope is disappointed that he doesn't suggest she go instead.

In their room Hester slumps onto the bed. 'Goodness knows why the lieutenant thinks I'd want to go out at the crack of dawn to fetch in dead rabbits when my sister is . . .' She is furious, all her grief turned to rage, and bangs her fist against the bedpost, wincing.

Hope puts an arm around her but she shrugs it off, saying, 'I wish Ambrose would get here.'

Hope feels the burn of more tears and watches Rafe remove his soot-smeared nightshirt to lean over the basin and splash water onto his face. His shoulder blades are like the nubs of wings. She gets up, taking a clean shirt

205

from the linen press, sliding it over his head and pulling back the covers for him to climb into bed. 'I'll never be able to sleep,' he complains. 'It's too light.'

Hester is filthy, her hair tangled into spikes. Her eyes look dead. Anyone would be forgiven if they mistook her for a lunatic.

Hope feels suddenly unsure of herself. Hester has always been so strong, has always held them all together, but now she doesn't even look as if she can hold herself together.

Hope passes her a laundered shift. She looks at it in momentary puzzlement, as if she's never seen such a thing before in her life. Pouring some fresh water into the basin, Hope wets a cloth, squeezing it out, giving it to her sister, then sets to work on the knots in her hair with a comb.

They don't speak and, in the silence, Hope finds a measure of reassurance in the faint sound of the clock in the other room, its regularity making it seem as if everything is in the right order, although she senses that nothing is.

Rafe sighs, his eyelids drooping. The two sisters lie on the bed, wide awake, contemplating the ceiling. The whole house is sagging, like an old woman's flesh.

Hester points towards the bulge. 'Do you think it's got worse since we've been here?'

'I don't know.' They stare at the swollen plaster. A beam creaks. Something rustles and whirs behind the walls, as if the house is whispering to itself. 'I sometimes wonder if this house won't eat us all alive.' Hope's voice is monotone, as if she has borrowed it from someone else.

'Don't go putting the frights on yourself. Things are bad enough without you imagining things too.' Hester sits up, makes sure Rafe is asleep, then looks straight at Hope. 'There's something I need to talk to you about.' Her voice holds a shard of ice.

'What is it?'

'The letters are not in the priest-hole. You're the only person who knows I hid them in there.'

Hope feels as if someone has snipped a thread deep inside her and she is unspooling. With everything that has happened she had forgotten about the letters. It seems an age ago, yet it was only the day before yesterday.

'Where are they, Hope?'

'I don't know.' The lie makes her burn. 'Melis kept saying there was something bad in this house –'

'Don't take me for an idiot.' They are talking quietly so as not to wake Rafe but Hester sounds abrasive even at a whisper. 'Melis had lost her mind . . . God rest her soul.' Her sister is shaking her head and Hope feels there is something she is not saying.

'But the knife. The dresser last night – falling like it did. The balcony.'

Hester's stare is as hard as a hammer blow. 'There is nothing bad in this house, unless you count young girls who are unable to tell the truth.'

Hope begins to cry. 'I'm sorry, so sorry, Hessie.' Between waves of sobbing she recounts what she knows about the letters.

'You *gave* him my letters?' Hester's arm twitches, lifting slightly, causing Hope to cower, waiting for a slap that doesn't come. 'Why didn't you ask me?' Hester is only just managing to contain her anger.

All Hope can think about is how pleased she had been to have a secret to share with the lieutenant. She had thought of no one but herself. Guilt grips her sharply, like cramp.

'I was trying to help you. The lieutenant said he would burn them, that Ambrose had ordered it, but I didn't see him do it. He may still have them.' Doubt rings through her voice.

'It doesn't seem likely, given he was set on destroying them. You'd better hope that Ambrose has some other . . . some other . . .' All the colour has fallen from Hester's face and she can't get her words out. 'He was aware of the importance of those letters.' She covers her face with her hands and, after a few moments, lifts her head and meets Hope's gaze with a seething look. 'I don't believe Ambrose would have given such an order.'

'The lieutenant said they were dangerous. Even you told me they were dangerous.' All Hope knows is that, once again, she has let her weakness for a man visit misfortune on her sister. 'I'm sorry.'

'It's no use being sorry now.' Hester stands and marches out of the room.

Hester

Felton is sitting at the table writing in his journal, which he slams shut, turning, half standing. 'Is there something . . . ?'

'What in the name of God do you think you were doing taking my letters?' I had planned to remain calm but can't hide the force of my rage. 'Did you burn them, as Hope says you did?'

'I regret to say they are destroyed, yes.'

'Regret,' I spit. 'Regret will not unburn my letters, Lieutenant.' I am jabbing at the air with my finger. 'I want an explanation.'

'It was wrong of me not to inform you. But I was acting on Dr Cotton's order.'

'If Dr Cotton ordered you to eat a poisonous mushroom, would you do so?' Disdain gushes out of me. 'Whether you were acting on his orders or not, you should have come to me. They were my papers, not his, not yours. *Mine.*'

'With all respect, my first priority here is the safety of you and your son, and those letters put you in too great a risk.'

I try to calm myself. I know nothing of this man. Suspicion begins to creep through me. 'Dr Cotton would never have ordered you to do such a thing and keep me in the dark.'

He hangs his head, like a disobedient child. 'It was my own decision to say nothing to you. I believed I was doing the right thing, thought it would prevent you from worrying, but now I see that it was an error of judgement.'

I arrange and rearrange my thoughts, holding him with a silent glare. With the letters gone I have lost my most potent weapon. The thought makes me flounder.

He continues, wringing his hands now, like a supplicant. 'Dr Cotton explained to me that he had begun discussions with the duke of the utmost delicacy, and that if the letters fell into the wrong hands everything might be jeopardized –'

'I don't believe you! He would have wanted *me* to know this. He would have written to tell me.'

'And I wouldn't believe either, in your place, but it is the truth – upon my soul it is.' He looks at me from under his brows, like a dog. 'He said he didn't want you to get your hopes up at this early stage.'

Through my tangled mind I concede that that is just the kind of thing Ambrose would say and this man has had ample opportunity to make away with Rafe, if that was his intention. I begin to sense myself treading on more solid ground, my anger and suspicions slowly abating. The thought of negotiations having begun with George is a flicker of light in the gloom.

I fumble for the chain around my neck, running my fingers down to find the enamelled ring: *Veritas nunquam perit*. There is no doubt that this is Ambrose's ring, delivered to me by this rueful man. It is the one solid fact I have to hang on to. 'Very well.' He visibly relaxes, his shoulders dropping. 'But remember this, Lieutenant. Under this roof, you do as *I* say. Is that clear?'

Hope

Hope can hear Hester shouting at the lieutenant as she tidies the bedroom. She has never seen her sister in such a rage and feels steeped in shame for being the cause of it. She gathers all the clothes that are scattered about the place, carefully folding them. Then she empties the pot, rinsing it, sweeps the dead insects off the windowsill and clears up a fall of powdered plaster in the corner.

Noticing a small stain on the hem of her skirt, she rubs the fabric together vigorously until just the ghost of the mark is left, hardly discernible. She sluices her armpits with water and clothes herself, fastening her dress as tightly as possible, so tight it hurts to breathe, as if the garment alone will hold her together, then tugs her hair into place, with pins that dig into her scalp. She puts on her shoes and stockings and takes a clean overskirt, tying it around her, stroking her palms over the neat squares where it was folded.

The room is pristine. Only the bed is unmade, with Rafe sleeping peacefully, his long lashes lying against his pale cheeks, like spiders. She carefully arranges the covers without disturbing him, looking around for something else to organize.

No amount of tidying will stop the dread spreading through her.

A door slams and she hears footsteps marching down the stairs, followed by a gentle tap at the door. She opens it to find the lieutenant.

'I owe you an apology,' he says. 'I hope I didn't visit trouble on you by asking you to keep a secret from your sister.' He is smiling that gap-toothed smile of his. 'It was wrong of me.'

Hope shrugs. 'It doesn't matter.'

He reaches out his hand and strokes a finger over her cheek, taking a step closer until their faces are mere inches apart. She is suddenly hot and is glad she laced her dress so firmly for she fears bursting out of it.

'Is it time to go out to the traps?' They spring apart, both turning to see Rafe wide awake.

The lieutenant laughs. 'Get dressed, young man, and we'll go.'

Once they have gone, she lingers a while, reluctant to go down and confront Hester. Eventually the scent of fresh-baked bread wafting up proves impossible to resist and she leaves the room, descending the stairs, forming an apology for her sister.

Something grabs her eye on the middle landing.

The door to the room where the dresser had fallen last night is ajar and she thinks something is moving inside, a shadow in the corner of her eye.

Instinct tells her to run but she finds herself drawn inexorably, one foot in front of the other, as if she has no choice, towards the door.

The hinge squeaks as she opens it slightly.

She steps over the threshold, breath held.

Thin shafts of light, from the cracks around the shutters, cut across the floor, illuminating the dust. Everything is as it was the previous night, the dresser fallen forward, its dust cover flung to its side, like a spill of milk. Her eyes follow the scatter of pewter dishes and cups.

She jumps back then, releasing a cry.

The cat is motionless on its side, pink mouth open enough for her to see its sharp yellow fangs.

Around its neck is a snare.

It is dead.

Hester

I can hear Rafe in the yard preparing to go, asking the lieutenant a litany of questions. Sitting at the table I inspect today's eggs for cracks. There are few this morning: last night's disturbance has upset the hens. Gifford is searching for his shovel, poking his head around the door to ask us if we are sure we haven't seen it. Margie pulls a loaf from the bread oven, sending a glorious aroma through the kitchen. Lark is whistling, just outside, where she is peeling potatoes.

Everything seems normal. But nothing is normal. The letters are burned. Melis is dead. I keep expecting her to come into the room and sit down. Then I remember, and grief hammers another nail through me. I cannot bring myself to think of what the heat is doing to her remains. I tell myself that her pain is gone, that she has escaped into the air and drifts through the house unencumbered.

Before the disturbance last night I had dreamed of Melis, so vividly it was like a visitation. *Hessie, Hessie, it's me.* She sat beside me on the bed. I could feel the weight of her, could touch her, could feel the warmth of her breath in my ear as she spoke. *No more George. You know what that means, don't you, Hessie?* I felt the sharp nudge of her elbow against my ribs. *Means you will be free.*

Despite everything, I have never wished George dead.

It seems too insurmountable a sin, and if I cannot know in my heart of hearts that I am good – a good person, a moral person, the person who looks after others – then who am I?

You think there is a reward for goodness, she had said. I have always believed that, but for all my trying to be good, the punishments have far outweighed the rewards. I consider whether I would be one of those rejoicing in the streets were Melis's deathbed vision to come to pass. I feel a thrill as I imagine it. Perhaps I am not as good as I have always believed myself to be.

Someone has left a few stems of lavender on the side. I take one, crushing the bud, bringing it to my nose, hoping it will soothe my agitated thoughts. As I am sliding it through a buttonhole in my shift, Hope enters the room. She is shaking, gabbling something about the cat in a voice as serrated as a hacksaw. 'We can't stay. We can't stay here.'

I try to take her arm but she will not be held. It is Lark who manages to calm her eventually. 'What's the matter? Try to breathe. Speak slowly.'

She can't speak without stuttering and all I can think is that I need her to be calm.

Lark talks to her sweetly, as if she is an infant. 'I expect she got herself caught up. I noticed a few snares lying around in the yard. Poor puss.' Hope sniffs and wipes her face with her cuff. 'Will you come and give me a hand in the barn? I could do with your help.'

I busy myself with ordinary tasks, until Rafe appears with a brace of rabbits slung over his shoulder, like a fur stole. The lieutenant is by his side, describing how to make a slingshot. 'It takes a lot of practice to hit anything with any accuracy.'

'Like Hywel?' says Rafe. 'He can hit a sparrow at a hundred paces.'

'I think that's very unlikely.' The lieutenant looks doubtful. 'Don't you want to show your mother what we caught?'

Rafe proudly holds up the rabbits for me to see. 'The lieutenant's going to show me how to skin them.'

I am glad to see him so content, but at the same time am perturbed that he seems so changed, the rabbits suspended from his hand, where his toy monkey might once have been. A jolt of loss comes with the inevitability of him growing up and leaving me with no one to care for. I want to stop time. It kicks the breath out of me.

'Is something wrong?' Rafe's voice draws me back and I see him take an object from his pocket. In my grief, I had forgotten the penknife and that he had lied to me in such an unabashed manner – another sign of his growing up. The thought sends new discomfort through me. His father is an accomplished liar, too.

'That penknife,' I say. 'You told me Lieutenant Bloor gave it to you.' Rafe is biting his lip and will not meet my eye. 'He didn't, did he?'

'Oh, but it *was* me he got it from.' The lieutenant is smiling.

'I thought you said you had no penknife.' Suspicion prods at me anew. I finger the enamel ring.

Rafe is shuffling from one foot to the other. The lieutenant is still smiling.

'I must have thought you meant something else. I'm so sorry,' he says, with disarming warmth. 'What with everything.'

'It doesn't matter.' I feel embarrassed now for making a fuss over a minor confusion.

'Would you object,' asks the lieutenant, 'if I teach your son how to skin and gut one of these?' He points at the rabbits.

'Of course not. It's very kind of you to be so attentive to him.'

The lieutenant explains to Rafe that it is better to let game hang for a couple of days, that it tastes better.

'You'll let me have one for the pot today, though, won't you?' Margie says. 'A rabbit stew'll do us all good.'

'Of course.' Felton, like a conjurer, deftly skins one of the carcasses, then demonstrates to a captivated Rafe how to remove the guts.

Felton

The house is deathly quiet. The afternoon heat has sent them all to rest inside. All but Felton, who sits under a tree in the orchard with his book. He stares at the page, not reading, unable to concentrate. The stench of the vagrant, urine and unwashed flesh, clings to him, though he has scrubbed himself several times since. It is the smell of his conscience. He bats it away. The last thing he needs now is a fit of morality.

He can't stop running over the conversation with Hester about the letters. There was a moment when he believed he was exposed but he managed to reel himself back from the brink. He convinced her with a lie and a measure of disarming remorse, but he must tread carefully. There is no time to lose – one more misstep and she will not be so easily persuaded.

There has been talk of the old man being sent to Ludlow tomorrow with Melis's body. Hester will not accompany them. Felton must persuade her out into the forest on some pretext. Her fresh-dug grave awaits. But she is a wilful creature and will not easily be convinced to leave the house. He cannot imagine what George could possibly have seen in her.

He wonders if Worley has arrived at Ludlow yet. It is of no use him being there if Felton cannot get word to him and, anyway, the man cannot show himself here as he would be recognized.

He needs a firm plan.

Picking an apple from a low bough, he slices it with Bloor's knife, finding its flesh crawling with maggots – like Hester, he thinks, innocent on the surface and rotten beneath. Flinging the fruit away, he notices that one of the bee skeps has been upended and is lying in the nettles at the edge of the paddock. Curiosity draws him towards it, only to discover that, not only is the fallen skep empty, all of them are. He cannot find a single bee, no sign even of any recent activity, just some vacant combs, brown and crusted with age and a few dead insects.

It makes him wonder what the mad sister was doing out here all the time and about the welts that covered her body. He has tried not to ponder on her disturbing visions but the disquiet will not entirely leave him. She had described George's death so vividly and the image has planted itself in his head.

Felton is a soldier, a rationalist: he has always wanted to see those who claim to know the future as charlatans, fleecing the weak and impressionable. But Melis . . . His blood chills as he recognizes that there may well be some truth behind her madness. George had said it. These women have been designing his fall. A new urgency takes hold in him, but he is bereft of ideas.

Returning to his book, which has been lying open in the sun, he notices that the page is charred where the magnifier had rested on it. Annoyance wells. It is the book from George and is dear to him. He notes, with a sardonic huff, that the obscured passage of text is an essay on Truth.

Gazing at the charred circle, an idea scores itself into his head, a new idea.

Hope

Rafe is making a paper fan. A bee hovers close, humming as loudly as a corn crake. Rafe tries to bat it away, exciting the puppy, which jumps up, snapping at it.

'You'll make it angry,' Hope tells him.

She imagines it is Melis come to haunt her.

She is darning Hester's stockings. It might seem a futile exercise, given Hester goes about barefoot, but it has a soothing effect, as if she may be able to put herself back together, one minuscule stitch at a time.

Rafe sits down on the floor and begins to rummage through the sewing bag, rearranging the pins in the pincushion to spell his initials. They are in the blue room, where the doors to the balcony have been secured with a plank nailed across them, a brutal reminder of her sister's fall.

She must not think of that.

There is nowhere Hope can escape the oppressive sense of the house turning on its occupants. She can tolerate this room only because she knows the lieutenant is a few steps away across the landing writing in his journal. She saw him through a knot in the wood of his door, couldn't stop herself peeping, and wants, desperately, to know what he writes, whether he writes about her, whether he thinks of her.

The room is unusually quiet, as if something is missing, or not quite as it should be. Sweat trickles beneath her clothes, but she refuses to go about in her shift, like her sister. Lark had said it was going to rain tomorrow, said she could smell it on its way. Hope doesn't believe her, not for a moment. Lark is not right about the lieutenant either. For what reason, other than jealousy, would she cast aspersions on the man sent to protect them?

Hope holds to this belief tightly, with both hands. She thinks she understands jealousy. It was always the reason Melis used to give her as a child, when the village girls didn't invite her to play with them. 'They envy you your prettiness,' she would say.

A sudden sharp pain burns her ankle, as if someone has held a flame to it, making her cry out.

'What's the matter?' The pincushion falls from Rafe's hand. His face opens up with sympathy.

'That bee must have stung me.' She lifts her foot, bringing it across her knee, rolling down her stocking so she can see, telling herself it is just a bee, nothing more sinister, but her imagination wants to take her down a darker path.

She finds the puncture, a red spot, and squeezes the sides of it gently, but no black sting appears.

'What is it?' Rafe peers at the bead of blood.

'I'm sure it was a bee, not a wasp, but I can't find the sting.' She has a momentary suspicion that Rafe has stabbed her with a pin. 'Open your hands.' He does as she asks, without hesitation. His hands are empty and she feels bad for having suspected him.

'Does it hurt?' He takes out his handkerchief to dab at the puncture. A small crimson smear interrupts the linen. 'Shall I kiss it better?' Without waiting for a response, he plants his lips lightly on her ankle. 'Poor you.' Then something seems to occur to him, and he meets her eyes with a limpid gaze. 'It might have been a queen. The queen doesn't leave her sting behind. She can sting as many times as she wants without dying.'

Hope hears Melis's voice coming from his mouth and suddenly has the feeling of having stood up too quickly, though she is rooted to the chair.

'Aunt Hope. Aunt Hope!' It is Rafe, waving the paper fan in front of her face, speaking with his own voice. 'What is it? Are you going to faint?'

She takes a few deep breaths. 'It's very hot, that's all. Let's tidy these things.'

As they are putting everything away into the sewing bag, she realizes what is not quite right about the room.

The clock has fallen silent.

With everything that has happened she has forgotten to wind it.

The clock stares, hands spread at ten past ten. The thought flickers into her head that that was the time Melis fell, that the clock is part of the house's conspiracy, but she reins in her imagination before it runs away with her.

No. Her mind is fooling her.

Hester

I didn't collect the eggs today. I can't muster the will to do anything but sit with my sister in prayer. I can hear Rafe and Hope descending the stairs, speaking in hushed voices, not wanting to disturb me.

The chapel is cooler than the rest of the house. A putrid sweetness hangs in the air. Her face is sinking, her eyelids hollowing. Someone has crossed her hands over her breast. Did I do it? I can't remember. Sorrow has rubbed away my sense.

Gifford will be leaving shortly with her and though I want, desperately, to say prayers at her burial, I cannot risk Rafe's safety. Melis would understand. The living must come first.

I notice one of the stained-glass panes is broken, a jagged aperture open to the sky. The trees outside rustle and murmur, the poplars whispering. Am I dreaming or has the stagnant air finally caught a breeze? I become aware of the faint smell of smoke. It must be from the kitchen chimney.

If the smoke is coming from the kitchen chimney why, then, can I hear, I am sure of it, the faint crack and spit of flames from this side of the house? A bonfire? Gifford must be mad to light one with everything so parched.

The sound becomes more insistent, the smell too, luring me out onto the landing where a large casement gives onto the yard. To my horror, I am confronted with the sight of the henhouse ablaze, thick tongues of flame licking skywards and a pillar of angry smoke rising, billowing up to obscure the trees behind.

I run down the stairs, two, three at a time, shouting, bursting into the kitchen to raise the alarm. Ordering them all to get to the well and draw up water to quench the flames, before the whole place catches. 'The wind's up. We've got to stop it.'

The lieutenant stands immobile, looking at me in stupefaction, as if he hasn't understood what I've said, before taking to his heels and rushing outside.

Hope is out of her seat hurling words in his wake. 'Rafe! Rafe's in there!'

I think I have misheard, but she says it again.

I crash across the smoke-filled yard towards the henhouse but am confronted by a jabbering wall of flame sucking up the wooden structure. Gifford is shouting about buckets. The entrance has not caught yet. I step forward into thick smoke, calling Rafe's name, my voice swallowed by the roar of the fire. Heat blistering. Lungs burning. A hand grabs me, pulling me back.

The lieutenant forces me aside, barging through, disappearing into the conflagration.

A deafening howl fills the air then, louder than the fire, louder than Gifford's shouting, louder than the wind picking up, louder than the barking dogs.

A sharp smack stings my face, bringing me to my senses. It was I who was screaming. 'Pull yourself together!' It's Hope, thrusting a bucket into my hand and dragging me towards the well. 'We need to put out the fire. Leave Rafe to him.'

Margie is at the well, winding the crank with a squeal, while Lark runs back and forth from the barn with the big milk churns.

Margie, strong as an ox, hauls each full bucket up and out and into my arms. I run to Hope, passing it to her, water slapping everywhere, then Gifford takes it, flinging it into the flames. On and on, pail after pail, churn after churn, but the fire seems to grow in the wind.

The lieutenant hasn't reappeared. A glut of dry matter is stuck in my throat. It is dread. No time to think. We continue. On and on. Each bucketful of water woefully inadequate.

My throat is sore, eyes smarting, tears pouring.

It seems a thousand hours but must be only moments later that the lieutenant emerges, just as the roof collapses with a crash, in a tower of flying sparks.

His face is black. Rafe is in his arms, *his* face black too. Upright. Moving. Alive. He is alive. The bucket falls from my hands. Water runs everywhere. I take him into my arms, welding him to me.

Shock has struck him dumb – struck us all dumb.

'Are you hurt?' I check his skin for burns. His hair is singed, his hands scorched but only slightly. It seems impossible that he has survived virtually unscathed. His grey eyes, rimmed in red, are round and bright in his sooty face.

'I'm sorry, Mother.' He is astonishingly composed, so stoic. 'I wanted to get the eggs as a surprise for you. You were so tired. But the door blew shut when I was inside and I couldn't undo the latch.'

'No, no, no, my sweetheart, don't be sorry.' I am gabbling with relief. 'Thank God.' I cling to his thin little body.

We are both shaking now, too shocked to cry. 'Thank God for the lieutenant. He saved your life.'

'Wind's pushing it towards the barn,' cries Gifford.

I wrap a wet cloth round Rafe's hands and sit him on the steps so I can help. We all know that if it catches the barn the house will be next.

Summoning all the strength we can muster, we continue lugging the buckets along the line, on and on.

Just as the flames have begun to diminish a new gust of wind blows, rattling all the doors and windows, shaking the trees, causing the flames to flare up again, higher than ever. Hopelessness descends and someone suggests we turn our attentions to saving the barn. The henhouse burns with renewed vigour while a ladder is found and leaned against the barn. The lieutenant climbs it, and containers of water are handed to him, which he heaves up with his one good arm to fling across the thatch. Even Rafe helps now, running to and fro to pass the empty buckets back to Margie.

The sky turns dark with a great boiling bank of black clouds, as if an angry god has doused the sun. We are all silently, hopelessly, praying for a downpour.

Then it comes, a sudden miraculous squall of heavy ram-rod rain, buffeting and drenching us all. And the flames are finally smothered. The rain stops as fast as it came, leaving the gutters gushing, the eaves dripping and the yard slick with mud, while a few surviving hens peck nearby, seeming oblivious.

Charred struts rise from the black pile of steaming embers where the henhouse once stood. I look back at the house, its twin, half expecting it, too, to be gone, but it is drenched in sunlight, its bricks a smug pink, windows shimmering.

Only now do I fully comprehend the horror of what might have happened had the lieutenant not been so quick to intervene. My relief is so great I feel unsteady, as if I am drunk. I lead Rafe back to the steps to sit, the lieutenant sinking down beside us.

'You saved his life.' I begin to thank him, the words seeming inadequate, but he holds up his hand, shaking his head.

'It's what anyone would have done.' Slumped by the door, head back against the brick wall, he looks not only dog-tired but distraught. I wonder if the incident has brought back the horror of the battlefield.

'It should have been me.' I am struck then by the truth of that fact. 'I am the one who always collects the eggs . . . Every morning.' Then it hits me, like a crack on the head. Melis predicted this: the fire, Rafe inside. I must blanch because he asks if I am all right. 'It is shock,' I say, by way of explanation, for how can I tell him that my sister knew this would happen?

I take Rafe into the kitchen, washing the soot from his skin and tending his scorched hands, anointing them with salve. Upstairs I carefully peel off his clothes and find him clean ones. He is silent and withdrawn, white with exhaustion beneath the smut. Waves of blessed relief break over me whenever I consider what might have happened.

'What's that?' He is staring at the nub of wax on the windowsill, the remains of the little figure he'd carved for me and I berate myself for not having hidden it. 'You said you would treasure it.'

I don't know what to say to him.

Hope sidles into the room on tiptoe, closing the door quietly and asking in a whisper after her nephew. She is still filthy, soaked to the skin and covered with soot and mud. 'This was what Melis saw, wasn't it?'

'I believe so.' I cannot continue to pretend and Melis is gone now, so what do I have to protect Hope from? 'Our sister predicted other things that came to pass. It was her curse.'

'But you always told me . . .'

'I know. I thought the truth would trouble you.'

She begins to cry, tears making runnels in the smears of soot on her face. 'Poor, poor Melis. I can't imagine how terrible it must have been.' I draw her into my arms, noticing an object in her hand, a blackened ring the size of a cup's rim.

'What is this?'

She holds it up, looking at it as if she'd forgotten she was holding it. 'I found it on the ground outside. It might have been what caused the fire.'

'What is it?' I can't make it out.

'It looks like the lieutenant's magnifying-glass. It must have fallen from his pocket.'

I can see it now, the metal ring and the protrusion where the handle was attached, the wood burned right away, the glass gone. Misgiving nips at me. 'Where was it?'

'Beside the henhouse. The straw's so dry, the sun would have lit it in no time.' She must read my expression because she says, 'What is it?'

'I don't know. Do you think he intended to –'

She interrupts me sharply. 'Why would he do such a thing?' She is the picture of indignation, as if I had accused *her* of setting the fire. 'There's no reason on earth. He's the one who saved Rafe's life. He's a hero!'

I can feel beads of moisture collecting over my forehead

and upper lip. Again and again the balcony collapses, my sister falling endlessly.

'I saw him.' We turn at the sound of Rafe's voice. 'I saw him while I was collecting the eggs. He was right outside the henhouse before the door blew shut.'

Melis is still falling, struts of the balcony crashing around her, and suspicion fizzes round my skull.

'The magnifier must have fallen from his pocket,' Hope repeats, her tone leaving no room for doubt.

'Or he put it there deliberately.' I don't want to believe it and ask myself why he would do that, unable to find a filament of sense to follow. I am racking my brain for some specific sign of his bad intentions but all I can think of is his kindness to Rafe and his sympathy when Melis died.

'Not you, too, Hester.' Hope is making angry staccato gestures with her hands.

'What do you mean – not me too?'

'Lark doesn't trust him either –'

I interrupt her harshly: 'You should have told me that.' As I say it, I realize I am being unfair. Had she told me, I would likely have dismissed her qualms as nonsense. I think of the burned letters.

Driven to know more, I scratch around in my head and remember finding Hope crouched over his box of papers, his leather journal in her hands, a guilty expression smacked over her face.

'The journal. That's where we will learn something about him.'

Hope is being wilfully naive, shaking her head, saying, 'You're wrong about him.'

'We shall see about that.' My voice is firm, firmer than I feel.

From the window I have a clear view of him slumped beside the well, like a sack of turnips.

His room is silent. I notice a puddle under the open window where the rain must have driven in. It has soaked into the rush matting, making the place smell like a hayrick. I keep alert for the sound of footsteps. I have to stand on a chair to reach the lintel, relieved to find the key there.

Unlocking the small chest, I remove the journal swiftly, tucking it under my shift, then replace the key and the chair. I wipe a wet footprint with my hem, still listening for the sound of his heavy tread on the stairs. As I am making sure I haven't left a trace of my presence, I see the volume of essays beside the bed and, unable to curb my curiosity, I open the frontispiece to read the dedication he'd guarded so vehemently.

For my blood brother, my first and dearest love. Ever yours with fondness and loyalty, your devoted GV.

It doesn't spring to mind until I am safely back behind the locked door of the bedchamber, the coincidence that GV also stands for George Villiers. Unease crawls up my spine. Perhaps it is no coincidence.

The unease takes hold as I begin to see another version of events, thinking of Melis's insistence that something evil inhabits this place. I want desperately to return to the comfort of ignorance but, steeling myself, I open the journal.

Felton

Felton is on the ground beside the well, crushed with fatigue, eyes gritty, throat smarting and dry, as if he has swallowed a fistful of powdered glass. The fire is out and the whole place has the stench of a battlefield.

Margie stops to express her gratitude. She uses the word 'hero', too. He is glad when she heads for the sanctuary of the kitchen. He opens his good hand. The ugly serrated scar on the mound of his thumb is visible through the layer of soot. The thought of what might have happened to the boy horrifies him, renders his heart as black as his hand. It is his incompetence rather than his conscience he should be addressing. He had simply assumed, on hearing some- one moving about in the henhouse, that it was Hester. It was always Hester. Each morning, since his arrival, she has collected the eggs. Had he only made sure it was her before he jammed the door – he rebukes himself mercilessly – he would not be facing this momentous setback.

The boy might have died. He has allowed himself to grow attached to the child. He mustn't give sentimentality room to breathe, or it will open a fissure in him, make him weak. The boy is just a boy – George's boy. It is his duty to deliver him unscathed to his father.

Gifford approaches the well, his gait uneven and pain- fully slow. He picks up the empty bucket, hangs it from the hook and winds it down. The winch complains. It needs greasing. He hoists it back up and leaves the full bucket beside Felton, patting his shoulder and meeting his eye with a nod of approval.

'What you did today,' is all he says. He is a man of few words but it is his tone that galls Felton. They all talk blithely of his bravery. If only they knew.

He nods in acknowledgement of the old man and picks up the bucket, swallows a measure of cool water, then pours some over himself, sluicing his face. He sits with his thoughts. The storm is long gone, the sky bright once more, the sun beating down again, drying his wet shirt.

The mother and her boy are inside the house. He thinks of the moment he delivered the child, silent with shock, into her arms and later when she had taken his hand, meeting his secret remorse with grateful eyes. *It should have been me.* He'd looked away when she'd said it, too quickly perhaps, for fear she would see the truth on his face. She was right – it *should* have been her.

Leaden with fatigue, he drags himself up through the silent house. On entering his room he senses that something is not quite as it should be. The floor is wet but it is only because he left the window open. He inspects his chest. It is locked, appears untampered with. He dismisses his suspicions as paranoia.

The phial of opium tincture draws his attention, like the star of Bethlehem. He drinks a generous quantity and flops onto his bed, waiting for the warm, heady swirl that makes everything matter so, so much less.

Before he knows it he has plunged into a deep, exhausted sleep, marred by hellish dreams of fire and demons.

The Arrow that Flieth
in the Dark

Nor dies Revenge, although he sleep awhile;
For in unquiet, quietness is feigned,
And slumbering is a common worldly wile.

Thomas Kyd, *The Spanish Tragedy*

Hester

I read in a horrified stupor, not stopping until I have finished it – every word. This man is up to his elbows in blood. In this outpouring, I have read of his love for George, of the lives he took in George's name: my sister, whose death was no accident, Lieutenant Bloor, whose identity he stole, Hywel, the poor innocent vagrant. But the death I had not expected to read of in this cursed journal is that of dear Ambrose Cotton, our protector – the man, I think . . . oh, God, no, *thought* of as a father in the absence of my own. I have read, too, of the mission with which George has charged the lieutenant, the mission that brought him here to the Hall in the Forest.

Make it seem like an accident.

Emerging through the tangle of anguish is the crushing sense that I have somehow cheated Fate. Melis was right when she said there was a wasp in our nest. It seems so very implausible that George could truly have believed my sister and me so great a threat. Oh, but he does. This journal describes a treacherous network of hate in which I sit enthroned, dictating a duke's downfall, a spider at the heart of a great lethal web.

I cast my mind back to that fateful morning at Littlemore Manor and the maid, Joan, appearing suddenly in the door to Ambrose's study, just as I had been explaining the correspondence to him. I remember feeling mistrustful of her at the time. Ambrose had described her as 'not the brightest button in the box' but it appears she was just bright enough to find herself in the pay of my tormentor.

George can't see that those cursed letters were never more than a last resort, a means of persuasion, that all I wanted was to keep my son. He is mistaken. I see now that implausible things happen every day and destruction is often wreaked in response to a mistake – wars are waged, people die. Melis died for a mistake, as did all the others he has murdered in George's name.

Rage fills me, the weight of it greater by far than my fear. There is no reward for goodness.

I slap the journal shut. 'Where is the pistol?'

Hope looks alarmed, seems unable to move or even ask what I have read. I rummage through the linen press until my fingers meet the cool metal barrel, pull out the weapon and hold it as if to take aim. It is considerably heavier and bigger than I remember, dwarfing my hand.

I ruminate about creeping into his room and shooting him dead while he sleeps: I can imagine the bullet shattering his skull, spilling his brains. I could feed him poisonous mushrooms from the forest or stove in his head with a mallet or push him over the banister to fall into the stairwell. I think of all these things, of course I do, I am not a fool, but neither am I prepared to give myself over so entirely to damnation. I am thinking, designing, planning our survival. His death will not free me: rather, it will send me to Hell. And George will simply employ someone else in his stead.

'What does he write?' asks Hope.

'He is not who he says he is. He was sent here by George

to' – I falter, cannot say in front of my son that he sought to murder me and Melis, he *did* murder Melis – 'to kidnap –'

'Me,' says Rafe. 'To kidnap me.' He doesn't seem in the least disturbed. 'My father must want me very badly.' His tone is peculiarly matter-of-fact.

Rafe has weighed all the evidence and distilled it to just this, which is correct, I suppose – the bald, precise truth. I can't find a way to explain to him that when his father wants something it is not because he loves it but because he must possess it – all the more so if it is out of his reach. How can I tell him that, to his father, he is merely a thing, not a person, no more real than the stuffed monkey that lies discarded on a corner of the bed?

'You'd better read it for yourself.' I pass her the journal. She takes it gingerly as if it might scald her. 'And Ambrose is dead.' Saying it is agony, but I cannot allow weakness to invade me.

The whites of Hope's eyes are mapped in red and tears catch in her lower lashes. 'What will we do?' She is petrified, slick with sweat, and shaking her head as if to rattle a marble from it.

I focus on practicalities, on survival, and load the pistol, remembering each step as Gifford taught me. The firearm seems to shrink, or is it me who is growing, fed on the feeling of power it gives?

'Are you going to –' Her voice quivers.

'Don't worry,' I tell her calmly. 'Look after Rafe.'

Rafe says what Hope couldn't. 'Will you shoot him?' He looks at me and picks up the nub of wax from the window-sill, beginning to soften it between his fingers, until its previous form is gone.

I don't answer him. Taking the gun, I creep to the

lieutenant's door and peer through a knot in the wood. He is on his bed, soot-smeared, fast asleep, the phial of opium tincture still clutched in his grimy paw. It seems doubtful he would be asleep like that if he'd discovered his journal was missing. The chest appears undisturbed, as far as I can see.

I return to the bedchamber. 'We're leaving. You, me and Rafe – as soon as it's dark.' I begin stuffing things into a bag. 'We'll just take the essentials.'

'Where will we go?' whispers Rafe.

'I don't know yet. We can't stay here.' I turn to Hope. 'I need you to go down and prepare some supplies for the journey. Hide them in the barn.' Evening is already beginning to filch the light from the room. 'Find Lark. She can help you saddle the horses and keep them out of sight.' I meet her eyes. 'But hurry, there's no time to waste.'

'What if he *does* wake?'

'He won't.' I wish I felt as sure as I sound. 'He's dead to the world. And if he does, there's nothing to say. Simply act as you would normally. Tell him he's a hero for rescuing Rafe.' The horrible fact of what might have happened in the fire returns, cracking through my brittle veneer. I expel the thought and continue gathering things together for the journey. 'He won't wake,' I repeat, in an attempt to give her a measure of reassurance, and myself, too, if I am honest. Hope seems so friable, as if she might dissolve, and I need her robust. 'Now go.'

She nods firmly, taking one backward glance at me as she walks to the door. I can tell by the set of her jaw that she has found some vestige of fortitude.

I lock the door behind her, trying not to let my mind drift to the possibility of another fire, with us trapped in the room, unable to unfasten the door. I reason that he would not risk Rafe's safety again – not deliberately. After all, one of the main purposes of his mission – all this senseless loss of life – is so George can claim his boy. The boy he likely wouldn't want if he were offered freely.

'Can Captain come with us?'

I hesitate. The answer is 'No,' but I say, 'We'll see.'

Melis's deathbed prophecy returns to me, as if she is whispering in my head. I imagine that assassin's blade finding George's putrid heart and am struck, for the first time, with such grim certainty that I will never be free as long as George lives.

Hope

Hope tiptoes, heart in mouth, down the stairs. She doesn't know which is greater, her fear or her shame.

Stupid, stupid girl that I am, to be taken in yet again.

At least Worley had flattered her, brought her small gifts: a ring of pretend gold.

This one has offered her none of that.

Foolish girl. Foolish, foolish girl.

The kitchen is silent.

Gifford and Margie must be resting, shattered in the wake of the fire. She hastily bundles together some bread and cheese, fills the leather flagons with water from the butt, now replenished by the storm, and packs everything into a satchel, which she takes out to hide in the barn.

The yard is still muddy underfoot and the stink of wet embers hangs in the air.

It seems in another lifetime that they were hauling buckets back and forth but it was only this morning.

Time is being deceitful again and she longs for the paralysed clock to spark back to life. What she does know is that it is the sixteenth day of August, fourteen days since they left Orchard Cottage, ten days since they arrived here. This knowledge fails to steady her.

Glancing back at the façade of the lodge, she sees the broken balcony, its struts and planks piled near the door, the ragged scars at the top where it used to hang. The sound of Melis crashing onto the steps echoes in her skull.

No.

But her thoughts spin away to the henhouse, how it had also lost its balcony, and suddenly she is imagining flames licking up the lodge itself, as if its fate and that of the miniature are intertwined by some terrible dark force.

Hope makes herself remember Hester's words: *The only evil thing here is the man sleeping across the landing.*

Lark is in the barn, legs astride a stool, milking, the liquid thrumming rhythmically into the pail. Immediately aware of Hope's arrival, she raises her head, somehow sensing Hope's disquiet. 'Something's happened. What is it?'

'We need your help.' Hurriedly she explains, adding, 'You can't tell anyone. Not even your mother, your grandfather. We'll leave as soon as night falls.'

In quiet haste, they bring the horses in from the paddock and begin to tack them up. The animals scuff their hoofs in the dirt and shake their heads, suspecting something is awry. Lark soothes them, whispering her secret language, stroking behind their ears, and blowing on the soft place between their nostrils, which instantly calms them. Hope has never encountered anyone who has such a way with animals.

'I knew that man was a wrong one.' Lark loosely buckles the girth straps and attaches the pillion saddle to the grey. 'I told you. You wouldn't have it, though. People think that because I'm blind I'm stupid.' There is a touch of bitterness in her tone. 'People believe what they want to believe.'

When Hope thinks about it, no one believed Melis either, yet she spoke the truth. Regret twists through her. 'That was a mistake. I see now. I was wrong not to believe you.'

She hadn't looked beyond her own problems to see Lark's: she had just seen a girl of her age living a simple life, a safe life, when in truth Lark's sightlessness has trapped her here with no experience of the wider world. She can see now that Lark had offered real friendship and she had been too blinded by her misplaced affections to recognize it.

Lark's hand momentarily seeks hers and Hope feels their friendship weave anew.

Lark passes her a hoof pick and they hastily check for stones and loose shoes, the horses obediently picking up their feet to be inspected. It occurs to Hope now that all those so-called hauntings, the knife, the cat, the fallen dresser, might have been conjured by the lieutenant to unsettle them.

She wants to believe it. It is more palatable than the other explanation.

They tie the horses up, ready to go. The whole process can't have taken much more than five minutes and Hope is thinking, as she dashes back to the kitchen, how pleased Hester will be with her.

The shadows are lengthening, and the light is thinning, birds are in their early-evening fluster. It will be dark soon and they will be gone. Hope balks at the idea of the forest at night, swallowing them, its unknown menace seeming almost as terrifying as the prospect of remaining here.

The kitchen door is slightly open and there, to her horror, is the hulking shape of Felton sitting at the kitchen table, his back to her, ladling yesterday's stew into a bowl.

She stops dead, unsure what to do.

He hasn't seen her.

She notices a meat cleaver on the end of the table nearest to the door, its iron head giving her a menacing wink as a low shaft of light catches its shine. She swallows, telling herself to keep calm, but can feel the prickle of panic as she imagines him wielding it.

As she begins to sidle away Felton turns, catching her in his sights. 'Where are they all?'

She contorts her face into the semblance of a smile. 'Resting, I expect.' There is a slight quiver in her voice but he doesn't appear to notice. He is smiling too.

The cleaver shimmers. He would disarm her of it in an instant were she to try what she is thinking.

'My arm's giving me trouble again.' He is rubbing his elbow. 'It was so much better.'

'It must be all the effort.' She thinks of him earlier on the ladder hauling heavy buckets to soak the thatch, to stop the spread of the fire that *he* started. 'You must have reopened the wound.' She is astonished by her composure.

'I don't suppose you'd take a look?' He begins to roll up his sleeve and undo the bandage, seeming completely at his ease.

She takes too long to reply because he says, 'What? You gone off me? I thought you liked me a little.'

There is that smile again.

He scoops a spoonful of stew into his mouth, speaking through it. 'And the scowl you're wearing makes me think otherwise.'

'No, no. I'm sorry. It's not that.' She is blathering nervously now. 'I just can't stop thinking about the fire. It's unsettled me. What might have happened.' She remembers

Hester's instructions now. 'If it hadn't been for you . . . You saved Rafe's life.'

He shrugs off the compliment. 'I'm no hero, just trained for such things, that's all.'

He pats the bench. 'Come and sit.' She feels his good hand at her back, remembering how, only hours before, the sensation had made her feel wanted, protected, safe.

Not now.

A brew of fear and revulsion threatens. Her face is close enough to his to smell his stewy breath and the smoke in his hair. The wound is like a mouth, its lips pink, gaping slightly, and she has to muster all her inner grit to stop herself running from the room.

'It doesn't look infected, has just opened a little. There's a pot of that salve somewhere.'

She stands, glad to put herself out of his reach. 'Who left this here?' She surprises herself by the levity of her tone and picks up the cleaver. 'Filthy thing on the kitchen table, Margie won't be pleased. Better put it away.'

She takes it outside and, dragging over a stool to stand on, hangs it on the high hook above the door, out of both their reach, resisting the urge to run as far and fast as she can.

Returning the stool inside, she goes to the shelves, feeling his gaze on her back. The small jar of salve is there. She pulls several pots down, pretending to look for it, while concealing it cupped in her palm.

'Hester must have taken it upstairs. Rafe had a scorch on his hand. I'll be back.' She manages to sound coy as she slips from the room. 'Don't go anywhere.'

He grunts, continuing to eat, bread now, wiping the bowl clean with it and shoving it into his mouth.

244

Hester

Darkness falls swiftly and I am thankful for the cover it will offer us. Hope's soft tread sounds on the stairs and I unlock the bedroom door, gathering our bags ready to depart, but am instantly aware that something is amiss.

'He's awake. He's in the kitchen.' She is frayed with panic, blathering about the lieutenant's wound and something about the pot of salve, which she is holding in her open hand.

'I need you to think.' I speak firmly, feeling the urgent press of time. 'Did he behave differently towards you?' I am trying to cobble together a new plan and wondering how he managed to get downstairs without either me or Rafe hearing him pass. I suppose he is accustomed to stealth.

Hope is heaving in great gulps of quaking breath. 'I don't know. I don't think so.'

'Now, listen to me.' I grip both her shoulders, forcing her attention to what I have to say. 'As far as he's concerned, we don't know anything.' He may well have discovered his missing journal and sniffed out our plan to flee but I have to calm Hope. 'Did he have his gun with him, downstairs?'

'I – I can't remember.' Her eyes are jittering madly to and fro.

'Never mind. He must have. He always carries it with

him.' I attempt to sound light, when in truth I feel as heavy as an anvil. 'He intends no harm to *you*.' I take Hope's hands, squeezing them. 'Remember that and hold your nerve. Wait here a moment.'

I pick up the journal and steal out onto the landing, listening down the stairwell. Once I'm sure it is silent, I tiptoe into the lieutenant's room, half expecting him to be behind the door with a blade. Everything is tidy. Only the linens are rumpled and marked with grey shadows of grime where he has been sleeping.

Quick as I can, I replace the journal, then cast about, looking under the bed and behind the door. Hanging beneath his coat, I find what I'm looking for, bundle it up and return to the bedchamber.

I fling the pouch of shot and powder onto the bed. 'He might have his pistol but it'll be of little use without this.' I don't mention the probability of him having some shot and powder in his pocket. It would only frighten her more.

'Listen to me carefully.' Hope is hunched beside Rafe on the bed, her arms wrapped tightly about her torso. I hand her the salve. 'You must go back down. He'll already be wondering what's keeping you.' I find the phial of sleeping draught, last used for Melis, and hold it out to her. 'Give him a drink and tip this in, all of it. It'll knock him right out. Shame it's not enough to . . .' Hope's look says she knows what I've left unsaid. 'Then see to his arm, make an excuse and come back here.'

Hope has begun to shake uncontrollably. I imagine him downstairs, wondering why she is taking so long, afraid now that he will come in search of her. 'I'll go instead.' My words are blunt. 'Lock yourselves in. I'll be back before you know it.'

I have no choice but to leave them, so, with the phial tucked into my pocket, I shut the door, hearing Hope turn the key.

I walk into the kitchen. 'Hope tells me your arm has flared up. I'm so sorry.' He regards me with a hollow look. Is he disappointed, I wonder, to see me instead of my malleable young sister? He doesn't ask where she is. I can see the hilt of his gun, hitched to his belt as ever. Its up-tilted barrel suggests it might be loaded. He wouldn't shoot me, I reason. Not with the Giffords so close by. It would be hard to make it seem accidental. But if he is desperate?

I put the salve on the table, and bustle about, taking down a length of muslin from the shelf. Noticing Margie's kitchen knife, I slide it out of sight beneath a cloth, should I need it. 'I don't know how to thank you for saving Rafe's life.'

He is unable to hide his awkwardness but I pretend not to notice, blithely saying we should drink a toast to him and that I believe there is a flagon of French wine in the cellar.

'Would you like some? It's the very least . . .'

'I'd like that very much.' He directs a look my way, then glances towards the cellar door, which is pinned open, gaping darkly. There is an alarming intensity to his gaze, a flare of something, and I realize I have made a fatal error.

I can hear Margie's warning: *Take care on those steps.* I can feel his firm shove on my back and myself tumbling over and over in the dark, cracking my head on the stone step at the bottom. If the fall doesn't finish me off, he can easily stave my head in with the butt of his pistol. That would do it. Fear trickles cold through me.

Delaying, I tear the muslin into strips and smooth the

salve onto his wound, noticing the fingers of his right hand are smudged, not with soot but with ink.

'What about that wine, then?' he says.

Dread curdles me as I think of reading the words that turned all I believed on its head, my heart squeezing tight as a fist at the thought of Ambrose murdered, of Melis cold in the chapel, of my own death brushing so close.

As if by magic, just when I feel my resolve buckling, Lark appears at the door.

'Can I smell stew?' She puts down her churn of milk and feels for a chair, scraping it back and sitting down. 'I didn't expect anyone to be in here. Who is it? No, let me guess.' She holds up a hand, sniffing the air. 'Lavender. That can't be anyone other than Hester.' She laughs, swiping her hair from her forehead. 'Tell me I'm right.'

Hardly able to believe that Lark has arrived in my moment of need, I laugh too, my fingers touching the stem of lavender that is in my buttonhole. 'And the lieutenant is here with us. I was about to go and fetch a jug of wine from the cellar. You can keep him company.' I rise. 'Would you like some as well?'

'I wouldn't refuse.' Lark has felt out a spoon and is dipping it into the large pot on the table, scooping stew into her mouth. 'Mmm. Delicious. It's always better the next day.'

Gingerly, I descend the cellar steps and am enfolded in the musty gloom where I find the flagon, returning quick as I can. Someone has already put three cups on the table and, thinking fast, I say, 'Good wine calls for glass, wouldn't you agree?'

The cupboard where the glasses are kept is just outside the kitchen door. Everything is layered in dust, rows and rows of glass and stacks of dishes that can't have been used in years. It makes me think of the great feasts that must have been held here, rowdy hunting parties and goodness only knows what. The place seems all the more dead for that thought.

I wipe three glasses on my shift and bring them into the kitchen, filling them with wine at the sideboard so I can't be seen from the table. I surreptitiously empty the draught into one, handing it to Felton after Lark has hers, so he can't pass it on. Then I sit, placing the jug on the table, holding up my own glass to make a toast.

'To Lieutenant Bloor. Our hero!' Lark echoes me enthusiastically and I touch my glass to hers with a chink. I observe the lieutenant shifting in his seat, his features tightening as I touch his glass too.

He notices I have seen his discomfort. 'Arm's aching something awful.' He cradles it to make his point and swigs back the red liquid.

I make conversation, breaking off hunks of bread and serving out the stew. When I put a spoonful into my mouth I realize I haven't eaten all day. Thinking of the long journey to come, I force myself to continue, although fear has stolen my appetite.

When Felton's glass is empty, I refill it. He begins to slur a little, his face reddening. He asks for more, yawning loudly, slumping over the table. His tongue is stained blue from the wine.

'I think it's time for bed,' I say.

The lieutenant makes an unintelligible sound and hauls himself to his feet, gripping the chair, which skids away beneath him. He lurches, stumbling, managing to get a grip on the edge of the sideboard, clinging to it to keep himself from falling.

Lark and I each take an arm and stagger to the make-shift bed that is still in the hall. The bed we made for Melis. Half lifting, half pushing, we manage to get him onto it, where he collapses, spread-eagled.

I slide my hand to the pistol in his belt, but he grips me with his great paw, suddenly alert.

'I was only going to put it to one side for your safety.' Remarkably my voice remains steady.

'No.' He is aggressive, pushing me away, slurring, 'I'm a soldier. Sleep with my gun.'

I withdraw my hand and he rolls over with a groan, making the weapon inaccessible.

'Good night, Lieutenant.' He is struggling to keep his eyes open.

'Sweet dreams, sweet Bridget,' he mumbles, and loses consciousness. He thinks he is with his sister.

He shifts again, half rolling back, the hilt of the pistol peeping out. I wait, watching, until his breath deepens to a rumbling snore, and try once more, easing the gun away little by little from under his body, until I am able to spirit it under my shift, triumphant.

I wait a moment, watching him, thinking how easy it would be to take that sharp kitchen knife and drive it into his chest. How easy, yet how difficult – unthinkable – to take a life, unthinkable for me. How does a conscience become sufficiently eroded to make murder banal?

Hope

They creep down, past the chapel. Hester glances to Hope, her expression pained. There is no choice but to leave Melis's body behind. Even so it feels wrong.

As they reach the hall, Hope glances in revulsion at the sleeping hulk on the makeshift bed.

She follows Hester, who holds Rafe's hand as they slink past him into the kitchen and out through the back door. It is a perfect night for travelling. The air is fresh and the moon, three-quarters full, spills its cool light over Lark, who is waiting by the gate with the horses and the puppy.

'Captain's coming with us,' Rafe says, in a gleeful whisper.

Hester wavers in her answer. 'Well, sweetheart . . .'

'The puppy has to stay.' Hope is firm and can see Rafe tensing, readying for an outburst.

Hester is on tenterhooks.

Hope squats to meet her nephew in the eye. 'I know you love him. But we can't bring him. He'll slow us down.' Rafe's mouth is pinched. 'We'll come back for him when it's safe. Lark will look after him, won't you, Lark?' He drops his shoulders, unclenching his hands.

'He can sleep in the barn with me.'

The child mumbles his consent with a shrug, and Hester looks relieved as she helps him up onto the grey.

The gate is shut with its big wooden strut firmly wedged

into place. Hope and Lark force it up, heaving together. A loud thump echoes through the night as it bursts from its slot and they all instinctively turn towards the lodge, expecting the lieutenant to burst from the door.

The house is cast pewter at night, its windows iridescent pools of quicksilver, a place in which sharp objects have a life of their own, where things scuffle behind the walls and cats become ensnared in traps. She thinks she can make out a face at the chapel window, a flit of light. Part of her refuses to believe Melis is gone.

They slip into the dark mouth of the forest where the moonlight struggles to filter through the thick vegetation. They can't see more than a yard in front, but Hope is just able to make out the pistol in Hester's hand. She has the lieutenant's firearm tucked into her own belt and doesn't know if it makes her feel safer or not, but focuses on the fact that in a few hours they will be in Ludlow at the Feathers, with its smell of fresh beeswax polish, its starched linens and nosegays hanging from the bedposts.

They move in silence.

The forest is alive with sound: a vixen shrieks; an owl wails and another, more distant, replies; something barks an alarm; a crashing and breaking of twigs comes from the undergrowth nearby.

Shapes appear, faces in the trunks of the trees, hooded figures, long arms. She counts in her mind to a hundred and then back to one, over and over again, as they move on slowly.

The path widens, moonlight shivering over it, and they have a view of the star-encrusted sky at last and space to push the horses into a canter. The thunder of their hoofs obliterates the forest noises.

Finally, they arrive at a clearing where the route forks.

'Which way?' Her whisper is loud.

Hester is scrutinizing the piece of paper on which she made a note of points on the journey from Ludlow. She can't read it. There is not enough light.

Hope feels her spirits leaking away but Hester points up at the sky.

'That's the Little Bear, and we need to go east, so it's this way.' She sets off down the wider of the two paths.

Hope is reassured by Hester's confidence, that she knows the stars. Were she alone she would be impossibly lost by now.

The fear of the lieutenant behind them has now become the fear of what may lie ahead. Two women and a child riding alone in the dark could easily fall prey to brigands.

The shadowy figures in the trees hold knives in their knotted fists, hunched, ready to pounce.

She takes a deep breath and returns to her counting, pushing away the dark thoughts, listening only to the steady drum of the horses.

Rafe begins to hum a tune faintly in the quiet, a song she has often sung him to help him sleep. She joins in with him and it dulls her nerves a little.

The path narrows once more, the trees becoming thicker, enclosing them, forcing them to slow down again.

A damp slap drags across her face.

She flails her arms to swipe it away, discovering it is nothing more than a trailing frond. Hester reaches out a hand to reassure her and they continue, pushing far into the arms of the forest, moving slowly until dawn creeps up on them, its glow casting the branches black, sharp shapes of leaves, in contrast with the paling sky.

Hope knows that dawn comes at about six in mid-August. It seems impossible that only fifteen days have passed since they left Orchard Cottage: a dozen lifetimes of events have been packed into that short period, none good.

'Not much further and we'll be out in the open country. Ludlow is only a few leagues on. A couple of hours at most.' Hester's unshakeable confidence is infectious, and Hope gives vent to a trickle of optimism.

They stop to rest the horses, allowing them to graze on the tufts of grass that line the path. A cock crows, sure indication that human habitation is close by and Hope's confidence grows. She unpacks the victuals, handing them round, and they sit on the ground to eat. Rafe is wan with exhaustion, leaning against his mother, eyelids leaden, barely able to stay awake.

She walks a little way into the trees to answer the call of nature. Looking up towards a branch above, where at least a dozen crows are squabbling loudly, she trips on a root and falls, jarring her knee, wincing as the pain shoots up her leg.

Sitting on the ground a moment to brush the earth off her clothes, she wonders why a length of new-looking twine is tied to a nearby branch. Something else catches her eye, poking out from the undergrowth.

She moves a little closer and sees, to her horror, what looks to be the remains of a human hand, half eaten away, seeming to spring up from the earth, as if planted there.

You're imagining things, she tells herself firmly, looking back at it, expecting to see nothing more than a growth of fungi, or a strange-shaped leaf.

It *is* a hand. Nails bruised. Skin grey.

She retches.

A crow swoops down to peck at it.

She tries to scream but, as in a nightmare, cannot generate any sound.

She runs, pushing her way through the morass, all the way back to where Hester is on her feet.

'What is it?'

Hope wants to explain but still can't find her voice, stuttering out a series of unintelligible sounds.

Rafe is tugging at his mother's skirt. 'Look, Mother.'

'Not now.' She is tired, her patience thin, but he persists and Hope still cannot find any words. 'Not now!'

'LOOK!' He shouts this time, forcing both women's attention.

They turn in the direction he is pointing to see the unmistakable hexagonal shape of the dovecot that sits on the roof of the lodge they left several hours before. Scanning lower she sees, between the trees, a hundred yards away, so clear it seems impossible that none of them had seen it before, the perimeter fence and the gate.

Hester blanches, white as a devil's dog.

Hope's stomach turns as if a snake is uncoiling inside her.

They hear the unmistakable high-pitched yelp of Captain.

'Cap–'

Hester claps her hand over Rafe's mouth to silence him and hauls him back towards the horses.

Hope removes the pistol from her belt, setting it to full cock with an ominous click.

Gifford's voice is in her head: *You have to grasp it as if you mean it. Imagine it is a fowl for the pot and you must break its neck.*

Felton

Felton squints. Light stabs at his eyes. As he moves his head a throb beats in his temples, drilling sharp pain into his skull.

Confused, he is unsure where he is, how long he has slept and has the instinct, a heaviness in the pit of his stomach, that he has missed something vital.

He rises, his head pounding so hard he has to sit cradling it in his hands until the agony subsides. His hair flops forward, stinking of smoke. Slowly his thoughts begin to line up and he eventually realizes where he is but has no idea how he came to be sleeping in the hall. He can't remember the previous evening, nothing at all, as if hours of his life have been stolen. He just remembers the fire and the terrible howls of the boy trapped, George's boy, and everyone deeming him a hero.

The light is streaming in through the east-facing window, so it must be morning, though he could have slept for a week for all he knows. He listens. A thick cloak of silence hangs over the place.

The house is too quiet.

His ears tune to the distant sounds outside – birdsong: the busy twitter of finches and the cockerel trumpeting out his crude tune. He can hear a distant whining and scrabbling, as if an animal has got itself shut in somewhere and is scratching pitifully at a door. A bolt shoots out there, and he hears Lark's voice, laughing: 'Get down, you daft beast.' It is the puppy, greeting her now, with a volley of frantic yelps.

Gifford's unmistakable gait limps across the yard and he shouts to his granddaughter, 'The horses are gone. Someone's stolen the horses.'

Felton springs up, wincing at the pain in his skull, in his arm. He feels for his pistol. It is not there. Rummaging in the bed, he is unable to find it. He throws open the front door. Gifford is standing forlorn at the main gate, his old musket slung over his shoulder. 'It wasn't properly latched. The horses have been stolen in the night.'

'Where are the women? The boy?'

'Upstairs, I reckon.'

Felton knows in his bones that they have gone. His first thought is that he has been exposed but, if so, why isn't Gifford pointing the gun at him? Trying to make sense of it, he thinks back but it is as if someone has filleted his memory.

The puppy runs up to him, jumping excitedly. He kicks it away. It makes a loud yelp, cowering. Felton, saturated in his own ineptitude, attempts to rearrange his muddled thoughts into a plan of action. They could have been gone hours. God knows where they will have got to. He struggles to make sense of it, failure pinching at him. His future obliterated.

'Give me that.' He indicates the musket, which Gifford removes and hands over. 'Go upstairs. Make sure the women are safe,' he says, knowing in his gut it is futile. The puppy is at the gate, now, scratching and whining. It has picked up a scent.

He shoves the gate with his shoulder. The puppy scampers out ahead of him. The track is empty but the animal has its nose low to the ground. The dog-lock is stiff on the old musket but it clunks into place.

He follows, keeping close to the cover of the trees.

Captain stops where hoof prints are clearly visible, heading away from the house. The puppy lifts its head, sniffing the air, and continues round a bend in the track.

With a frisson of excitement, he spots the unmistakable black and white markings of the pony among the bushes lining the path.

'I've got you,' he whispers. His blood is up. Fate has offered him one more chance to see this mission through. The puppy gallops now and Felton can hear the boy's delight on seeing his pet.

In his mind's eye he sees Hester splayed on the ground, blood pooling across her breast. A terrible accident. Mistaken for a horse thief.

Is it too implausible, he wonders, to imagine Hope reassuring him? *A terrible accident – how could you have known?* She has proven her credulity already, so it seems possible he could dupe her once more. There is a flaw in this plan, but he can't quite put his finger on it in the tangle of his mind.

He can hear footfall behind him.

Someone has followed him out.

Glancing back, he is relieved to see it is only the blind girl.

'Stop,' he hisses, continuing on, keeping an eye behind. 'There's danger ahead.'

She doesn't stop, is moving towards him, faster now she has heard where he is.

He picks up his pace, musket aimed forward, rounding the bend to be confronted by the black eye of another gun, his gun, in the outstretched hand of – not the mother but Hope, her features sharp with hate.

The mother stands behind, with the two horses. He can't see the boy.

They hover in stasis for what seems like aeons but is only a fraction of a moment. He is aware of Lark moving to the side, his mind whirring on whether the daft girl in front of him has the courage to pull the trigger. He cannot quite see if her arm is trembling. The barrel looks steady, perhaps steadier even than his, and he remembers, his throat constricting, Gifford talking about what a gifted shot she was. 'A natural', he'd called her.

There is something about the determined set of her mouth that tells him not to underestimate her. He assesses whether he can get a sightline on the mother, but she is obscured by the horses. His scheme crumbles.

He hears Hester say, 'Go!' and from the edge of his vision he sees the boy speeding towards Lark, who leads him away out of danger.

Felton shifts slightly.

A crack explodes.

Her shot flies towards him.

He fires simultaneously, his trigger finger squeezing before he has instructed it to – a soldier's reflex – the ancient musket booming and recoiling violently against his shoulder.

Her bullet thuds into a tree behind him, splintering through the wood.

He watches her fall back, crashing into the long grass with a violent expulsion of breath, half cry, half howl.

Hester

Hope lies motionless on the ground.

All falls to a deathly hush. Even the birds are shocked.

The lieutenant is the first to move, groping in his pocket, patting himself down, apparently unable to find what he seeks.

Rafe, in Lark's arms, begins to bellow as the piebald staggers, dropping to its knees with a groan, then falling heavily onto one side, a red flower blossoming on its flank.

I become aware that Hope is moving. She is reaching for the ammunition pouch. It takes me a moment to understand that Hope has not been hit: the weapon's kick had thrown her off her feet.

The lieutenant leaps forward, eyes white with rage.

I lunge, brandishing my own weapon, lifting it, looking straight along its barrel, as I was taught.

The lieutenant stops in his tracks.

I tell Hope to get to safety, realizing what the lieutenant understood moments before, that he has used his only shot.

Fear moves over his features, his gullet shifting up and down, the useless musket wobbling in his grip. He must be pondering whether I have the mettle to kill him. Does he not know that a mother will do anything to protect her child?

I draw Margie's kitchen knife out from inside my jacket, holding it in my free hand. In this moment, grazing so close to danger, close enough to smell the chaff on Death's robe, I understand that I fear nothing, not even my own obliteration.

'Drop your weapon!' My command is firm.

He obeys instantly, tossing the gun into the grass between us. I can hear Hope comforting Rafe. I resist even a glance at my child and remain absolutely focused on the disarmed man before me. The man who was sent to kill me and steal my son.

'On your knees! Hands on your head!'

He drops down instantly, brings his hands up, the injured one only able to reach his ear, the pain of the movement visible on his face.

'Now right down, on your front.'

He does as I say without question. His face is in the dirt. I keep the pistol ready. 'If you move even so much as a muscle . . .' I plant my foot on his back.

I tell Hope to take Rafe inside with Lark. My voice is steady, my mind clear. 'Find Gifford. He'll have to finish the pony off.' I can hear the poor beast wheezing heavily behind me; the bullet must have punctured a lung. 'Tell him he must take the grey, ride to town and get help – someone he trusts. Give him what he needs from my purse, then go upstairs to the bedroom. Lock yourself in there with Rafe. Lark, you stay in the kitchen with your mother.'

Hope protests. 'I can't leave you alone with –'

'Just do as I say.' I have no doubt that I will survive, not even a splinter.

I walk slowly round the prone soldier, lifting his shirt

with the tip of the knife. He doesn't appear to be carrying a blade of his own and I only notice now that he isn't wearing his boots. He must have heard the commotion and rushed out without thinking. His feet are filthy, hard black pads on the underside, like a dog's.

'You must have thought me such a fool. I've been so kind to you. But who is the fool now?'

He doesn't respond. I order him to get up. 'Slowly, no sudden movements.' He rises, spitting the dust and grass from his mouth. His eyes are ringed so dark they seem bruised and their whites are tinged yellow. The effect of the sleeping draught.

'Turn around.' He cringes visibly, bracing himself for a shot in the back of his head – the ultimate humiliation for a soldier. It is tempting but, if I am honest, for all my new-found courage I don't believe I have it in me to do such a thing. I can see, only too clearly, the consequences. George would see me hanged for murder and Rafe would be his. I cannot let that happen.

I clutch his shirt collar at the nape, tugging it tightly until he emits a guttural coughing, and press the barrel of the gun between his shoulder blades.

'Dr Cotton was like a father to me. Perhaps you didn't know that.' A stink rises off him, of sweat and ash and something else, something rotten, fear, I hope.

His neck is thick and muscular. I know he could crush me easily with his one good arm. But I have the loaded gun. Power is a physical sensation, I discover: an intense, swelling euphoria teamed with absolute clarity of thought. I know exactly what I will do.

I am aware that this must be how it feels to be a man, as I march him, obedient as a broken horse, back across the yard, into the house. We mount the stairs to the blue room, where I order him to remove the fire back-plate. He crouches to do so. His whole body is quaking now, the fabric of his shirt blistering against his back where it is stuck to the sweat.

The panel scrapes back, revealing the black hole behind. He glances back at me, to see if I mean it. My rigid demeanour tells him there is no choice but to submit to my will. How humiliating it must be for a man like him to yield to a woman.

'Get inside!' I give him a firm shove with my foot. He crouches, crawling meekly into the priest-hole. I heave the back-plate into place. I know perfectly well that once the hearth is lit and the iron plate too hot to touch, there will be no escape for him.

I hurry to build the fire, making a pyramid of logs and filling its heart with kindling. Taking the tinderbox, I tease sparks from the flint, causing the soft fibres in the box to smoke. I blow gently until it glows, then tip the nascent flames into the dry sticks. They flare up fast. I watch, entranced, as ribbons of flame crack and scintillate, jabbering upward into the flue.

Now the immediate danger has passed, I lean against the wall closing my eyes, feeling spent, fancying I can hear the humming Melis used to say was the house whispering. I can feel her in the air. I miss her horribly, as if part of me has been ripped away, leaving raw exposed flesh.

A shot is fired outside. I look out, expecting to see Gifford having dealt with the poor piebald, but it is Margie I see stalking back through the gate with the old musket in her hand. I start to think through our next steps. Gifford will be able to lead us through the maze of forest that had us bewitched into circles last night. Plans clog my head. Margie and Lark can keep the fire going until I've worked out what to do with the prisoner. I am reassured by the thought of the woman shooting the pony without apparent qualm. She seems capable enough of looking after herself.

But I can't see Gifford in the yard, or the grey.

I throw another log onto the fire and run downstairs, finding Margie and Lark in the kitchen. 'Where's Gifford?'

'He's gone already. To Ludlow, for help, like you said.' Margie folds her arms across her chest.

'When? When did he leave?' Tension begins to coil round me.

'He left immediately. Been gone a good twenty minutes or so.'

I am re-forming the plans in my head.

'Prepare to leave,' I say. 'We can take the mule and the cart?'

'Is he in the priest-hole?'

I nod. 'We have no time to lose.'

'We'd be safer here.' Margie has folded her arms firmly and I prepare for a battle of wills.

'I must insist.' I give no room for a refusal, yet the recalcitrant woman is shaking her head.

'My father will be back before nightfall with help.'

'There's no time to wait for him.'

'We'd be better off on foot,' says Lark. 'The mule's on her last legs.'

'But with the child . . .' Margie is increasingly fixed. 'The lieutenant will be out of his hole and on our tails in no time. A strapping man like that. Catch us up easily.'

I can see I haven't considered properly all the possible

eventualities of a trek on foot through the forest with an eight-year-old boy and only a half-dead mule for transport.

'What is your opinion, Lark?' My heart is sinking.

'She's right. We're safer waiting here. At least we will know if someone's approaching and can be sure of exactly where the lieutenant is.'

I resign myself to a wait, slumping onto the bench, despair pinching at me.

'He'll be back by nightfall, I'm sure of it.' Margie tries to sound bright. 'We can take it in turns to look out and the yard-dog will warn us of anyone approaching.'

She makes it all sound so straightforward but I am teeming with qualms, particularly about the fate of my prisoner. Under normal circumstances he should be brought before a magistrate. But forcing that eventuality would risk our exposure.

I fill a basket with firewood and carry it back upstairs. I look in on Hope and Rafe in the bedroom and tell them we will leave as soon as Gifford returns. We have all day to prepare for our departure. All day for me to devise a plan for the man in the priest-hole.

I return to the blue room, feeling, only now, the exhaustion from the previous night's futile trek. Fatigue has seeped deep into my bones but it is not physical tiredness alone. I am tired of running, of hiding, of the subterfuge, the relentless fear. Even if we do get safely to Ludlow we still won't be free.

Desperate thoughts run through my mind. I can see the great web of George's influence, remembering, vividly then, like a hallucination, the man, Worley, in my house with my son in his grasp.

Resistance has made me brittle, pieces of me breaking away until I no longer recognize myself. This is no life – no life for my son. But I have no idea how to escape, understanding, with a crushing sense of despair, that I remain as much a captive as my prisoner.

Feeding the flames and counting the minutes until Gifford's return, I feel the final vestiges of my tenacity disperse. Had I the capacity for true cruelty I would let the lieutenant starve in there. But even had I such, I remind myself that this man's death would merely remove the immediate threat. The true threat is out there, beyond my reach.

What is it they say about the devil – that he wears the finest clothes?

I jump, startled, as a crash shudders through the house, and a *whoof* of air makes the flames in the hearth gutter.

Hope

Hope scrambles from the bed, dragging her nephew with her.

The room is filled with a thick cloud of white dust, and rubble cascades from a vast hole where the ceiling has collapsed.

They fall out of the door into Hester's arms, just as another large section of ceiling cracks and plummets, fragmenting, sending out a new billow of dust.

Cowering in the doorway, they wait in silence for the cloud to settle. Shock is making Hope shake uncontrollably. The old bowed ceiling was already cracked, she reminds herself. But she begins to become aware of something, a dense shadow moving about the room, making shapes, mutating in and out of different forms, now a bird, now a wolf, now a horse, now a cat.

'What is it?' Dread roots her, her body becoming dense, legs leaden.

She can't find her voice.

She wants to speak, to say the man's a demon, that he has brought the devil here, invited him in. She is thinking now of how they were drawn in circles in the forest, as if something was pulling them back to the house against their will, and then, half gagging on the memory, her mind running off. 'He is raising the dead. I saw it, coming up from the earth, a human hand.'

She attempts to slam the door, to imprison that infernal ever-moving thing, whatever it is. But Hester is holding on fast, white knuckles tightly gripped around the handle, watching, entranced, eyes like plates following the demonic shape as it flits about the room.

With a sickening twist at her core, Hope understands: the lieutenant has bewitched her sister. She glances down towards Rafe, who is sitting on the floor on the landing coated with white dust, knees tucked up, hands over his ears, eyes tightly shut, while the unholy shadow continues to fly round the room, shape-shifting interminably.

Alarmingly, Hester begins to laugh as she follows the thing with her eyes. 'Melis,' she is saying, between gasps, 'Oh, Melis!'

Hope's head spins, her body feeling detached, as if it belongs to someone else. She wants to shake some sense into Hester, drag her away, tell her Melis is dead, force her to see that they must escape before the house bewitches them all.

But Hester is possessed already.

'Look.' She is pointing, entranced, eyes wild, following the circulating shape, still laughing. 'It's Melis, forcing me to listen to her.'

'Come away. Shut the door, I beg you.' Hope tries to prise Hester's fingers from the latch but her sister has been invested with a monster's strength and will not be moved.

'No. No. Can't you see?' She bends for a scrap of paper on the floor, reading something from it – a rhyme, a spell.

Hester

I take in the scene – the collapsed ceiling, the air dense with white dust, and the shadow droning as it travels about the room, its shape forming, un-forming, re-forming, now sinuous, now dense, in a state of constant alteration. Hope is in a frenzy, trying to pull me away, saying we must escape.

I shake her off.

A light touch brushes over my cheek, vague as a current of cool air. Melis? If she had wanted my attention, she has it now. It is as if she drove her will into the very fabric of the building and burst forth from it to make me listen.

I still have the fragment of paper in my hand. It is covered with a spider scrawl of words. I don't need to read them. I wrote them myself, to remember Melis's parting words. *The bees know it – honey and sting. Sweetness and sharpness. That is what you need. You must make it happen.*

The dust settles slowly in the room, air clearing, everything frosted in white. As I step inside sound fills my head, the hum of the house amplified a thousand-fold, obliterating all other sounds, a dirge for her.

In the corner, where the rubble of plaster is deepest, amber tears ooze down the wall, forming a glossy pool on the floor. The house weeps for her too. A beam of sun strikes the liquid, casting it gold. I crouch, dipping the tip of my finger into it. It clings to my skin, oozing as I lift my hand to my lips, viscous threads dangling in thin air. Golden tears for Melis.

'No!' Hope is shrill with fear. 'Don't!'

It rings around my mouth, taste-buds pinging with sweetness. I am tempted to get on my hands and knees, lick it from the floor, every last sticky golden drop.

Among the broken splinters of wood and great slabs of plaster I can see the great form, rent in two, splayed open to reveal the mystery of its inner workings, its exquisite geometrical chambers. It is miraculous in its perfection.

I hear Melis whisper, *It is nearly time*, and I know I must find a way to make it happen. My conscience is vanishing.

Hope is frozen in the doorway, horror etched over her features. Her mouth opens but she is unable to speak, her gaze following the ever-changing shape.

I unlatch the window, pushing it wide. The shape slips out, leaving only the echo of silence.

'Bees,' I say. 'A beehive in the attic. The weight of it's made the ceiling cave in.' I can see now how the fall of the balcony has weakened the fabric of the house, set in motion a series of collapses. I point to the sticky pool. 'Honey.'

Hope is still cowering on the landing, bewilderment breaking over her features. Understanding dawns slowly until she coughs out a small laugh of relief. 'A swarm. I thought – I thought –' She expels a new spate of laughter. 'I thought he'd bewitched you, the lieutenant. You were behaving so strangely. The paper. I thought you were making a spell.'

'Oh, Hope! It's not a spell. I wrote down what Melis said to me on her deathbed and left the paper beside the bed. She saw George's death.'

Hope gives me a sideways look and, if anything, appears more confused than before. 'How was it she could see the future?'

'Time doesn't necessarily behave as we expect.' I notice her crumple, as if I have said something truly awful when I meant to comfort her. Some things resist explanation.

I glance at the paper, still between my fingers, trying to comprehend what Melis wanted by telling me my kindness is my failing. I have scrawled a date there: the twenty-third day of August.

'What day is it today?' I ask.

She is counting on her fingers. 'It is the seventeenth day of August. Why?'

Less than a week until the date on which Melis envisaged George's death. What do you want me to do? I ask my dead sister silently.

Hope is harbouring a glut of questions but I have no answers for her and send her and Rafe downstairs to Margie, while I return to tend the fire in the blue room.

Melis's whisper is in the flames. *It's nearly time. You must make it happen.* George has a world of enemies. Surely someone will do the deed, some discreet assassin, some disaffected soldier, a political act. Melis's seed has been planted in me. I have never truly wished someone dead, but now I do: I wish George dead.

To have admitted it, even unspoken in my mind, feels like a dangerous transgression, a chip off my soul. But it is not enough to wish it: someone must act on it. My whole life I have wanted to be good but now Melis's words clarify, like butter, and I begin to sense the power of my sting.

Felton

The fire cracks and spits in the coffin-sized space, consuming him in its blistering jaws. The iron plate, the thickness of a thumb, is the only barrier between him and the flames. He burns his wrist brushing against it, shrinking back as far as he can, the smell of singed hair invading his nostrils. Dark presses tight around him. There is no room to move. His body begins to seize up, his joints complaining, the fizz of pins and needles running up and down his legs. The agonizing throb has returned to his arm.

He has a new grudging respect for Hester: she, too, has been entombed in this place more than once, and without apparent complaint. The boy also. He is his father's son, after all. Felton had dismissed the woman, so diminutive, believed her to be weak, but the fortitude and ingenuity that led her to confine him in this hole has made him see he misunderstood her. She is a formidable adversary.

She held that gun to his back without a tremor. He wonders, with growing dread, whether her ruthlessness will stretch to leaving him to starve to death. How long would it take? A week – ten days? He hasn't even the means to end his own life, has no idea, even, of the passing of time. Perhaps he *is* dead and this is Hell.

He clings to a small residue of hope that Worley, awaiting word from him at Ludlow, will take it upon himself to set out for the lodge. But why would he? A desperate sense of futility assails him in the dark and he longs for his opium tincture to quell it. He thinks of George and the dead sister's prophecy. He might have been able to warn George, at least, but he can do nothing now, not even save himself.

Delirium begins to claim his mind, people from the past, shadows drifting in the dark. George floats by, jewels glinting. He is dazzled, as he was on their first meeting, his heart erupting. There had been other men since, strings of meaningless encounters, but George had always been the only one. He can feel the sting of his jealousy, ugly and mean-spirited. You cannot claim a man like George. He has to be shared with the world. He never minded the women but the men – he loathed George's male lovers. He cleaves to the knowledge that he was the first. He had claimed the unknown territory, set his banner there. Felton whispers to him, warning him he has failed in his mission, 'I love you still,' but George dissolves into the air.

The past taunts. The beating that killed the boy in that grubby back alley . . . Young, so young, too young to lose his life. He squats in the corner, face caved in, flesh rotting and green. He counts all those he has killed, unable to calculate the number, most in battle. They are all in here, crowding the space. Here is Dr Cotton, laughing at his failure, blood spewing from his mouth, Lieutenant Bloor, innards spilling, and Melis, bones poking through parchment skin. 'We will never leave you,' they chant over and over again. And here is Hywel now, a hole blown through his guts, joining in the chorus.

Bridget arrives, blinding him with her brightness, hovering on a pair of swan's wings. 'See what you have done,' she whispers. 'Sinner. Sinner. Sinner. This will give you a taste of Hell . . .' Her words are swallowed by the crackle of the flames. All those dead and yet the woman, the mother, who would see George brought to his knees, refuses to die, like some devilish cat with nine lives.

Hester

The lieutenant's room is gloomy but cool, with its shuttered window. The bed is unmade, the linens still streaked with ash from yesterday's fire, exactly as they were when I last came in here.

I flick through the pages of his books, search the pockets of his coat and look under his mattress, not knowing yet what I am seeking. My mind thrashes around for an idea, and I hope I might find something in this room to give me power over my prisoner.

Searching the contents of his chest, I pull out the journal, then a mess of bills and letters, inspecting each in turn. From what I can gather, he is deep in debt, but I suppose George intended to pay him well. At the bottom of the box I find a packet addressed to a Lieutenant Felton. This must be his true name. It is secured by several unbroken seals, one depicting a set of scales, suggesting the contents must be legal documents.

I rip it open. Inside is a sheaf of papers. *The Last Will and Testament of Elanor Felton, née Wright.* Scanning the first page, with references to a son being her sole surviving relative, I assume it is his mother's. It is dated only a few weeks ago, and I wonder why it was unopened, but as I take in the paltry list of effects it becomes clear. He must have been aware that his mother had nothing to leave him.

Flicking through the pages, something falls out from between them. It is a letter, yellowed and pocked with age. *For my own dear brother* is written in faded ink on the front and scrawled above, in another, more recent, hand, is: *Found among Mistress Felton's effects.* It, too, is unopened. I carefully pick away the seal. The paper is brittle, coming almost apart at the crease when I unfold it.

When you read this, beloved brother, I will be gone to another place. Whether it will be a better place I do not know. But this earthly life has become a world of unbearable pain and shame, so better to risk eternal damnation in the taking of my own life. It is possible I will be shriven for my sin. Our Father is a forgiving God. I must grasp that thought, even as I fade away.

But mine is not the only life I take. It is my unborn child's also. Damning proof of my first, and lesser, sin of fornication. Though the truth is I was given no choice in the participation of that act. I beg of you, beloved brother, to ensure, should they discover my condition after my death, that my yet unformed child's father shall never know I murdered his flesh. I tried to tell him of my state, but my letters were all returned unopened. I held on to the hope he would return and make me an honest woman even as I felt his infant grow in my belly, but my hope has slipped away, now, to despair.

I know George is beloved of you and you of him, and that in telling you this you will not only have lost a sister but also a friend. But George is not, was never, friend to anyone but himself. As I sense my breath shortening, I hold the hope, wish, dream that you will make him pay for his ruin of me, your only and most loving sister. I cannot demand you take revenge. What a black word that is. No, no, sorry, it is my anguish giving vent. Do not listen. You must do as you see fit but I wish that he would know what he has done to me.

My love for you is infinite, dearest brother, and I pray, God willing, we will meet again in the world to come. I cannot bring myself to consider that I go to eternal damnation. I beg, humbly, miserably, your forgiveness for depriving you of your sister, Bridget. Pray for me, brother, with all your heart.

The thought of Bridget and her letter, unread for so long, rends me apart with sadness. This girl, speaking from beyond the grave, is another me, her unborn child another Rafe. I am thrown back to the time when I discovered I was carrying George's child, the crushing shame, the humiliation, the knowledge that my virtue was lost for ever, and he, the real sinner, remained untarnished, his dignity, position, everything, intact.

'How am I even to know if the child is mine?' he had said and, with that, marked me a whore. Like Bridget, I was so green, so unwise, and neither did I have any choice. I had the means, my father's house, to take myself away and lead a quiet life with my sisters and my son, the life George has now stolen from us.

On learning of Bridget's tragic fate, I acknowledge my own strength. I think of all the young women, down the years, barely out of girlhood, who have fallen victim to the whims of glittering disingenuous men, only to be cast aside. Hope is one too.

Together we are an army. *Revenge. What a black word that is.* Rage rises in me like bile, sharpening my sting. In my mind's eye it is I who thrusts the blade into George's breast, can see the horror on his face, can smell his fear. I am both appalled and thrilled. Was that what my sister envisaged when she used her final breath to exhale the word 'justice'? But in doing it I sacrifice myself, my life, my soul, and leave my son an orphan, history repeating differently down the years.

This will turn him. I look round, half expecting to see Melis behind me, but the room is empty.

I recall the lieutenant, not long after his arrival here, talking about Bridget and how she died of an ague. It dawns on me then, the fickleness of chance. Had the lieutenant opened his mother's will and discovered the letter between its pages, had he known the truth of his sister's fate, he would not be here now, following George's orders. Nothing would have changed my fate, though. George would have sent a different killer to my door.

Unless – an idea emerges, half formed, scoring its way through the weft of my mind – the lieutenant had already taken his revenge on the man who as good as murdered his sister.

The full realization of the power of this letter settles into me as a tentative plan begins to form.

Hope

Hope wheels the cart, with Lark, to the kitchen door so they can pack it, ready to leave as soon as Gifford returns. Her thoughts circulate like the swarm of bees. It is easy to see how the mundane can take on a disturbing significance when nerves are shredded as hers have been.

It will be a great relief to get away from this blighted house and the monster hidden in the priest-hole.

'What do you think will happen to him?' she asks Lark. She doesn't know what to call him. He is not Lieutenant Bloor – that is all she knows.

Hester has been tight-lipped about any plans she may have. She had barely spoken, save to ask Hope to oversee the loading of the cart in preparation for their departure. She has been shut in the blue room keeping the fire going and reading ceaselessly – papers, letters, that man's journal. Hope can't understand why she wants to go over and over it. She will not explain. They have all become so choked with secrets.

They have started to load, when Lark turns to her. 'I'll miss you, Hope.'

'Aren't you to come with us?'

Lark shrugs. 'I don't know.'

'You can't be left here with . . .' There is no need to name him. They fall to silence and Hope is left to consider that, whatever happens, she will eventually end up else-where and Lark here. It is her home, after all. Hope isn't sure about anything, except that now she has found a true friend it will be a wrench to leave her. Lark seems so woven into the fabric of this place it is hard to imagine her any-where else.

'Is that everything?' says Lark.

It is not. Neither of them wants to mention Melis's body.

It is Margie who eventually calls them in and leads the way to the chapel. She stops outside and mutters a prayer, then hands them each a napkin, which they tie over their noses and mouths. Even so the stench of putrefaction is strong enough to make Hope retch the instant the door is opened.

Flies throng about her sister's remains.

Only her face and hands are visible.

'It's not her. She's gone to a better place,' Lark says quietly, taking Hope's hand tightly. Hope lets it rest there, only breaking from Lark's grip when Margie asks her to fetch some of the old dust sheets from the unused rooms.

Margie and Lark, moving efficiently, swaddle the body, tight as a baby, in several layers. Hope expects her to be feather-light, like the cast-off skin of a snake, but it takes all their strength to lift her, get her down the stairs and onto the cart.

More flies collect once they are outside and Hope can't help but think that they have laid their eggs in her and that the eggs will hatch to maggots, which will eat away at her until she is reduced to mulch.

Tears prick at her eyes. She wipes them away. The sweet, rancid stench of putrefaction lingers on her fingers and she rubs her palms vigorously on her clothes but has the sense she will never be rid of the smell. She is suddenly rigid with the sense of her own mortality and wants to scream, make a pact with the devil to keep herself alive for ever.

It is as if the veil in her mind that protects her from the truth has been drawn back, exposing her to the horror of the finite nature of everything.

She can see in her mind's eye all the edifices that mortals think permanent crumbling away, vegetation engulfing them, armies of insects breaking them down until nothing is left but a scar in the earth where they once stood. This house has already begun its descent. Soon it will be nothing, just the ghost of a house.

In a desperate impulse to cleave to the living, she grabs Lark, who, seeming to understand instinctively, draws her into a tight embrace. They stand like that, rocking back and forth. Lark smells of hay and her body, strong, alive, tight against her, makes her feel suddenly, strangely, inappropriately, aroused.

They wait and wait for Gifford's return. Night falls and he still doesn't appear, making them all restless with wondering where he has got to. Hope and Lark tend the fire to give Hester a chance to rest. No one mentions the man in the priest-hole. The two girls sit, wrapped up together, bathed in firelight, whispering and sharing secrets.

'To think I believed you were jealous.' Hope nods towards the fire. Lark knows exactly what she means. 'What a fool I was.' She puffs out a small laugh.

'I *was* jealous.' Lark pauses, running a hand down the curve of Hope's cheek. 'Just not in the way you believed. Not because I wanted *him*. But you.'

Hope doesn't know how to reply. Her silence makes the air seethe with awkwardness. She stands to throw a log on the fire. Pale early light has begun to flood into the room, casting a silvery glow over Lark, making her seem other-worldly, like some forest sprite.

'Someone's approaching,' says Lark, just as the yard-dog begins to bark, and then comes the definite sound of hoofs becoming louder

Hope tenses, ready to alert Hester and Rafe.

'It's my grandfather,' Lark says. 'No need to worry.'

'How do you know?'

Lark smiles. 'It's the dog. That bark is a greeting, not a warning.'

It seems to Hope extraordinary, a supernatural ability, rather than the effects of Lark's blindness, that makes her hearing so acute.

They rush down to open the gate. Gifford trots in, lead-ing two solid horses. He is followed by two strangers, rugged men mounted on a pair of huge bay geldings. Each carries a musket. Margie seems to know them, running over with a greeting, introducing them as the Carter brothers, saying she's known Will and Jem since they were infants. Lark leads the animals to the trough and loosens their bridles.

Gifford hands Hope a letter. 'For the mistress,' he says. She inspects the back but there is nothing to indicate who it is from.

Hester

The sight of the cart below, bearing the swaddled remains of my sister, laid out as if on a funeral bier, drills a new chink in my heart and my loathing for the wretch in the priest-hole swells until I am engorged with venom.

I prod the fire, still unclear about how to achieve my aims without risking anyone's safety. My mind flits, as if it is attempting to solve a puzzle of logic: how to transport us all to Ludlow safely, with a corpse, a child, a blind woman and a killer. I hear Melis's faint murmur in the purr of the flames, *honey and sting*, and I know already that the lieutenant is going nowhere.

Hope bursts in. 'They're back. We can go.' Her face is flushed, straggles of hair stuck to her damp forehead. 'Gifford's brought two men with him – brothers. Will and Jem Carter.'

'Remember, we know nothing about them.' I don't like to burst her ebullience. I glance out and see them leaning against the gate smoking.

'Margie says she's known them since they were babies.'

'Well, that's something, I suppose.' I recall the maid at Littlemore, Joan, her butter-wouldn't-melt expression as she placed her tray of food on the desk beside the incriminating letters, and Ambrose's assurances that she was his cook's daughter, raised beneath his nose. Still someone turned her, squeezed my secrets out of her. I notice what appears to be a letter folded into her hand. 'What's that?'

'I almost forgot.' She holds it out. 'It's for you.'

I take the paper, scrutinize the seal, which reveals nothing, but the handwriting of the address – *The Feathers Inn, Ludlow, to be delivered to Mr Gifford, for his house guest* – is familiar. It looks like Ambrose's hand but that cannot be. I rip it open, scanning the text.

I have been delayed at Littlemore by an unexpected difficulty but will soon be able to make haste to the lodge and hope to high Heaven this missive finds you alive. All I can say is beware the guard I sent you. Bloor is murdered. The man is an impostor and means you ill . . .

My hand has found its way over my mouth and through my fingers I am saying, 'How is this possible?' I scrutinize the text, seeking some hidden clue that will explain how Ambrose, whose murder the lieutenant confessed to unequivocally in his journal, has been able to write to me.

I hand it to Hope, my mind churning. It seems the only explanation – that it was written before his death.

'What's this?' Hope holds it up, tapping her finger to point out a smudged line at the bottom. 'I can't make it out.'

It is a quotation in Latin. The sort of thing Ambrose was fond of adding to his correspondence. I scrabble among the papers on the table, finding a magnifying-glass. With a lurch of sadness I recognize it as the one Melis used when she was clipping the wings of her queens to prevent the bees from swarming. 'It says the truth never dies. And there is what looks like a date. But it's barely legible.'

'Let me see.' Snatching the letter, she holds it closer to

the window to peer through the lens. 'It's dated only three days ago. The lieutenant was already here by then, so he can't have murdered him.' She takes my wrist, shaking, smiling, almost laughing. 'Ambrose must be alive.'

Her elation is like sunlight spilling into the room and I loathe to douse it. 'The date proves nothing.' My voice is flat and hard. The lieutenant's description of killing Ambrose was vivid, down to the sensation of the blood soaking into his sleeve. I have no doubt in my mind that the deed was done. 'I'm sorry, Hope, but it must be a trick, an attempt to expose our location. A forgery . . . a good one.' Even down to the Latin quotation, which matches the one on the enamel ring.

I return to the window, placing both hands against the glass to search the blanket of trees for any sign, any unexplained movement in the foliage, to suggest Gifford was followed here.

Lark appears in the doorway. 'My grandfather would like to know when you will be ready to go. The horses have been fed and watered, so . . .'

'Would you ask Gifford to send the men out to search the forest nearby? I want to be sure they weren't followed.'

I am glad to have a little more time to finesse the plan that is formulating in my head, its various parts beginning to fit together.

It is only six days until the twenty-third.

My things are scattered all about the room, and Hope begins to collect them together, folding them into a bag. 'There's no need.' I tell her.

'Quicker if I help you.'

'I'm not coming.' Hope seems to think I don't mean it, as she continues packing. I take the bag from her. 'I mean it.'

'Am I staying here with you?' Rafe approaches me, slipping his hand into mine.

'Listen, sweetheart.' I meet his gaze directly. 'I want you to go ahead with Hope. I will follow. Better that way.'

'What if I say I won't go?' He has set his mouth in a stubborn line.

'Sweetheart.' It is hardly surprising he doesn't want to be separated from me but I can't let myself think of that now. 'You will be with Aunt Hope.'

'I'll only go if I can take Captain with me.' He thrusts his chin up defiantly.

'Very well, then.' Triumph spreads over Rafe's face as I relent. 'He can go in the cart.'

Hope looks worried. 'Are you sure it's a good idea? Why don't we all go together? And what about him?' She points to the fireplace. 'He should be brought before a magistrate. Made to pay.'

'We can't risk involving the law at this stage. If George were to find out . . .' I feel perfectly calm now my plan is coming clear. Hope knows well enough that to try to change my mind or to ask for the reason behind my decision to stay would be futile.

'And Melis – you want to see her properly buried, don't you?' Hope's tone has an edge to it and I can see that she is making a tremendous effort to stifle the onset of tears.

'You will have to take charge of that, Hope. Margie and Gifford will come with you. They'll speak to the Ludlow sexton.' Melis's death seems very distant, as if it happened in another lifetime. 'I will say my prayers once this is all over. Go to the Feathers, take rooms, and wait there. One of the men can stay here and the other can go with you. I'll be hard on your heels.' I wipe a tear from her cheek.

'Promise.' I can see a question forming on her lips. 'Don't ask, because I cannot tell you.'

Lark has crept back into the room to say that the men are conducting a search and I ask her if she'd be willing to stay here with me. 'It won't be for long.'

'I'm happy to help in any way you need.' She takes both of Hope's hands and gives her some words of encouragement. 'You are stronger than you think.'

I hope it is true.

The men return, assured that no one is lurking among the trees. I have looked the Carter brothers in the eye. They seem honest and I have no choice but to rely on my instincts.

Picking a few wild flowers, I lay them on Melis's body and kneel beside her a moment in prayer, then take Hope to one side, out of Rafe's earshot.

'Be strong, darling one. And if anything happens to me –' distress shoots into her eyes – 'which it will not, you must get word to Bette Cotton. She will know what to do.' She nods. I can see she is using all her fortitude to hold herself together.

Hope bids farewell to Lark and mounts one of the horses. Without too much ado, I kiss Rafe and help him onto the pillion saddle behind her, noticing that he wipes away my kiss with the heel of his hand.

Hope is back in the breeches, sitting astride, hair scraped away under a straw hat, a loose shirt and a kerchief tied around her neck. She even had Jem Carter fooled. I overheard him asking Margie who the young gentleman was and whether he would be staying at the lodge or travelling to Ludlow.

The party trundles into the cool green clinch of the forest, so different during the day, its dank, dappled floor and gently swaying vegetation harbouring none of night's threats.

I wander through the house, like a spectre. The bed-chamber is covered with white, as if there has been a snowfall, and the broken hive oozes, making dark runnels through the dust. Something is suspended from the hook behind the door. On closer inspection I see that it is Rafe's monkey, hanging from a snare attached to its neck. My mind snaps instantly, uneasily, to the dead cat.

'Surely not. Rafe wouldn't . . .' I find myself saying aloud. But I don't know the extent of the invisible damage that has been done to my son by the trauma of recent events. I think of him trundling into the forest, and want to bring him back, to protect him from his demons.

I must accept that I have done the right thing in sending away the two people I love most in the world. I had no choice, if I am to see this through, and I will if it is my last act on this earth.

Felton

Felton hears someone calling him. A siren song . Bridget? The dead speak in this place. 'Lieutenant.' But why doesn't she use his given name. Is the voice coming from within or without? He shifts, propping himself on his elbow the better to listen, but all he can hear is the crackle of the fire.

Then it comes again: 'Lieutenant, can you hear me?'

It is Hester.

Is it Hester?

He tries to answer but his mouth is arid. He clears his throat, which is painfully raw, and when it finally comes his reply is barely audible. 'Yes.'

'Would you like some water, something to eat?'

He must still be in the throes of delirium. Her tone is too friendly. His sick mind has conjured this up.

He gulps in a blast of foul air. 'Are you in my imagin-ation?' His voice cracks and wheezes. Despite his struggle to tether his mind, a sensible part of him is aware of how unhinged he sounds.

'I understand how confused you must be. I know what it's like in there.'

He tilts his head in the direction of the voice, seeing the finest line of orange light at the edge of the back-plate. Keeping his eye on it, he feels better fixed in the space with it, less prone to drift into disorientation. His thoughts begin to arrange themselves into a semblance of order. This is not his mind playing tricks.

'How long have I been in here?' As he says it, he realizes he has no idea. Through the muddle of his mind, he remembers Worley waiting for him in Ludlow and wonders if he has been missing long enough for the man to come looking for him.

'Two days. You must be parched.'

'Why are you being kind to me?'

'I'm not a monster.' Her voice is soft and tempting.

Am I a monster?

I am a monster.

'Besides,' she continues, 'everyone deserves a chance to repent.'

His suspicion is aroused. 'Repent?'

'It would ease your conscience. No person alive is entirely bad. I know you have the capacity for goodness.'

His head swims but he keeps his gaze adhered to that sliver of light. Even the knowledge that she is his enemy, George's enemy, is not enough to make him able to resist her kindness.

'Your sister was truly good, wasn't she? I have been reading all about her in your journal.' The thought of her reading his innermost thoughts, all his sins there in black and white, makes him feel sliced from scrotum to throat on a coroner's slab, the entirety of him exposed, nothing left of his heart but a shrunken black node.

'You loved Bridget very much, didn't you. I have lost a sister too, remember. We have that in common.'

Why would she bring up her own sister in such a way, knowing he is her murderer? He becomes convinced that this must be a precursor to retribution. He girds himself to be hauled out and shot through the head, but as this thought takes shape he wonders why, if she was going to shoot him, she didn't do it before. He returns to the horrifying thought that he will be left to starve, the worst kind of death.

'If you intend to kill me then, I beg of you, make it swift.' He is ashamed at how pathetic he sounds and clings to the forlorn hope that Worley will come.

She ignores his pleas, continues talking about her sister.

He pictures her seated on the floor, in her shift, feet bare, hair awry, leaning up against the wall beside the hearth, the pistol cradled in her small hand. 'I loved Melis more than I loved myself. Her loss was too much . . .' She stops a moment, and he wonders if she is drying tears on her sleeve. It is impossible to imagine her in tears – the diminutive, resilient woman who held a gun to his back and marched him up to this place, compelling him to crawl inside by the sheer force of her will. 'Melis had visions. But you know that. She saw our father's death. I have never told anyone. And she saw her own – you witnessed it . . .' She goes on and on. Felton wishes she would stop, wants to block his ears, but something – is it fear? – keeps him listening.

'It would seem her predictions were strangely accurate concerning death. It makes me wonder if she was also right about George's. An assassin with a knife, it wouldn't surprise me, given all his enemies. I suppose we will know soon enough. The day she predicted for such an event is not far off. What do you think, Lieutenant?'

He expels some unintelligible sounds. It is too much for him to take, this talk of George's death, when he is festering in this hole with every bone and muscle of his body hurting. 'From what you have written you loved – still love – George dearly. Do you love him as much as you loved Bridget? I think you loved Bridget more.'

'Stop!' he manages to shout.

'Do you ever wonder if she suffered? There is no worse pain than the thought of a loved one's torment.'

He brings his hands over his ears now and can hear his blood surge, like the sea. Mention of Bridget has brought back long-suppressed feelings, a numb limb prickling painfully back to life. He sees the woman's ploy now. If she means to bring him anguish, she is succeeding. He should have killed the bitch when he had the chance.

'I'm sorry I have made you stay so long in there. You see, I had no choice.'

She is quiet for some time. And he is left with his thoughts spiralling out of control in the dark until he forces his eye back to the shred of light. George is in danger and he is powerless even to send warning, but more than that the idea of Bridget's suffering is too much to bear. 'Are you there?'

No answer.

He waits.

All he can hear is the fire and the interminable rasp of his own breath.

The orange sliver wavers.

He drifts.

Bridget is lying next to him. Her skin is cold and waxy. He is dead too. Panic rises in the tight space, filling it. He is drowning. He is boiling. This is him for eternity – in this black hole. Bridget, her corpse pressed up against him, is muttering something about revenge. And George is there with them too now: his teeth are pearls falling from his mouth in a clatter of laughter.

Are you laughing at my misfortune, George? Do you hate me because I failed you?

The woman is speaking again. Drawing him back from the lip of Hell. 'Are you hungry?'

He hears a loud splash and fizzle. The sound of water thwacking onto the hearth-stone, dousing the flames.

'I should warn you I am armed, and I have a guard at the door, also armed and ready, so any false move and you will not live long enough to regret it.' Her voice is terrifyingly steady.

He can't help but admire this woman, with her hidden reserves of courage. *I am armed*: there is hardly need for that in his pathetic state. She could topple him with a prod from her smallest finger – if he is even able to stand.

The iron plate scrapes and an oblong of light falls in beside him. Something, an object, drops in with it. It is soft and gives beneath his fingers. Bread. Its yeasty aroma stabs his tongue. 'Here.' She passes in a bottle of water and also, with great care, a lit lamp, its flame protected by a bell of glass. He immediately considers the glass as a means to escape, its broken edge run over the thin skin of his inner wrists.

His life would slip away and then . . . An image of Hell appears to him, a painting he once saw in the Low Countries, of terrible beasts and unimaginable tortures. It makes his will to live suddenly strong.

Gulping the liquid, he feels himself revive miraculously, like a plant after rain. He stuffs the bread into his mouth. It is a heavenly assault of flavours: fruity, rich, malty, buttery and sweet, as if it has sat beside a tray of cakes while they were dusted with powdered sugar. After barely three mouthfuls he is already full to bursting, his gut creaking and burbling agonizingly back to life.

He can hear that the fire has been relit, can feel its heat surge through the space, which seems larger now it is illuminated. A new optimism surges into him. This small act of kindness makes him know he can persuade her to release him. He must first convince her of his contrition.

Hester

I have unpicked every phrase of his journal until I know the way he is welded together better than I know my own self. I have read and reread his sister's letter. This letter is the key to his soul.

In order to enact my plan, I need to feel as confident as I can that the others have made it safely to Ludlow. And I must be certain that my prisoner has reached the furthest outpost of his despair – though certainty is a luxury in short supply. But I know what it's like in that godforsaken hole. I have no doubt he is a broken man, without the tincture he relies on so greatly.

I tell Lark and Jem Carter I am not to be disturbed.

Once I am alone, I douse the fire with a bucket of water once more, and wait in silence.

'Hester?' His voice is feeble. My name sounds like someone else's on his lips. I hardly know who I am any more. I am certainly not the same woman I was three weeks ago. I wait for him to speak again and eventually he repeats my name.

And he says: 'Are you able to forgive me?' It is an indication of remorse, a sign he can be moulded to my will.

'It is not my forgiveness you should be asking – it is the Lord's.'

I inch closer to the hearth, legs, feet, dress black with

ash, mouth pressed up to the warm iron. 'Your whole life has been destroyed, all your potential come to naught because of George's actions. Think of the man you might have been. Now what are you? A crippled ex-soldier reduced to nothing. Think of all those other men whose lives he stole too, your comrades in arms, their lives, their families' lives shattered by George's whims and misplaced pride. You know the truth. You know he sent them all to a certain death. And for what? To play at being the Great Leader of Men. You know the truth. We are all expendable to him – even you.'

I can feel a coolness in the air about my head, sense Melis still watching me, hear the breathy hum of her whisper: *Honey and sting, sweetness and sharpness, and sharpness, and sharpness.* 'It's a wonder someone hasn't run a knife through George before now. But God knows who would have the courage. It would be an act of true sacrifice.' I let him think on that a moment.

He doesn't answer.

After some time, I hear him sigh deeply, and when he finally speaks, he asks again, with more force this time, 'Are you able to forgive me? I beg of you.' A moment later he asks again, more pitifully even than the first plea.

I don't answer. Instead I say, 'Let's get you out of that hole.'

The back-plate is still warm to the touch and, loaded pistol in one hand, I grip my fingers round its lip, gaining enough purchase to heave it aside an inch at a time. I have a momentary glimpse of myself as another would see me, filthy with ash and smut, the image of a madwoman, but I have never felt saner.

A rancid stench is released as the lieutenant edges out

with excruciating slowness, groaning and wincing, a ghoul, skin grey, eyes blank. By the look of him, cowed, remorseful, pathetic, he is ready, but if I have learned anything it is that appearances can be deceptive. His reaction to his sister's letter is what will tell me if he can be moulded to my will.

Felton is disoriented under the steely gaze of the pistol's eye.

Her glare is fervent, terrifyingly so.

But he is out.

He imagines kicking the weapon from her hand, getting her about the throat – snap – scaling down the building and into the arms of the forest. It is a fantasy. He is too weak to stand unsupported, has to cling to the mantelshelf.

She pushes a stool towards him with her foot. He slumps onto it gratefully as she draws something from her pocket, holding it up in her free hand. It is his phial of tincture.

She must see the craving scored through him as she says, 'I expect you've been missing this. I'd wager you'd give almost anything for a dose of it now.'

She is right. It is the only worldly thing he wants in this moment. It might help obliterate the agony of his mind – knowledge of the deeds he has committed – for a while, perhaps, at least. But he is aware, too, that there is no escape from himself.

She holds up the phial to the light. 'Almost empty. Here!' She tosses it towards him. He fumbles the catch and it falls into his lap, rolling off, onto the floor. He folds his body forward, reaching for it, every part of him creaking and painful. Picking it up, he removes the stopper, draining every last blessed dreg.

She offers him a drink of milk, which is warm and gluey, passing through his gullet to sit in his stomach, like a bag of gravel.

'I think you should read this,' she is saying, holding out a piece of paper and a small magnifying-glass. 'It is addressed to you.'

The paper is discoloured and stiff with age. It takes a moment for his eyes to focus, and when they do, it is like a kick to the gut, knocking the breath out of him. Bridget's hand spidering over the page. Disbelieving instantly, feeling duped, but looking again. *When you read this, beloved brother, I will be gone to another place.* It is Bridget's. 'What is this? Where did you find it?'

'It was between the pages of your mother's will.'

'I don't understand.' But he does understand. *Whether it will be a better place I do not know. But this earthly life has become a world of unbearable pain and shame, so better to risk eternal damnation in the taking of my own life.* That sealed package contained more than his mother's will. His head is spinning, as if the past has slid the floor out from under his feet. His mother had kept this from him. An ague, she told him, caused Bridget's death. She lied. The old welling hatred for his mother burgeons.

'Read it.' Hester steps to the far side of the room as if to give him privacy to read his sister's words from beyond the grave.

He feels disembowelled. Bridget is brought to life in these lines of text. It is her tone of voice, unmistakably, her choice of words. Oh, God! His heart is levered open and out of it emerges new truth that amends all he thought he believed.

I hold the hope, wish, dream that you will make him pay for his ruin of me, your only and most loving sister. I cannot demand you take revenge. What a black word that is. No, no, sorry, it is my anguish giving vent. Do not listen. You must do as you see fit but I wish that he would know what he has done to me.

He is flung back to the last day he saw his sister, her bruised wrist, her desperate tears, not caused by concern for his safety going to battle, as she'd said, but by George's violence.

Great sobs of grief rack him, a frantic outpouring for his poor blighted sister. He can feel her unimaginable pain and torment, too, for himself, the fool who has spent all his life loving a shadow, loving a fraud, the man responsible for his cherished twin sister's death. He howls and rages, not caring that Hester is witness to his shame.

He opens his hands, the hands that have snuffed out so much life and all in George's name. He was blinded by the gleam of George's gilding, unable to see the festering monster that lay beneath. But his eyes are unveiled. He sees it all, how George has so easily exploited his love, and how easily he draws people into his thrall. He understands now, something he has never before understood, the sheer power of vengeance, how it creates its own force.

Hester

I pass him a handkerchief, which he wipes over his face. Then he looks up at me with hollow eyes. The letter is in his fist, pressed tight to his heart, anguish scored over his features.

'What do you intend to do with me?' He creaks gradually to his feet, like an overfilled bucket being winched up from a well, to stand unsteadily before me, arms splayed, hands open. 'If you intend to shoot me, please make it quick.'

Rather than leaning away from him, which is my instinct, I do the opposite until the gun is a foot from his chest, quashing the part of me that feels afraid now he towers above my small frame.

'If I do so, I cast myself into eternal damnation.' I lower the weapon. 'It is what *you* intend to do that concerns me.' He seems not to know what to do with the smile I toss him. 'I should remind you there is an armed man outside the door, who is unlikely to be as accommodating as I.'

He is haggard and gaunt, the stubble over his chin flecked with steel, but the two days incarcerated with almost nothing to eat have not eroded the bullish shoulders and thick neck. Even so, I know I must show not the smallest iota of fear. 'Now you know the truth about George.'

He sinks back onto the stool.

'It must be the bitterest of blows to discover the true fate of your sister.' He shakes his head, as if refusing to believe what he knows to be the truth. 'I can't imagine her suffering. To take her own life and that of her unborn child, to cast herself into the blackest of sin, she must have been beyond despair.' I want him to feel it, to feel that despair, to know that George caused it, for his heart to be upended irrevocably.

A look of profound sorrow passes over his features and I know I have reached the tender part of him.

'I'm sure she watches over you. My sister watches me. The dead guide us, if we allow them to do so. You loved Bridget very much, didn't you?' He is nodding, and I sense my message is beginning to penetrate. He holds his sister's letter in a shaking hand.

'Look what he has reduced you to. Those who rub close to George Villiers risk a bad end. I should know. I was another Bridget. But you are aware of that.'

After what seems an age suspended in febrile silence, he directs a blighted look my way. 'Did your sister make other predictions that came to pass?'

I nod slowly. He is on the brink of bending to my will. I sense Melis close by and can picture her vision as if it is my own. This time I see, in thrilling clarity, the lieutenant plunging the knife into George's breast. His hands are sticky with blood. George's expression is horrified, terrified. George always believed death was for other people.

'Oh, yes, she saw many things. She saw the fire and Rafe in it.' I try to keep my voice steady. 'Had I been more inclined to listen to Melis, recent events might have turned out differently.'

He drops his face into his palm, as if to shut out the world, exposing a rind of dirt around his collar.

'Do you want to know what she whispered to me just before she died?' I know I have planted a seed of curiosity in him, can see it in the way he looks up at me and nods. 'She said it was your hand she saw thrusting a knife into George. Not some nameless assassin's, but *yours*.' I watch his expression as my lie sinks in, first doubt but then something else, more ruthless.

He is staring at his hand, fisting and unfisting it, shaking his head slightly.

'Think of Bridget – her suffering.'

He sits upright with a sharp inhalation, his forehead ploughed into horizontal furrows. 'I am mired in sin.'

'You have been used. A man like George is difficult to refuse. I can see you have been deep in his thrall. You are not the only one. The devil has a powerful pull.'

He is scrutinizing the letter through the magnifying-glass. 'Bridget must have her revenge.' His eyes ferment with hate – hate for George – and I know my job is done.

'I'm going to release you.' I see something new in his expression now: surprise, hope, determination, it is hard to say which. I grab the collar of his shirt, bringing my face right up to his until I can see his black-clogged pores. 'If you think you are going to go looking for my son, you will not find him.' Droplets of spit land on his skin. 'He is long gone, now. Could be anywhere.'

He meets my gaze with a straight look. 'Your boy belongs with you, not that devil.'

'You know what it is you must do, don't you?'

'I do.' He fixes me with a bludgeon-like stare.

Melis's breath is heavy in the shell of my ear. After all

the not-knowing, now I know. I have won. Now I am sure, absolutely sure. A small throb of exhilaration starts in my temple. I have pulled back the bowstring, inserted the arrow. He is my arrow. He is my sting.

Night has fallen by the time he walks out of the gates, glancing back once or twice. I stand with Lark and Jem Carter on the steps watching the lieutenant's departure, staying there until he is out of sight.

'You must never speak of this.'

They give me their word. Lark is shaking her head. 'I don't know why you let him go.' She echoes the small uncertainty that still flickers inside me.

'Mercy has its own rewards,' I say lightly. They must think me detached from my senses, both had tried to make me change my mind.

'He's bound to seek out Rafe at Ludlow.'

'I made it clear to him that they had travelled on further.' I can see the concern in the stiff set of Lark's posture.

'Do you think he believed you?'

I had been so sure of my plan, so certain I'd set him on a direct path to destroy George, but now shards of doubt are crashing into me. 'I do, yes. He was repentant. He seeks God's forgiveness. Who am I to stand between him and the Lord?' I wonder if she can detect the deceit in my tone.

She simply shrugs and says the livestock needs tending, before loping past the charred skeleton of the henhouse towards the paddock.

I enter the lodge, slowly mounting the stairs, past the empty floors to the blue room at the top, where I stand at the window looking out, imagining the lieutenant moving towards my adversary. My arrow is in flight, propelled inexorably towards its target. The forest is a dark blur, my own vague reflection cast in the glass. I do not recognize the hard woman who gazes back at me.

For the first time I become aware of a silence so absolute it cannot be quantified in any normal measure of quiet. Melis has gone from here and I envisage her at the lieutenant's shoulder as he moves through the night, whispering to urge him on, away from this place, far away into another world. *Have your revenge*, she is murmuring. *Our revenge.*

Hope

It is Rafe who hears him first, running to the door, where Will Carter is trying to prevent him from entering. Hope can't believe her ears on hearing the familiar voice and follows her nephew to see him launching himself into the arms of Ambrose Cotton.

Hope is stunned to silence. She has wept for Ambrose, grieved for him, the nearest she has had to a father, and here he is, very much alive. He looks pallid, quite unwell, and his clothes are covered with dirt from the road.

'We thought you were gone – murdered by the lieutenant.'

'He tried his best.' He pulls open his shirt to reveal a bandaged torso. 'The wretch knew what he was doing. Thought he'd got me right in the heart. Under normal circumstances I'd have bled to death in minutes.'

'I remember,' says Rafe. 'Your heart is in the wrong place.'

Hope is recalling, with a sense of wonder, Rafe sitting on Ambrose's lap to listen for the heartbeat on the right side of his chest. It seems to her nothing short of miraculous, as if something divine has intervened to spare him, making her feel that they, too, are under its protection now.

'Where's Hester – Melis?' He searches the room with his eyes, a look of horror dropping over his features as

Hope recounts what they have endured these last days. She tells him of Melis at peace now, enfolded into the sacred ground of the Ludlow churchyard. She, Rafe and the Giffords had said prayers over the grave. She is gone, but when Hope lies in bed at night, in that moment between sleeping and waking, she still sees her hitting the stone steps, the shock thrusting her breathlessly to full consciousness. And she tells him Hester is still at the lodge.

His brow crumples and she thinks he is going to cry but he rams one fist hard into the opposite palm. 'How could you – how could you have left her there?'

Gifford and Margie are silent, both looking to Hope to explain that Hester gave them no choice. 'She insisted.'

'Surely you must have been able to see the idiocy of such a plan.' He has begun to pace, like a caged animal.

She tells him that they left a guard with Hester and that the lieutenant is in the priest-hole with a fire lit to prevent his escape. But nothing she says appears to soothe his qualms as he replaces the coat he has just removed and makes for the door.

Before leaving he turns. 'I'm sorry. It's not your fault, Hope. I shouldn't have lost my temper.'

They watch over the banisters as the doctor descends the staircase and shouts for his groom to find fresh horses. The well-dressed guests milling about the hall of the Feathers turn to look at the ranting grime-covered man marching past them, barking orders.

'Come,' Hope says, trying to sound bright, 'let's go down to the yard and wave him off.' Rafe glowers at her, slapping away her proffered hand, harder than is necessary, and stamps ahead down the stairs, his puppy following at his heel.

She does her best to hold her patience with him.

The yard is in a flurry of activity. An army of grooms is untacking and tacking up horses, brushing them down, pumping water into buckets, filling nosebags with oats. There is a metallic hammering where the smith is replacing a lost shoe. One horse is nervy, thrashing about, hoofs skidding on the cobbles, causing all the others to shift out of its way, and a dog is caught, yelping as it jumps aside.

Ambrose is asking the landlord if he knows of any local men who might join the pair of armed men who travelled with him from Oxford. Hope doesn't want to have to consider what he thinks might confront him on his arrival. Hester's confidence had lulled her into a sense of security that she now realizes was false. 'I need trustworthy men, who can leave immediately. And ...' Ambrose looks around, lowering his voice '... if anyone comes looking for me, I haven't been here.'

'Understood,' replies the landlord.

'Can't I go with him?' asks Rafe, yanking at Hope's sleeve.

She sinks to her haunches to meet his eyes. He ties his mouth into a rigid little knot. 'Ambrose will bring your mother back here.'

'He didn't *say* that.'

'You must stay here with me for the time being.'

'You can't make me stay with you, if I don't want to.' He remains tight and sullen.

She takes a deep breath. 'They'll be riding through the night. It's not safe.'

'We rode through the night before. And if anybody tries to hurt us I'll *deal* with them.' He makes a thrusting motion with his fist and his face has set into a chilling sneer.

It would be a wonder if he had come through so much hardship and not been affected by it, but there is something profoundly unsettling in his expression, which she has never seen before.

Ambrose intervenes, crouching beside them, patting Rafe on the shoulder, as he might a comrade. 'I need you to stay here. Who else will look after your aunt Hope? It's a very important job. Do you think you're up to it?'

Rafe seems to thaw slightly. Hope is impressed by Ambrose's handling of the child but reasons that he knows her nephew well. He tutored him almost daily. She is reminded, with an ache of longing, of their peaceful life at Orchard Cottage, wishing all this would be over.

When the men are mounted and ready to leave, Ambrose beckons her, leaning down and cupping his hand to her ear, saying, 'Make sure you stay close by him.' He nods towards Will Carter, standing in the doorway to the inn, who nods back. 'I'll send word as soon as things are clear. But lie low here. Stay in your rooms and keep up the disguise, even in private, in case of gossiping maids. If you need anything, send the Giffords out.'

She wants to ask him to give Lark a message but somehow can't find a way to put it. Had she time, she would have sent a letter, a private word, but of course Lark cannot read and Hope wouldn't know what to say anyway.

Once they have left, she tries to distract Rafe by suggesting they go inside and watch them departing from the upstairs window. He shrugs, without looking at her, and her heart sinks at the thought of keeping up his spirits for she doesn't know how much longer.

It is busy inside, with a raucous table of men drinking

and playing cards, laying down bets on a game, and a few more loitering about.

She pushes Rafe ahead as they move slowly through the crowded hall towards the stairs. Captain, who has been following them obediently, is distracted by a cat under a table, giving chase, skittering and wriggling round the feet of the card players and away towards the kitchens. Will Carter, following close behind, offers to retrieve him while Hope and Rafe make their way towards the stairs.

Beside them the landlord, a vastly fat fellow with a bulbous red-veined nose, is calling to someone, his voice booming through the busy hall. 'We've managed to find you a bed for the night, Mr Smyth. A gentleman has had to leave unexpectedly.'

A figure emerges from the shadows, walking unsteadily towards the host. 'Finally, I can leave the godforsaken fleapit I've been staying in. I take it the linens will be clean.'

Nausea sweeps over Hope and she stumbles slightly. She recognizes him instantly, the superior tone, the foppish get-up, the neat chestnut beard, the red jacket. It is not a Mr Smyth but Worley, drunk and swaying only inches away, between her and the stairs.

She turns her head, so he can't glimpse her face, hoping her male outfit will put him off the scent.

'Of course the linens will be clean. What kind of establishment do you think this is?'

'And I wonder,' Worley is slurring and places a hand on the landlord's arm, clasping it tightly, as if needing to steady himself, 'is a Dr Cotton among your guests?'

The landlord is umming and aahing, as he shuffles through the pages of a ledger. 'I had to turn away a Dr something – the name was not Cotton, though. It was a few days ago so I doubt he's still in the vicinity, even if he is the fellow you seek.' Worley stumbles, righting himself on the landlord's arm again. 'You're most fortunate that I'm able to find you a room at all, Mr Smyth.' The landlord is trying tactfully to free himself from Worley's grip.

Hope grasps Rafe firmly by the hand, and while Worley's attention is distracted, she inches past him to mount the stairs. But as they meet the bottom step, Rafe protests, with a loud 'Let me go!'

Worley's gaze snaps round.

His head is swaying, face ruddy and sweat-shining.

Hope starts to climb but it is too late.

He looks at her, gaze swimming, then away.

Relief floods her as she hauls the complaining child up another step.

But Worley returns his eyes to her, recognition alighting.

'Fancy seeing you here.' He emits a breath that stinks of beer. 'And this one.' His smirk is triumphant as he chucks Rafe on the cheek.

'Get off me.' Rafe wipes the place where Worley has touched him and Hope fears for an instant that the man is going to smack him.

'You can't fool *me* with this.' He pinches the fabric of her man's coat. He is close, uncomfortably close, speaking at a low, intimate growl, and his foetid breath makes her want to retch. 'You were all woman last time I saw you. If only they knew . . .' He throws out a lecherous laugh. Hope remembers his fingers asserting themselves beneath her skirts and she hates herself for her previous credulity.

Not any more.

Not any more.

Drawing herself up to her full height, and standing a step above him, she invests her tone with all the disdain she can muster. 'Mr Smyth, is it? I can assure you I have never encountered you before in my life and I think I'd likely remember a fellow who turns himself out in the way you do.' She runs a derisive look up and down his lurid clothing, then turns to the landlord. 'Would you kindly ensure that this drunken oaf keeps his distance from my family and me?'

She starts to climb the stairs, head high, perspiration simmering beneath her clothes. Halfway up she becomes aware of a tussle below: the landlord is insisting that Worley not follow her up the stairs.

'Run.' She lets go of Rafe's hand. 'Fast as you can. To the room. Shut yourself in.' He flies up, Hope trailing behind.

She is almost at the top, dares not look back, can hear now, someone, Worley, hammering up behind. Rafe is swallowed into the dark corridor off the landing that leads to their rooms.

She turns momentarily. Worley is almost close enough to touch. The fat landlord lumbers in his wake, wheezing loudly.

Worley grabs her wrist. His grip burns. 'Got you!' Spit showers her and the stink of his breath mingled with her fear makes her feel faint.

With a sharp downward movement of her arm she breaks from his hold, astonished by her own strength.

Worley sways, almost losing his footing, and rights himself but wobbles drunkenly again, reaching out to clutch at her, a silent, petrified plea scrawled on his face.

Hope steps back minutely.

He is grappling at thin air, arms floundering.

He teeters, wavering, for an elongated moment, on the lip of the top stair.

She watches in appalled anticipation as time seems to falter.

Then he tumbles backwards, past the landlord, who can do nothing.

He plummets over and over, head colliding with the edge of each wooden step, an ominous thud, thud, thud, thud as he falls, finally to slump on the floor at the bottom.

The hall is silenced, and a crowd gathers around the broken shape in its crimson jacket. His head is haloed to match his coat, as a pool of blood expands on the flagstones.

Empty and numb, Hope sits on the top stair, her face sinking into her hands, not wanting, not daring to look.

'He's dead,' someone announces.

The landlord has reached her, places a big sweaty hand on her shoulder. 'I'm so sorry, sir,' he is saying, clearly shaken. 'I'm so sorry. I shouldn't have . . . I should have stopped . . .'

'It's not your fault. He was drunk.' She knows, her voice surprising her with its steadiness, that had she not taken that minute backward step, she could have grabbed his collar and pulled him in. He might have fallen forward instead of back and suffered nothing more than a bloody nose and a sobering dent to his dignity.

'I could have caught him.' She realizes, with a heavy feeling, that she shouldn't have said this.

The landlord looks at her for what seems an interminable time. 'And have him pull you down, too? A slight fellow like you? There was nothing you could have done. And, as you say, he was completely soused.'

But Hope is thinking back to the broken balcony, the strange symmetry of events, and how she had instinctively reached out to haul Hester back, with no thought for her own safety.

Her conscience jabbers.

Only she will ever know whether her infinitesimal backward movement, the difference between life and death, was deliberate.

Hester

It is the dead of night but I am up, sitting in the dark, thinking of what I have set in motion, willing the lieutenant on, when the yard-dog starts barking. I hear horses, heavy footfall on the stairs, voices, imagining a consignment of guards sent by George.

The priest-hole is beside me, gaping, ready to suck me in. But I cannot make myself move.

The latch rattles, the creak of the door, a scrabbling sound and something jumps onto me. I push it off. Wet slides over my face.

'Leave it,' comes a command. 'Here, Caesar!'

I cry out, paralysed with fear, believing myself in some kind of waking dream in which the dead have returned to haunt me.

'Hester. It's Ambrose.'

The dark shape moves towards me. My breath is shallow and I am shaking uncontrollably. 'It can't be you.'

A yellow glow leaks into the room. Jem Carter is in the doorway, holding up a lamp. I rub my eyes, repeating, 'It can't be you.'

'It is me.' He reaches for my hand. I expect his to be cold, but it is warm and alive.

Ambrose is alive! I am lost for words. There is nothing to say when someone you love has returned from the dead.

'My letter didn't reach you, then?'

'I thought it a forgery.'

'Even with the quotation? I was sure you'd know it was from me . . . I've been out of my mind with worry ever since Bloor's murder was reported.'

I am remembering the lieutenant's horribly vivid description of sinking a knife into Ambrose's torso. I had believed him. Everything, my plans, my future, my son's safety, now seems built on quicksand. 'The lieutenant was sure he'd killed you. Why would he have lied about that?'

'He tried his damnedest. Left me for dead with a blade in my breast.'

'That was the delay you spoke of in your letter? And Rafe, have you seen him? Is he safe?'

'All safe at the Feathers with Hope.'

I allow myself a small ration of optimism and, rising from the pallet, I wrap my arms round him. He winces, bringing his hand to protect his chest. 'I'm so very sorry,' he is saying, 'about Melis.'

I wish I could cry but I feel completely dried up.

'Where is he?' Ambrose's tone is suddenly rigid: he has noticed the open entrance to the priest-hole.

I falter. 'Gone.' I am glad the dim light means he can't read my expression. 'Escaped.'

'How? From there?' He is pointing at the hiding place. 'Did he force his way out? Did he hurt you? What was your guard doing at the time?'

'No one was hurt.' I can't bring myself to tell him that I deliberately allowed the lieutenant to leave, furnished him with supplies for his journey even. He would think me a fool for placing so much trust in what seems now little more than a hunch. I know what I saw in the lieutenant's eyes, but it defies logical explanation.

'We must get out after him. How long since he escaped?'

'I don't know. It was already dark.' I glance at the clock. It has said the same time for several days now. I don't know how long I have slept, don't know if the lieutenant has had enough time to get well away.

He makes for the stairs, calling his men to feed and water the horses, arm themselves and prepare to return to the forest, girding them for a manhunt. 'Make yourself ready, Hester. Fast as you can. It's not safe to stay here. If he was on foot, we've a chance of catching him.' He races down ahead of me.

'But what about Rafe?' I call down the stairs, desperate to delay them. 'Shouldn't we get to Ludlow and be sure of Rafe's safety before hunting down the lieutenant?'

'We'll split up. My men can search for the lieutenant and the rest of us will make for Ludlow. We'll have to move on from the Feathers.'

'Wait.' I am insistent but he is already at the bottom and out of the door. 'It's so dangerous at night. And you, you . . .' I don't know how to stop them, can't tell him that the lieutenant is the arrow I have aimed and fired at George. 'You cannot be well enough. You're wounded.'

I envisage my whole plan falling apart. 'What will you do with him when you've caught him?'

'We'll worry about that when it comes to it.' He is brusque and musters his men. 'Be sure your weapons are loaded.'

Felton

The lieutenant stalks through the leafy gloom. He had been desperately weakened by his incarceration but freedom is intoxicating and has invested him with renewed vigour. The moon is up and almost full, but the light barely penetrates the canopy of trees. It is mercifully cool, after the infernal heat of the priest-hole, and the ground gives off the scent of loam and fresh decay. He is sensitive to the vibrations of the earth, nose primed for the whiff of tobacco smoke and sweat. Nothing must prevent him from his new mission. He will get retribution for his sister, if it is his last act on earth.

He travels light – his only weapon the blunt penknife that the child had stolen from him and returned to him at the gate by Jem Carter. He had precious few belongings before and has fewer now. Hester had packed him a parcel of food and drink, and given him a few crowns, more than enough to get him to Whitehall.

He feels their approach first, as if something is altering the shape of the air. A squirrel interrupts its nut gathering to sit upright, tufted ears twitching, before scampering away. Soon he becomes aware of the unmistakable thrum of horses at a canter. It fast becomes louder. He relies on all his old instincts to tell him how many riders there are: three, four, perhaps.

Scrambling up a nearby tree, he watches the dark shapes of the party of riders heading towards the lodge at a pace. He wonders if perhaps it is Worley with a band of men come to his aid. What he would have given, only a few hours ago, for Worley to appear. How things have changed.

He jumps down from his perch and hurries on, running twenty paces, walking twenty, stopping only to read the stars for his direction.

It is not long before he hears horses approaching once more, a larger party this time, from the direction of the lodge. He tucks himself behind a dense thicket of brambles, alert. They are close.

One shouts, 'You go on. My horse is lame.'

He hears the thunder of hoofs as some continue towards Ludlow. But others, four at least by his assessment, have halted right beside his hiding place. He daren't look but feels he could reach out his arm and touch them. He hears the thump as one dismounts.

Fear sharpens him. He holds his blunt little blade in his fist. Sunk home in the right part of the neck, it might cause some damage. He has surprise on his side, should he need it. He knows he can't fight them all off. He might have done once, when he had the use of both arms and his body was primed for combat. He hardly dares breathe.

A man is talking to his horse, lifting its legs, and Felton can hear the scrape of a hoof pick. A cloud of biting midges gathers about his head and he has to use all his self-control to stop the urge to swat them away.

'Just a stone!' the man says, and Felton is sure he can hear the soft thud of the offending object falling to the forest floor. Then a whistle and a call. 'Come, Caesar.'

He hears the hound before he sees it, the crack of twigs

and the stutter of its sniff as it prods about in the bush where he is hidden. It stands still, training a pair of dark eyes on him. He wills it away.

The man whistles, calling the hound's name again. Caesar's ears flatten slightly. He ignores his master, continuing to pierce the lieutenant with his stare. He very slowly reaches out the back of his hand towards the long muzzle. The hound smells him and licks the salt sweat from his palm with its agile tongue. Another whistle. It bounds off. Felton expels a lungful of air.

'He's coming.' It is unmistakably Hester's voice, which gives him a measure of relief to know she is unharmed. 'Come, boy.'

He can hear the pat and stroke, the man's foot sliding back into the stirrup, the creak of leather as he heaves his weight into the saddle.

'What is it, Ambrose?' she says.

His innards shrivel to hear that name. The doctor lives? It is impossible, unless – the thought is dark and grim, but nonetheless he unfolds it tentatively in his mind – unless it is the devil's work, the doctor raised from the dead. He tells himself not to be a fool. Perhaps he has lost his touch with a blade.

'Caesar's picked up a scent,' the man says.

Felton can hear the hound's purposeful sniff, close by once more, and girds himself for exposure, not moving a muscle, but the animal moves on, away from him, the riders following. He waits a while to be sure they have gone before continuing.

He moves off the main track, taking a narrow more southerly trail, pressing on through the thick vegetation, keeping his mind focused on his destination. By dawn he arrives at the edge of the forest where the land opens out into pasture, bleached to yellow by the sun. He stands a moment to work out his route, stretching his stiff limbs. It will be harvest time soon and a field of oats shimmers almost blue in the easterly light, a gentle breeze addling it.

He marches as fast as he can, passing hedgerows filled with blackberries, which he picks as he walks, not minding that they are still slightly tart. Coming upon a stream, little more than a ditch, he crouches, scooping the cold water into his mouth and over his face. Removing his boots, he dips his blistered and bloody feet into the trickle and dampens his shirt to cool himself as he moves on across the open country. Soon the sun beats down hard and there is no shade to be found.

Walking some distance, he arrives at the sprawling outskirts of a small town. It is market day and the place is teeming with people packing up their stalls. The bells ring for Evensong. He considers going inside the church, seeking some kind of redemption. He doesn't, of course. He is beyond redemption.

He slakes his thirst at the town pump where, as luck would have it, he finds a man so drunk he can barely stand. His horse, a fine-looking thing, is grazing at a nearby verge. Felton persuades the fellow to take a couple of crowns for it. He seems delighted. And so he should be, for it is a criminally good sum for an ordinary gelding.

The horse is high-strung, shying at everything that moves, making Felton wonder if the drunkard didn't get an even better deal than he'd initially thought. But the animal and he settle eventually into an uneasy alliance.

'I'm coming for you, George,' he says, as he girds it into a gallop.

Hope

Before Hope has even broken her fast, the magistrate arrives to ask her a few questions about Worley's death. She had anticipated this and asked Margie to cut off her hair the night before. Margie had tried to persuade her it wasn't necessary but she was sure she would have to remove her cap out of respect to the official. Wistful, watching the long black curls fall to the floor, she sensed that, with her hair, she was losing the final shreds of her innocence. And good riddance to it, she told herself. It was her innocence that had caused them all so much trouble.

The magistrate is a tall, thin man, with gimlet eyes and patchy white stubble on his chin where he has been poorly shaved. She removes her cap, running a hand through her cropped hair, and looks directly at him, before making a small polite dip of the head. 'How can I be of help to you, sir?'

Taking her into an empty room, he scrutinizes her, making her feel her secret is visible through her skin. He enquires about her reasons for being at the Feathers and she explains, as Hester told her, that she and her younger brother are awaiting the arrival of their parents.

He doesn't seem particularly interested in her responses, barely looks at her until he says: 'One or two witnesses have told me that the deceased, Mr Smyth, seemed to recognize you.'

His eyes bore into her and he leans in closer.

Heat creeps up her body, flaring onto her cheeks.

She wants to ask him to open the window, but daren't.

'He must have mistaken me for someone else.' She is trying to keep her hands still, resting loosely fisted on her knees, which she keeps splayed as a man would, despite her instinct to cross them. 'I can't think of any other explanation,' she adds.

'By all accounts he was very drunk. Would you agree that was the case?'

'I would agree so, yes.'

'Well, I don't know . . .' He pauses and all she can think of is that he will uncover her, that he knows she is a liar, that she could have prevented the man from falling, that he can see the truth seeping from her pores.

She prepares herself.

He lifts an arm. She recoils slightly. He brings his hand down onto her shoulder. 'Dreadful business.' He pats her, as a kindly uncle might his young nephew. 'Dreadful accident.'

'Accident' is the word everyone has used to describe Worley's tumble down the stairs, so it is the word she uses too, packing up her conscience and hiding it deep within.

Later that morning Hester arrives with Ambrose, announcing that they are all to travel to another inn a half-day's ride away. It is a subdued reunion. Marks, dark as bruises, circle Hester's eyes and she is as pale as vellum. Lark is with them, seeming diminished outside her domain, relying on Hope and Margie to guide her down the stairs and out to the stables.

They leave as soon as the horses are watered.

The lieutenant isn't mentioned and Hope says nothing of Worley, though the Giffords recount the gruesome details of the drunken Mr Smyth who fell to his death on the stairs. It seems barely to register with Hester.

Hope wonders if the lieutenant is dead. The series of terrible events seems now like the darkest of nightmares, too distressing to have happened. But Melis is in the Ludlow churchyard – that is a fact.

The sickening image of Worley's corpse crooked on the flagstones, blood pooling, keeps flashing through her mind, making guilt riffle through her, like a thief's fingers in a bag.

They are a large party, with the three Giffords and Ambrose's two men, as well as the Carter brothers, for protection. They make good progress on the route, stopping after a couple of hours at a quiet clearing to rest the horses and stretch their legs, sitting in the cool grass, passing round a flagon to take a drink.

'I know how to set a trap and skin a rabbit,' Rafe tells Ambrose.

'Who taught you that?' says Ambrose. 'Was it Lark? She's a wizard with snares.'

'No, it was the lieutenant.'

Now that the man has been mentioned they all become starched, save for Rafe, who is describing exactly how a rabbit trap works, miming with his small fingers the tying of the slipknot.

They arrive in the middle of the afternoon at a remote

turnpike with a tumbledown coaching inn, where they take a suite of gloomy rooms above the stables. From there they have the advantage of being able to hear any comings and goings, but it is a far cry from the luxury of the Feathers, with grimy bedding and vermin scuttling behind the wainscoting.

Hester is distant, sitting in a huddle over a map with Ambrose, discussing quietly where they will go next. Hope hovers nearby, feeling left out, ignorant of their plans, as if she can't be trusted, although Hester has told her it is for her own protection. She knows it is not the same but she is reminded of the clench of wretchedness she always felt when ostracized by the Iffley girls.

It is as if her secret has built a barrier between her and those she loves. All she can think of are the reasons she doesn't belong, remembering the cheesemonger in the market, fixing her with a hard sapphire stare that assumed her guilty no matter what.

She slips from the room and down to the stables where the Carter brothers are keeping an eye on Rafe, as he teaches the puppy to obey his commands. He is a strict little drillmaster, dealing out punishments when Captain is not obliging, despite the men's suggestion that the dog might respond better to rewards.

The brothers are eating and Jem offers her a lump of hard cheese on the point of his poniard. She shakes her head. 'Something wrong?' he asks.

She attempts a smile and seeks refuge inside the stables where she can hear Lark in one of the stalls, talking quietly to the big roan mare, as she rubs it down. 'That's better, girl, isn't it?'

Hope watches in silence with just the rhythmic shush-shush of the brush passing over the horse's flanks and the animal's occasional whicker of contentment. After a while Lark seems to sense her presence. 'Who's there?'

'It's me.' She stops herself saying her name in case someone overhears and becomes curious about a boy named Hope.

'Come here.' Lark beckons her and she sidles round the large animal, a rich dung smell rising up from the straw underfoot. 'We'll be leaving in the morning, going home.'

'I wish you weren't.' Hope thinks of the lodge buried in the forest with its ghosts.

'Livestock needs tending . . .' Lark pauses, resting her head against the mare's neck. 'I'll miss you.'

Hope feels something quicken deep inside her and exhales a trembling breath. She doesn't know how it happens, but they have come together, her body warm, hands cold, breath hot.

'Something has changed,' Lark says, pulling away. 'You're different.'

A shard of sorrow sticks in Hope's craw.

Lark, who can hear the blink of an eye from across a room, who can smell rain a day away, who can untangle a single thread of birdsong from a distant cacophony, has detected her guilt.

Hope is transparent to her, all her failings visible: the foolish girl who allowed Worley to ruin her, was taken in by the lieutenant and, much worse, the woman who took – deliberately – that minute backward step.

She feels the cold pain of rejection spreading into her heart.

But Lark says, 'It's this.' She is running her hands over Hope's cropped hair. 'You've cut it.'

They begin to laugh, foreheads pressing together, fingers interlocked, neither wanting to be the first to let go, and Hope seals away her secret shame, hiding it deep in an inaccessible recess of her mind.

Felton

Felton makes swift progress, has funds enough to feed himself well and pays for a few hours' rest at a roadside inn. There he learns, from talk in the dining room, that George has gone to Portsmouth to raise an army: he is planning to return to the war in France. Felton revises his route and heads for the south coast.

He stops in Winchester to buy himself a set of clothes that will pass muster in George's entourage and chooses a serviceable knife of ordinary metal, waiting while the merchant grinds it for him.

'Where are you going?' the man asks, and when the lieutenant says he's on his way to Portsmouth, adds, 'I hope you're not thinking of signing up to the duke's army. Only a lunatic would be mad enough to serve under that villain.' The whetstone squeals as he presses the blade to it. 'He hasn't the skill to lead an army, too swollen with his own importance to listen to anyone's advice.'

'I have no intention of joining up. Seen enough of war in my time,' is all Felton says.

The cutler demonstrates the sharpness of the knife by slicing an apple cleanly in two, seeming very pleased with himself.

'Overstepped himself, the duke. Thinks England belongs to him. No good'll come of it.' He spits on the ground.

'What day of the month is it?' Felton asks.

'The twenty-second, I believe. Summer's on the wane.'

Tomorrow, thinks Felton.

The cutler holds up the blade, admiring it, then slips it into a pouch and hands it over. 'Be careful. It's sharp. You wouldn't want any accidents.'

A huge crowd awaits George in Portsmouth harbour. People jostle and push. Someone jolts Felton's arm hard, sending a painful spasm juddering through it, which makes him think the infection must have returned.

'Here he comes, the varlet,' shouts a voice nearby. The crowd ripples, febrile, hot with rage. They are men like him, fighting men, soldiers, sailors, accustomed to the brutality of combat. And, like Felton, they all hate George.

A boy on his father's shoulders waves a fist, his reedy voice crying, 'Who rules the kingdom?'

'The King!' roars the crowd in response.

'Who rules the King?'

'The duke!'

A drummer starts up, banging in time with the chant.

'Who rules the duke?'

'The devil!'

The boy, flushed now with power, the crowd in his control, continues, 'Who killed the devil?'

'We did!'

'We did!'

'We did!'

By the devil, Felton realizes they mean George's old adviser, Lambe, and he is assailed suddenly by the thought of that old man's brutal death, torn limb from limb.

The crowd surges. Something is happening. He manages

to haul himself onto a bollard the better to see. And there he is, George, in all his splendour. He goes bare-headed, no hat to spoil the tumble of his curls. A big diamond in his ear catches the sun, flashing. The chant continues, increasing in frenzy, but George appears oblivious, smiling and waving as if they are hailing him.

Felton weaves his way to the arched stable entrance of the Greyhound Inn, where the entourage is headed. A new chant goes up:

> *'Let Charles and George do what they can,*
> *The duke shall die like Dr Lambe . . .'*

The horde of snarling faces combines to make a monster with a single desire. It would take just a single man to pull him from his horse. But none of them would dare. They are bold only in numbers and all are daunted by his power. George knows it. That is why he is so relaxed in the saddle, swaying easily with the rolling gait of his horse. Felton knows it too. Hester's words filter to his mind: *It would be an act of true sacrifice.*

George passes almost close enough for Felton to reach out and touch his horse, a magnificent animal. Felton calls to him but his voice is lost in the uproar. George doesn't wait for the mounting block to be rolled over and leaps down in one lithe acrobatic movement, meeting the cobbles like a dancer.

Immediately advisers cluster round him, one briefing him about something as he strides towards the door. He advances through the yard, wearing his confidence like a suit of armour, but Felton sees a weakness that is invisible to others. George's hand trembles slightly and he glances behind, the whites of his eyes bright, towards the gates being swung to. The crowd has riled him.

As luck would have it, Felton's old comrade Fiske is on the main gate, and waves him inside with a greeting, assuming him part of the entourage. Another crowd mills in the hall, this one smiling and obsequious, here to pay homage to the man who has more power than the King.

With a toss of his splendid hair, George disappears behind a sturdy oak door, strapped across with steel braces. A pair of sentries is left on guard. Each wears an ordinary sword, but Felton can see the slight bulge where their poniards are tucked, waist-high, at their backs, and the uneven hang of their jackets where their pistols are concealed.

Felton approaches, citing an appointment with the duke, but the guard makes clear that he has been ordered to admit no one. 'No exceptions.' He gives Felton a sympathetic look.

Felton loiters for some time, scanning the place for signs of anyone behaving suspiciously, and eventually the hangers-on begin to disperse. They have realized that the great man has retired and will not emerge now until morning. Through a window that looks over the street Felton can see that even the angry crowd has reduced to a few clusters of drunken diehards, still chanting but with diminished zeal.

He seeks out the landlord to ask if there is a bed for him. The man looks him up and down. Even though Felton is dressed in the good suit he bought in Winchester, disdain is written on the man's face. He says he doubts Felton could afford his establishment even if there were a vacancy.

He leaves the Greyhound. It is breezy out by the port, now night is falling. He stops at an apothecary for opium tincture, grateful for the blunting effect it has on his pain and also his nerves. After cruising about the increasingly rowdy taverns, he wanders away to watch the sunset, a scape of vivid orange and pink casting the masts of the ships in stark contrast. Eventually, he seeks out a boarding-house behind the port, the kind of place where his good suit means he is greeted like a lord.

The room is under the eaves and has a single small window with just a shutter, no glass, and a heart-shaped hole carved at its centre. It couldn't be more convenient if it had been by design, for through it he has a view straight into the Greyhound. George's rooms are on the first floor, tantalizingly close. He knows they are his because they have splendid vast casements, larger than any others in the building. He can see a woman moving about, the wife he supposes, whom he has never met, a blurred shadow against a simmering glow of golden light. He also has a view of the staircase and watches the servants buzzing up and down to bring the duke and duchess their evening meal.

He kicks off his boots, pours himself a measure of the brandy the landlady has procured for him and swills it back. He lies on the bed, head swimming pleasantly, and puts his mind to working out how best to gain access to George.

His new knife lies on the table, its blade luminous in the candlelight. He can hear Hester saying, *It was your hand Melis saw.* Its seductive brilliance makes it seem like some fine-honed thing cast in gold and set with precious stones. It is impossible to see beneath the gleam that it is nothing but a tenpenny knife made of nickel. He picks it up. It is like George, cheap but with enough shine to dupe all except the most astute. What was it Bacon said of beauty? That it was rarely found with virtue.

That chant rings round his head:

> *Let Charles and George do what they can,*
> *The duke shall die like Dr Lambe . . .*

He drains the bottle of brandy. His eyelids droop, his head lolls, and he forces a sharp intake of breath to resist the urge to sleep. But despite his efforts he is back at Saint-Martin in the death-stalked chaos. A great gaping mouth roars, a black hole bearing down on him. He slices his sword but his arm is heavy, too heavy, and a blow knocks the weapon from his fist. He plunges backward into mud. A scream rings out, a gasp, and he shoots upward off the pillow.

Dread continues to surge through him even once he is fully awake. He makes himself stand and walk to the basin where he splashes water over his head and face. His bowels are loose. Night terrors are the curse of soldiers. In the barracks the small hours are punctuated with their screams. But they never talk of it. None wants to seem weak.

He resists sleep for most of the night, while his hatred simmers and he reads Bridget's letter over and over: *I cannot demand you take revenge. What a black word that is.* Her words give force to his resolve, and by sunrise on the twenty-third day of August he is ready.

He rises from the bed, still fully clothed. His mouth is arid and he is aware of the dry pip, pip, pip of his heart as it musters courage. Sitting at the table in the window, under the curious gaze of a great hook-beaked gull perched on the sill, he takes a clean sheet of paper and writes his message: *He who is not prepared to lay down his life for God, King and country is a coward and does not deserve the name of gentleman or soldier.* Let them all believe this a political act. He won't have them digging up Bridget's past. He signs his name, tucking the fold of paper inside his hat, which he puts on along with his boots, then brushes down his jacket. He is ready.

He presses his eye to the heart-shaped hole and waits for George's shadow on the stairs.

Hester

I can hear laughter rising from the yard where the men are playing blind man's buff with Rafe. Hope and Lark, deep in conversation, are hitching the grey to the cart. They seem to go together, Lark cool and calm as milk, and Hope sweet as honey. Milk and honey. Moon and sun. I envy Hope her innocence.

It warms me to see the ties of their friendship tightening, but the Giffords are returning to the lodge today. I long for home, but we will ride later for another inn and then another, until the danger is gone, if ever.

It is the twenty-third of August today, or so Hope has informed me, which means that today is the day. It is all I have to cling to but seems now so unlikely: the look in the lieutenant's eyes that had made me so certain is fading in my memory until it is flimsy and perforated as a leaf skeleton.

Rafe has a handkerchief tied around his eyes and is staggering about, the men skipping out of his reach. They don't notice but I can see that Rafe has tilted his head upward and I suspect he is able to see under the blindfold, which explains why he seems to have an uncanny sense of where the men are.

Last night I had found him asleep with his hand clutched round the hilt of Jem Carter's poniard. The sight made a brace of sadness tighten round my heart – to think he feels the need to protect himself at such a tender age. It explains, at least, Margie's wandering kitchen knife. I had slid it from his grip and returned it to Jem, telling him I had found it in the yard. The memory of his monkey strung up, like a criminal, on the back of the door, niggles at me. I haven't mentioned it to Hope. Some things are better left unsaid.

Ambrose comes in, sallow from his injury and the subsequent journeying across the country before he had time to fully heal. He seems altered in a way I cannot quite pin down, harder, marked by the nearness of death. I wonder if I, too, have been visibly ravaged by the same force. I suppose I must have.

I am transformed inwardly – that much I know. I allow myself a brief moment of mourning for the good person I once was, the person who regarded kindness above all other virtues. I am no longer her.

'I have settled the account with the landlady,' he says, 'and have told her we are making way for Hereford.'

'And where, really, will we go?' I am tired, so tired of chasing my own shadow. 'Worcester, as we discussed?'

'It's a big enough city to get lost in for a couple of days.'

'Let's walk outside a little. Stretch our legs before the ride.' I take his arm and we go to a small orchard at the back of the inn. The place is neglected, the fruit falling, forgotten, and the grass overgrown. The heat is no longer the force it was. It is an ordinary English August day, with white clouds, a refreshing breeze and the air alive with the scent of earth and herbs from an early-morning shower.

'Tell me about Bette. Is she recovering well?' It seems an age ago that we were at Littlemore Manor and Ambrose had been stricken with worry about his wife, yet it is less than a month.

He doesn't reply. His expression has caved in and he emits a long, sorrowful sigh.

'Oh, dear Lord! I'm so sorry.'

He is simply shaking his head and I understand it is too painful for him even to think of, let alone speak about. When we find what we are looking for in life, it can be ripped from us in a moment.

'I know you have told me you don't want to talk of it,' says Ambrose, 'but I have decided to take action. I intend to approach the duke myself.'

It is unspoken but I understand that, with Bette gone, he feels he has nothing left to live for. I grip his arm. 'You can't do that.' A tremor hangs at the edge of my voice. 'You'll hang for it.'

He stops in his tracks, turning to face me. 'What are you thinking? That I intend to assassinate him? I mean only to try to convince him to see sense. I have borne witness to the destroyed letters. My word still counts for something. It is our only course.'

My mind is so contaminated by murder and vengeance I cannot think clearly. He must know such an approach will fail, that George would have him behind bars on some trumped-up charge within days.

My thoughts are back with the lieutenant – my sole hope.

Today, I think, today.

It will be the blackest secret.

My black secret.

Felton

George finally appears on the stairs.

To another eye, through that heart-shaped hole in the shutter, he would be just the blurred shape of any man but Felton would know him anywhere: the swagger, the slight upward tilt of his chin. Felton feels his pull, strong as a spring tide, sucking him in. *You are my demon, George.*

He runs his finger absently over the puckered scar. The mark of his loyalty. The mark of his frailty, his blindness. He forces himself to think of Bridget, to put a vivid picture of her into his mind. He must prime himself.

He cannot see beyond the deed. He knows there is nothing beyond. He is not certain now that he is ready for sacrifice.

Felton slips out of the back door, unseen. The yard is empty, save for a tethered goat that stares at him with probing eyes as he passes. He can hear the clatter of the Greyhound's kitchens, where they are preparing the duke and duchess's breakfast. Fiske is on the front door again. He paints on a smile for his old comrade. The door swings open smoothly on oiled hinges and – easy as a hot knife through lard – he is inside.

There is a great hubbub of preparation, boys running about with pitchers and platters. Nobody sees Felton. He is just another of the duke's men. The hall is packed with them, the atmosphere ebullient. There has evidently been some kind of good news and everybody fizzes with it. Felton hears a loud guffaw of laughter from the parlour. It is George's laugh.

Then he appears and they part to allow him to pass, as if he is Moses and they the Red Sea. He stops to talk to one of his advisers. The man's head bobs back and forth as he explains something, and as he takes his leave he bows reverently, as if George is a god.

George moves on, brushing past Felton, their sleeves actually touching.

'Felton!' He stops. 'No one informed me of your arrival. How did you gain entry?' The breath catches in Felton's throat. But George smiles. 'Never mind that. Have you good news for me?'

Felton is struck by how familiar yet unfamiliar he is, as if someone has replaced his old friend with a magnificent marionette. The crowd presses about them. George orders them away. 'For God's sake, give me some space.' They back off instantly, turning away, and George leads him to a quiet alcove.

'Where's my boy?' George, who has his back to the room, turns to flick his eyes over the throng, now at a respectful distance. 'Is the mother dealt with?'

'I need to speak to you about that. It's of grave importance.' Felton feels suddenly incapable, his resolve wavering. He could throw himself on his old lover's mercy, confess he has failed, beg his forgiveness.

'What is it?' George has picked up the anxious note in Felton's voice.

Felton looks to where the guards are posted at the far door. He is trained to kill, has killed more times than he can remember. He can picture the pattern of George's rib-cage, the organs beneath, the lungs, the stuttering heart, if he has one. But what if he fails, as he failed to kill the doctor?

'Tell me!' George rests an arm over his shoulders, as if they are good friends, lovers still.

There is some kind of disturbance at the main entrance. The guards move to deal with it, the crowd turning as one away from them, towards the door.

This is Felton's moment.

He thrusts his blade, precisely, between the jewels encrusting George's beautiful jacket. It slides invisibly through the fabric and skin, meeting a slight resistance as it pushes into the layer of muscle, between the ribs, right to the hilt. He feels already the wet warmth of his lover's blood on his fist, knowing by the thick flow, its surprising heat, that this time he has met his target.

George looks at him, not instantly understanding. Then, glancing down, alarm registers as he sees a small red patch on his white breeches.

Felton smiles and whispers, 'This is for her.'

George falls slightly towards him, like a drunkard. 'That bitch turned you.'

'Not *her*, no.' *He thinks I mean Hester.* 'This is for Bridget.' Felton's cuff is soaked. His good suit stained.

Confusion jostles across George's features. 'Bridget? Who?'

He doesn't even remember her.

The crowd must think the two men are embracing.

Hatred crystallizes. Every drop of admiration Felton had ever felt is gone in an instant. 'My sister, who took her own life. She was carrying your child. You raped her.'

Dread smears across George's beautiful face.

Felton pushes him away slightly. He staggers. He meets Felton's gaze again momentarily, then drops his eyes to his breast, where Felton's fist is awash now with his bright foamy blood.

The dying man tries to say something but his mouth moves wordlessly. Is his belief dented that he is one of God's chosen? Is he begging for deliverance?

They both know it is too late for that.

This moment, which has seemed eternal, comes to an abrupt end.

Felton flings his hat to the floor – the note tucked into it – and before the gathering comprehends what has occurred, he spirits himself away through the distracted melee towards the kitchens.

But he can't resist a final look.

George is wrenching the tenpenny knife from his breast. He inspects it in disbelief, as if it is the ghost knife in that play. Felton hopes he registers what an inferior weapon it is. It drips scarlet.

George looks surprised. Has he forgotten he is mortal?

In the kitchens they have no idea of what has taken place in the hall. Felton walks calmly through. His senses are alive. He smells the meat roasting on the spit, hears the glug and slosh as a bucket is emptied in the yard and feels the brush of breeze over his skin from the half-open door. A lad carrying a dead goose by the neck stops to stare at his blood-soaked cuff but says nothing.

He is almost out of the back door when the guards arrive.

He considers running – he could maybe disappear in the complex of twittens around the port, board a vessel for somewhere – but no. It may seem inconceivable that he has not prepared for the aftermath. His sole preoccupation has been the deed itself, and he wavered on that until the final moment. Now it is done he finds himself bereft of purpose.

He doesn't resist. A prayer circulates silently in his mind. He wonders if God is listening – after all he is a sinner and must pay the price for the lives he has taken. God loves a sinner who repents – isn't that what Hester said?

He is marched through the hall past horrified faces. Perhaps they thought the duke had the power to cheat death. Outside, as he is pushed onto a cart, he can see the hostile crowd already gathered, chanting.

'*The duke is murdered!*' cries someone. The news takes hold and a great cheer goes up, moving like a wave through the port. 'By that man's hand!' Someone is pointing towards Felton. The cheering multiplies, becoming louder and louder, all for him. They think he is a hero. The irony is not lost on Felton.

Hope

Hope is setting mouse traps along the shelf where the bee skeps are lined. She has located the queens, ensured there is enough honey in the combs to see the colonies through winter, and wrapped the hives in oilcloth to protect them from the worst of the weather.

It will be Christmas in a month.

She and Hester have their work cut out, just the two of them keeping Orchard Cottage, now Melis is gone. With the honey season over they are taking in mending and embroidery so the house is piled high with other people's musty clothes and they keep finding needles embedded in the upholstered arms of the chairs.

The August heat is a distant memory. It has rained for days but this afternoon it is dry, so Hester has suspended the rugs over the fence and is beating them, half obscured in a cloud of dust.

Hard work helps blot the bad memories and they never talk about what happened. They both have their secrets. But they are free.

News of George's death had come at the tail end of August. They were riding into Stratford, a bedraggled bunch, grinding along in a heavy silence, wondering if they would ever be able to return home, when a cheer went up from a group of men in the town square.

Ambrose sent Jem Carter to find out what was going on.

'You won't believe your ears.' He was bristling as he returned. 'The duke's been assassinated.'

It was all Hope could do to prevent herself from cheering, but when she looked at Hester, who had a hand over her mouth, she seemed about to burst into tears. She had never seen her elder sister cry.

Carter was going into the gruesome details of the stabbing in a Portsmouth inn: '. . . his blood ran everywhere.'

Pamphlets were being passed round, and as the news spread, more people were gathering in the square. Someone produced a keg of ale and a song started.

'He had it coming to him.' Ambrose couldn't hide the smile flickering about his lips. 'By whose hand?'

'Some fellow by the name of Felton. He's been captured and will be executed.'

Hope noticed a look pass between Hester and Ambrose, his eyebrows slightly raised and she glancing away to the ground. Hope knew there was something they hadn't told her: more secrets to prise them apart.

'Who was this Felton?' Hester said.

'Disaffected soldier. Some officer who served in the duke's army at Saint-Martin.' Carter was warming to his topic.

His brother was reading from one of the pamphlets. 'Fellow's being hailed a hero in some parts.'

'Can't say I'm surprised,' said Ambrose.

'That's my father, who's dead,' came a small voice from the pillion seat behind Hester.

'And good riddance to him.' It blurted out of Hester seemingly before she realized what she was saying. Rafe leaped down from the horse and scampered into a nearby alleyway.

344

They all ran in search of him but it was Hope who found him eventually, sitting on a flight of steps, burying his head in his hands. He had run a fair distance and they were both out of breath. Hope sat beside him without saying anything as their panting subsided.

Eventually he looked up. His face was pinched, eyes dry and flaring with anger, little hands gripped tight. 'Everyone's happy he's dead.'

Hope didn't try to explain. She just folded her nephew into her arms and held him. After a time he sat up, with the same dark look on his face. 'He promised me a horse.'

Three months have passed since. Rafe's birthday has come and gone. He is nine now and every day the sisters give thanks that he is with them and not at court.

Hester props up the rug-beater and steps into the lane. 'Ambrose is here,' she calls to Hope, who can see him now, approaching on horseback. He dismounts, with a cheerful greeting. Bette's death and his injury have taken their toll and he seems to have aged a decade in recent months, walking stiffly with a stoop he never had before.

'What's that I can smell?'

'Rabbit pie,' Hester tells him, as they enter the kitchen. 'Rafe trapped the rabbit himself. Skinned and gutted it without any help.'

There is a moment of silence and Hope wonders if they, like she, are remembering the lieutenant.

He is never mentioned at Orchard Cottage, as if he never was.

'Where is young Rafe?' asks Ambrose.

'He'll be in the outhouse.' Hester leads the way round to the back where they can see the child, deep in concentration, cross-legged on the floor tying a length of twine. He doesn't look up, though he must be aware of their arrival. Since their homecoming, Rafe has turned in on himself, become a taciturn presence, which Hester is convinced is only a phase. 'He'll grow out of it.' But Hope wonders about the invisible scars beneath the surface of his tender skin that have pulled him out of shape.

'What are you doing?' asks Ambrose.

'Tying snares.'

'I hear you're becoming a wizard with them.'

Hope remembers Ambrose using exactly the same expression about Lark, which causes her to smart with longing.

'I have something for you. A belated birthday gift.' Ambrose takes Rafe's hand and leads him outside to where his horse, a compact, fine-looking creature, is snatching at a few stray clumps of grass. 'A young man of nine years needs something to ride, don't you think?'

Rafe breaks into a rare smile. 'Is he really mine?'

As we watch him ride the horse round the yard, Ambrose begins to talk about a number of staff he has had to let go at Littlemore. 'You were right, Hester. My cook's daughter, Joan, was spying for him. To think I've known her since infancy.' He continues, talking about the new arrangements he has decided to make. 'I've found a buyer for the Hall in the Forest and persuaded the Giffords to come to Littlemore. Margie's such a fine cook and they have shown us all such loyalty, I don't want to leave them to a new owner I know nothing about.'

'All three of them? Even Lark?' A small thrill catches in Hope's breast.

'I wanted to talk to you about Lark. We were wondering if she might come and help you here. I know how short-handed you are now . . .' He stops himself before mentioning Melis's absence. 'I'm afraid she's insisting on bringing her goats.'

'I can't think of anything better.' Hester claps her hands. 'What a tonic she will be for us.'

Hope runs her fingers through her hair. It has already grown a few inches. She is thinking about their laughter in the stables at that tumbledown coaching inn, heads pressed together.

Hester

Ambrose announces gleefully that Felton was hanged today, just as I am cutting into the rabbit pie. I stop a moment, knife in my hand, and shake my head minutely, gesturing in the direction of Rafe. I don't want it discussed in front of him, not when he is so happy about the horse, not ever. But he seems to be paying little attention.

We discuss the Giffords' arrival as we eat. Hope is cheerful, as if someone has stoked a fire in her. I try to join in with their merriment but can't help dwelling on the fact that both men are dead by my invention and wondering what that suggests about the state of my soul. I may not have wielded the blade but I have to live with the knowledge of what I set in motion and must pay the price on the Day of Judgment.

When Rafe has gone to bed – we all sleep together these days, Hope, Rafe and I, a habit we acquired at the lodge – Ambrose brings up Felton once more. He raises a glass to the triumph of good over evil. I sip the wine – it is slightly sour. Secrets tangle about me, a welter of untruths. There is a hardness to me now – the price of survival.

Once Ambrose has left, I break a sprig of lemon balm from the bunch in a jar on the table and set a pot of water to boil to make an infusion. When it is done, I pass Hope a cup of the hot, fragrant liquid.

'Lemon balm always reminds me of Melis.' I am struck with an image of her covered with stings. We don't speak for a while, listening to the sound of a distant dog howling.

'It's a wonder, really,' I say, 'that we weren't all stung, with that great hive in the loft.'

'I was, by a wasp in the blue room.'

This is the first time we have spoken about our time at the lodge.

We fall back to silence. I am reminded of Melis's death-bed prophecy. Would it have happened without my intervention? I will never know. I blow gently on the hot infusion, scented steam rising over my face.

As we go up to bed, Hope is talking about Lark and which room we will give her when she arrives. It is good to see her so happy.

We undress in silence, just the soft sigh of my dress falling to the floor and the sound of Hope folding hers carefully. Some habits stick fast.

I hold up the candle to look at my sleeping son in the middle of the large bed, on his back, one hand behind his head, eyelids twitching in a dream, and I know it was all worth it.

I slip between the cool sheets, sinking my head into the pillow, as I count my blessings. A sudden sharp pain rips through my temple. I shoot up with a cry, holding my hand to my head, the pain still smarting.

Hope rushes to my side. 'What is it?'

'Something stung me.'

Together we inspect the pillow.

'It's this!' Hope has an object between her thumb and forefinger. It is one of the long, sharp leatherwork needles.

Rafe has been roused by the commotion. I look at him.

349

He is haloed in a golden circle of candlelight. I catch a cruel smile flicker over his face. I recognize it.

Melis whispers: *We've a wasp in our nest.*

'It must have fallen out of the sewing basket,' Hope is saying. 'Are you all right? Shall I fetch the salve?'

I am still looking at Rafe.

That cruel smile is not his father's.

It is mine.

Author's Note

The Honey and the Sting sprang, not from the life of a notable, or notorious woman, as with my previous novels, but from two central ideas: the corrupting effects of power, and revenge. Both were drawn from the Jacobean drama that has long fascinated me. In these revenge tragedies, women are invariably cast as the catalysts for the collapse of moral order. I wanted to turn this around, give women – ordinary women – the opportunity to resist the patriarchy, to fight back, to have retribution. As such my novel, though it is set in a specific past, might be regarded as more fantasy than history.

Frances Bacon said of revenge that it is a 'kind of wild justice'. In his essay, Bacon, a lawyer by trade, is arguing for the law as a tool for an ordered vengeance rather than the chaos of self-generated revenge. However, I couldn't help but think of those without access to the proper process of the Early Modern justice system. This seeded my central characters as outsiders, the kind of invisible women whose stories would never have been a matter for the historical record.

Early Modern women were the chattels of their fathers, husbands or brothers, they were obliged to obey and be silent; if they resisted, they were punished. Women who spoke out of turn, commonly derided as nags or scolds, might be forced to wear iron bridles and led about town like animals, as a warning to others. Men were sanctioned to beat their disobedient wives with a stick no wider than the thumb, as long as they avoided killing them. In marriage a woman was required to be sexually available to her husband whether she wanted to or not. Rape was considered the defilement of the property of a man, rather than a crime against a woman. Women who didn't belong to men were unprotected and those who lived apart – old women, unmarried women – were often regarded with suspicion and susceptible to aspersions of witchcraft. It was this class of vulnerable women, whose lives went unrecorded, that I wanted to address in *The Honey and the Sting*.

Though the three sisters are purely fictional creations, the two men at the heart of the novel are not. However, I have taken great liberties with my depiction of George Villiers, Duke of Buckingham. He was not guilty of the crimes described in the book and I imagine most historians will balk at my characterization of him. The real Villiers was an intriguing figure, the lover of a king, about whom many rumours of corruption circulated, even that of regicide, and who managed to wriggle out of Parliament's attempt to impeach him. But he exists in my novel as a fictional emblem of moral turpitude. I felt this was fitting as he was a man in possession of more charisma than ability, who was supremely powerful but used his power to promote himself above all. Parallels in political leaders of today are entirely intentional.

By 1628, the year in which the novel is set, Villiers had become a figure of loathing in the wake of a series of ill-managed military campaigns, the aforementioned rumours of regicide and the failed parliamentary impeachment. Many had come to expect he would meet an inauspicious end. Indeed, his close advisor, the occultist Doctor Lambe, had been brutally torn limb from limb, as described in the novel, a gruesome act which was widely regarded as a proxy attack against Villiers. The story of his assassination by John Felton at the Greyhound Inn in Portsmouth is true. Very little is known of Felton's life or the reasons behind the murder. Most deemed him merely a disaffected soldier motivated by having been passed over for promotion. It is possible that he had known Villiers as a young man and that they were educated at a military school in France together, as I have depicted. His biography is, at best, vague, but these possible connections provided a tempting background for fiction.

It was Villiers' treatment of his sister-in-law, Frances Coke, that particularly sparked my imagination. She was an heiress, forced into marriage with Villiers' deranged brother and then hounded into hiding by Villers, with her young son, under a charge of adultery. Frances was headstrong and determined not to be subjugated by her formidable brother-in-law. Her story became a jumping-off point for the novel. I had initially hoped to include her in the narrative, but ultimately found myself limited by the bounds of her biography, and so my trio of fictional sisters sprang to life.

Each of the sisters, all outsiders in their own way, were inspired by different sources. It was Frances Coke's determination to protect her son at all costs and resist Villiers' domination that gave rise to Hester. Through her I wanted to explore the question of the lengths a mother might go to to protect her child.

The idea for the visionary Melis came from a curious figure, Eleanor Davies, an early seventeenth-century prophet and author. Davies correctly predicted several events of political significance, one being the demise of Charles I;

another was, significantly, the assassination of George Villiers. Much like Cassandra, she was ignored, considered mad and endured imprisonment in Bedlam.

For Hope I drew my inspiration from Miranda Kauffman's recent book *Black Tudors*, in which she demonstrates that Early Modern England was a place of greater racial diversity than has long been supposed and that people of colour were not exclusively slaves or servants. Hope represents this largely forgotten cohort.

These three sisters are every-woman: ordinary, yet extraordinary, each of them outsiders, resisting oppression in their own way and, though the price is high, each of them is in some sense triumphant.

NEWPORT COMMUNITY
LEARNING & LIBRARIES

Acknowledgements

I have discovered that writing fiction doesn't become easier with experience and so I am particularly fortunate to be surrounded by a number of brilliant people who have guided me expertly in the creation of this novel. Firstly, I have a huge debt of gratitude to Jillian Taylor, who helped shape *The Honey and the Sting* from an amorphous mass of disjointed ideas and dealt patiently with me when I threatened to abandon the project altogether. Thank you also to Maxine Hitchcock, and the team at Michael Joseph, my agent, Jane Gregory, and her team at Gregory and Company, all of whom I couldn't manage without. Special thanks go to Hazel Orme for her hawk-eyed copy-editing, Stephanie Glencross for much-needed early help, Lauren Wakefield for her beautiful cover design and my dear friend, Glyn Reed, who gave me confidence to keep going when I was losing hope.

7/10/20

Newport Library and
Information Service